Elsie Ross

THOSE FRAGILE YEARS

THOSE FRAGILE YEARS

A CLAUDIA NOVEL

by

ROSE FRANKEN

THE BOOK CLUB
121, Charing Cross Road,
London, W.C.2

MADE AND PRINTED IN GREAT BRITAIN BY
WYMAN & SONS LIMITED, LONDON, READING AND FAKENHAM

CHAPTER ONE

EVERYTHING about living with Julia and Hartley was wonderful, except living with them. "The cook couldn't be nicer," Claudia told David, as they were going to bed one evening. "She lets Bertha use the kitchen to fix the baby's food, and Agnes thinks Matthew's an angel. She's not so petrified of the dog any more, either."

"Which one is Agnes?" David asked. "The one with the teeth?"

"The one with the teeth is Fanny. She takes care of Julia, looks after her clothes and makes her bed and all that sort of thing. Agnes does our floor, but they both wait on the table."

"They sound overworked," said David dryly. "Who makes Hartley's bed?"

"Watkins. Along with polishing silver. Julia's lucky to have a chauffeur who'll do more than just drive. She really manages beautifully with only four to help, plus a laundress, and a man for heavy cleaning."

"Beautifully," David agreed.

"We mustn't be so nasty," Claudia right-about-faced. "If Julia and Hartley weren't nice enough to take us in, we'd be in a fine fix coming back to New York without a roof over our heads. Don't sit on the bed."

"We could always go to a hotel," said David, who hated to be beholden to anyone, even his brother. "Why shouldn't I sit on the bed?"

"It's not good for it, and it's not ours. And as for a hotel, what hotel is going to take a Great Dane?" She couldn't bring herself to add, "and a baby and Matthew." A month ago—a lifetime ago—she would have said, "A Great Dane and three children." She turned away and fumbled blindly in the bureau drawer for something, anything. She felt David's arms encircling her. "Darling, don't try to be gay."

Their gaze met in the mirror. There was pain in his eyes, too. She buried her head against him. "It's easier to be gay," she sobbed, "than it is to be anything else."

"I know," he said, "I know. Gaiety covers more. But not from me, darling."

"But I can't keep crying on your shoulder," she protested angrily. "Every time I do it, I could kick myself."

His lips pressed against her hair. "Whose shoulder would you prefer?"

"I'm a grown woman. I oughtn't to need a shoulder."

"I need one," said David, "and I'm a grown man. We've lost our eldest son. We're entitled to grief. Don't fight it. Pain is a part of life."

"Pain is all there is," she answered.

He didn't remind her that she had a husband and two children to go on living for. He merely said, "Claudia, give yourself time, dear."

"I have. It'll be five weeks next Tuesday, and still I can't seem to get hold of myself. He was so well and happy, and then all at once for there to be nothing. I keep thinking what's the meaning of it, why did it have to happen!"

"I don't know why. I wish I did." He took her in his arms again. "Cry it out, don't hold it in."

Every time I see a little boy crossing the street," she sobbed, "it brings it all back."

"With me too, darling. It's something we'll both have to get over."

"But it gets worse every day instead of better. Every day it seems to get harder——"

"Until one day," he said, "it will begin to get easier."

"What makes you so sure?"

"Because you love me, and I love you."

She couldn't hurt him by saying she didn't believe it was as simple as that. She wiped her eyes and blew her nose and said instead, "I think I'd better take one of Hartley's sleeping-pills."

"You won't need it," he said, and added with gentle implication, "you'll sleep to-night."

A kind of terror invaded her. "Dear God, don't let me let him down again——" She loosed his arms from around her. "It's getting late, you told me you had to meet a contractor to-morrow at quarter to nine. And, incidentally, what's the idea of making such an early appointment?"

"Contractors work for a living even if architects don't."

"John can meet him instead. He promised me he'd see to it that you kept decent hours."

"John's my partner, not my nursemaid. Anyway, he has to drive his mother in from Greenwich in the morning for a cardiogram."

"If Mrs. Payne is that sick, she ought to have a companion

6

to go around with her. She relies on John entirely too much, she ought to realize he's married now. I wouldn't say this to Candy, but I do think it was a mistake for them to spend the summer with John's mother. It's even difficult being under one roof with Julia, and she's only a sister-in-law, and she minds her own business. Why are you looking at me that way?"

"I didn't know I was looking at you in any particular way. I was just wondering why you're so interested in John and Candy all at once."

"Have I ever not been interested in Candy since she was a child? And doubly, now that she's grown up and your partner's wife? Besides, I think she misses Elizabeth terribly. A girl needs her mother at a time like this. I mean, a first baby, and adjustments of all kinds."

"You're talking to make talk," he told her quietly. "And your hands are like ice. What are you afraid of?"

"Nothing," she insisted shakily. "Not a thing."

"I'm glad," he said. "Because sometimes I get a little afraid that grief will take us away from each other instead of bringing us closer."

She could feel her cheeks grow hot. "All of a sudden, you're full of the silliest ideas. Which do you want, a bath or a shower?"

He touched the tip of her nose with his finger as if to put a full stop to her pretence. "Which do you?"

"A shower's quicker, but I don't like getting my hair wet."

"Wear a cap."

"I don't like wearing a cap. Anyway, I'm all right, I took a bath this morning."

"I took a shower this morning," he said.

"Then what are we arguing about?"

"You began it," he mentioned. "I didn't."

At the last moment she couldn't resist the luxury of the enormous Turkish towel spread invitingly over a cane armchair beside the tub—an innovation that Julia had borrowed from England. Or perhaps it wasn't the towel so much; it was that she wanted to put off going to bed. Nervously she fingered a row of bath-oils on a hanging shelf, turning away a little so that David could not see the emptiness in her eyes. "I think I'll take a quick dip," she decided. "What shall I smell like, a rose, a violet, or a pine?"

"No pine," he said. "And a rose has thorns, and a violet shrinks. Be yourself, and that'll be fine with me."

7

If there was another meaning behind the pleasantry, she chose to ignore it. " I might as well smell expensively as long as I have the chance to," she retorted flippantly, as she started the water. " Besides, Agnes expects all the towels to be used up every day. If it wasn't for Agnes, I could skip a bath now and again and no one would be the wiser. I think that was the 'phone——" She stopped the water to listen. " It is. Who has the nerve, at this ungodly hour ? "

" It isn't so ungodly, it happens not to be nine o'clock yet. I'll go."

It was Julia, calling from downstairs, to ask if she and Hartley could pop up for a little visit. " Certainly," said David, " glad to see you," and said " Damn " as he put the receiver back on the hook.

" Your voice was not running over with hospitality," Claudia chided him. " After all, they couldn't be sweeter to us, and they never intrude."

" They're intruding now," he grumbled. " I thought they said at dinner they were going out somewhere."

" They must have changed their minds." She felt guilty. She had sent out a call for help, and it had come at the expense of Julia and Hartley's evening, and David's desire to be alone. " Darling," she murmured, " I'm so sorry——"

He held her tightly. " Are you ? "

She nodded, loath to bring another lie to her lips. It was kinder to let him think what he wanted to think.

Abruptly, he put her away from him. " Let's hurry and get into bed, and maybe they won't stay long."

" My bath. I could jump in and out of the tub in one second."

" Jump in and out afterwards."

" Afterwards is a nuisance. I jump immediately or not at all, so it's not at all. Get in your own bed, or Julia will be embarrassed, poor thing."

They were barely ensconced beneath the covers when they heard the portly bellow of Hartley's cough coming down the hall. " If you coughed as much as Hartley, I'd be worried about a flare-up," Claudia remarked.

" People who have something to cough about, don't," said David. " Not that I have anything to cough about any more," he assured her quickly. " Come in ! "

Julia and Hartley entered, more like company than as if it were their own home. Claudia was glad that, ever since the fire on the farm, she'd made a point of never going to sleep

8

without tidying up; she'd dumped everything helter-skelter into closets and drawers when Julia said she was coming up, and outwardly, at least, the room was as neat as a pin. She observed Julia noticing out of the corner of her eye, for which Claudia didn't blame her. There was nothing worse than planning a lovely guest-room and having guests make a mess of it.

"Why didn't you tell us you were in bed already?" Julia exclaimed apologetically.

"What's the difference?" said Hartley. "Claudia looks very sweet and fluffy in bed."

It was a surprising compliment on Hartley's lips, and very possibly he was moved to say it because he suddenly missed Julia's being fluffy in bed. In or out of bed, Julia looked like a well-groomed Madonna, although this evening she came rather close to being pretty. She had changed from the severe satin house-gown she had worn at dinner to a flowered *negligée*, and her smooth dark hair had curled up a little with the heat. "You ought to wear things like that more often," Claudia told her. "You look like a different person."

"I'm afraid I do," said Julia. "Actually, I can't bear myself in anything that isn't tailored, but when we decided to stay home this evening, I thought I might as well be cool."

"So did I," said Hartley. He too had changed into a silk dressing-gown with a muffler tied round his neck, which, if not exactly summery, did very well by his slightly doubled chin. Hartley and Julia always took going to bed quite seriously, just as if they didn't sleep in separate suites of two rooms each. "The name without the game," thought Claudia.

"You youngsters," Hartley went on, "have got us old folks in the habit of turning in early."

"Old?" Claudia scoffed politely. She prodded David with a look. It wouldn't hurt to carry on with a little small talk, but there he lay without opening his mouth. Fortunately, Hartley had no sense that he might have interrupted anything and only the deepest concern for their well-being showed in his eyes as he stood beaming down at them. "Everything you want to make you comfortable? Air-conditioning working all right?"

"Everything," said Claudia.

"Perfectly," said David, still not killing himself.

"How about a couple of theatre tickets once in a while?" Hartley persisted. "To break the monotony?"

"It isn't monotonous," said Claudia. "We never did go out very much at nights."

9

"It would do you good, occasionally," Julia suggested.

"Why?" said David.

"David means," Claudia hastened to cover his perversity, "that you mustn't have us on your minds. We're fine, really."

Hartley cleared his throat. "The thing is, Julia and I think that perhaps you're a little too fine. I mean to say you don't have to keep a stiff upper lip for our sakes. Frankly, I don't see how you can be so stoical. When David had to go away for his health, that was bad enough, but losing Bobby——" Hartley cleared his throat again, and passed his handkerchief across his forehead, a habit he'd developed when agitated. Claudia watched him, pinning her mind to the everlasting freshness of that monogrammed square of linen. Keeping your mind away from your feelings was one way not to drag your heart to your sleeve and wear it there. A heart, and especially a sick and bleeding heart, belonged where it had been organically placed, discreetly hidden from view.

"What's the use of blubbering?" David answered Hartley obliquely.

"No use," said Julia, "but most people do, particularly when they haven't got very much to blubber about."

Claudia caught David's eye, and they smiled faintly at each other, because he had said almost the same thing about coughing. It was true, too. Hartley coughed from cigars, and Julia's life was sad with emptiness. Neither of them had ever known any trouble to speak of, beyond an operation apiece and more than the usual count of allergies. Personally, Claudia always felt that she wouldn't be caught dead with an allergy, and she didn't encourage them in the children, either. If Matthew's nose ran, it ran of its own accord, and not because he was near a dog or cat, or couldn't eat eggs; and in due course of time it stopped running of its own accord, without benefit of tests and injections. Bobby hadn't even needed braces on his teeth, he'd inherited an excellent bite from both David and herself. All in all, they'd always been an old-fashioned family when it came to modern improvements in health. That's why it was so ironic for David to have come down with T.B. Except for the malaria that had stalked him after the war, he'd never known what it meant to be ill.

The sound of her name brought her back into the room.

"Claudia hasn't heard a word I've been saying," Julia announced.

"Yes, I have. What was it?"

"If you'd heard," Hartley smiled, with his wonderful literalness, "you'd know."

"She didn't want to hear," said David maliciously. "Julia thinks it's time you came out of your shell, and began to see people ; she's having a dinner-party to-morrow evening."

This time she evaded David's eyes, for Julia's suspended social calendar had been hanging over their heads for weeks. If only they could keep on going to bed every night at nine o'clock ; it wasn't any shell, it was exactly what the doctor had ordered for David the next few months. They were used to it, after almost a year in an isolated little cottage in the mountains, when there wasn't anything else to do, literally or figuratively, except go to bed—with David on the porch outside her window.

"Please go ahead just as if we weren't here," she begged Julia. "We don't need company, really."

"This isn't company, though. Just my niece who's back from her honeymoon, and perhaps Candy and John. I haven't seen them since the baby was born."

"If it's family," said Claudia, "that's different."

"And possibly another couple or two," Julia slipped in casually, like a dose of castor-oil sandwiched in orange juice.

David immediately looked suspicious. "Dinner jacket ? "

"Not if you'd rather not," Julia told him with a lenient smile.

"Nonsense," Hartley objected. "It'll do him good to get spruced up again." Black tie, or even white tie, held no hurdles for Hartley, with Watkins doing all the leg work ; but resurrecting David's studs and cuff-links and stiff shirts was going to be something of a project at this point.

"If it's to be formal," Claudia came to his rescue, "you'll have to count me out. Everything I own is either too short or too long."

"Then we'll do a little shopping first thing to-morrow," Julia suggested brightly, as if it hadn't been in the back of her mind all along.

"That's a good idea," David chimed in like a snake in the grass. "It's time you had some new dresses."

Claudia felt trapped. It was a conspiracy plotted by Julia and Hartley, and entered into at the last minute by David. What were they afraid of, that she was going into a depression ? Well, they needn't worry about it, she wasn't that sort. And yet what did it mean, waking up morning after morning, with that sick lump of inertia weighing her down ? Why did she feel this vague panic at the thought of seeing people ? For what reason was she holding herself aloof, even from David ? Perhaps he was aware of it, perhaps he knew that she was drifting off to a small island of her own making, surrounded by thoughts and feelings in which he had no share. Yes, it was a little frightening. " If David thinks it's high time I had a new dress," she said aloud and with effort, " then it's high time that I got one."

" I said ' dresses '," David corrected.

" That's right, my boy," Hartley applauded. " Don't let her get away with anything."

" We'll start early," Julia planned, " before it gets hot."

" I wish you wouldn't drag around with me," Claudia protested. " You and Hartley have both put yourselves out too much for us as it is."

" You have," said David, " that's true."

" Now, will you listen to those foolish youngsters, Julia ? "

Julia's eyes gave up. " I've told them over and over that we don't know they're around, they're so little trouble."

The words had no sooner left her lips than the door banged open, and Matthew appeared. " Bluff doesn't feel good," he announced, using a new approach. It was usually himself who was stricken by a sudden ailment, which never got him anywhere, except back to bed.

" What's the matter with the dog ? " David asked, like a jumpy mother.

" He doesn't feel good," Matthew repeated.

" Did he tell you so ? " Claudia enquired caustically. " David, don't be gullible, this is a ruse." (How much Matthew looked like Bobby, standing there in his pyjamas, with his face flushed and his hair tousled. She could almost make herself believe, for a moment of sublime insanity, that unreality was real.)

" What's a ruse ? " Matthew asked with interest.

Hartley tweaked his ear. " A big boy of seven ought to know what a ruse is. A ruse is one of those cakes in a paper box with whipped cream on it."

Charlotte Russes belonged to another era, but Matthew was an opportunist. " I'm hungry," he ventured hopefully.

" You're not," said David. " Good night."

" And button your pyjamas," Claudia threw in for good measure.

Matthew stolidly stood his ground, " I am so." He buttoned a button. " And Bluff doesn't feel good."

" Matthew——" David began warningly.

" I'll carry you back," Hartley interceded, with the sudden taste of fatherhood in his blood. " Piggy-back," he added rashly.

" Not with your bad leg," said Julia. " You'll break both your necks."

Matthew regarded his uncle with disdain. " I'm too old for piggy-back. That's only for babies like Michael."

" My mistake," Hartley apologized.

" He can walk by himself," said David sternly. " Matthew, I'll give you until I count three to leave this room."

Claudia could see that it was on the tip of Matthew's tongue to ask what would happen after the count of three, but he thought better of it. He inched towards the door. " I could clean up after Bluff," he mentioned in leaving, " if I had a piece of cardboard from one of Daddy's shirts."

It was a masterly exit. A small silence fell upon the room. " I'd better investigate," David finally decided.

" I'll go with you," said Claudia. " Turn round, Hartley, while I get into my bath-robe."

" I'm not looking," said Hartley. " But take it easy, I don't see why you're so upset over a little thing like this."

" That's because you've never seen," Claudia replied silently, " and it's never a little thing." She couldn't help admiring Julia, who sat on quietly with a fixed smile on her face, like a well-born hostess ignoring catastrophe. Julia's carpets on the guest-room floor were hand-tufted, and nailed wall to wall.

They found Bluff lying near the elevator, with his massive head sunk between his paws. He rolled his eyes and gave a mournful sigh. " Shame on you," said Claudia.

His tail thumped feebly in reply. " He says he couldn't help it," David translated generously.

Claudia bridled. " I wish you were as charitable to your own flesh and blood. If your baby misbehaves, you say he should know better."

" He should. Watch where you're going."

" I am." She picked her way gingerly for a few more feet, and then stopped short. " There's not a hint of anything," she declared. " I bet Matthew made it up."

" Matthew ! " David shouted. " Come here ! "

Matthew came out of his room. " You told me to go to bed," he said grievedly.

" Why did you say Bluff didn't feel well ? "

"Because I could hear him," said Matthew, and pointed to an obscure recess in the hall.

"Oh, Bluff, how tasteful of you!" Claudia exclaimed in immense relief.

"Some damn fool," said David, scowling downwards, "has been giving that dog chicken-bones. It's lucky they didn't splinter."

"Splinter or not," said Claudia, "who's going to clean it up?"

"I will," said David.

"No, I will," said Claudia. "Where's Bertha?"

"I don't need Bertha. Get me a couple of newspapers, and a pail of water and some ammonia," he ordered with a large air of efficiency. "And some rags, if you have them."

Claudia regarded him coldly. "I always carry rags with me. Can't you think of a few more things you'd like?"

"Here comes Aunt Julia," Matthew remarked affably.

Julia's colour turned a shade paler. She quickly averted her eyes. "It's all right," Claudia hastened to assure her. "It could have been a lot worse."

"This is nothing," said David, with a nonchalant wave of his hand.

Julia obviously felt that they were exaggerating the situation in reverse; hailing from a long line of Boston forbears, however, she rallied beautifully. "Accidents can happen in the best of families," she murmured.

"This is more of a topographical error than an accident," Claudia explained.

"Where's a pail?" David reiterated.

Julia almost said, "Don't bother," but it would have been carrying politeness to impracticality. Claudia gave her a little pat on the shoulder. "Go on back to Hartley, and take David with you. Matthew and I will do the honours."

Matthew clutched at his abdomen in a manner that was both horrid and contagious. "Was that necessary?" Claudia inquired frigidly. "Now for being so funny, you mayn't help me. March."

Matthew weighed the alternatives, and came to the conclusion that bed was the lesser of the evils, only to reappear with a new piece of information. "The baby's awake," he reported. "He knocked over a glass of water by the crib, and he's soaking wet."

"He and what else," thought Claudia in dismay, hoping that Julia's velvet chair had escaped a drenching. Julia must have been hoping the same thing, because she smiled gallantly and gave forth another axiom. "It never rains but it pours," said she.

"If you think this is pouring," David told her, "you ought to be around when we're really in top form." He spoke jokingly, but Claudia knew the memories that seared him. Always, in these minor crises of the family, there had been Bobby. . . .

"What is wrong?" Bertha had climbed up four flights of stairs, and stood red and puffing in their midst, with her arms full of freshly ironed clothes. "Bertha!" Claudia protested. "You'll kill yourself; use the elevator."

"I would rather walk," said Bertha. She took in the scene at once. "Ach, chop-bones!" she diagnosed, without her glasses. "Wait until I put my wash down, and I will attend to it."

"God bless Bertha," said David devoutly.

"Check up on how damp the baby is!" Claudia called after her.

"Bertha's not so young any more," Julia remarked. "She ought to take things a little easier."

"She ought to," Claudia agreed, "but she won't."

Julia chose her words with care. "Nevertheless, it really isn't necessary for her to wash and iron. I explained to her that all she had to do was to put everything down the chute each morning. Hilda's an excellent laundress, I've had her for years."

Claudia read between the lines. Hilda undoubtedly resented any invasion of her premises, although Julia was too tactful to say so. Even David sensed a crisis in the offing. "You'd better tell Bertha to curb her passion for laundry," he advised through a mouthful of toothpaste after Julia and Hartley had gone downstairs.

"I have," said Claudia, "a dozen times. And Bertha's told everybody in the kitchen a dozen times never to give Bluff bones. In short," she summed up, "all is not gold that glitters. Julia doesn't show it, but she probably feels the same as we do. Everything's wonderful about having us here, except having us."

"And the moral of that is," said David, "a rolling stone gathers no moss, so why don't we begin to look for a place of our own?"

She glanced at him quickly to see whether he was in earnest. "David, use your head," she said, a little sharply. "And let me have the toothpaste if you've finished with it."

"Squeeze it from the bottom," he adjured her. "What do you mean, use my head?"

"Because it would be silly for us to take on the responsibility of our own place, now."

"Why would it?"

His question was so reasonable and detached that it put her on the defensive. "You know perfectly well, why," she came back at him impatiently. Our plans are uncertain, and rents are high, and we're very well off as we are. Julia and Hartley simply turn themselves inside out to make us comfortable. Look at the way Watkins takes you down to the office and calls for you every day——"

"Very nice," said David dryly, "but it won't kill me to use the subway."

"You're better off not using it for a while. And it isn't just you I'm thinking of. The children live in the park, and as for me——" She laughed shakily. "I don't have to lift a finger."

"That's right, you don't," said David.

He came round to her and put his hands on her shoulders, and turned her round to him. "Only you happen to like lifting fingers," he said. "And I happen to know that you've given me a lot of reasons, but not the real one. The real reason is that you're afraid to start living again."

"I don't want you to shoulder any more responsibility than you have to!" she insisted desperately. "What's to be gained by overworking? The one thing we've got to be careful of is a flare-up."

"I won't overwork and I won't get a flare-up," he said. "You ought to know by this time that you can trust me."

"You really have been good," she acknowledged, "and I know how hard it is for you to hold yourself back."

"We're talking about you, not me."

"You think it would take my mind off, do me good to start housekeeping again. You're about as subtle as Julia was about the dinner-party to-morrow night."

"Do we have to be subtle with each other?"

"No, but there's no sense even discussing it. We won't be able to find an apartment. I hear there's nothing to be had except in the new buildings, and they're a thousand dollars a room, and no room. And they look like cheese-boxes; the architect in you would simply writhe at the way they're put together and zoom up overnight."

"What about the old buildings?"

"Nobody's moving out of them."

"Have you looked?"

She pulled away from him. "David, please. You don't have to give me something to fill my days. I'm managing quite well."

"You're managing very well," he said. "To look at you no one would guess."

"Guess what?"

"That you'd gone away and locked the door."

Her heart skipped a beat. He knew, then, that when he held her in his arms, she wasn't there. She couldn't bear his knowing, she couldn't bear the hurt in his eyes. "Don't be silly," she said unsteadily. "That's a silly thing to say."

This time he touched his finger to her lips, as if to stop the lie between them. "Run on to bed," he said. "I think I'll take that hot bath you didn't take, it'll make me sleep."

Her arms went out to him in gratitude, and for an instant they clung together, but there was nothing within her that she could give to him. She was more barren than Julia. "Good night," she whispered.

"Good night, my darling." He let her go.

Her hands were trembling as she poured a glass of water from the thermos-bottle on the night-table, and reached into the little drawer for Hartley's pills. Only a few left. She must remember to ask him for some more.

She put out the light. Her bed stood waiting, like a lover. The smooth, cool sheets embraced her aching limbs, and the pillow was soft beneath her head, and the darkness covered her with gentleness. Already the world was beginning to fade out. The thin shaft of brightness beneath the bathroom door and the hard splash of water in the tub were in another dimension. Consciousness slipped away from her, and ecstasy replenished her empty body. Only a little longer now . . . and somewhere, in the vastness of space, she would find Bobby. . . .

When morning came, she would know that she had dreamed of him, but in the night he was more real than life.

CHAPTER TWO

"You cried in your sleep," David said, as they were eating breakfast.

Weariness clung to her like cobwebs. "I had a night-mare——" It was too horrible to talk about. She broke a

17

piece of toast and put it down again, repelled by the very thought of food. "Usually, I have such wonderful dreams," she faltered. "I can't remember about last night—it was all mixed up—Bobby was in some kind of danger, and I tried to run to him but my legs wouldn't carry me. I screamed, but he didn't hear me."

"You mustn't," said David gently, as if she could help it.

"Don't you dream of Bobby?" she asked him in wonder.

"I try to tune out before I go to sleep," he said.

"I tune in," she confessed.

"I know."

"Is it wrong?"

"You'll have to be the one to answer that." He put the tray aside and pushed back the covers. "It's late, I have to hurry. This business of eating breakfast in bed is fatty degeneration of the soul, and if Julia thinks she's doing us a favour, she's not."

Claudia closed her eyes. She didn't have the energy to go into it again—Julia wasn't doing any of them a favour. Julia found that it made an easier household to have breakfast served in the rooms, like a hotel, with a flower on each tray to boot. Claudia was almost certain that David liked it, because he kept insisting so violently that he didn't. Which was just as well. When—or if—they did go housekeeping for themselves again, he wouldn't have to suffer this outrage to his manhood. There'd be no trays, no flowers, and no ice for the orange-juice. . . .

She must have dozed off, for the next thing she knew, he was bending over her, dressed and ready to leave for the office. "Sleepy-head——"

"It's not me, it's those pills. They take a while to wear off."

"They're a rotten habit to get into. It's only quarter past eight, though, so go back for another nap. I'll 'phone you later."

"No, wait, I'm awake. Is Watkins driving you down?"

"I didn't tell him I had an early appointment. I'll take the bus."

"I bet you'll take the subway. You've been aching for a whack at it."

He gave a sheepish grin. "Makes me feel like a man again. What about having lunch with me as long as you're going to be downtown?"

18

"What was I going to be downtown for?"

"Shopping. With Julia. Remember?"

"No. I forgot. And I hope she forgets."

"You go," he exhorted her. "Call me if you get finished in time." He dropped a kiss on the top of her head. He was eager to be gone, eager to start the day. Her lids drooped. How lucky he was to have a profession that he enjoyed, and enough energy to want to take the subway. ... Only quarter past eight ... as if that were early ... The few times she'd ever stayed in bed so late were when she had a sore throat or a baby. ... She remembered when Bobby was born, that women were still taking their time to get over childbirth, and it had been a couple of weeks before she'd begun to feel like herself. She remembered the first time she'd given him a bath, and how her mother had stood by, watching, and showing her how. It was comforting to try to believe that her mother and Bobby were together, again. She felt almost jealous that she wasn't with them. ...

She didn't hear the door open, but she heard Bertha say, "Shhhh——" as from a great distance. She lifted her eyes with effort. Bertha was about to tip-toe out again, holding Michael by the hand. He wore a sun-suit, and he was fat and sweet, like Bobby had been at that age. "Come back," said Claudia, "I'm up."

"We wanted only to tell you goodbye before we went to the park," Bertha said.

"To the park already? What time is it?"

"Nine o'clock."

"I must have fallen asleep."

"Yes," said Bertha, "you were asleep when we came in. You are tired. You need to rest."

"I've been resting for a month."

"Do not be in such a hurry with yourself," said Bertha. "You have had a hard year. No, no, Michael, naughty! Take out the horsie from your mouth. That's Bertha's nice good boy."

"What about the glass of water that Bertha's nice good boy knocked over last night?" Claudia remembered to ask.

Bertha looked blank. "The baby did not spill any water," she said.

"Oh," said Claudia. She was silent for a moment. Then she said, "I'd like to talk to Matthew; where is he?"

"Bluff wanted to go out, so he went downstairs to the yard with him."

" How's the carpet ? " Claudia enquired, off the top of her mind.

" Fine," said Bertha. " You would not know if you did not know. Mrs. Naughton, don't worry about Matthew. If he tells stories, it is because everything is strange to him, nothing is like it used to be. It is hard for all of us. You are tired, and I feel like I must wash and iron, and Mr. David needs the office, and Matthew lies a little."

Bertha didn't say it in words, but she meant that Matthew missed Bobby, too. It was true. Claudia knew that she ought to spend more time with him, she ought to try to find out what was going on in his confused and lonely little heart, but there was no motherhood in her. She had nothing to give him, except her sorrow and her weakness. After Bertha had gone, she buried her head in the pillow to smother the sound of her weeping. Bobby had never been so lost to her as at this moment. She could not find him even in her dreams.

It might have been minutes, or hours, later that Julia telephoned to say that she had made an appointment for eleven o'clock. " I spoke to Miss Tate," she said crisply, " and she'll have a number of dresses put aside for us to choose from."

" Who's Miss Tate ? " Claudia asked without interest.

Julia had the perspicacity to avoid going into detail. " I couldn't live without Miss Tate," she said, and digressed to more pertinent matters. " I called Candy this morning, but she doesn't think John will want to go out this evening because it's his mother's birthday and he'll probably want to stay at home with her."

" Oh," said Claudia, who could never see why plain birthdays should stop the clock, so to speak. She had an immediate vision of John, Candy, and Mrs. Payne sitting in Mrs. Payne's long, Victorian drawing room in silent observance of the fact that more than threescore years ago she had happened to be born in exactly the same way as everybody else on earth was born. As Bobby had been born. . . . When you had only eleven little birthdays to celebrate —Why, oh why !

" However," Julia went on, " the Woodburns are in town overnight, so I asked them instead. They're a very important contact for David, so you have to look especially nice."

Claudia recognized the high degree of organization that had already gone into the making of Julia's day. It made her tired to contemplate the spending of so much energy. "It's now three minutes past ten," Julia continued brightly, "and Watkins will be waiting downstairs at twenty to eleven."

Claudia's excuses wilted. "I'll be there," she gave in meekly.

This meant that she had no time to waste, especially if she was to be any sort of credit to Julia. She jumped out of bed and washed her hair, which killed two birds with one stone as far as her nails were concerned. Then she unearthed her best lingerie, and also a new girdle that she kept putting off wearing. It made her as flat as a pancake, and the slip and panties were a sin to hide. Julia had given them to her a long time ago, and she'd been saving them. She didn't know what for though. It wasn't as if she were going to have any more babies and had to go to the doctor every so often. She remembered how she always wore her best things when Bobby was on the way——

Too bad that she couldn't wear her underwear outside, she reflected, as she put on her old navy-blue dress over the finery underneath. She stuck an out-dated beret on her head, and admitted to her unexciting reflection that it was indeed high time that she got herself a new outfit.

The thing to do was to say it before Julia had a chance to say it. "I hope I won't disgrace you," she apologized, as Watkins opened the door of the shining limousine for them.

Unexpectedly, Julia became her ally instead of her critic. Although she didn't attempt to pretend that Claudia was a fashion-plate, she glorified her dowdy appearance into something of a spiritual triumph. "You had more important things to fill your mind this past year. Taking care of a sick husband, for one."

Claudia winced. She hated to think of David as a "sick husband". She was too much of a coward to ask the question, and waited until the car was threading its way majestically down Fifth Avenue. "Don't you think he looks and acts pretty well?" she finally asked.

"Who?"

"David."

"David? He's in splendid shape. If he keeps on behaving himself for another few months, I don't think you need have a moment's worry about him," Julia assured her with so much fervour that Claudia's heart began to beat normally again. She tried, out of sheer gratitude, to evince a little more interest in their destination. "Is the Miss Tate you spoke about one of those frightfully expensive places?"

"She isn't a place," Julia laughed. "As a matter of fact, though, she's an institution. Would you believe I haven't bothered to have a thing made to order since I've known her? Very often she'll send something up to the house without my seeing it, and it'll be perfect. She has so much initiative and skill that she's got herself a following of the best-dressed women in New York."

"She sounds wonderful," Claudia murmured, feeling that Miss Tate was going to be much too rich for her blood. Her apprehensions, however, were considerably lessened when the car stopped in front of a large department store, instead of one of the small and outrageously expensive establishments that labelled the major part of Julia's irreproachable wardrobe. "Why, this is where I bought the dress I have on!" she exclaimed in surprise.

"Let's not hold that against the shop," said Julia, with one of her rare flashes of humour.

"This dress was very nice in its day," Claudia defended.

"But its day is over," Julia smiled, doing herself unusually proud, thought Claudia.

The vast main floor was cool, and almost empty of shoppers in the off-season of early summer. "This won't be bad," said Julia, only to find that the sixth floor was a stuffy mass of women. "Oh, dear, what wretched luck," she deplored, "we've hit a sale."

Claudia couldn't see what was wretched luck about it. On the contrary, she thought it was great luck. David always said she was like a drunkard when it came to anything reduced, whether it was a pair of shoes or a chandelier. "Only, please," he used to beseech her, "don't buy me any reduced ties." The upshot of it was that whenever she did find a bargain, she'd never tell him the marked-down price until he admitted that he liked it at the regular price.

"I hope," Julia was saying, "that Miss Tate doesn't keep us waiting. Let's sit down until she comes."

They found a couple of chairs, still warm from the last occupants. "Oh, dear," Julia bemoaned on general principles. She sought comfort in replenishing her lipstick, whereupon Claudia made hay and headed towards a long rack of evening gowns. She reached for a flowered silk not too unlike the *negligée* that Julia had worn last night, and peered at the sales-tag dangling from one of the sleeves.

A hundred and eighty-five dollars, reduced to fifty-eight ! She peered further before letting herself get too pleased about it. Size twelve. This was really luck of a high order, even though she wasn't mad about prints as a rule. Nevertheless, they were practical, and this particular one was unusually attractive in design. And why shouldn't it be at the price it was reduced from ? She captured the dress not a minute too soon, for a fat woman, who was raping the entire rack, willy-nilly, almost got it. " Marvellous values," the woman wheezed, snatching a hideous green satin on the way.

" Marvellous," Claudia agreed. She tucked the print over her arm, and went back to Julia, who hadn't even missed her. " Why don't you sit down while you can ? " said Julia, closing her compact.

" I am," said Claudia.

It was all perfectly timed, because a moment later Julia said, " Here comes Miss Tate."

Miss Tate almost didn't reach them, because the fat woman, weighted down with dresses, waylaid her frantically. " I can't find anyone to wait on me ! " she puffed. " Are you busy, Miss ? Can't you wait on me ? "

Miss Tate looked through and beyond her. " I have a customer," she said coldly.

Her coldness melted into an effusive warmth as she skated up to Julia. " My dear, I was so *happy* when you called me this morning," she exclaimed in a husky voice that sounded just like Julia's, " but it's a shame you had to run into a madhouse of a sale ! " She gave her other hand to Claudia. " And this is the little sister-in-law ! She has a darling little figure, hasn't she ? I have some lovely things put away for you, and don't ask me how I did it with the place swarming with women, but I've got the big corner room waiting for us ! I simply told the floor manager, ' Sale or no sale, Mrs. Naughton is coming in, and I will *not* take her into a hot cubbyhole '."

" Splendid," said Julia, rising.

Claudia rose, too, and inconspicuously annexed the flowered gown. Miss Tate, however, had eyes in the back of her golden head. " Sweetie, you don't want that dress," she said gently. " It's one of the sale things."

" Is it ? " Claudia said innocently.

" Put it down, darling." Julia's tone was patient ; she might have been talking to a child who had picked up something unpleasant from the gutter. " Now come along."

Claudia came along, but she managed to hang on to the gown, anyway. In the end, economy proved its own reward, because it was the only thing that looked anything near decent on her, except a plain white linen street dress at a hundred and ten dollars which was robbery, pure and simple. Miss Tate looked horrified when Claudia said so. "But, my dear, it's a Flora Rosenbach!" she protested.

Julia nodded approvingly. "It's very definitely Rosen-bach. It does nice things to the hips."

"And the sleeve detail," Miss Tate pointed out. "I couldn't believe it was only marked a hundred and ten!"

"Only," Claudia echoed.

The "Flora Rosenbach" (a name which wouldn't have stood a chance on anything except an expensive gown) was merely the beginning. It appeared that the little linen frock, as Miss Tate lovingly called it, was basic, and needed a large floppy linen hat, a linen purse, a tangerine scarf and tangerine sandals to complete it. "Now it's perfect!" she explained, standing back like an artist surveying a completed picture. "It simply cried out for the proper accessories."

The printed silk, on the other hand, didn't cry out for a single thing. It was full of flowers, and that was all it needed. Indeed, Miss Tate didn't so much as ask Claudia if she had the proper evening slippers to go with it, so Claudia volunteered the information that she had a pair of silver pumps that would be just the thing. "Pumps," she announced, as if to convince herself, "never seem to go out of style." Miss Tate permitted the statement to go unchallenged. Her heart was in the "Rosenbach", and in the little Jouet Original that turned out to be a little too original. "I look like a clown with all those ruffles around my neck," Claudia rejected it firmly.

"It's chic," Miss Tate tempted. "Frightfully chic, and not expensive for what it is. Only two-twenty-five."

"Walk over," said Julia.

"There's no use walking," said Claudia. "I wonder what time it is, I'm supposed to have lunch with David."

Julia consulted her wrist-watch, and discovered it was five minutes to one. "I had no idea it was so late," she cried, aghast. "You'll never make it, Claudia, you haven't even had the white linen fitted yet."

Claudia brightened. "Then why don't we just forget the white linen, as long as I have the print to wear to-night?"

" Please, please, *please* ! " Miss Tate entreated, clasping her hands in anguish. " Pass up the Jouet, if you insist, but not the Rosenbach ! Sweetie, you look so *divine* in it, with that big floppy hat, hubby will adore it ! Now, please. Pretty, please ? "

" The dress and everything that goes with it," Julia broke in calmly, " is being charged to my account."

Julia was sweet, but David was proud. " No, don't, I have an account here," Claudia said.

" Pay no attention to her, Miss Tate. Claudia, why don't you let me call David while you're having the alteration done ? It'll save time."

" I wish you would, and tell him to eat a decent lunch and not have sandwiches sent in, and to come home early, no cheating."

Miss Tate looked startled, and then she took it all in a spirit of good, clean fun. " These adorable newly-weds. I'll go and get the fitter right away."

" Miss Amy," Julia specified.

" Absolutely. I told Miss Amy not to do any of the sales things, we'd be needing her." Miss Tate linked her arm through Julia's in a very special way. " And when you're finished 'phoning," she said, without moving her lips to make it more important, " I have something to show you, a little import came in this morning, it hasn't been put in stock yet. It's a little gem of tailored simplicity." Miss Tate opened her lips, and removed her voice. " No one has seen it, because it's *simply you.*"

The door closed behind them. Yes, Miss Tate was a clever woman, she knew her trade, but there were other things in life besides clothes. *Pretty please*, indeed. " She's a *silly* woman," Claudia decided, irritably, " and I've been sillier." Suddenly she hated the flowered silk, with its ignominious seduction into forgetfulness. For a little while she had let Bobby slip away from her, but now there was only emptiness again, and a longing that was like a physical pain, shattering and unbearable. She sank into a spindly gold chair, so tired, all at once, that she could scarcely stand up. The aching memory of the dream that she had had in the night swept over her anew. It was as if she were in a shadowy realm, too close to earth, too far from Bobby. He had needed her in the dream, and she had not gone to him. The helplessness of her body had stood between them.

It was hard to breathe against the agony that ripped her.

She walked to the long window at the far end of the room, and opened it to let the air in. In the street far below, buses lumbered past, and horns tooted, and people hurried along as if they knew where they were going. Poor things, they didn't know, any more than Bobby had known. Death was imminent in their living. There was so little to separate one world from the other. It was a thought to end all thinking, and with the end of thinking there was the end of the pain. How simple it was, and final. She opened the window a little further——

"I knocked, but I guess you didn't hear me."

Claudia turned. The room was a dark blur after the brightness of the sun outside, and her knees were soft beneath her. It took a little time for her vision to clear, and sanity to return. It must be Miss Amy, of course, standing there in the doorway. Her badge was the rosette of pins dangling from her waist. The pins glistened like tiny diamonds against her black skirt, and her tape-measure was a necklace worn open round her neck. "The traffic is so noisy with the window open," she offered in apology. "Which dress needs the alteration?"

Claudia wet her lips. "The white linen."

The fitter slipped the dress off its hanger. Her movements were unhurried, and her voice made a pleasant sound in the room. "It's too bad that Miss Amy had just left the floor for her lunch period," she mentioned.

"Oh," said Claudia. "Then you're not Miss Amy?"

"No, I'm Miss Rose. I have a great many of Miss Tate's customers, though."

"It doesn't make a bit of difference," Claudia made an effort towards politeness.

Miss Rose returned her smile. "She reminds me of my mother," Claudia thought, from a long way off. Her mother had the same kind of soft hair, half grey, and although her face wasn't old, there had always been age there, so that they had never been taken for sisters, the way it often happened these days, between mother and daughter. Claudia remembered a challis dress, with tiny pink buds on a white ground, and narrow coral velvet ribbon for a trimming. It was her best dress for a long time. Claudia remembered her mother, sitting on the floor, turning up the hem, the way Miss Rose was doing now. . . .

"White linen has such a fresh clean look."

"Not for long," said Claudia. "I mean, I have a dog

who'll change that fresh clean look with one swipe of his paw."

Miss Rose smiled again. " What kind of dog ? "

" A Great Dane."

" Oh, they're tremendous, aren't they ? I guess you live in the country where he has plenty of place to run."

" No, we live in New York. That is, we're staying in New York. We used to have two Danes, but that was when we had the farm."

Miss Rose sat back, and let her hands fall idle in her lap. " I love a farm," she said a little wistfully. " Did you have cows and chickens ? "

" And pigs. Sheep, too."

" That must have been a real farm," Miss Rose said.

" It was."

" A farm is such a wonderful place for children."

" Wonderful," Claudia agreed softly, remembering how Bobby had loved it.

" I'd hate to bring up a child in New York if I could help it." Miss Rose put some pins in her mouth, and went back to the hem. " A child should be brought up where there's trees and flowers, and maybe a brook. Have you any children ? "

Claudia nodded. " Boys. Have you any children ? " she went on hurriedly, not really interested, but wanting only to keep the conversation away from the dangerous edge of the personal.

" My little girl would have been just about your age," Miss Rose said.

It was a strange reply, for surely she could not mean that her daughter was dead. No one could talk about the loss of a child so quietly and unemotionally. " Oh," Claudia murmured ineptly.

Miss Rose put the last pin into place. " The dress looks worlds better now that the hem is up, doesn't it ? "

" Yes. Miss Rose, I didn't quite understand. Is your daughter—not with you any more ? " It was a hard question to ask, but she had to ask it, she had to know. It wasn't curiosity, it was a need to learn the secret of such quietness and acceptance.

Miss Rose pulled the skirt into line and readjusted a seam before she answered. " She died when she was fifteen. Pneumonia. She was only sick two days. It was before they discovered all these wonderful serums that they have now."

" How did you live through it ? " Claudia asked in wonder and in awe.

" Sometimes I look back and ask myself the same question," Miss Rose admitted. " I guess the answer is that you live through anything you have to. One thing I've always been grateful for, though, was that my husband didn't have to live through it. She was our only child, and the sun rose and set in her as far as he was concerned, so I was glad he was spared the suffering. He was killed in a building accident six months before Elise was taken."

" Oh, God."

Miss Rose glanced up. " There now, I shouldn't have bothered you with my troubles." She got to her feet and started to unbutton the large linen buttons down the back of the dress. " Is there anything else you bought that needs fitting ? "

" Just the print, but Miss Tate said it didn't need anything done to it."

" This one ? " Miss Rose picked up the flowered gown, and looked at the ticket on it. " My, but you're in luck," she exclaimed. " I fitted this dress in a size eighteen last week, and my customer paid almost two hundred dollars for it, and look what it's reduced to." She smiled. " It's nice when nice things happen to nice people."

" But why should dreadful things happen to nice people," Claudia protested angrily. " To lose your husband and your only child within a year—I don't see how you can stand the loneliness."

" You get used to it, after a time. I have a nice little two-room apartment in Brooklyn, and I have my radio to listen to at nights, and I belong to a lending library, but usually I'm so tired when I get home that all I can do is a little dusting and straightening, and go to bed. When it comes right down to it, there's a lot of people worse off than I am."

" I don't think I could feel like that," said Claudia.

" When you live a little longer," Miss Rose told her, " you'll realize that death isn't the worst thing. When I think what Miss Tate lives through, with her husband paralysed in a wheel-chair for the past ten years, and no hope for him, I'm thankful that I haven't got that kind of heartbreak to come home to every night in the week. Honestly, I watch her fly around here, so interested in each customer on the outside, and I say to myself, just like you said about me a minute ago, ' How does she do it ! ' "

"I don't know," said Claudia humbly, thinking of the endless months of David's illness and convalescence. "There's nothing harder than watching someone you love suffer."

"That's what I meant. It's worse than your own loneliness." Miss Rose gathered the white linen over her arm. "I certainly did talk too much. Usually I hardly open my mouth, except about the dress I'm fitting. But I guess a person needs to talk once in a while, it's good for them."

"It's good for the other person, too," said Claudia.

Miss Rose laid her hand for an instant on Claudia's shoulder. "It's nice of you to say so, but you've got plenty of time before you have to begin to worry your head about all the grief and suffering in the world. You just enjoy this pretty white linen dress, and if Miss Tate finds anything else for you, I'll be glad to come back."

"Thank you," said Claudia. "Thank you more than I can say, Miss Rose."

Miss Rose turned at the door with a puzzled little laugh. "Why, there's nothing to thank me for, child, it wasn't much of an alteration."

"It was a very big alteration," said Claudia.

CHAPTER THREE

DRIVING home in the car, she said to Julia, "Did you know that Miss Tate's husband has been helpless in a wheel-chair for ten years?"

"I didn't even know she was married," said Julia, and mentioned, as an afterthought, that she was sorry to hear about her husband being ill. "She does do the most amazing job," Julia went on. "I could have walked out in that little import, except for the sleeves. And I must say Miss Rose re-set them quite as well as Miss Amy would have. I had Miss Vera last time, and the dress was never really right after she fitted it. Funny little group of women, aren't they, with their pretty names, and their dusty black dresses? They're like a small regiment of anonymity."

Claudia wanted to tell Julia how wrong she was. She wanted to tell her about Miss Rose's lonely little flat in Brooklyn, but Julia wouldn't have known what that kind of loneliness meant. She'd probably say, "It's better to haved loved and lost than never to have loved at all," but the sharing of loss wouldn't have come from her heart. Not that Julia wasn't kind and generous—there wasn't a year that she didn't give fifteen per cent. of her personal income to charity, but she had no real identification with the suffering that she helped. She wasn't attuned to people like Miss Rose, or Miss Tate, for she had no parallel of experience within her own being. It was as if she were going through life with but half the equipment of living, knowing only the suffering of her own soul in search of fulfilment. It was sad, in a way, because perhaps that was the greatest of all pain.

She felt Julia's touch on her knee. " Was it awfully tiring for you to-day ? "

" No, I'm glad you made me go."

" So am I." After a moment she said, " Let's throw that navy blue away now, shall we ? "

It was going overboard to throw it away. " Wouldn't Agnes like it ? "

Julia looked a trifle sceptical. " She might. Hasn't Bertha some cousin, though ? "

Claudia got the point at once ; Agnes was accustomed to imported cast-offs. " Bertha has lots of cousins, she'll be delighted."

Bertha was so delighted that she wouldn't accept the dress. " It is much too good," she demurred. " I will sponge and press it, and you will be very glad you have it for rainy days." She unpacked the flowered silk from its many layers of tissue, and held it up to study it. " It is beautiful," she approved. " Beautiful-quality material. But it should be beautiful for fifty-eight dollars. Why not ? "

" Why not indeed ? " Claudia agreed. There was no use in aggravating Bertha by telling her what it had sold for originally. On the other hand, she had no intention of telling David what it had been reduced to. As if she had a Chinaman's chance of fooling him. It was the first question he asked when she put it on that evening. " It looks nice," he said (which was a rave from him when it came to clothes), " a hundred-and-eighty-five reduced to what ? "

" Very funny," she returned, and stalked off to kiss the children good night, leaving him with one eyebrow stuck half-way up his forehead.

When she came back, he was having trouble with his collar button. She smiled sweetly. " This is only the beginning of your trouble, my love. You're missing one stud, you'll have to use a safety pin."

"Damn. What's the idea of getting dressed up to eat supper at eight o'clock? It's almost time for bed."

"Don't look to me for sympathy until you're ready to act like a human being. David, tell me truthfully, does it actually look reduced?"

"No, darling, it looks twice the price."

"Then why did you think it was a sale dress?"

"Because I know you from the old country."

She was partly mollified. "Then guess how much."

"You told me. A hundred and eighty-five."

"Reduced to what, ass?"

"Sixty."

"You have a nerve, that's more than two-thirds off!"

"Ninety," he hazarded obediently.

"Fifty-eight. And stop grinning. I bought another one at the regular price. I'm not fooling. A hundred and ten dollars. And not even silk. Bertha'll have a fit when she sees it. Only Julia's paying for it."

He got on his high horse. "I'll pay for my wife's clothes. Reduced or unreduced."

"I said you would, but she said ridiculous."

She couldn't help feeling pleased at either alternative.

It wasn't one of Julia's most successful parties, probably because everybody good was out of town. Hartley, on the contrary, liked New York in the summer-time, and always insisted that it was the best vacation resort in the world. This evening he had the air-conditioning turned on full force, and everybody was cold, although it was close to ninety outdoors.

The food was superb, as usual, but the guests were dull. There was a middle-aged couple from the south, who turned out to be the whole works in a soft drink, which they drank at the table instead of champagne. "Greater love," David muttered for Claudia's benefit, "hath no man."

The Woodburns, Julia's idea of a good contact for David, turned out to be dull in a different way. They were quite old and over-youthful, and had just returned from a trip round the world in their private yacht. Julia mentioned how fortunate she was to have caught them before they departed for Newport, but they could have been leaving for Brooklyn, the way they said foist for first and thoid for third.

" How come ? " Claudia murmured to David.

" Super well-bred," David whispered back. " Nobody born can be better born than that."

" We live and loin," said Claudia, and David gave her a pinch under the table. The honeymooner who was Julia's niece caught him at it, and got quite pink, probably from association. She was one of last year's débutantes, and might have looked lovely in the newspaper with plenty of tulle. The groom, Claudia had gathered during cocktails, had gone straight from West Point to the bride's coming-out party, and doubtless a uniform had done for him what the tulle had done for her. At any rate he had three names, each one quite undistinguished in itself, but when strung together, they made an imposing effect.

" Skeezicks said that when they went abroad for their honeymoon," David volunteered in the elevator on the way upstairs, as soon as they could decently say good night, " that they insured their wedding gifts for a hundred thousand dollars."

" Fancy that," said Claudia. " You pushed the wrong button, this is Julia's floor."

" Now fancy that," said David, and pushed another button.

The door slid open, and Bluff was there, officiously barking his welcome and wagging his tail. " Quiet, you clown," David growled at him affectionately.

Matthew appeared before the door had a chance to close. " Bluff woke me up," he announced.

" For anyone who's just been woke up, you look awfully awake," Claudia commented.

David frowned. " This is getting to be a habit, young man. Back to bed with you."

" Wait, just a minute." Claudia knelt on the floor, and held him to her in a rush of tenderness. " Matthew dear, why can't you go to sleep ? What's bothering you ? "

" I do go to sleep, but I wake up again." Tentatively, he lifted a curl of her hair. " And when I wake up," he continued plaintively, " I haven't got anything to do."

" That's good," David inserted *sotto voce*.

Matthew eyed the flowered silk with mingled reactions. " Why did you go downstairs in your nightgown ? "

" This isn't a nightgown, it's an evening dress. I used to wear them once in a while, don't you remember ? "

" On the farm ? "

32

" Not so often. But sometimes."

" I hate the park," he digressed abruptly, and with fervour.

" I don't blame you," said Claudia. " It can get to be too much of a good thing. Any other hates on to-night's agenda ? "

He was distrustful of long words that he couldn't understand, so he ignored the question. " Why can't we go back to the farm ? " he demanded with his lower lip thrust out.

" We sold the farm," said David, " and if you ask me ' why ' again, I'll bat you one."

" I know why," said Matthew.

" Then you know more than I do," David mumbled under his breath.

" But why can't we buy another farm ? "

" My son," said David, with his voice using quotation marks, " farms do not grow on trees."

" Trees grow on farms, though," Claudia mentioned in a small voice.

She was aware that David gave her an odd look. Then he said, " Run on back to bed, Matthew, and don't wake Bertha."

" Bertha's downstairs, she's ironing."

" Ouch," said Claudia. " Come on, then, I'll tuck you in."

" No, I will," David said. He lifted Matthew in his arms. He wasn't supposed to lift anything, but Claudia made no protest, because she knew that the way he was lifting Matthew would never hurt him. Matthew seemed to be giving himself into David's arms, and it was all somehow very easy and gentle. She left them alone, and went into her room.

It was a little while before David followed her. She was already undressed, and ready for bed. She was standing in the middle of the floor, winding her watch. " He's a nice youngster," David said, taking her to him.

Tears came to her eyes. He had always said that about Bobby, just in that tone of voice, but he had never said it about Matthew. " Yes, David, he is."

He kissed her eyes. " Don't cry, darling."

" I'm not. It's strange. I'm quite happy, all at once." She heard herself say the words, and she felt a little shock that she had said them. " Is it wrong ? " she whispered.

He shook his head. " It's the rightest thing that ever happened."

" It's even more strange," she felt her way gropingly, " because to-day I was so desperate and lonely that——"

33

"That what——?" he coaxed her softly.

"I'm ashamed to tell you."

"Don't be."

"I stood by an open window, and I think I would have jumped out if someone hadn't come in."

He smiled a little. "You wouldn't have jumped out."

"How do you know?"

"Because I know."

"You have a lot of trust in me."

"A lot," he said.

"But it wasn't my courage that made me ashamed," she had to make him realize, "it was the courage of another woman who'd lost her husband and her only child, and who hasn't a soul in the world, and yet she had the strength to talk about it as quietly as I'm talking now."

"And you, my darling," David told her softly, "had the ears to listen."

They didn't talk again until he, too, was ready for bed. "Why didn't you ever tell me," she said, before they put the light out, "how much I had to be grateful for? You've got your health back, and there's Matthew and Michael——"

He shrugged. "You're a smart girl," he told her blandly. "I knew you'd get round to finding it out for yourself. Shall we have the air-conditioning or the air?"

"The air," she said.

He opened the windows. Claudia took a clean handkerchief from the drawer of the night-table. She saw the bottle of sleeping-pills. "Two left," she said speculatively. "I suppose it pays to give them back to Hartley."

"Pays who?" said David.

"Pays Julia." It was funnier in its implications than she meant it to be, and spontaneously they laughed. Then horror came into her face. "How could I——"

He laid his lips on hers. "Because you love me."

A little later, they laughed again before they went to sleep, and it was like a healing hand upon her heart. It didn't take Bobby away from her, it brought him closer, because she was close to David, and he was a part of David. "Remind me," she murmured, with a delicious drowsiness stealing over her, "to rumple up the other bed in the morning."

"Don't," David advised her sleepily. "Agnes might just as well get used to it."

It was morning before they knew it, and before they knew

34

it the door-knob rattled and the door burst open and Matthew was there. " Knock ! " David bellowed, from his pillow.

" On wood," Claudia supplied *sotto voce*.

" Why do you and Daddy sleep in one bed ? " Matthew enquired in vague disapproval.

" Any objections ? " said David. " It's a quarter to eight, why aren't you out in the park already ? "

Matthew bridled. " I haven't had my breakfast yet ! "

" Dear me," said Claudia, " Bertha must be losing her grip."

" Bertha says," Matthew related thoughtfully, " that the park is coming out of her ears. How does a park come out of somebody's ears ? "

" It doesn't," David assured him. " It's just a slang expression for a bellyful."

" Bertha says," Matthew continued, " that if we lived in the country, I could play out by myself. She said she could put the baby on the porch, even."

" Maybe we will live in the country," said David. " Mother and I were talking about it last night."

Matthew's interest took a flying leap into the future. " I don't like New York. I want to go back to the farm."

" Matthew——" David began warningly.

" But why can't we buy it back again ? " Matthew saved himself.

" Now you're being worse than silly," said Claudia, with a feeling of sickness at the very thought. It was hard enough to imagine any house in the country without Bobby, much less the farm. David must have guessed the way she felt because he pressed her hand and said, " Out with you, Matthew, I have to get up now."

" You can get up," said Matthew magnanimously.

" Thanks," said David.

Something in his voice warned Matthew not to go on playing with fire. He edged slowly towards the door. " Aren't we going to live with Aunt Julia and Uncle Hartley any more ? " he filled in his time.

" Naturally not," said Claudia, " if we decide to go to the country."

" I hope we have our own elevator to ride up and down in like we have here."

" Hope," said David. " See where it'll get you."

Matthew was encouraged to linger. " Bertha says Aunt Julia is your sister-in-law. Is Uncle Hartley your brother-in-law ? "

"Just mine," said Claudia, wondering what she was so possessive about. "He's Dad's real brother."

"Why?" Matthew asked.

She was a fool to have been lured. "Goodbye, Matthew, have a nice trip," she answered pleasantly.

"I'm not going anywhere," he said surprised.

"Oh yes, my lad, you are!" Claudia felt the top sheet slither away as David emerged from beneath the covers. Matthew vanished before his father reached him. David returned, and sat on the edge of the bed.

"Your sheet's slipping," Claudia mentioned with a catch in her voice.

"Let it slip," said David. He put his arms round her. "Darling, morning changes things, and if you don't want to, don't."

"How do you still feel about it, David?"

"The same as last night. It'll be good for all of us. Especially Bluff. It's criminal to keep a Great Dane cooped up."

"Cooped up in a five-story house off Fifth Avenue. Poor thing."

"I meant criminal for Julia. Claudia, seriously, if you're not ready to make the move, we'll forget about it until the autumn."

"The children ought to have the country for the rest of the summer. Only I'm so full of fear," she faltered. "When we talked it over before we went to sleep, I felt fine about it, but now I'm shilly-shallying again. Oh, it isn't only your health that worries me," she broke off with honesty. "When it comes right up to it, I just haven't the courage to face a home without Bobby. Last night I was ready, and this morning I'm not. It's like pulling myself up a step and sliding back two steps."

He laid his cheek against hers for a moment. "It's the other way round. You're pulling yourself up two steps, and only sliding back one step."

"How do you know?"

"Oh, I watch you occasionally," he returned lightly.

"I oughtn't to slide at all."

"Mrs. Strong Lady God."

"I almost am, when your arms are round me."

"That's a step up in itself."

"You know too much," she said unsteadily.

It was only by the skin of their teeth that they got the

other bed to look a little slept in before Agnes appeared with breakfast. They dawdled over it, like a honeymoon. " That poor bastard Skeezicks," said David, out of a clear sky. " Julia's niece looks like she's going to have blue veins on her forehead after the first baby. I'd better get shaved."

" Yes, she does. I'll come in and sit with you."

It ended up like old times, with a bathroom full of Bertha and Bluff and the baby. He was good and late in leaving. She clung to him briefly. " Remember. A decent lunch," she impressed upon him, meaning it, but wanting the last moment of nearness. " And don't come home too late."

" I will, I won't," he promised. " Oh, and look, darling, if you've really made up our minds, you'd better tell Julia."

" What'll I tell her, when she's been so wonderful to us ? "

" Tell her that's why we're going to stop imposing on her."

" That won't work. She'll say, ' Don't be absurd, you know very well that Hartley and I love having you here '."

" Tell her she's a liar," said David cheerfully.

" You're such a help," said Claudia.

This being Julia's massage morning, it was a good time to catch her in bed before her masseuse arrived. What Julia had to massage, Claudia couldn't imagine, for there wasn't a bump on her from top to bottom. David was of the opinion that she would benefit greatly by a couple of bumps here and there, but Julia apparently wanted to stay like a stick, which, possibly, was sour grapes, because she'd never had the faintest sign of a hip, back or front.

Julia looked up from the *Wall Street Journal* as Claudia entered. It was always difficult to reconcile Julia's Madonna-like face with a hard business head, but even David had to concede that she had a flair for stocks, and he had invested a good half of the money from the farm on her sound advice. " The market's certainly bullish," Julia mentioned with a deceiving flavour of lustiness, and reached for her bed-jacket.

" Oh, don't be silly, it's too warm to be modest," said Claudia, to whom a bull meant something else entirely.

" It is muggy," Julia agreed. She slipped the jacket over her nightgown just the same. She was even modest in front of Hartley. " They should see the way David and I run round," Claudia murmured inwardly. David was fussy about her going barefoot, of all things, but there his fussiness stopped.

" You're looking really rested this morning for the first time," Julia commented.

" I did. I mean, I am. Julia, have you a minute ? "

" Of course. What can I do for you ? "

" The point is, you've done more than enough already,"
Claudia opened negotiations.

" Don't be absurd," said Julia. " You know how Hartley
and I love having you here."

" Oh, dear," thought Claudia.

" Bertha popped in with the youngsters on the way to
the park a little while ago," Julia went on brightly. " She
wanted us to see Michael in his new overalls."

" Bertha should have her tail kicked. She can't get it
through her head that showing off that baby can be a bore,
even to his parents. David had to stop in the middle of
shaving this morning to admire him. Really, the only way
he could get rid of her was to begin to take off his towel."

Julia flushed slightly. " That's fairly drastic, isn't it ? "

" Yes, but it always works."

Julia changed the subject. " What do you think ? Bluff's
finally making up to me ; he gave me his paw and took a
piece of toast off my tray."

" That was big of him," said Claudia.

" He spit it out again," Julia confessed, " as soon as he
discovered it didn't have any butter on. How on earth does
Bertha manage to get them out to the park at the crack
of dawn every day ? "

" That's another point, Julia. She hasn't anything else to
do. She hasn't got enough to keep her busy. Neither have I."

" I should think you're both entitled to a good rest,"
said Julia. " You've been through more this last year than
most women live through in a lifetime, and Bertha's stood by
like one of the family."

" She has. But she doesn't loaf gracefully, and I really do
think it's time that we started in for ourselves again, and
stopped complicating your household."

Julia tried her level best to look upset at the prospect of
having her home to herself again. " You're a foolish girl,"
she protested valiantly. " It's no complication at all, and
far from being a trouble, we've enjoyed a little bustle and
excitement around us."

This, of course, was just so much patrician idiocy, particularly after Bluff's recent bustle on her lovely beige carpet,
and although it was past history (having happened during
the first week of their stay), his tail had knocked an invaluable
piece of Chantilly porcelain off an invaluable Louis Fifteenth

38

table. Julia hadn't batted an eyelash at that catastrophe, either, and Hartley had affirmed, with his undaunted love of cliché, "dogs will be dogs". He'd always wanted a dog, and children, too, which was as far as he got, what with one thing and another, so actually their being there wasn't as much of a hardship on him as it was on Julia. Still, she was a perfect gentleman about it, and even now, she carefully schooled from her voice any hint of relief. She merely said, "What have you in mind when you say ' starting in for yourselves '? Buying a place in the country again ?"

" Anything but," Claudia firmly rejected the idea. " No, but what we would like to do is to get the children out of the heat, and rent some inexpensive little cottage within travelling distance for July and August. Then, nearer the autumn, I can look for an unfurnished apartment in New York."

" It makes quite sound sense," Julia acknowledged, "except that you ought to find your apartment now, before you go to the country. If you wait, you won't get anything fit to live in."

" I thought we'd have a better chance if we waited until the rush was over."

Julia laughed. " Those days are past, my child. You've been away from New York so long you have no conception what the apartment situation is. Let me call Mary Keyes and ask her what she has on her lists."

" Who's Mary Keyes ? "

" She was married to Kenyon Keyes. He died a couple of years ago, left her without a cent, and she went into real estate ; she's made a great go of it, and is very clever about getting the right thing for the right person."

" She sounds like another version of Miss Tate," said Claudia. " Not that that isn't good," she added hastily, "only I'd rather find my own apartment, it's more fun." Fun. As if anything in the world could ever be fun again. Moreover, Julia's idea of the right apartment was probably the sort of thing her niece had signed up for—a duplex with a terrace facing the park in a brand new building, whereas both she and David preferred a modest old building on a modest side-street, with three nice bedrooms, dining room, living room, and kitchen. If there happened to be a small extra room to use as a study, so much the better, but it wasn't essential at this stage of their depleted resources. " I know exactly what we want," she concluded aloud.

"Then all you have to do is to tell Mary, and she'll save you a lot of running around," Julia overrode her in a firm voice, and reached for the telephone beside her bed. "Miss Casey, get me Mary Keyes. It's early, so you'd better try her hotel. Call me back when you reach her."

Miss Casey had a little office with a switchboard off the library on the floor below, and, according to David, cost less than not having a secretary, because she was a deduction. In fact, he had gone on to explain, Hartley and Julia couldn't afford their income any longer, and had to take losses in the stock market to keep their heads above water. "Poor things, my heart aches for them," Claudia had retorted, not believing a word of such a fantastic tale.

The telephone buzzed. "Mary's on her way to the office," Julia reported.

"That's good," said Claudia, "I'll start out by myself."

Fortunately Miss Casey announced the arrival of the masseuse a moment later, and diverted Julia's mind. Claudia rose with alacrity from the ottoman beside the bed. "I'll let you know what luck I have. Goodbye."

"Wait a moment. Listen to me." Julia put her thin and entirely beautiful hand on Claudia's arm. "Please believe that you haven't outworn your welcome with us, if that's what you're afraid of."

"You're very sweet, Julia," said Claudia, quite moved, "considering that we've been cluttering up your lives for over a month."

"Just a month," Julia corrected, giving herself away ever so slightly, "and we expected you to stay much longer."

Claudia shook her head. "It would be an easy way out for us, but the sooner we face the business of living by ourselves again, the better."

"Psychologically," Julia admitted, "I suppose that's true." She hesitated. "If your minds are really made up, we might as well go ahead with some building plans we've had drawn up for the house."

When it came to doing things for the house, Julia and Hartley always spoke of it lovingly as if it were a living thing. "By all means go ahead," said Claudia, "but how can you make it more perfect? You've already changed the façade and put in marble baths and panelled rooms and an elevator——"

"The elevator only runs as far as the top floor," Julia interrupted.

" How high do you want it to run ?   Through the roof ? "

She meant it to be witty, but Julia was quite serious.
" Not through, but to," she explained.   " We want to
extend the shaft, and make a solarium with an awninged
terrace."

" It'll be wonderful, but such a lot of work, isn't it ? "

" It's a major operation," said Julia happily.   " It'll
probably take all summer."

" You're looking forward to it, aren't you ? "

" Yes.   Hartley and I both love that sort of thing."

" Then you're even more of a fool than I thought," Claudia
told her in deep affection.   " I suppose you'd have just let
us stay on and on, and given up the solarium."

" Of course," said Julia simply.   " You can still stay."

" I'd like to see myself."   Claudia dropped a quick, shy
kiss on Julia's cheek.   " I'll start looking for a cottage and
an apartment right away, and with any luck at all, you'll be
rid of us within a week."

" You're an optimist," sad Julia.   " But knowing how you
function, it wouldn't surprise me."

" Me, either," said Claudia.

She ran upstairs, not bothering to wait for the elevator,
which was busy going for the masseuse.   It was a matter of
noblesse oblige at this point to move with as much haste as
possible.   And a very good thing it was that she couldn't
change her mind.

CHAPTER FOUR

WHEN she entered her room, she noticed, with a renewed
appreciation of Julia's impeccable system, that Agnes had
come and gone.   Both beds had already been made, looking
as if butter wouldn't melt in their mouths—and a bowl of
fresh sweet-peas supplanted yesterday's vase of roses.   She
was glad that the roses were gone.   She couldn't bear the
fragrance of them.   She couldn't bear anything that was
beautiful.   She couldn't bear to see the sky at sunset or
listen to the chirp of a bird at dawn.   What would the country
do to her, she thought in sudden panic, with its vast greenness
and solitude ?   If it weren't for David and the children,
she would prefer to stay in New York where the grating
noises and hurrying crowds absorbed her pain, and kept the

41

aching of her heart from tearing her to pieces. Beauty, without Bobby, was the distillation of all suffering. It was like a blinding light that she could not bring her eyes to face. If Julia had known how she felt, she wouldn't have had fresh flowers put in her room every day. She couldn't say to Julia —or even David, " The fragrance of a single rose brings everything back——" There had been so many flowers for Bobby, most of them roses.

The telephone rang. If it were Mary Keyes, she was tempted not to answer it. Then again, it might be David, and that would be a fine how-do-you-do if she let it ring.

Miss Casey's tidy voice said, " Oh, Mrs. Naughton, I was afraid you'd gone. Just a moment, Mrs. Payne is calling you——"

The connection was blurred. Miss Casey tried with rigid patience to regain the lost thread of her contact with the long-distance operator. Claudia waited. She could never think of Candy as Mrs. Payne. A short two years ago, she'd been a round-cheeked hoodlum in blue jeans, playing baseball with Bobby on the lawn, her taffy-coloured hair flying out in thick little braids behind each ear. Then, overnight, she'd slimmed down and grown up into a lovely seventeen, and a little later John had come into her life, and they were married. " My partner's wife," David would tease her, terribly pleased, but finding it hard to get used to the idea.

Suddenly, free of the cacophony of sound, Candy's clear young voice bubbled out over the wire. " Claudia, I'm so *excited* ! " she began, without preamble. Candy talked like her letters, blocks of round, square handwriting, guiltless of salutation or conclusion. " How are you ? " she added as an afterthought.

" Fine," said Claudia. " What are you excited about ? Did the baby gain ten ounces again this week ? "

" We don't weigh her until to-morrow. No, I'm excited about your moving ! Tell me, are you coming out to Greenwich ? It's as nice as any place close to New York, even a little nicer, maybe, if you don't mind its being on the stuffy side."

" We hadn't got round to thinking where we'll go—we only just made up our minds this morning. How'd you find out so fast ? "

" Well, how do you think ? David told John naturally, the minute he got to the office, and naturally John 'phoned

42

me right away ; he's crazy for you to come out to Greenwich, too. And before I forget, Mother Payne says to tell you that there's a wonderful place just down the road from here, and for *nothing* ! "

" What's ' for *nothing* ' ? " Claudia enquired with interest.

" She doesn't know, but the family's all died off, and it's in the hands of the bank, or something, and Mother Payne says that always means a bargain."

" It sounds dusty."

" I don't think so, there's a caretaker."

" Not that kind of dusty."

" Oh. I know what you mean. I couldn't say, I've never seen the house itself, it sets way back from the road, but the gates look very imposing."

" I don't think we want gates," said Claudia dubiously.

" You can always take them down. Come on out on Saturday, anyway, and look at it."

" Better find out first what the rental is, and for how long."

" It isn't for rent, it's for sale."

" Forget it, then, we're not buying."

" Oh," said Candy. " John didn't mention whether you were or weren't. He just said you'd decided to move to the country."

" But just for the summer," Claudia specified with finality. " I'm going apartment-hunting this morning so that we can get back and settled by the time school opens in September. Matthew's behind, as it is."

" Oh," said Candy again. " I must say I'm disappointed. I wish we hadn't decided to give up New York and live in Connecticut, I'd much rather be near you."

" Don't be silly. Besides, we had our share of country-living ; it's a phase everybody ought to go through. Have you seen anything yet that you like ? "

" We haven't begun to look. Mother Payne says, what's the hurry ?—she loves having us."

The phrase sounded familiar. Claudia ruled a smile from her voice. " What's the matter with the house with the gates ? "

" Too near," said Candy briefly.

It was Claudia's turn to say " Oh."

" We don't want gates, either," Candy added. " Mother Payne's just calling me from downstairs to tell you to come for lunch Saturday, and she'll have a real-estate agent line

43

up some houses for you. Wait a moment." Candy broke off to listen. "But she says not to expect too much choice this late in the season," she relayed obediently.

"I'm glad it's late in the season, because I do expect quite a reduction in rent," said Claudia. "It's out of season for apartments, too, so we ought to have good luck all round."

"I'm not so sure about apartments," said Candy doubtfully. "I only know that the very minute we put Mother's on the market, it was snatched right up, even though we're not going to give occupancy until October on account of not wanting to put her things in storage until we know what we're going to be able to use. You have a lot of stuff in storage, haven't you?"

"Not a lot. All we kept were the eighteenth-century pieces—the Sheraton table and chairs, and the Chippendale sofa and David's desk——"

"And the low-boy, I hope," Candy interjected. "If you sold it with the farm, I'll never forgive you. I'm not as crazy about old furniture the way Mother was, and you and David are, but I just loved the way that low-boy used to stand in the dining room bay, with a bowl of flowers between the candlesticks——"

"We kept it," said Claudia. "The candlesticks, too."

Candy gave a small sigh. "That's a relief. I can't wait until you're all settled down again, it'll be like old times——"

A thick little silence fell upon her words, as if, thought Claudia, Candy suddenly remembered that it could never be like old times. "I have to ring off," she said hastily. "I hear the baby crying, and if I don't run"—a note of grimness took the lilt out of her voice—"Mother Payne will be there ahead of me, picking her up and spoiling her like nobody's business. You wouldn't believe it, but she's spoiled already."

"I believe it," thought Claudia, as she hung up the receiver. Poor Candy needed another ten years added to her age to pull her safely through the next few months. She'd been full of young and generous impulses when she'd offered to spend the summer with her mother-in-law, wanting to brighten Mrs. Payne's last days with the joy of a first grandchild. Claudia, however, had a strong suspicion that John's frail little mother would outlive them all with her bad heart, and now Candy was slowly forming the same opinion. "Poor John," Claudia abruptly switched her sympathies. If a man loved two women, he needed one of them to be wise.

The telephone rang again while she was changing to low-heeled walking shoes. Miss Casey said, " Mrs. Keyes called, but your line was busy. She left a message that she'll pick you up at two o'clock."

" Oh, dear. Look, Miss Casey, would you call her back and tell her it isn't necessary ? "

" She's probably left the office by this time, but I'll leave word with her secretary."

"Thanks," said Claudia, washing her hands of Mary Keyes.

It was only ten-thirty when she emerged to the street, but already the sun was rolling a blanket of heat across the pavements. The tree-lined street, with its proud rows of private houses, wore the jaded look of a fancy lady. Summer was not becoming even to the loveliest city block.

She turned east and crossed Madison Avenue, pausing to glance at a large bronze placard against the outside of a old nice corner building. SIX, SEVEN, AND EIGHT ROOM SUITES. What could be simpler, and why would she need the kindly but unnecessary offices of Mary Keyes ? True, it was only a stone's-throw from Julia, but it wasn't as if Julia were her mother-in-law.

She stepped into the cool expanse of marble lobby. A green-liveried doorman closed a heavily ear-ringed lady and her Pomeranian into a taxi-cab with an obsequious bow, and returned to his post, dusting off his white gloves. " Much too expensive," Claudia decided. " We can do without the white gloves." Still, there was no harm in asking, especially if she cut down on a room.

The doorman did not seem to hear her. " I'm interested in a six-room apartment," she repeated.

He became quite tall as he looked down on her. " There are no apartments, Madame," he informed her from a great distance.

Since the bronze placard had informed her otherwise, she could only surmise that this was a case of flagrant discrimination. " My good man," she felt like telling him, " I might not have a Pomeranian, but I do have a Great Dane." Instead, she said coldly, " In that case you ought to remove your sign out front."

He continued to look down his nose at her, but a dash of Irish accent spoiled the effect. " Sure, and why don't you read what it says, Lady ? " he retorted smartly. A limousine drove up to the door. He sprinted forward, alert and attentive, leaving Claudia suspended in outrage. She started back to the corner to make him eat his words, only she had to eat them herself, for there it was, like a little whisper in

45

italics across the very bottom of the sign : *No Vacancies.*
" What are they ashamed of, why don't they come out and
say so in plain language ? " she muttered.

If she had had any sense, she would have known when to
quit, but no, she had to go on, and on, down one block and
up another until, finally, she had so many feet in one shoe
that she couldn't take another step. " This is positively my
last try," she promised herself, as she approached a tall,
narrow, red-brick edifice, bursting with modernity and
bulging terraces like small tumours all over its front. White
chalk crosses on bare windows gave an effect of a giant
tick-tack-toe game, and a large working sign clearly announced
in round figures and fractions, that $3\frac{1}{2}$–$4\frac{1}{2}$ and $5\frac{1}{2}$ ROOMS were
available for immediate occupancy. " So I'm not proud,"
Claudia shrugged. Michael was so little he might fit very
nicely in half a room.

" Only two three-and-a-halfs left," the doorman told her.
He wore a painfully new uniform that hadn't yet fitted to
his body, and his manners hadn't worn off yet, either. " Try
across the street," he advised her. " I heard they have a
vacancy."

It was the first decent word that anyone had spoken to
her all the morning. She thanked him profusely, and hobbled
over to a dingy-looking apartment house directly opposite,
where she found no doorman and hardly any elevator man.
It took him some time to appear, and when he did, he was
quite elderly, and quite deaf. " I'll call the super, have a
seat," he said, and disappeared.

Claudia had a seat. It was wonderful to sit. She enjoyed
it as much as her feet did, and while she waited she tried to
like the old-fashioned lobby, with its high-backed velvet
chairs, and musty odour. Anyway, it was preferable to
the passionately modern *décor* of the new buildings. The
" super " turned out to be old-fashioned, too, with no coat
on and a Danish accent, done in monosyllables. " Sublet,"
he greeted her. " Seven rooms."

Her spirit revived. " That's just what I want ! "

" September."

" Good," she approved, catching his rhythm. " What
rental ? "

" Twenty-three hundred. O.H.E."

Twenty-three hundred was more than they wanted to
spend, but it was certainly the cheapest thing she'd come
across so far. She wondered what the O.H.E. meant. A

whole new language of initials had sprouted up, and she could never get them straight. The only initials that had ever made any sense to her were F.D.R.

" Want to look at it ? " the super asked.

" Of course," said Claudia. She wasn't going to let three little letters bother her. " This is quite an old house, isn't it ? " she made conversation, as the elevator crawled noisily upwards.

" Thirty-forty years." He pulled the car to a halt. She followed him down a narrow hall to a door marked " 4B." He rang the bell, and the door opened. " Okay, Mrs. Lacey," he said with an air of having done his duty, and went downstairs again.

Mrs. Lacey switched on a lamp in the dank, onion-smelly foyer. She was dressed in slacks and wore a bow in her hair, and was too old to look young. " I do wish he'd announced ! " she deplored breathlessly. " You've caught me with something boiling over on the stove, so would you mind, please, beginning with the kitchen ? " She flew off in the direction of the onions. " It's a lovely big kitchen," she threw back over her shoulder.

Big was all it was. Claudia wondered, with a sinking heart, how many coats of white enamel it would take to cover the bilious green of the antiquated wooden dish-cupboards. She noted the warped and yawning drain-boards, and knew that that way lay madness and cockroaches.

Mrs. Lacey rescued a potful of bubbling something-or-other, and led the way through a swinging door. " This is the dining room," she explained redundantly. " Also unusually large for an New York apartment. That's a seven-foot sideboard on that wall, and you hardly notice it."

" I notice it," thought Claudia, trying to picture what the room would look like without it, and without the garish Oriental rug and the heavy maroon draperies across the windows. " May I see the rest of the apartment ? " she asked faintly.

" You certainly may," Mrs. Lacey generously acceded. She pushed open a pair of french doors which were curtained in what might have been ecru net, and Claudia found herself in the living room, which was just like the dining room, only more so. The windows were swathed in heavy maroon draperies, this time done in blue, and one large and two small Oriental rugs covered a poorly varnished, softwood floor. " This room, of course, faces the street," Mrs. Lacey elucidated, neglecting to mention what the dining room faced. "And you can see the street from the master-bedroom. It's really a wonderful apartment, and the only reason I'm renting it and selling the furniture is that my husband is moving his business to Hartford."

"I see," Claudia murmured, not realizing that she didn't see at all. "I wasn't interested in a furnished apartment," she mentioned as an afterthought.

Mrs. Lacey's mouth became very small and thin and ugly beneath the crimson exaggeration of her lipstick. "Didn't the super tell you this was a frozen rent?"

"Now that I think of it, yes," Claudia admitted, belatedly putting two and two together and arriving at O.H.E.

"Then you understand that the lease has two more years to run at twenty-three hundred. I'm asking thirty-five hundred for the furniture, just as you see it, rugs and all. It's absolutely nothing for it. Why my dining room set alone was almost a thousand dollars new."

"But I don't need a dining room set. I'm afraid I couldn't use any of your furniture."

"Then this is just a waste of both our times," Mrs. Lacey said, with her voice getting very shrill and high. "I should think anybody'd know that you just don't expect to get a frozen rent like this without buying something, either a grand piano or the furniture or something."

"I'm sorry. I didn't know. You see, I've been away from New York for almost a year."

"The housing shortage has been going on for a lot longer than a year," Mrs. Lacey enlightened her with severity.

Her eyes were too hostile to try to explain about living on the farm for ten years before that. The only thing to do was to take herself out of Mrs. Lacey's hair, and lunch, as fast as possible.

The super was fixing a hinge on the entrance door as Claudia hurried towards the fresh air. "Didn't like it," he hazarded.

"Didn't like it," she answered.

"Didn't think you would," he said.

It was an admission of utter defeat to take a taxi for only a few blocks. She leaned back against the hot leather seat and closed her eyes. The taxi-driver waited, poised for action. "I ain't no mind reader, Miss," he reminded her.

She gave him Julia's address with an apologetic smile.

It was a one-way street, and when she got there, the meter had the nasty look of being ready to drop another nickel. "You can stop at the corner," she decided hastily. "I'll walk those few steps." Immediately she'd said it, she felt like Mrs. Lacey round the mouth, so she made herself part with a twenty-cent tip, which was a lot for a thirty-cent fare. In return, he reached round, stretched out his arm, and opened the door for her. His opinion of women tippers seemed to go up.

As she trudged along, she saw three specks trudging from the opposite direction, and then she saw Bluff, bounding ahead to a tree. She whistled. He put his leg down and lifted his ears and wondered where the whistle came from. When it finally dawned on him, he almost knocked her over, he was so pleased to see her. "It's Mother!" she heard Matthew shout, and he, too, started towards her at a run. "Where were you?" he demanded.

She pushed the hair out of his eyes. Bobby's hair was always in his eyes before he began to train it back. "My, what a dirty face," she said unsteadily. "I was shopping."

"Did you buy me anything? Bertha took us to the zoo."

"I hear you went to the zoo," she managed with a wooden smile, as Bertha and Michael joined them at the stoop. "Bluff, will you please stop that, you'll knock me over!"

"He thinks you've got something for him," said Matthew hopefully.

"Well, I haven't."

"Don't ring, I will use my key," said Bertha. "You look tired, Mrs. Naughton."

"So do you," Claudia refrained from saying. They were all hot and tired, and without roots, moving like strangers through the orderly beauty of Julia's house. "What are we having for lunch?" Matthew asked, mechanically.

"Something nice," Bertha promised.

His apathy sharpened into interest. "What?"

"Ice-cream."

"What else?"

Bertha favoured him with a hypocrite's smile. "You will see." On the way upstairs, she whispered to Claudia. "I asked the cook for calves' liver."

"You certainly make life hard for yourself."

"Liver is healthy," said Bertha, who also clung to spinach. "Why don't you have your tray with the children?"

The last thing Claudia felt like was a tray with the children but she said "all right" because Bertha and Matthew were lonely, too. The baby was too little to be lonely, but he wasn't too little not to like calves' liver. Bertha had to cut it in tiny pieces, and camouflage it with apple sauce.

Miss Casey telephoned while they were still eating. She was terribly sorry to say that Mrs. Keyes had been unreachable all morning, and was therefore keeping her two-o'clock appointment. "That's good," Claudia acquiesced meekly. "I'll be waiting for her."

"Who's Mrs. Keyes?" Matthew wanted to know.

"Don't talk with your mouth full.—A friend."

"What kind of a friend?"

"In need.—Swallow."

"I am.—Is she coming here?"

"Yes."

"Can I see her?"

"'May I see her?'—No."

"Why not?"

"I know a little boy who did not wash his teeth this morning," Bertha came to Claudia's rescue.

"I didn't use them overnight," he defended, pushing a piece of calves' liver round his plate.

"Eat," said Claudia.

She reminded herself of the super.

Mary Keyes was quite different from what Claudia had expected from her name, which sounded slim, tailored, and youthful. On the contrary, Mrs. Keyes was on the old side, and had an important figure with a shelf out back. She wore a hat of violets atop her grey hair, and gave the impression of having an invisible velvet ribbon around her ageing throat.

Her out-of-dateness fairly oozed social background as she greeted Claudia from the leather sofa in Hartley's library. "Dear Julia's one of my favourite people," she said by way of an overture, and the least Claudia could say in return was, "Mine, too."

"I've got some really charming apartments to show you," Mrs. Keyes continued.

"This I would like to see," thought Claudia, and was about to say, "Let's go," when Mrs. Keyes got it in ahead of her. "Shall we look at them at once?" she said.

"I'd love to."

Mrs. Keyes moved over an inch. "Very well, do sit down, my dear, and we'll begin."

Claudia sat, feeling like the White Queen in reverse.

"Miss Casey gave me an idea of your approximate requirements, and of course you need a fairly large place." Mrs. Keyes rustled into a commodious briefcase as if in search of it. "I'm quite sure that you can get the Jarvis' duplex, although it isn't on the market yet. However, I happen to know that they're divorcing. Let's me see that's fourteen rooms and six baths, and perfectly delightful."

Evidently Mrs Keyes did not realize that the David Naughtons were the very poor relations of the Hartley Naughtons, and the kindest thing to do was to put her straight immediately. "Seven, or even six rooms," said Claudia firmly, "will do us very nicely. And we can't afford much rent."

Mrs. Keyes folded the list that she had withdrawn from the briefcase, and put it back again. "What do you mean by 'much rent'?" she asked carefully.

Claudia's spurt of courage failed her. She cleared her throat. "As little as possible," she left it to Mrs. Keyes' imagination.

"In that case, this might answer your purpose," she said, and fished out a large, heavy floor plan for Claudia's inspection. "Five and a half rooms in the seventies off the park."

Claudia opened the plan with interest. "Oh, good. I've been wanting to see what those look like." She wasn't an architect's wife for nothing, and it didn't take her long to find out what the half-room was. "Why, it's a jog!" she discovered.

Mrs. Keyes must have misunderstood her, because she explained that bathrooms didn't count as rooms—the half-room was the dining alcove.

"It's a jog," Claudia insisted stubbornly, studying the lay-out. "It's a jog where the kitchen isn't. And I don't see a window in the kitchen."

"There seldom are," said Mrs. Keyes, with a slight chilling of tone. "In the modern apartment, we're getting away from dining rooms and kitchens."

"What do people do for eating?" Claudia enquired, with something of Matthew's persistence.

"Many of the new buildings provide for maid and restaurant service."

" But that's awfully impractical with children."

Mrs. Keyes conceded the point. " I daresay it is, if you want to keep them at home."

" We do," said Claudia tersely. " We always have."

" Fortunately," Mrs. Keyes checked up, " I see that this particular building does not have the hotel service, and the maintenance is accordingly quite a bit lower than average. You can get five-and-a-half rooms on the third floor for twenty-two hundred. Which is absolutely nothing, considering it's deductible."

" It is ? " Claudia hadn't realized that rent, like Miss Casey, was deductible, and twenty-two hundred was a hundred less than the horrid Lacey apartment. She studied the floor plans with renewed interest. " The kitchen's awfully tiny and the bedrooms are, too, but maybe it will look larger in the flesh. It's worth seeing, anyway, and I'd like to very much. This afternoon, if possible."

" But I thought you didn't want an apartment until the autumn ? "

" I don't."

" Splendid. I'm certain this will be ready by October. I passed by on the way here, and I noticed that the foundation was in, and once the foundation is ready, it goes up very quickly."

" Then the building isn't built yet ? " Claudia said blankly.

" If it were completed," Mrs. Keyes differentiated nicely, " I venture to say that you would not find one of the lower-priced suites available. The apartment that I quoted you is excellent value. Excellent. A purchase price of twenty-one thousand for five-and-a-half rooms is very little indeed for a high-type co-operative."

" Co-operative ! " Claudia echoed in a bleat. " You mean you have to buy the apartment ? And from a floor plan ? And without a dining room ? "

" People do, my dear."

" Then people are crazy," said Claudia.

" Possibly," Mrs. Keyes returned enigmatically, " but all I can tell you is that they're selling like hot cakes." She closed her briefcase with an air of finality. I'm afraid there's very little else that I can suggest to you, much as I'd like to be of help. Unless——" She paused, with a plump jewelled finger to her lips. " Come to think of it, I might have just the thing in a rental," she said slowly. " I really might. Although I urge you to consider that, with the maintenance deductible, as I said before, a co-operative apartment is something that should not be lightly considered."

"I'm not considering it lightly or any other way," said Claudia. "I wouldn't buy the most wonderful house in the world now, much less an apartment. What about the idea you just thought of?"

"Ah, yes." Mrs. Keyes opened her briefcase again, and fished around in it. "It's Madame Rosa Schumann's apartment, but I don't believe I have the listing with me. No, I haven't. However, I remember very clearly that it has a dining room, and the house and management are very nice. Very nice."

"Where is it?"

"In the fifties, not too far from the Fifty-ninth Street entrance to the Park for the children."

"And my husband could almost walk to his office, he's on Forty-ninth and Madison. But I suppose the rental is exorbitant."

"I can do things for you on the rental," Mrs. Keyes confided mysteriously. "I know Rosa very well, and I can persuade her to accept a good bit less than she pays. And all she pays is thirty-four hundred, which is exceedingly little."

"It's not little for us, though," said Claudia, "but perhaps if we can get it for less, I'd better look at it, anyway. What about the furniture?" she added distrustfully.

"It's unfurnished," said Mrs. Keyes. "Rosa never lived in the apartment. She signed the lease and went abroad, and now she's decided to stay in Paris for a year or two. You know how these opera stars are. That's why I'm certain that she'll be glad to get rid of her lease, even at a loss." Mrs. Keyes rose, and held out her hand. "My dear look at it, anyway, and if you like it, we'll see what we can do. I'm sorry I can't go with you, I have another engagement. But I'll give you the address, and you can look at it any time you wish."

"I'll go right away," said Claudia. "It sounds too good to be true."

Driving down in the taxi, she tried to anticipate what the catch would be, other than a rental which was beyond their limit. She was, however, much impressed when she saw that it was a corner building on Park Avenue, easily thirty or forty years old, but with a distinction that the apartment house off Third Avenue had lacked. "I like it," she decided at once. She liked the doorman too. He

53

had no gloves on, and he looked like somebody's uncle. He would probably be very nice to the children.

The elevator man was very nice, too. He took her upstairs, along with a pretty Chinese woman, and two men who weren't talking German, so it must have been Russian. "United Nations," the elevator man mentioned resignedly, after he had let them out on their respective floors. "The place is full of them."

"Do they allow dogs in the building?" Claudia remembered to ask.

"We have a couple," he said, "so I guess they do."

"So far so good," she thought in relief.

The car stopped on the eleventh floor. "Apartment A," he directed her. "Go right in, the door's open. I've got another call, I'll be back for you."

"Thank you," said Claudia.

There wasn't a dark corner in the whole place, she could see that as soon as she stepped inside. There was a nice square foyer which gave on to a large living room, with big windows, and shining parquet floors, and a white marble mantel-piece. It was very handsome if you liked it. "I could learn to," she decided firmly.

The dining room adjoined the living room and was quite a bit smaller, but it was legitimate and no jog. The thing to do was to see the rest of the place before she let her hopes run away with her.

The foyer turned at right angles into a short hall. At the end of the hall there was a spacious bedroom, with windows facing west and north—or south and east, she was never sure which was which, especially so high up. The bathroom had a window, too, and it was a sincere, candid bathroom with a great big tub and oversized basin, which David would appreciate ; and there was white tile on the floor, which Bertha would appreciate. Actually, she was afraid to look at the rest of the apartment, she was so certain that something must be wrong with it. But no, the two remaining bedrooms were entirely adequate, with a tiny modern bath between them. The off-centre position of closets and windows gave a clue to the fact that this must have been one very large room, divided into two. "That's all right," Claudia forgave it readily, "it's perfect for Bertha and the children."

Indeed, every bit of it added up to perfection. Something was missing, though. What hadn't she seen? The kitchen, of course ! She'd forgotten about the kitchen. She retraced

54

her steps to the foyer and opened a door near the entrance. It turned out to be a coat closet. She opened another door, and it was another coat closet. "Lots of closets," she noted with satisfaction. She was trying to puzzle out where the kitchen was when the elevator man returned.

"Like it, ma'am?" he enquired amiably.

"Very much, but I seem to have mislaid the kitchen."

He had a nice sense of humour. "A lot of people don't find it straight away," he said. "It's off the dining room. I'll show you."

She followed him back through the living room, into the dining room. She studied the wall space, deciding that there might be room for only six of her Sheraton chairs, because she noticed, for the first time, that for some odd reason, there was a mammoth Venetian blind running the entire width of the wall opposite the windows. It wasn't unsightly, in a modern kind of way, but it didn't seem to belong to the rest of the apartment. "What on earth is that for?" she asked the elevator man.

"That's the kitchen, ma'am," he said. "Want me to pull it up for you?"

She could only nod her head in abject acceptance, for already she could see little white enamel feet peeping out from beneath the lowest shaft of the blind. The enamel feet belonged to an ice-box, a gas-stove, and a sink. There they stood, all in a row like a counter in a drugstore. If Bertha were to stand in front of them, most of her would be in the dining room.

"People don't go in much for cooking these days, but some of the tenants have regular dinners here once in a while," the elevator man volunteered encouragingly.

"But why didn't they put in a door, at least," Claudia wailed, "and make it into a separate room?"

"Board of Health," he explained. "Have to have ventilation. This is what they call a Hollywood kitchen."

Claudia clung desperately to a vanishing dream. "Are they this way all over the house?"

"Not the fours," he said. "The fours have a regular kitchen, but no dining room."

"I'd even prefer that," said Claudia, compromising like crazy.

"Only two bedrooms," he reminded her, "and anyway they're all rented, ma'am."

She was too disappointed to say anything more. As

she passed through the living room on the way out, she took one last longing look at the lovely size of it, and the spotless floors, and the brightness, and even the mantel. "These was nice apartments in the old days," the elevator man offered, as if reading her mind. "Twelve rooms, this one was, and now it's a five and two threes, and the landlord gets four times the rent he used to get."

"Homes seem to be going out of style," said Claudia bitterly.

"Ain't it the truth," said the elevator man.

Hartley was in the hall when she reached home, talking to a man with a long measuring-stick in one hand and a blueprint in the other. Claudia recognized, with an emptiness in the pit of her stomach, that Hartley wore the engrossed and completely happy look of a man about to re-do his house. "Well, well, well," he greeted her, affectionately, and put his arm round her and introduced her to the contractor. "Julia tells me you and David are going to leave us?"

"Yes," said Claudia, trying to be very gay about it, "I've just been looking at apartments."

"No hurry, no hurry," said Hartley, "we don't want to get rid of you, we've got pretty fond of having you around here. See anything?"

Claudia didn't have the heart to tell him the truth. If they had to live in one room and a venetian blind, she wasn't going to interfere with his solarium. "A couple of things," she said, not going into what they were.

"Splendid, splendid," said he.

David came home a little while later. "I see by the contractor downstairs," he greeted her, "that we've burned our bridges behind us. What did you find?" He kissed her. "Hello."

"Hello."

He tossed his hat on a chair and took off his coat. She brought a silk bathrobe from the closet—one of Julia's many birthdays gift throughout the years—and laid it across the bed.

"Thanks," he said. "Shall I shower now or later?"

"Later." If she didn't start talking soon, she'd burst. A delayed fury was sweeping over her. "That horrible woman's furniture!" she choked. "And almost three hundred a month for no kitchen!"

56

"All right, I can see you're steaming, begin from the beginning."

"It's not funny," she protested. "The world is going to pot, and nobody's lifting a finger to stop it!"

"Could be," he said. "Look, why don't we both take a shower and cool off?"

It wasn't a bad idea. Luckily, they didn't have to get dressed again, because Julia 'phoned up from downstairs to say that she and Hartley were dining out, so wouldn't they like to have trays in their room? "We'd love it," said Claudia gratefully. She was so tired that she couldn't move.

For the first time since Bobby's death, she slept like a log the whole night through, but in the morning she wakened with the pain in her heart sharper than ever. What did it matter where they lived? Yesterday it had seemed to be important; the past and the future had given place to the present, and the minutiæ of living had acted as an anæsthetic laid upon an open wound. David would say that yesterday she had taken a great step forward, but she knew differently. There was no healing in an anæsthetic. To-day the power of it had worn off and once again there was only the past, aching with memories, and the future yawned ahead of her, empty and meaningless. If David knew that she was backsliding into a vast inertia and depression, he gave no hint of knowing. He finished his coffee and handed her the newspaper, folded into a neat oblong. "I checked a few apartments that might bear looking at," he said. "There's one on Washington Square, and a couple on the West Side that don't sound too bad."

"Julia won't like visiting us there," Claudia remarked, "but I'll see what they are, anyway."

She took a bus across the transverse. The difference between the East Side and the West Side was, she concluded, largely mental, because the park and the reservoir were just as beautiful, perhaps a little more beautiful, from the opposite angle. There were, however, many more dentists and baby carriages on the West Side, and she could see why Julia felt as she did, although it was nothing you could put your finger on.

Fortunately, Julia was spared the embarrassment of her husband's brother living on the wrong side of the city, because one of the apartments that David checked had been rented the previous day, and the other one turned out to be on the second floor rear, and dark as pitch.

As she waited for the bus to take her back across the transverse, she debated the wisdom of going all the way down to Washington Square on another wild-goose chase. Still, the Square had an alluring sound, and she might as well just cover all the feasible neighbourhoods and get it over with.

When she finally found the address, it was blocks over from Washington Square, and nowhere near as alluring as it had sounded in the paper. The apartment was on a little side-street that dashed across a crowded thoroughfare, and lost itself in a jumble of small shops and tenements. Instead of baby carriages, there were a number of artists painting pictures on the sidewalks with berets on their heads, and she knew that David wouldn't be able to take it. Besides, there were rows of pushbuttons in lieu of an elevator, so she didn't go beyond the vestibule. Not that she was too proud for pushbuttons, but she couldn't see Bertha wading through easels, and climbing up steep flights of stairs with Michael plastered to her hip.

" You and your ads," she upbraided David that evening.

" Sorry," he said. " They read nice."

" They all do. I suppose the only thing left is to go out to Greenwich in the morning, rent a house, and I'll keep coming into town every so often until I find something that's at least livable."

" I guess that's the thing to do," said David. " I'm looking forward to a whiff of the country, aren't you ? "

" Yes," said Claudia.

" What's the matter ? "

" Nothing."

He drew her down beside him. " What are you afraid of, darling ? "

" I wish you weren't so damn smart," she mumbled.

" Would you rather spend the summer in town ? "

She laughed shakily. " We burned our bridges, remember ? "

" Hartley and Julia wouldn't mind postponing their solarium, they know it's hard to find an apartment."

" I wouldn't dream of it. I'd be ashamed to give in to a whim."

" When are you going to learn to be a little more gentle with yourself ? "

" I don't have to be," said Claudia. " You're gentle enough for both of us."

58

"These are hard days," he said simply.

Claudia wondered whether David's desire for the country would help to heal the pain that lay hidden so deep within him. If it did, he must have that healing if it was hers to give. She couldn't bring herself to tell him that she was afraid of beauty.

CHAPTER FIVE

JOHN and Candy were planning to meet them at the station, but Hartley said, " Nonsense, why take a train when Watkins could drive you up in the Rolls ? " And Julia added, " I'm glad the white linen was delivered in time for you to wear it."

" Wear an expensive new dress to rent a house ! " Claudia expostulated.

" What are you going to do, save it until you're an old lady ? "

" Julia's right," David chimed in. " Wear it."

So she wore it, hat and all, and felt extremely stylish as they sped along the Parkway. It was hardly anything of a trip, and before they knew it, they were drawing up in front of the Llewelyn Real Estate office on Main Street, as Mrs. Payne had taken the trouble to arrange.

John's mother was very much like Julia, with a directly opposite approach. She always had at her finger-tips a " little furrier ", or a " little tailor ", or a " little cabinet-maker ", who could deliver a better job than anyone else at half the price, whereas Julia never patronized anyone who couldn't deliver a better job for twice the price.

Mrs. Payne had undoubtedly made Mr. Lewellyn promise that he would personally undertake to find them a great bargain. Indeed, she must have painted so vivid a portrait of their unhappy plight that he was apparently prepared for anything but a Rolls Royce and a glimpse of Claudia's white elegance.

" Oh, dear me," he exclaimed, in an agitated but delighted sort of way, and hurried back to his desk for an entirely different listing. " Damn," said David gloomily, " this is going to be a waste of everybody's time."

" We should have come by train, and I should have worn my blue," said Claudia. " It just goes to show never be what you're not. I wonder is that frightfully good English Mr. Lewellyn talks with, or a slight impediment ? "

" Both," said David. " He comes from one of the oldest families in Greenwich."

" How do you know ? "

" You can tell it."

After a few minutes, Mr. Lewellyn came hurrying out again. He had a very faint limp, more like a hop, and he was thin and sandy, as if his blood-line had run out. As he climbed into the soft, cushioned seat of the Rolls, he confessed, with a shudder, that the houses he had lined up for them would never, never in this world have been right for them. " One or two of them," he confided, " aren't even in Greenwich."

" We're not committed to Greenwich," David assured him tactfully, for he, like Candy, felt that it was on the stuffy side. " What do you say, Claudia ? "

She tried to look interested, but suddenly she didn't care where the houses were, or what they were like. That suffocating blanket of depression was beginning to enfold her again. She huddled back in the car, closing her senses off from the nostalgic impact of country smells and country sounds, and dreading the moment when they would return to Mrs. Payne's for luncheon, and she would have to hold Candy's baby in her arms. What would David say if she were to admit this final cowardice of her soul ?

The morning passed in a blur as they drove from one house to another, all of them expensive and over-furnished. More often than not, they didn't get out of the car. " This is not for us," David would take the initiative, and Claudia would nod agreement, even if it were only a matter of too many shrubs, too well cut. Mr. Lewellyn, however, couldn't understand their peculiar aversions, even though he acknowledged each succeeding defeat by saying, "Sure*ly*," in a plaintive little uphill refrain. It was obvious that he was quite unhappy about the whole thing, especially as it was growing late. " I told Mrs. Payne that I'd have you back for a one-o'clock luncheon," he said nervously, " and I think we just have time to stop in at the Grey estate, which is practically next door to " Grasmere." Mr. Lewellyn liked to refer to houses by their writing-paper names, and Claudia remembered that " Grasmere", austerely engraved, headed Candy's letters when she was visiting her mother-in-law. If the Grey estate was next door to " Grasmere ", it was probably the place with the gates. " It's another waste of time," she murmured to David, " but Mrs. Payne will never forgive us if we don't look at it."

Oddly enough, they both liked it. It was a stone house, not too big, set far back along a line of tall maples, with broad easy lawns, beautifully kept by a very old Italian gardener. The rooms had been stripped of all the important furnishings, but there was enough to do with for the summer —bed, and chairs, and a sofa or two, and only an occasional scatter rug on the polished floors. " This is exactly the kind of place that's a joy to rent," said Claudia, breathing a sigh of relief. " Not an ornament in sight."

" It's my idea of a nice place, too," said David.

Mr. Lewellyn was entranced. " I just had a feeling you'd adore it, and I think—rather I hope," he corrected himself a bit coyly, " that I can get it for you at a marvellous bargain. Would you believe that the house alone cost seventy-five thousand to build ? "

" Yes, I'd believe it," said David. " What's more, it was built about 1932, when building was good and labour was plentiful."

" You never said a truer word," Mr. Lewellyn concurred most solemnly. " You couldn't duplicate it to-day at twice the price, to say nothing of the property and the landscaping And yet I think—I only *think*, mind you—that an offer of fifty-five would buy it. With, roughly, four-and-a-half acres of land."

" It's remarkably fine value," David acknowledged, and for one breathless moment, Claudia thought that he was tempted. " It's excellently designed and handsomely constructed," he went on, " but as Mrs. Naughton said, it's the kind of house we'd like to rent, not own."

Mr. Lewellyn looked ready to weep. " But why not ? It's got everything you want, as far as the neighbourhood and—excuse the expression—swank. What I mean to say, it's an *estate* for the price of a bungalow."

Claudia felt that now was the time to explain, once and for all, that the Rolls was merely borrowed for the day, and that the white linen and floppy hat added to a deceptive note of " swank " that was leading Mr. Lewellyn down a very wrong alley indeed. Mr. Lewellyn, however, didn't give her the chance to correct his erroneous impression. " I know, I just know," he rushed ahead, with his voice fairly wringing its hands, " that the bank will definitely not consider a rental, and oh, oh, oh, how I hate to see you lose this lovely place ! Particularly since Mrs. Payne happens to be one of my favourite people——"

He sounded like Mary Keyes, and Claudia was sure at this point that people who had favourite people were not among her favourite people. She was glad when David said in a tone that could even put an end to Matthew's arguments. " If the bank isn't interested in renting, Mr. Lewellyn, there's no use in discussing it any further."

" You see, we're not interested in *buying*, we just want a house for the summer," Claudia reiterated.

Mr. Lewellyn bit at his pale lips. " Then I must simply find you one. Suppose I call for you after luncheon, and we'll try again ? "

" Suppose," David suggested gently, " that you show us some of the houses that you had originally intended to show us ? "

" I will," said Mr. Lewellyn, " but I know just as well as I know my own name that you won't like them and it'll be an absolute waste of time."

Claudia thought it was better not to catch David's eye.

Candy and John were waiting for them at the *porte-cochère* of the big Victorian house that John was born in, and that his mother intended to die in. It was a hard combination to beat, and one glance at Candy's face was enough to tell Claudia that she wasn't beating it. Candy was sunburned, and she had her shape back from the baby, but there was a strained look in her eyes that didn't belong there. John looked a little strained, too, beneath his fine tan. " They're so happy, they ought to be happier," thought Claudia. She returned Candy's bear-like hug and gave her forehead to John's brotherly kiss, and wished that she could give them a piece of her mind fresh with the impact of seeing them. " You fools, don't you know that nothing matters as long as you have each other and the baby ? " But she was tongue-tied when it came to holding forth, for which David was eternally grateful. He couldn't stand women who went around scattering seeds to sow fine souls.

" Quick, tell me, did you get a house ? " Candy cried. " I can't bear it if you didn't——"

" We didn't," said Claudia.

" Did you look at the Grey place next door ? " John asked curiously. " I hear it's quite a find."

David nodded. " And worth a lot more than they're

asking for it. If you and Candy want to settle out here, you ought to consider it. How is it you haven't seen it ? "

" Candy didn't want to," said John without rancour.

" We'd better go in," said Candy quickly. " You're ten minutes late and the soufflé's collapsing by inches. I know David could live all his life without a soufflé, and John thinks they're all front and no back, but Mother Payne's Annie has been making them every Saturday for lunch for the past twenty years, so that's that."

" Julia's Annette makes them too," said Claudia, " so stop griping."

Candy giggled. " I never realize how much I miss you, until I see you," she said. " And I adore your new outfit, it's stunning. The baby's asleep, thank goodness ; I'll show her off after lunch. Come on, hurry, I bet Mother Payne is having a fit."

Mrs. Payne's restrained version of a fit was a slight rising of colour up along her neck, and a chilly remoteness to her voice. " You naughty children," she greeted them, " I am afraid luncheon is ruined."

" I'm terribly sorry," said Claudia contritely, and, as an example to Candy, she bent down and placed a kiss on Mrs. Payne's cheek. It was a withering cheek, even though she wasn't as old as she tried to seem. The kiss that Claudia gave her melted her into warmth, and for the moment she forgot about the spoiled luncheon, and held eagerly to Claudia's hand and asked her about the children, and the apartments she'd looked at, and did Mr. Lewellyn show her some nice places this morning, particularly the Grey place ?

Claudia went into great detail and thought how easy it was to be nice to someone else's mother-in-law. In return Mrs. Payne said that David looked remarkably well, so much better than before he was ill. " I'm so glad," said Claudia thankfully. Mrs. Payne never said that John looked well, she always fretted that he seemed a little tired, which was one of the things that filled Candy with confusion and resentment. It was pleasant for a wife to hear that her husband looked well and rested. " John's put on weight," Claudia offered for what it was worth. " I've never seen him so fit."

Mrs. Payne said, " I see Thomas getting ready to announce luncheon." She leaned heavily on John as she got to her feet, and her progress to the dining room was slow and unsteady. Claudia hadn't realized that she had become so feeble. Or had she? Candy said that she put it on; if no one was watching her, she was downright spry.

Thomas was serving the correct but uninspired dessert of cut-up fruit and home-made cookies (Julia's lunches were of the same ilk, nicely balanced and restrained), when the sharp wail of the baby wafted down from upstairs. "There," Mrs. Payne announced, with a degree of satisfaction, "I knew it. She's not comfortable with that formula."

"But it agrees with her, she's gaining on it," Candy protested. "She's just spoiled, she'll have to cry it out."

The baby kept on crying, and Candy made herself keep on eating. Mrs. Payne said nothing further, but Claudia noticed the colour deepening on her neck. Finally John said in an undertone, "Darling, let me bring her down."

"I'll do it," Candy surrendered.

Mrs. Payne looked after Candy's slim departing figure. "The modern theory," she observed, "seems to be against Nature's intention that a mother nurse her baby."

"I didn't nurse Matthew or Michael," Claudia mentioned in Candy's defence. She didn't add that David was ill at the time of Michael's birth, and her mother had died the morning that Matthew was born. But she'd nursed Bobby. The years rolled back. Life had been wonderful and secure when Bobby was born. She remembered the miracle of love against her breast, and David bending over her, and the touch of her mother's hand. . . .

Candy missed her mother, too. It was in her eyes as she gave her baby into Claudia's arms. Mrs. Payne wasn't smart enough to know it. It was all their faults.

"The baby's staring up at you as if she knows you," said Candy tremulously.

"Perhaps she does," said Claudia softly. It was as if she were holding Bobby.

Promptly at two, Mr. Lewellyn drove up under the *porte-cochère* in his dusty sedan, and gave three precise little honks to his horn. Candy and John followed them outside. "Stop back afterwards and tell us if you found anything," Candy begged.

"Why don't we go along?" said John. "Maybe we'll see something too."

"I'd adore to, but we'd never get back in time for the baby's four o'clock bottle."

"Mother can give it to her."

64

" Your mother bounces her afterwards, and she spits up."

" You'd think Mother hadn't raised a fine, stalwart specimen like me," John essayed half jokingly.

" Beginner's luck," said Candy. " You were her first. And only," she added, with a grim little tightening of her lips.

" Candy needs a helping hand," David remarked soberly, as they drove off.

" Yes," said Claudia.

" It would be good if we found a place near-by, and you could sort of steer her straight over this rough going."

" The blind leading the halt," said Claudia, with a little laugh.

They could talk, because Mr. Lewellyn was busy driving in the front seat. " We'd better go in my little car," he'd advised. " Some of the places I have in mind are off the beaten track, and hard to find if your chauffeur doesn't know these roads."

It hadn't made any difference to Claudia, but David wasn't too happy about it. He thought everybody but himself was a bad driver. Mr. Lewellyn wasn't too good, Claudia had to admit it. " The next house I'm going to show you," he confided, passing gaily through a red light, " is one of those I told you isn't in Greenwich proper."

" That's good," Claudia murmured. The first two houses had truly justified his prophecy, one was a spanking new bungalow on a barren corner plot off the centre of town, and the other was just rooms full of decent mediocrity. " Now this place," Mr. Lewellyn continued, '' probably won't suit you, either. It's just a shot in the dark, but it just might do for the summer, because there's loads of grounds, and water, although the house itself, I must warn you, is frightfully old and run-down. That's why the rental is so cheap."

" What kind of water ? " Claudia asked, " and how cheap ? "

He didn't hear her, for another car swerved barely in time to avoid a collision. The driver leaned out of the window and cursed at them, and David said, under his breath, " Don't talk to him while he's at the wheel, or we'll all get killed ; the damned idiot's near-sighted."

Suppose they did get killed, thought Claudia, without the healthiness of fear. She'd be with Bobby. At this moment, she wanted Bobby more than anyone else in the world—more than Matthew or Michael—almost more than she wanted David. It wasn't that she loved him less, it was

65

because this beautiful summer day, reaching its peak of beauty made the ache in her heart unbearable.

"The odd thing about the place I'm about to show you," Mr. Lewellyn's silky voice broke into her reverie, "is that you're actually in the township of Banksville, but you pay taxes in—I believe it's Northcastle—and yet you use the Greenwich station and the Greenwich telephone exchange. So "—he paused to chuckle—" you're really suspended in the middle of nowhere. It always amuses me."

David was less amused than pleased. He didn't like to be pigeon-holed. "We seem to have left the estates behind us," he commented in approval.

"Not entirely," said Mr. Lewellyn. "We're going to pass one any moment." He took his hand off the wheel to wave towards a high brick wall. "That's the beginning of the Jameson place. The tooth-paste magnate. It cost half a million."

The tooth-paste wall seemed to go on for ever, and then, all at once, a winding road of pretty little cottages appeared, with small artistic signs out front that stated, in jolly hospitality, "The Martins", "The Salisburys", "The Smiths". One even went so far as to say, "The Drakes Live Here".

"Ah, now here's a place called ' Elsirob '," Claudia cheered David up, "in case you prefer it."

"I wouldn't be surprised," he shrewdly deduced, "if that wasn't a combination of the wife's name, which is Elsie, and the husband's name which is Robert."

"Darling, that's quite clever of you," she rose to his mood. "And here's another provocative name we're coming to, ' Oak Lawn '. Maybe because there's oaks on the lawn."

"Come to think of it," said David after a moment, "we never called the farm anything."

"No, we didn't," said Claudia. "Why didn't we ? "

He put his hand on her knee. "Because you're a nice girl."

"Maybe we should have."

"I'm glad we didn't. I like thinking of it as just the farm."

"I don't like thinking of it at all," she confessed.

"You're still a nice girl," said David.

Suddenly, Mr. Lewellyn surprised them by ejecting his hand and waving it loosely, although there wasn't a car in sight. Then he slowed carefully to a crawl, and made a right turn into a road that led past a field of daisies, rippling in the breeze like a soft white coverlet. " Isn't that just too beautiful ? " he sighed in ecstasy. " It's good farm land around here."

Claudia knew enough to know that daisies meant poor farm land. She had almost wept when David had ploughed and harrowed and fertilized a meadow full of daisies, to get a catch of emerald green alfalfa, which had been his pride and joy.

" Now this property," Mr. Lewellyn turned back in his seat to explain, " adjoins the property I'm going to show you. It was originally part of a tremendous farm that used to be here. In fact, if it won't prejudice you too much, the house that's for rent was used by the herdsman and his wife up to last autumn. Then all the cattle were sold off."

" That won't prejudice us," said David, as they passed twin silos looming up behind a red barn.

" Provided it's clean," Claudia qualified.

" Frankly, it isn't," Mr. Lewellyn prepared her. " That's why I hesitated to show it to you. To be absolutely frank, it's not the sort of place, really, that I can picture you in, but perhaps for just the couple of months that's left of summer it might do."

" How far is it to the station ? " David asked.

" If you take a short cut, which we didn't, it's only a few miles. But you're not far from the Parkway, if you want to drive to New York. It's convenient enough, and yet it's in the middle of nowhere, as I said before. Oh, drat ! " he broke off lustily. " I passed the turn-off." He stopped the car with a screech of brakes, and went into reverse, grinding his gears until they groaned. " Here we are. ' Deep Pond Lane '. This is almost a private little road, although technically it isn't. I mean to say, it's the only house on it, and the property extends in both directions."

" Nice frontage," David remarked.

" And it's a pretty name, ' Deep Pond Lane '," said Claudia.

" It's really not a pond at all, it's part of a river that widens out about half a mile further on into quite a considerable body of water," Mr. Lewellyn explained. " Oh, now there's the house over there, you can just about see the roof of it through the trees."

" It's an old one," said David, as they rounded a turn.

" The porch is tumbling off," said Claudia.

" I warned you, it's not your kind of thing," Mr. Lewellyn protected himself. " And yet they've got an asking-of price almost as much as the Grey estate. Forty-two thousand. So of course, they'll never sell it, and that's why it's for rent.

Four hundred for the rest of the season. It's worth more than that, frankly, if you like water, except that the inside is quite dreadful, really. Oh, *drat*!" He fished through his pockets with one hand. "I haven't brought the keys, but I'll let you out in the front, and I'll climb in through the kitchen window and open the door for you."

The house sat quite far back in a neglected square of lawn. "The road's been moved," said David. "That's why it's set the way it is. All old houses were on the road."

"Then this is an old house," said Claudia. "I mean really old, not just run down."

"Really old," said David. "The porches are just stuck on by some amateur carpenter."

"If you take them off in your mind's eye," said Claudia slowly, "it would look a little like the farm."

"Very much like the farm," said David in an odd voice. "Even though the farm was a salt-box house, and this is a hip-roof."

"That's what I thought it was," said Claudia, "but the porches made me not sure. A hip-roof house in Connecticut isn't very usual, is it ? "

"It's rare," said David. "I've only seen two or three that are worth restoring."

"Is this one worth restoring ? "

"It has the old shingles and the old doors, and if they haven't raped the inside, I'd say it was."

"I don't know much about it," said Claudia, humbly, "but so would I."

The front door opened after much rattling, and Mr. Lewellyn beckoned them to enter. He had a smudge down one cheek, and his suit was streaked with dust. "Whew ! If you have the courage, come on in. These floors must be about a hundred years old ! "

"Closer to two hundred," said David as he stepped across the threshold.

Mr. Lewellyn sighed ruefully. "I'm afraid you just can't make do with it," he said. "It's worse than the last time I showed it. Or maybe I didn't notice the torn matting, and the nasty curtains. To be frank, it's nothing but kitchen furniture all the way through. The panelling's quite interesting, though, if you happen to like old panelling. But, good heavens, the house isn't *livable*, with this awful stuff."

"No, it isn't," Claudia agreed. "Not with all this dirt, and with those sagging porches. They're not safe."

"The back one is," Mr. Lewellyn assured her. "That is to say, I walked across it. And you can see the river from it. It's quite lovely, as far as property goes. There's about thirty-eight acres—all cleared land—but of course that wouldn't interest you."

David's lips moved. "It might." Claudia wondered whether he had really said it, or whether she imagined that he said it. She must have imagined it, because Mr. Lewellyn was apologizing profusely. "I'm so sorry I took your time. There's no need going any further. The bedrooms, as I recall, are just as dilapidated."

David had already started back towards the entrance hall. "I'd like to look upstairs."

"But believe me, it just isn't livable," Mr. Lewellyn protested. "I don't see how the owner can leave a house in this condition. For any price. Only pigs would rent it."

This made it rather awkward. "Well, you see, it isn't the sort of house that anyone would want to rent," Claudia tried to soften the shock. "That is, we wouldn't be interested in renting it, because, as you say, there's too much to be done to it. It needs an architect to love and understand it, and bring it back to what it was." She put her hand in David's. "I hope my husband feels that way about it, too."

"I do," said David, and the way he said it sounded as if they were being married, and he was promising to love and cherish her until death should part them. Only there was no death, while there was love, and Bobby was quite close all at once. She was used to his coming and going, but this was different. This was peace in her heart. Was it the river, running through green meadows? Was it a sense, suddenly, that this shabby little house, sweet with years, was meant for them? Perhaps Bobby, too, had been lost and lonely, but now that he knew that they were home, he had come back again.

She followed David up the old stairway with its handrail worn to the softness of velvet, and was glad that Mr. Lewellyn did not bother to go with them.

Later, they walked down towards the water. Behind them, they could hear Mr. Lewellyn close the window and lock the door. It was right that he should do so, for the house belonged to them, and not to strangers. Poor Mr. Lewellyn. He didn't know what to make of them. "I'll wait for you in the car," he'd told them, a little dazedly. "Take your time. Don't hurry."

There was no hurry. They paused to watch a great big robin strutting along as if he owned the earth. "Did you ever see anything so fat?" Claudia exclaimed. "It must be more than a robin."

David smiled. "That's all. Just a robin." He bent to pick a single rose that lifted its head above a mass of weeds. "There's been a garden," he said.

He gave the rose to Claudia. She touched her lips to it. She knew that it was more than a rose. It was three steps up.

They kept on walking until they reached the river bank, and then they stood for a long while, watching a brace of wild ducks fly for cover in the tangled brush of the opposite shore. How Bobby would have loved it! She couldn't have said the words aloud, and yet, as if in this quiet spot their souls were one, David finished her unspoken thought. "It's going to be a nice place to think of him in," he said.

CHAPTER SIX

MR. LEWELLYN wasn't very happy as he drove them back to Mrs. Payne's. "I don't know what she's going to say about this," he finally laid down his cards.

"She's not our mother-in-law," Claudia reminded him. "Stop worrying."

"Yes, I know, but still and all," Mr. Lewellyn murmured, and almost hit an old lady crossing to a bus-sign.

As it turned out, he hadn't worried for nothing. Mrs. Payne was horrified at the whole thing. "But nobody in his right mind," she affirmed flatly, "would buy a house and thirty-eight acres of land in five minutes! Especially," she added, fixing David with a disapproving eye, "an architect."

David was so pleased about the house—to say nothing of the thirty-eight acres—that he could afford to be affable. "Nobody but an architect would dare to be so indiscreet," he said, and gave her a sunny smile, although Claudia could tell that inwardly he felt that it was none of Mrs. Payne's damn business. "Besides," he went on, using up the rest of the smile as long as he had it on his face, "it took us longer than five minutes." He glanced at his watch. "Mr. Lewellyn picked us up at two, and now it's all of ten to four."

Mrs. Payne was literal until it hurt. "I was speaking

figuratively. And as it happens, you were rather late for luncheon." Shades of the fallen soufflé resided within the stiffness of her voice, although everybody thought she had forgotten it by this time. Candy managed to catch Claudia's eye. " Now you can see what I go through," her gaze implored.

Claudia deliberated. Whether Candy's problem with John's mother was generic, or merely an acute condition of temporary proximity, was increasingly difficult to determine. Whichever it was, she decided that nothing could be gained by adding fuel to an already burning fire. " I think Mrs. Payne is perfectly right," she swung round. " It isn't normal suddenly to decide to buy up half the countryside. No wonder she's disgusted with us."

" Not disgusted, my dear," said Mrs. Payne, somewhat softened, " it's just that I feel a little responsible, under the circumstances. I don't want to see you and David rush into anything you'll regret."

" We never regret," said Claudia.

" You might regret this, though." Mr. Lewellyn's sepulchral prophecy issued from a dim corner, where he had selected, as a self-inflicted punishment, the most uncomfortable of Mrs. Payne's uncomfortable drawing room chairs. Since he was clearly the " circumstances " to which she alluded, it was inevitable that sooner or later she would aim the whole weight of her disapproval in his direction. With a degree of courage surprising in one so pale and thin, he up and beat her to it. " Surely, Mrs. Payne," he protested, " I do hope you believe that I wouldn't have shown them that particular house if I so much as *dreamed* that they were in the market to buy ! "

" Only we weren't," Claudia insisted. " We had every intention of finding an apartment in New York for the winter."

Mr. Lewellyn twisted his hands in supplication. " Surely. That's what you told me. But if you've changed your minds, and have decided to live in the country, why don't you buy the Grey place ? It's ideal. Price, the neighbourhood, everything. Ideal."

" And I have reason to know," Mrs. Payne squelched any grandiose ideas of price that Mr. Lewellyn might be cherishing, " that the bank is most anxious to settle the estate, and the property can be had for even less than they're asking for it."

"I'm ready to submit an offer for fifty-five," Mr. Lewellyn ventured in eager co-operation.

"Less," Mrs. Payne stated inexorably. "I told my son that it was the opportunity of a lifetime to make a really magnificent investment——" She paused to peer round the room for John, but he had vanished, several minutes past, to fetch her medicine for palpitation. Her accusing gaze found Candy instead. "Neither he nor my daughter-in-law," she finished coldly, "have so much as driven up the road to look at it."

Candy's eyes dropped guiltily. She couldn't say to John's mother, "It's too near," although, in her secret heart, Mrs. Payne probably knew the reason for Candy's stubborn disinterest.

"Of course you must remember that, nice as it is, the Grey place hasn't any water," Claudia inserted tactfully.

Candy threw her a grateful look. "No, and I'm mad for water!" she cried.

"You can do without water with a young baby," Mrs. Payne observed tersely. "A river, where there are children, is courting disaster. It isn't safe."

Safe. There was no such thing as safety. Bobby had been alive and well one moment and in the next moment, all that could die of him was lying beneath the wheels of a truck. The image returned to snatch the peace out of her heart and to fill it once more with agony and rebellion. It had seemed so right to have come upon the little house out of nowhere, and as suddenly named it home, and theirs. Yet now, back in Mrs. Payne's drawing room, something had happened to disturb that immense obedience of the spirit. What mesmerism had possessed them to want to burden themselves with a tumbledown house and thirty-eight scraggy acres? It wasn't like David to be impractical and foolhardy; he was doing it for her sake, so that she could grow her roots again, and know a place that she could call her own. As if she ever could, without Bobby. Mrs. Payne's warning about courting disaster had brought back not only the fear of death, but the fear of life. True, she could not have meant to destroy the sense of peace on the river bank, but it was hard for outsiders to tread for ever lightly over broken hearts. After a little while even friends began to forget, as it was right they should. . . .

She felt David's strong clasp round her fingers, as if he knew the agony screaming through her. "I don't quite

72

agree with you, Mrs. Payne," he said quietly. "We can't live in eternal caution, and I think that a river, where there are children, is a wonderful thing."

Mrs. Payne submitted gracefully. "Æsthetically, yes. And it won't run away," she added with a playful smile. "As long as you want to buy a place, take your time, look around, and if you still want that particular house, it'll still be there."

"Sure*ly*," Mr. Lewellyn chirped in. "It certainly will be there, no one's bought it so far. And I have a listing of dozens of houses for sale. Literally dozens."

"But they don't want dozens," Candy burst out. "They want this house, and I can't see what the argument's about!"

"There is no argument," Mrs. Payne informed her in chilly reproval. "I was merely trying to be helpful, but I agree with you, I mustn't meddle." Injury crept into the abrupt ageing of her voice, and the little red spots came out along her neck like a danger signal. Candy bit her lips. "I didn't say you did!" she denied, a trifle hysterically, which meant she had probably told John his mother meddled, and John hadn't been very tactful in transmitting his wife's sentiments. At any rate, Mrs. Payne appeared to have stored her little grievance away for a rainy day, and now she had aired it just enough to show she had it. She straightened the ends of her delicate white lace collar, and said, "I'm very glad that you said what you felt, because I daresay Claudia and David were too courteous to tell me it was none of my business."

It hit pretty close to the truth. "No, really not," Claudia protested, a little too feverishly. "In fact, I think we ought to listen to your advice."

She could feel David's puzzled eyes upon her, not sure whether she was carrying politeness to a degree, or whether she meant what she said. She was glad that John's return to the room allayed further discussion. He came in, bringing an objective freshness and a glass of water and two tablets. "Well, let's get started if we're going to see the place while the sun's out," he said, with innocent heartiness.

Nobody made a move. Mrs. Payne swallowed the two pills and held the glass aloft, while she looked about for the coaster that John had neglected to bring. She started to put it on the table beside her, and in loud silence thought better of it. Mr. Lewellyn sprang forward. "I'll take it," he offered, eager to re-establish his good standing, and after a moment of helpless indecision he walked out to the hall with it.

"What's the matter ? " John asked of the room in general. "Why so quiet ? Do we go and see the house or don't we ? "

"By all means," his mother replied. "You go, too, Candy. I'll keep an eye on the baby."

Candy refrained from remarking that she'd had every intention of going. "The baby'll sleep until her next bottle," she said evenly. "I've already asked Annie to look at her occasionally."

"That wasn't necessary while I'm here," Mrs. Payne remarked with raised brows.

John put his arm around her. "But you won't be here, you're coming too."

"No, dear. I'd only be in the way."

John's lean face tensed a little. Candy put out her hand to her mother-in-law. "Oh, please do come along with us, you won't be in the way, ridiculous, what gave you that idea ! "

It was easy to see that she was being overly persuasive for John's sake, and David followed her example with good intentions, but a minimum of grace. "Perhaps you'll change your mind, Mrs. Payne, when you see the place," he suggested, a little too politely.

Claudia thought, "He's spoiled, because Mamma was never that kind of mother-in-law." Outwardly, her mother had reacted exactly the same way as Mrs Payne when they'd bought the farm the year Bobby was born, but she hadn't been able to hide that she was as excited about it as they were. "Lunatics," she always called them. David had adored her mother ; it was too bad that it couldn't be that way with Candy and Mrs. Payne.

In the end they succeeded in coaxing her into going with them. She was putting on her hat in front of the hall mirror when she spied the half-filled glass of water that Mr. Lewellyn in desperation, had stuck behind a vase of flowers on the console. The afternoon was humid, and the bottom of the glass had sweated more than usual, leaving a nasty damp grey circle on the rosewood finish. She rubbed at it with her handkerchief while her nostrils spoke her mind for her.

"I'm sorry," Mr. Lewellyn murmured abjectly.

"It'll disappear with a little wax," John cheered them both up. "Forget about it, come along."

Claudia knew from experience that it would take something more than a little wax, but Mrs. Payne went the whole

74

way and said that the table would have to be completely refinished. Her irritation directed itself towards Candy's yellow shorts and halter. " I hope you're not going dressed like that," she said.

" You mean undressed like that," John modified. This time he put his arm round Candy instead of his mother, and bent to touch his lips against his wife's bare shoulder. " I like it. It's no worse than a bathing suit," he said.

" But she isn't going bathing," Mrs. Payne replied, " and it's very undignified to run around with nothing on. You seem to forget that she's a married woman with a baby."

" I wish you wouldn't forget either ! " The words escaped Candy's lips before she could call them back. " I'll change," she mumbled hastily.

She turned and rushed up the curved stairway, with its impressive Victorian balcony, and Claudia was almost certain that she had seen tears of embarrassment and frustration in Candy's clear young eyes. John must have seen them, too, because he said, with faint impatience, " Mother, why hold us up with a silly thing like that ? "

" There's no one over there to see her, anyway," David added, and looked as if he'd like to wring Mrs. Payne's neck.

" Whether there is or not," Mrs. Payne maintained, " there's such a thing as one's self-respect. I simply can't get used to the lack of modesty in the younger generation."

John gave a forced laugh. " Now come off it, Mother. Only a few years ago you went sailing with your blue jeans rolled up and not much else on besides."

Mrs. Payne flushed. " That was quite another thing. There was just your father, and you and I." She sighed. " It seems more than a few years ago, those happy days. I'm an old lady now."

What she meant, and not too subtly, was that John's marriage, rather than her husband's death, had succeeded in making her into an old lady, and ridiculous though it sounded, Claudia suddenly realized that it was true. She would always remember her first impression of Mrs. Payne— a tiny grey-haired woman of such formidable vitality that Claudia felt abashed to admit that she had never been salmon-fishing in Canada, or mountain climbing in the Alps, or duck-shooting in the Carolines. " And she can still play a right smart game of tennis," John had added proudly to the list of his mother's accomplishments.

"She's just wonderful," Candy had worshipped in awe.

Privately Claudia had felt that there was black magic in Mrs. Payne's athletic brand of motherhood. What was the purpose of it? One could always find any number of playmates one's own age, but Nature had arranged only one mother to a family, and preferably the motherly kind.

Time proved her right, for all at once, shortly after John's marriage, Nature had her innings, and Mrs. Payne suffered a severe reversion to type. It was as if the borrowed years of her youngness had caught up with her, and she took unto herself all the female prerogatives she had hitherto disdained. John, baffled and dismayed, went with her from one specialist to another, and quite naturally, Mrs. Payne's over-pushed body was beginning to show signs of wear and tear. There was nothing of immediate concern, however, beyond a rise of blood-pressure and a tired heart, but the diagnosis was sufficient to enable her to retire in a blaze of glory to a state of semi-invalidism. It was too bad, according to David, that none of the doctors chose to examine her mental processes, but to be fair about it, he had to concede that Mrs. Payne presented no conspicuous problem of psychic disturbance. What problem there was fell to John and Candy, and neither was facing it. Candy had youth, but Mrs. Payne had age, and age combined with filial devotion could be a fearful opponent. "Poor John," thought Claudia, as they waited in the hall for Candy to return. "Why can't he see it? Or does he try not to see it?"

Candy saw it, but she wasn't doing anything about it except letting it destroy her. All the joy had vanished from her face as she came running down the stairs a few minutes later, in a striped cotton dress that hid her slim, sunburned limbs, and gave no sweetness to the young lift of her breasts. Mrs. Payne smiled gently upon her. "That's better," she said. "I've always liked that little dress."

"I loathe it," said Candy shortly. "It was the first thing I could grab and I didn't want to keep everybody waiting."

"All right, let's go," said John quickly. "You look nice, darling, whatever you wear."

"Thanks." She hurried ahead to the porch, and again Claudia saw that her eyes were flooded with tears. She knew, without knowing how she knew, that it hurt almost as much when John was sweet as when he wasn't.

"This household is in a mess," David muttered at her side.

"No more than most," Claudia returned, "when two women in love with the same man live under the same roof."

"A good kick in the pants might help the situation," said David.

Claudia wanted to ask him whose pants, but Mrs. Payne, leaning heavily on John's arm, had come up behind them. "It's turned a little chilly," she said. Her gaze wandered to Candy, who was already ensconced in the red leather seat of John's tan convertible. "I think you ought to pull the top up; Candy oughtn't to run any chances of catching cold so soon after the baby."

"You're not supposed to take having babies seriously any more," Claudia put in, to avoid an issue. "You're supposed to get up and hustle the next day."

"I don't subscribe to it," Mrs. Payne flatly declared. "That's possibly the reason why so many women can't nurse their babies, and have shattered nerves after childbirth."

"Oh, dear, what did I start?" thought Claudia unhappily. She was glad when John ended the argument. "Candy loves the wind in her face," he said brusquely. "Now look, Mother, you lead the way in the closed car with Mr. Lewellyn, and the rest of us will pile in the convertible and follow up."

"Sure*ly*," Mr. Lewellyn applauded. "I just hope Mrs. Payne won't mind a set of chains in the back."

It had occurred to Claudia to wonder what chains were doing in his car in the middle of summer, but the fact remained that they were there, and Mrs. Payne shied away from them as if a poisonous snake were coiled against the dusty seat. "I'm always more at ease in my own car," she demurred, "and it will hold all of us comfortably. John can have it out of the garage in no time."

Mr. Lewellyn turned to Claudia. "Why can't we all drive over in your lovely Rolls?" he went Mrs. Payne one better.

The moment was ripe to finally disillusion Mr. Lewellyn as to the rightful ownership of the car. "Oh," he said, looking very let down indeed. "I see."

"But of course we'll drive over in it," Claudia conceded generously.

"It isn't here," said David, with his patience running out. "Watkins took it to the village to have air put in one of the tyres. Now let's get started or we'll never get back to New York at this rate."

"It'll save a lot of time and fuss if I get Mother's car," said John, quite resigned about it. He leaned over the leather seat and lifted Candy in his long arms. "Come along with me, keep me company."

"John, put me down!"

"Shh," Mrs. Payne cautioned, "you'll wake the baby."

"He hurt!" Candy protested a little wildly. "I wish he wouldn't *do* that!"

Mrs. Payne sighed as Candy, still struggling in John's arms, vanished from earshot. "The child worries me," she said. "She isn't acting like herself."

Claudia wanted to retort, "She was looking forward to driving over with just the four of us in the open car, but it got to be too much of a crisis." It seemed petty, though, and on the face of it a rather inadequate reason for Candy's behaviour. She said, instead, anxious for a little respite from the tension, "I'll 'phone Bertha that we'll be late getting home, not to keep the children up."

"That's a good idea, I'll do it," said David, and disappeared like a flash.

"That's a filthy trick," she ground out under her breath.

"It's *such* a lovely day!" Mr. Lewellyn made sprightly conversation. "Yes, indeedy."

"We need rain," Mrs. Payne returned in a sepulchral voice. She plucked a less than perfect rose leaf from the lattice-work against the *porte-cochère*. She had an excessively green thumb, and took prizes right and left for her floral achievements. "If Candy would only take an interest in the garden," she continued with her little sigh, "I'm sure it would be very relaxing for her."

"It wouldn't be relaxing for me," said Claudia, who adored flowers, but had no talent whatever for making them grow. "Besides," she went on, enjoying a sense of utter perversity, "it's hard to take an interest in anyone else's garden."

"This isn't anyone else's garden," Mrs. Payne corrected her gently. "John is my only child, and everything I have including this house and all that's in it, will be theirs after I'm gone."

"Better they than me," Claudia inwardly thanked her stars, knowing that Mrs. Payne prided herself on never throwing anything away. But Mr. Lewellyn rose to the occasion and said, "No one can say you're not a wonderful mother, Mrs. Payne, only let's hope we'll have you with us for many, many years to come."

"Yes, indeedy, amen," Claudia finished silently. She was relieved to hear the loud coughing of the ancient limousine, since it meant that they should soon be on their way. Unhappily, the coughing stopped, then it began, and stopped again. "John must be flooding the motor," Mrs. Payne frowned. "If they don't realize that haste only makes waste, we'll be standing here for the rest of the afternoon."

It was what everybody was afraid of, and it was a work of art how Mrs. Payne managed to shift the blame. "Wonderful little woman," Mr. Lewellyn persisted, after Mrs. Payne had hurried off in the direction of the garage, forgetting to walk old. "You should have known her before she became ill."

"I did," said Claudia shortly.

"She's a lesson to all of us."

"She is that," said Claudia.

Mr. Lewellyn swallowed his Adam's apple, and made a fresh start. "It's too bad your sister's such a nervous little thing; it almost seems to be the modern trend to have a neurosis these days," he remarked with a little laugh, and almost a lisp. "Everybody you meet goes to a psychoanalyst, heaven only knows why!"

"Candy doesn't, and I've never known her to be nervous, and she's not my sister," Claudia nipped him in the bud.

"You're not sisters?" Mr. Lewellyn exclaimed. "Now whatever gave me that idea!"

"I haven't the slightest notion," said Claudia wondering what was keeping David so long. "We're not even related," she added spitefully.

Mr. Lewellyn had to re-orient all of his preconceived notions. "Then you weren't a Van Doren before you were married?" he began, taking first things first.

"No," said Claudia. "Just a Brown."

"One of the Mattingly Browns?" he suggested hopefully.

"Plain Brown."

"Oh," said Mr. Lewellyn. This bit of information, coupled with the discovery that the Rolls was merely loaned for the day, was disappointing. "But I heard somewhere that Candy had made her home with you and your husband in that lovely apartment on Beekham Place?" he pursued doggedly.

"That was her mother's apartment," Claudia continued to knock down his efforts to build her up. "Candy's mother was one of our closest friends."

" Yes, of course, of course, I see the whole thing, now. I daresay that when Mrs. Van Doren died so unexpectedly, you took the child under your wing, after a manner of speaking, and that was how she came to marry your husband's partner. So romantic, wasn't it ? " He did not wait for her to agree, but rushed ahead to get it all out of his system, as he had been bursting to do for the past several hours. " Naturally I know who the Hartley Naughtons are, they're always in the society columns, and that's where I got mixed up. You're Julia Naughton's sister ! " he deduced triumphantly.

" Sister-in-law," said Claudia feeling as literal as Mrs. Payne.

" Sur*ely*. At long last, I have it all straight, stupid me ! " Mr. Lewellyn gave a heave of satisfaction, and lapsed into silence while he digested these various social tit-bits. He'd probably been burning with curiosity all morning, and Claudia felt an odd surge of respect for Mrs. Payne, who might mind other people's business, and yet didn't indulge in promiscuous gossip. She was close-mouthed as a well-bred clam. As for Mr. Lewellyn, it was more than ever difficult to believe that he came from one of the finest and most prominent families in New England, as Mrs. Payne had verified at luncheon. However, Claudia decided that there was probably one to every old blood-line, like a black sheep in reverse.

" Oh, here they come," Mr. Lewellyn suddenly exclaimed, and sure enough, there was Mrs. Payne's mammoth old car lumbering up like a glorified truck, with the three of them perched high in the front seat. " Where's David ? " John shouted above the roar of the motor. " We're finally ready ! "

" Telephoning, I'll go get him ! "

She found him in the powder-room, or what passed for a powder-room in Mrs. Payne's Victorian mansion. Mrs. Payne was not one for remodelling, and the powder-room, along with the rest of the house, had stolidly withstood the inroads of modern beautification, and remained a downstairs lavatory, guiltless of any embellishment beyond its substantial white tiling and old-fashioned but commodious equipment. " I'm here," he called out, when he heard her looking for him.

She paused for an instant before she opened the door with her heart thumping against her ribs, and her body going cold and damp with the terror of association. Just a year ago it had happened this way—they had gone sailing on John's boat, and David had disappeared into the miniscule washroom, and she had heard him cough, and she had pushed open the

door. . . . Was it happening again ? Her legs buckled beneath
her. And then the door opened, and there he stood, drying
his hands on one of Mrs. Payne's large linen towels. "The
circuits to New York were busy, so I cancelled the call.
What's the matter ? "

"Nothing," she said unsteadily.

"You don't look like 'nothing'."

"David, are you really all right ? "

"No. Mrs. Payne gives me a swift pain."

"She can't help it," said Claudia, her relief coloured with
charity. She laughed tremulously, ashamed to tell him about
the fear that had swept over her. "I'm a fool ; come on,
everyone's waiting."

"With a little luck and no more talk," said David, "we
ought to be back in town by dinner time."

Luck was not with them. A few hundred yards up the
road, the tidy stone pillars of the Grey estate stepped out
into their path. It was impossible to ignore them, and
Mr. Lewellyn, still currying favour the he had so grievously
lost, leaned forward to lightly tap Mrs. Payne's shoulder, and
said, "Don't you think that, as long as we're passing, we
ought to take just a little tiny peek ? We can drive up and
around and right out again."

"That's a very sound suggestion," Mrs. Payne approved,
with forgiveness in her tone. "It will give us some idea of
comparison in the two places."

John turned in his seat, and looked back at them doubtfully. "I don't imagine Claudia and David want to spare
the time," he said.

"Surely a couple of minutes more or less won't matter,"
Mr. Lewellyn carried on for Mrs. Payne.

"Go ahead," said David, as resigned as John had been
about using the convertible.

The grounds were even more attractive than Claudia
remembered in her first quick appraisal of them. She hadn't
realized how nice a gravel drive-way could look when it was
freshly raked, and she noticed how the grass was cut, so that
it was like a velvet carpet, newly swept. Great spreading
rhododendrons put out early blossoms like gigantic red bows
on pompous women, and beckoned them towards the house.
"Now isn't this perfectly charming ? " Mrs. Payne demanded.

"It is awfully nice," Candy granted reluctantly. "At
least the outside is."

"The inside is, too," said Claudia. "I'd really have

rented it in a minute if it was for rent and not for sale."

"But if you like it so much, I can't understand why you *don't* want to buy it!" Mrs. Payne exclaimed.

"I can't understand it, either," Mr. Lewellyn moaned.

"Because it's not our kind of place," Claudia patiently explained.

"It looks like anybody's kind of place," John commented. "Not too much upkeep, slate-roof, copper leaders, and stone that'll never need painting."

"You don't get this kind of building to-day, at twice the price," said David.

The old caretaker caught sight of them, and emerged from behind some shrubs with pruning shears in his hand. "Hello, Tony!" Mr. Lewellyn called to him with beaming familiarity. "You remember me, I came this morning!"

Tony's leathery face cracked into a smile. "I have key, I open door right away!"

"We might as well take a quick little glimpse, as long as we're here," said Mrs. Payne.

David looked crucified, but Claudia whispered, "Let's. It'll be fun to compare."

It wasn't fun. The house wore too well on a second visit. "It's not so large that two people would rattle around in it, and yet it's big enough for a whole family," John summed up. It was on the tip of her tongue to say yes, and wouldn't it be perfect for him and Candy, but she dismissed the idea as heresy. Candy could never stand the strain of living so close to John's mother.

And then Candy discovered the powder room, and fell in love with it, as anyone would, because as powder rooms went, it was very superior. It was as gentle as a breeze, with pale marble walls and lavender curtains. "I wonder if the curtains go with the house," said Candy, quite object-struck.

"The marble does, anyway, and the curtains are easy enough to duplicate," John told her, just as if they were going to move in the next day.

Mrs. Payne said, looking very happy, "I knew you'd like it. If the place that Claudia and David want to buy is even nicer than this, I don't wonder that they've lost their heads over it."

Claudia gave a feeble smile, and David didn't say anything except, "We like it." They both knew that the Grey estate had successfully cooked the goose of the little house on the river, as Mrs. Payne had probably intended it should; and truthfully, the more Claudia saw of the firm plaster walls and lovely straight library panelling, the more she had to admit that John's mother wasn't so wrong. David must have been feeling a few pangs of indecision himself, because he said under his breath, "If you're so crazy about it, say so before it's too late."

"Anyone would be crazy about it who wasn't crazy," she retorted.

"Well, come along now, children," Mrs. Payne carolled to them, with the perfect timing of an artist. "All we wanted, you know, was just to take a peek at the place."

"Mr. Lewellyn says Mrs. Grey fitted out the whole top floor as a playroom for her grandchildren when they came visiting," said Candy. "Couldn't I just take a dash up to look at it?"

"Provided it's a dash," said David.

"I'll go with you," said John.

When they came down, Candy reported: "There's a ping-pong table and a huge hobby-horse, and lots of trains all set up." Later, as they were driving off, she mentioned, a little wistfully, "It was a lovely powder room. . . ." The way she said it took Claudia back to Tennyson and the sixth grade. *She had a lovely face. God in His beauty lend her grace, the Lady of Shalott.*

"In every particular," Mr. Lewellyn agreed fervently, "it's a little *bijou*, house and grounds and all. That's what it is, a little *bijou*."

"It's pretty nice," said John.

Mrs. Payne didn't say anything. She didn't have to.

They rolled along in silence for a space. "We seem to be leaving Greenwich," she remarked.

"I think I mentioned that the house on the river isn't in Greenwich, actually," Mr. Lewellyn said.

"But we use the Greenwich station and the Greenwich telephone exchange," Claudia inserted. "So you see we really have the name without the game."

"I should think it would be a rather questionable property investment," Mrs. Payne commented. "The neighbourhood appears to be getting somewhat mediocre." She glanced with disfavour at the gay little signs that informed the passing public that the Smiths, the Salisburys, and the Martins, all lived next door to each other in a row. "We don't like fancy little signs either," Claudia confessed, "but you can't have everything, and anyway, somewhere along here there's a big tooth-paste mansion with a mile of high brick wall."

When they came to it, Mrs. Payne mistook it for an

institution. "No, no, surely not," Mr. Lewellyn set her straight, "that's the Jameson estate. You can't see it from the road, but it's modelled after an old French château at a cost of a million dollars."

It had only been half-a-million a little while ago, and Claudia was appreciative of his generosity. However, a hidden château could not entirely take the curse off "Elsirob", the little shingled house with the pink shutters. "We'll have to pass it day after day unless one of us burns it down," she thought with a sinking heart. To make matters worse, she hadn't remembered "Oak Lawn", a few yards farther along, with its scrubby oaks and a glimpse of clothes-line dangling in the rear yard. Mrs. Payne's hanging yard was discreetly hidden behind an immaculate white fence, and all her garbage pails were sunk modestly in the ground. The Grey estate had sunken garbage pails too, Claudia recalled, nicely contrived and camouflaged. She was as sensitive to the proper disposition of garbage as Candy was to a powder room. Each to his weak spot, she reflected.

"Now we're coming to the beginning of the original farm land," David announced quite pompously.

"I adore the looks of a red barn, especially with silos," Candy said.

Mrs. Payne said, "Farms that aren't used become a great burden."

"That's right, they do," David assented cheerfully, and let Mrs. Payne read between the lines whatever she wanted to. She read the worst, and said, "Not even farmers can make farms pay these days."

"Oh, a couple of cows and some chickens mightn't break us," David returned airily. He might have gone on into sheep, simply to be unruly, if Mr. Lewellyn hadn't burst out feverishly at that moment, and said, "I'm so sorry, turn right, up this little road!"

The old limousine did not like being taken by surprise, and baulked noisily at the rugged curve. "This is so *country*!" Candy marvelled. "It's hardly more than a few miles away, but it's like a different world from Greenwich!"

Claudia was about to say, "That's what we like about it," but she concluded that it was wiser not to teach the younger generation how to shoot, so to speak. It was time that Candy learned the gentle art of tact, if not diplomacy. Mrs. Payne had been married in Greenwich and John had been born there and it behoved no one, particularly a daughter-in-law

84

to cast aspersions on a way of life that had maintained itself for over a quarter of a century behind the privacy of an English box-hedge that was as fine, if not finer, Mrs. Payne was wont to say, than anything in England.

There wasn't even a fence to mark the boundary of the little house by the river. There it stood in the middle of what had once been a lawn, and was now just a tangle of tall grass and weed. Claudia's heart sank. She realized, of course, that the whole place was run-down and needed building up, but after the magnificent good health of the Grey estate, the peeling paint and sagging porch made it look like little more than a shanty in comparison.

" Why are we stopping here ? " Mrs. Payne asked.

" This is it," Mr. Lewellyn stated baldly.

Mrs. Payne, for once, was speechless. David didn't wait for her to regain her voice. He was out of the car before John had time to turn the motor off. " There's no way of driving up to the front door yet," he shouted back over his shoulder. " There's a big fallen log over the path, so you'll have to walk it ! "

" The porch is falling off, too." Candy's voice was very small.

" That's nothing, it has to come off, anyway, it doesn't belong," said John. He stood, squinting at the house through the sun. " Hip-roof," he said.

Claudia nodded, thankful that he was an architect and knew all the answers.

" What do you think of it ? " Candy asked, still in that same small voice.

" I reserve judgment," he replied, and strode after David across the lawn.

" That's fair enough," Mr. Lewellyn concurred, with a nervous little laugh. " Shall the rest of us walk up and look too ? "

Mrs. Payne did not budge from her seat. " I don't believe it," she said flatly. " Claudia, are you and David actually serious in wanting to buy this tumbledown shack ? "

" Yes, I'm afraid so." Claudia felt that her voice was as small as Candy's.

" And how much did you say they wanted for this——— ? " Again Mrs. Payne lost her power of expression.

" Forty-two thousand," Mr. Lewellyn supplied.

" The Grey place is thirteen thousand more," Claudia reminded her quickly.

" You mean they're *asking* fifty-five ? " Mrs. Payne found her tongue.

" Forty-two is only the asking price for this, too, and if they both come down, it'll amount to the same thing."

Mr. Lewellyn again gave his nervous little laugh. " Ladies, ladies, I can't promise anything, I'll do my best, but this is a rising market, you know."

" It's a falling market," Mrs. Payne contradicted firmly. " The peak of these ridiculous prices is past."

" It's silly to discuss price," Candy said, " until you've really bought the house——" There was a note of doubt in her voice that did not escape Claudia. Even though she didn't want to take sides with her mother-in-law, Candy was plainly not impressed with their choice.

Mr. Lewellyn held out both his thin moist hands to help Mrs. Payne alight. " Sure*ly*. That's an excellent suggestion. Suppose we look inside, shall we ? "

Mrs. Payne climbed down from the car with obvious reluctance and excessive difficulty. The procession towards the ramshackle porch was as slow as a funeral cortège. " The river is simply breath-taking," Candy exclaimed with a burst of enthusiasm, but once inside the door she couldn't say anything except, " Look how wide the floors are, I adore the old nails——"

Mrs. Payne said, " Where have John and David disappeared to ? "

" I hear them upstairs," said Claudia.

" I'll wash my hands," Mrs. Payne told her, " while you two join them. The steps are too steep for me." Her tone indicated that she had already washed her hands of the entire project.

" There's a little bathroom off the maid's room," said Claudia. " Let me take you."

" No, no, I can find it. You show Candy round."

" I don't see much point in going any farther," Claudia called a halt when they'd reached the kitchen. " You don't like it, either." She smiled faintly at Candy's give-away silence. " There isn't even a powder room."

" I don't even see where you'd fit one in, either," Candy returned seriously.

" We couldn't, unless we built on. Company would just have to go upstairs to powder."

" I don't care," Candy blurted out. " I hope you buy it, anyway, I'm so happy to have you nearby, I can't see straight.

86

Of course, I must say," she added honestly, "that I think the Grey place is much nicer in every way except the river."

"And the old nails."

"You're making fun of me. No, but really——" She lowered her voice discreetly. "Maybe you ought to go back and look at the Grey place while this is still fresh in your mind."

"I don't have to," said Claudia. "I remember everything about the Grey place." She'd remembered everything that was worth remembering about this place, too—the simple grandeur of age, and the peace that had come to her when she had stood by the river with David. Now the river sparkled into the room, full of diamonds. There was an elm leaning over it that was part yellow with the sun and part yellow with blight. She was glad that there weren't many elms along the bank ; they'd lost almost all of them on the farm. It was too bad about elms, they were such stately trees to be so humiliated. Perhaps they'd be able to save the ones that were here. Certainly there would have to be a great deal of clearing of the overgrown brush, careful clearing so that the natural beauty of the shore-line wouldn't be spoiled. If you took out too much, the wild ducks would have no place to nest. There were no wild ducks on the Grey estate, no clearing to be done beyond a few fallen leaves in the oval lily-pool in the garden. There might be an occasional frog in the lily-pool—Bobby had loved frogs, there had been lots of them round the brook on the farm—and she had never been able to eat frogs' legs again in a restaurant, although David told her that that was silly, she ate chicken didn't she ? Yes, she'd eat chicken, but she drew the line at goose. How tame the geese had been, walking around on endless tours of inspection as if they owned the whole farm, and honking their heads off if strangers came. Geese were wonderful, and not enough appreciated unless you knew them. But you couldn't have them without water—so there'd be no geese if they bought the Grey estate. A fine reason to buy a place. It wasn't the only reason, though. In spite of the peeling paint and sagging porch, there was that sense of peace that lingered in the shadows on the river, and the confidence with which the little house sat behind the great bride and groom hemlocks. As if it belonged there. As if it were waiting for David and herself to walk in through the door and call it home.

She was aware that Candy had finished with her brief

inspection of the kitchen. There was nothing to admire as there had been in the Grey kitchen. The Grey kitchen, in addition to having everything else that was the last word in modern equipment, boasted a stainless steel plate-warmer in the butler's pantry. As far as Claudia was concerned, it was dotting the " i ", for Bertha's dishes were always piping hot from putting them on the overhang part of the stove, but now Candy said, " If you ever wanted one of those wonderful plate-warmers, where would you put it ? "

" In the powder room we haven't got."

" Let's find John and David," said Candy lamely.

" Let's," said Claudia, knowing that Candy needed John's moral support. If John was disappointed in the house, too, it would be much easier for Candy to say what she felt.

They found David and Mr. Lewellyn in the master-bedroom but John was nowhere to be seen. The room was not large, but it was square and airy. The wide boarding of the pine floors shone like honey with the sun on them, and the old glass in the mullioned windows gave a new magic to the river. " It's a home," Claudia thought again. " It's our kind of home." There would be quietness in going to bed at night and waking up in the morning, within these simple, pleasant walls. She looked at David. His face told no tales. He was standing with his arm on the wood-carved shelf, talking to Mr. Lewellyn, and when he saw her he held out his hand. " Darling," he said, " Mr. Lewellyn makes very sound sense. He thinks we ought to rent the house——"

" Rent it——" Claudia echoed. It was incredible. Why, she had already bought it and moved into it. She had never expected this right-about-face. She glanced around for John. Perhaps John felt as his mother did, and between the three of them, they had succeeded in changing David's mind.

" Where's John gone to ? " Candy saved her the trouble of asking.

" He's in the attic," said David. " Here he comes."

John came in, blowing dust off his hands. " No great shakes of an attic," he reported. " There never is, in this type of house."

Candy looked relieved at the no-great-shakes, and took it as a verdict. " It certainly seems as if this type of house wasn't built for convenience," she said. " I mean, take the Grey place, for instance. It's so functional."

" You're talking about modern construction and planning at its best," John explained. " This house isn't in the same category. If David doesn't buy it, he ought to have his head examined."

"Doesn't buy which?" Claudia queried, a little bewildered.

David looked at her. "What do you mean, 'which'?"

"The Grey place, of course," said Candy. "Who wouldn't?"

"Actually," John seemed deaf to the interruption, "I didn't know there was an old hip-roof in this vicinity. If it weren't for the big hemlocks on either side of the entrance, I'd have said it was moved down from New Hampshire or Vermont."

"That's an interesting theory," said Mr. Lewellyn. "Very. In fact, I'll try to find out something about its history just as soon as ever I get back to the office. You see, as a rule I don't handle properties outside Greenwich, and I only had this down as a short summer rental. It's been on the market for sale too, of course, but no one's bought it because no one's realized what a fine old house it really is. I didn't," he confessed. "I'm frank to admit I really didn't! I was born and bred in a house just about the vintage of Mrs. Payne's——" He broke off in consternation. "Where *is* Mrs. Payne, by the way?"

"Waiting for us downstairs," said Candy. "And John's trying to be funny. Don't let him pull your leg, Mr. Lewellyn."

"I don't think he is," said Claudia gently. She knew just how Candy felt, for hadn't she felt exactly the same way about the farm? She'd never forget the first time she'd seen the little salt-box house sitting in the bend of the road, looking like something a child might draw, with slanting lines and a chimney. From the way David had raved about the old doorway and the old panelling, she'd expected no less than a Palladium mansion. It took time to become an architect's wife, and Candy had a long way to go. Even now, she was doggedly resisting the idea that classic beauty lurked in the purity of this shabby little run-down cottage. "What about the porch?" she demanded distrustfully. "Is that supposed to be wonderful, too, just because it's hanging by one ear?"

"Now the porch I happen to know about," Mr. Lewellyn contributed eagerly. "A dirt farmer rented the place during the war, and tried to make a go of goat's-milk. He built the porch himself."

"He didn't make a go of that, either," said David. "It'll take a carpenter less than a day to rip it off. You'll see a big difference without it, Candy."

89

John said, "As a matter of fact, it's about the only thing you'll have to do to the house, David, until you're ready to build on."

"Sure," said David. "A little soap and water, and our own furniture and the grounds attended to and it's livable. When we can afford to, we'll add a library downstairs, facing the river, and put in a dressing room up here for you, darling." He put his arm round Claudia. "So you still like it," he said exultantly. "I was afraid as hell you'd change your mind."

"I didn't, but you did," she accused him. "The first thing you said to me when I came upstairs was that we oughtn't to buy the place, we ought to rent it. I haven't recovered from the shock of it yet."

David laughed. "Oh, that was Mr. Lewellyn acting like a real-estate agent. He says if we negotiate a sale now, it'll be weeks before we can take possession. And it will."

"The miserable red tape of title search and all the rest of it," Mr. Lewellyn enlarged. "This way, if you start off renting it, the owners are supposed to have the lawn cut and the house cleaned up, and the utilities in running order."

"Oh," said Claudia, "that's wonderful, and I think it's very clever of you," she mentioned politely.

"Moreover," Mr. Lewellyn puffed up like a pouter pigeon, "I intend to apply the rental to the purchase price. And on an all-cash proposition, as your husband proposes, I might be able to get them to do better than forty-two thousand. I'm not certain that I can, but I'll make every effort."

"That's wonderful," Claudia said again.

"Leaving it like this," he impressed upon her earnestly, "gives you every chance to look at other properties."

"This is where we came in," David interrupted with a grin. "How soon can we take possession?"

"Let me see. This is Saturday," Mr. Lewellyn meditated, looking very important. "I should say that if I go straight back to the office I should be able to contact the owners, and have everything in ship-shape by Wednesday."

Claudia mentally discounted the ship. "I saw an old vacuum cleaner in the hall closet, I hope it goes until we can get our own out of storage," she said.

"I'll come over and help," Candy offered happily.

"Bertha and I will be much too busy to have you help us," said Claudia.

Candy's laughter bubbled over. She looked suddenly about twelve years old. How up in the air she could be one minute, thought Claudia, and how down in the dumps, the next. It was as if her tears were half in laughter, and her laughter in tears. It wasn't an ordinary change of mood, as most people were given to, nor was it like grief or loneliness that kept shifting about in one's heart to be accommodated for all time in the very texture of one's being. No. This that was happening to Candy was different, and it was a little frightening. Perhaps Mrs. Payne's outmoded theory was correct and Candy was suffering a delayed reaction from the long hard labour of bringing her baby into the world. Perhaps it was the loss of Elizabeth, and the substitution of Mrs. Payne to provide the mothering she needed. " I'm glad we're going to be near her," Claudia decided.

" Children ! " Mrs. Payne's voice floated up from the bottom of the stairs. " What on earth are you doing up there ? "

" I forgot all about her," said John guiltily. " We'll be right down, Mother ! "

Candy clapped her hand over her mouth to stifle a squeal of merriment. " Who's going to break the news to her that the house turned out to be wonderful—— "

" I will," said John.

" This I must see and hear," said Candy.

Mr. Lewellyn's courage appeared to desert him abruptly. " I'll join you in the car," he said. " I'd better see that all the windows are closed."

Claudia and David followed him through the rooms, loath, with a single impulse, to leave the little house. They marvelled, again, that it was exactly the right size for them, even more than they needed—three smallish bedrooms and two larger rooms. " Some day," David planned, " we could throw two of the small rooms together."

" I'd hate to buy a house there wasn't anything to do to," said Claudia.

" So would I," said David.

Mrs. Payne could have saved her breath. " You can sink a fortune into this cottage," she prophesied darkly as they made their way over the fallen log back to the car. " And, mark my words, you'll end up with it costing you more than the Grey place, with nothing to show for it in the bargain."

" Except the house they happen to want," John reminded her. " And, anyway, Mother, I told you they're not going to buy it straight off, they're going to rent it, so they can still change their minds if they want to."

Give Mrs. Payne a finger and she wanted a hand. "It's not even fit to rent. Bertha's not going to be happy in that kitchen."

"That kitchen," Claudia informed her, "is pure gold next to what we just had all winter in the mountains. Bertha cooked on a wood-stove, and we pumped our water."

"That was a case of necessity," Mrs. Payne argued. "David was ill, and everything else was secondary. But now he's on the road to recovery, thank God"—(It wouldn't hurt you to say he *has* recovered, thought Claudia rebelliously)—"and there's no need to put yourself through anything you don't have to, especially when you've got every comfort with Julia and Hartley. Candy tells me that even the guest-rooms are air-conditioned, and really, much as I'd love to have you out here near us, I do believe I'd rather see you stay in town just where you are."

"That's right nice of you," Claudia retorted silently, but David's patience was at dangerously low ebb. "We've been there over a month, and enough's enough," he said tersely.

"Nonsense, they don't feel that you're outwearing your welcome," Mrs. Payne assured him, playing fast and loose with their hospitality. "In fact, I happen to know how much they love having you."

"They do," Claudia interceded hastily. "But they'd also love not having us, because they want to make a solarium, and summer's the most logical time to get it done."

Mrs. Payne was momentarily diverted from the immediate problem. "What on earth do they want a solarium for?"

Claudia didn't try to explain that Julia and Hartley weren't hankering for the sun, it was merely that a siege of building gave refreshment to a marriage that had never quite achieved the heights of passion.

"Look, Mother," John told her with a trace of David's impatience, "there are two types of people, those that like to fuss over houses and those that don't."

"I guess I'm the type that doesn't," Candy admitted. "Because, honestly, I could just move into the Grey place and be perfectly happy with what somebody else has done."

"Provided it's been done well," Mrs. Payne amended in a salute to Candy's judgment and taste. "This child knows a good thing when she sees it." She put her hand on her daughter-in-law's arm in a fleeting moment of attunement, and Candy looked a little scared, as if she had put her foot into something and didn't know how to get it out again.

CHAPTER SEVEN

WHEN they were alone, driving back to New York, Claudia meant to talk to David about Candy, but suddenly she couldn't think of anything else but the little house, with the lengthening shadows surrounding it in mystery as they'd looked back upon it. " It was lovely, wasn't it ? " she said.

" Yes," said David, without having to ask her what was lovely. He took her hand and held it, not saying anything more. This was another of the high spaces of their marriage that she would always remember. There had been many of them, she reflected humbly, some of them happy, and some of them full of sorrow, but always they had been together. She remembered the day that David had told her that her mother could never get well. . . . She remembered that last hour in their bedroom at the farm before the war took him overseas. . . . She remembered the way they had walked out of the doctor's office after he'd found out that he must give up working for a year. . . . And there was another day, driving back to New York over this same road, sitting quietly, with her hand in David's, as she was sitting now, knowing that they had left Bobby alone in a place of stone monuments that spoke the strange and awful language of death. Claudia had left her heart there, too, for it had seemed that there was nothing to come back to, not even Matthew and the baby. It was a sin to have felt that way, but she could feel no other way, for her heart had died. Now, suddenly, it was alive again. This buying of a home was more than the buying of a house. It was a new beginning. They both felt it, and so it was not necessary to try to put it into words. She said only, and very softly, " I feel as if I need never go to the cemetery again."

David nodded. " I know. I know."

They didn't talk again until they reached the city limits. The same sun that had wrapped the little house in gentle shadows was burning angry fires in a thousand windows as it sank behind the Palisades. " I'm glad we won't have to live in an apartment in New York," said Claudia.

" So am I," said David. " And I'm glad we kept our old station-wagon."

" Oh, I meant to ask you, can we get it out of cold storage by Wednesday ? "

" I hope so."

" Yes, because we won't want to borrow the Rolls for moving all our luggage and the baby's stuff. There'll be a lot to do," she added, " and the nice part of it is that, all at once, I feel like doing it."

" That's good," said David. " That's awfully good."

" It's the first time I've wanted to do anything. I can tell you now that I even dreaded going to the country for the day. The stillness. And the beauty. Beauty hurt like a terrible pain twisting my insides. It doesn't, any more. It takes away the pain."

David pressed her hand. " That's good," he said again.

Traffic held them up in mid-town. The city had turned out for a breath of air, and the park looked untidy and cluttered with humanity. " Bertha will never want to look at another green bench as long as she lives," Claudia mused. " How she loathed sitting with her hands in her lap from morning until night."

" Something tells me," said David, " that her sitting days are over."

She was certainly not sitting with her hands in her lap when they arrived home. Being traditional to a mania, she always reserved Saturday night for a general clean-up of nails, ears, and hair. Matthew was still smarting from his close association with hot water and soap as he bolted out of the bathroom in a rush of belated mutiny, and no clothes. " You should've taken me with you, there wasn't anybody in the park to play with, why does Bertha have to cut my toe-nails when they aren't even long, even ! "

" How do you do, dear Mother," Claudia suggested pointedly.

" Very nicely, thank you," said David.

" Hey, stop it——" Matthew resisted ineffectually, and then surrendered to a sheepish smirk, and once more it was hard not to let time roll back and imagine that it was Bobby standing there, with his shoulder-blades sticking out like little wings, and the polite sunburn of the park leaving the rest of him heart-breakingly white and tender. It was only this year that Bobby had begun to fill out with the solid bone and muscle of puberty. " Where's Bertha and the baby ? " she asked over a suddenly closing throat.

" Here I am.", Bertha's round face emerged from behind a cautious opening of the bathroom door. " Matthew, such a way to run around naked, a big boy like you !—Come in,

Mrs. Naughton, quick, I have the baby in the tub ; if I leave him long he might slip——"

To Bertha's fond eyes, beaming with pride, there was nothing immodest in the rolls of fat that overflowed down Michael's little stomach and made plump pink sausages of his arms. " He's obscene," David declared, peering in at him.

Bertha mistook the word for some higher translation of pulchritude, and readily conceded that Michael was one of the most beautiful babies that had ever been born. Michael got the idea, and wrinkled his nose and laughed a noiseless snuffling little laugh. " Don't be such a show-off," David admonished him.

" Ach ! " Bertha decried, beginning to think that perhaps " obscene " wasn't the word she thought it was, " he is not showing off, he is just glad to see you ! "

" He doesn't know we're alive," said David callously. " Where's the dog ? "

Claudia wiped her mouth of the soap that had clung to the back of Michael's fat neck. " Yes, where is he ? "

" Uncle Hartley borrowed him," said Matthew. " He's downstairs keeping Uncle Hartley company while he gets dressed."

" When did that love affair begin ? " asked David, looking very pleased for Hartley, who was a dog-lover by birth, if not by marriage.

" Upsidaisy ! " Bertha puffed with ostentation, to show how heavy Michael was as she lifted him out of the tub. " Now let Papa see how nice you can walk."

Michael was no longer in a mood to show off. He stood nailed to the floor, obdurate and remote, with an opaque and unblinking stare curtaining his eyes.

" You've insulted him, David," Claudia chided. " Michael, your father apologizes. Now walk.—Bertha, we found a house ! "

" I wanted to ask you ! " Bertha cried.

" What kind of a house ? " Matthew shouted. " Is it in the country ? "

" Not only is it in the country, it has a river," David let out.

" A river ! Boy—— Has it got an elevator too ? "

" No, Mrs. Payne, it has no elevator," Claudia informed him coldly. " David, it's awfully hot in here."

" It is," said Bertha. " Better you both go and rest before dinner, and I will come in later and hear all about the house."

" I want to hear now ! " Matthew insisted shrilly.

"Mamma is tired," said Bertha. "First she lies down a little."

Bertha was an angel, Claudia thought gratefully. She'd been wondering how she could preserve the happiness of the day without spoiling it by urging David to rest when he came home. "Bertha's right, I'm simply dead," she caught on with alacrity. "I only hope I can have dinner sent up on a tray."

"Miss Julia said by all means you should if you want to," said Bertha. "I have only to ring the kitchen and let them know not to set the table for you."

"Kid your grandmother," David told them. He went whistling to the bedroom, and Claudia found Bertha's eyes and they both smiled. "He's so much better," Claudia whispered, "and the house is wonderful, I'll tell you later——"

She found David affably exchanging amenities with Fanny, who was turning down the beds. He kept calling her Agnes. "Idiot," Claudia enlightened him after she had departed with an armful of used towels that hadn't been used because they'd been away all day. "I've told you before that Fanny is the one with the teeth, and she does Julia's floor."

"Then this was still Agnes," said David doggedly, "because she was doing us. Agnes has teeth, too."

"Not as many or as far out, and anyway it couldn't be still Agnes, because she went to her sister's wedding this week-end and Fanny's standing-in for her."

"Slumming," David amended, noting the exquisite arrangement of his old bathrobe across a chair. "What do we tip them when we leave?"

"Oh, God," said Claudia, "I don't know. Isn't it awful, there are so many of them. You'd better let me do it when it comes to Agnes and Fanny. They really do look alike in uniform, and Agnes should get more. We'll have to tip Watkins a lot, too," she added gloomily.

"At least twenty-five plus a couple of fine neckties," said David.

"Ouch," said Claudia. "It'll mount up to a fortune. However——" She lay down on the soft bed, savouring anew the impeccable opulence. "We've certainly been living in luxury. Our bedroom in the country is going to look like a pea-nut beside this."

"There's still time to change our minds and stay," said David. He lay down beside her. "Want to?"

"No, I love pea-nuts."

" But think how pleased Mrs. Payne would be with us if we came to our senses."

" I feel sorry for her," said Claudia.

" Not me. She's one of those mothers that sad young playwrights are writing bad young plays about."

Claudia smiled. " I was thinking this afternoon how spoiled you are, because Mamma was so different. Mothers-in-law aren't usually so wonderful, you know. But they've got something on their side, too. Even Mrs. Payne."

" It seems to me she's doing her damnedest to mess up John and Candy's life."

" They're messing it up themselves. Candy's trying to pull John away, and he's letting himself be held. They haven't grown up enough to be free inside, so that it doesn't matter."

" That doesn't excuse Mrs. Payne."

Claudia shrugged. " It's not Mrs. Payne's problem. She's old. Or thinks she's old, which is worse. It's up to John and Candy to handle the situation with a little wisdom and understanding."

" You talk most saintly," David told her with a grimace. He carried her hand to his lips. " Maybe you're right, though. A marriage grows strong on the things you go through together."

" It either grows strong or it busts up," said Claudia soberly, " and that's what I'm afraid of with John and Candy."

Because David made no answer, she knew that he was afraid of the same thing. They lay for a long while without saying anything, and then he put his arms round her.

" Darling, you're tired," she whispered.

" I'm not. I feel fresh as a daisy."

" You're fresh," she couldn't resist, " but I don't know about the daisy part."

After a while, she said, " That I should ever live to see the day I'd be glad that Julia and Hartley didn't dine until eight o'clock."

" We've sure been in luck." David glanced at his wrist-watch. " Do you know what time it is ? It's a quarter to already."

" If it's as late as that, I'm starved."

" Yes, that soufflé was not geared to last us through thick and thin," he remarked.

" Well, cheer up," said Claudia, " our trays ought to be up any minute, so hop in your own bed or Fanny will look like a startled gazelle. Remember she's accustomed to

Hartley and Julia not only in separate beds, but in separate rooms."

" They're crazy," David complimented her obliquely.

He didn't move a second too soon. " Shall I place the table between the beds ? " Fanny enquired.

" Sure*ly*," said David.

Claudia gulped on a cavaire canape that she caught on the fly. " Such fanciness," she gloated. " There must be company for dinner."

" Just a single gentleman, Ma'am," said Fanny, which showed that all was not deaf that seemed it.

" Who ? " Claudia asked inquisitively, since Fanny had broken the ice, so to speak.

" I don't know, Ma'am. Just a single gentleman was all I heard."

Hartley and Julia appeared at that moment to return Bluff in person. He was up on both beds in a single bound. " Ugh," said Claudia, wincing away from his great sloshing tongue, " go kiss your father. But watch the soup ! "

David barely rescued the silver tureen from tipping over. " Come here, you great big clumsy baboon," he commanded in a voice that dripped tenderness. " Hello, Julia."

" Hello," Julia returned, not quite recovered from the tottering tureen.

" He's a great pup," Hartley proclaimed robustly. " I enjoyed every minute of him."

" You mean every yard of him," said Julia.

" What did he knock over ? " David enquired apprehensively.

" Yes, what did he ? " said Claudia. " You took the words right out of my mouth."

Julia laughed. " Nothing of any consequence, really."

" Only my humidor," said Hartley. " And mashed my best cigars." He studied David with an eye that was more fatherly than brotherly. " I must say you're looking pretty chipper after a long trip to the country and back."

" Yes, you look fine," said Julia.

" He should," Claudia murmured demurely. " I mean, driving in a Rolls, why not ? "

" The Rolls is there for you to use any time you want it. Too bad, if I'd known you weren't going to be tired to-night," Hartley went on, " I'd have told you to come downstairs for dinner, we're having an interesting chap."

Since Hartley's interesting chaps invariably turned out to

be Soft Drinks with fishing camps, or Social Registers with yachts, or Banks with indigestion, Claudia didn't think they were missing very much. In this particular instance, in view of the cavaire and *filet mignon*, the expected guest was probably no less than a whole Oil Well.

" Sorry," David said, looking anything but.

" This chap," Hartley elaborated, " is a young newspaper man, just back from Formosa with some lantern slides. He can do with a good dinner and a sympathetic audience."

Ordinarily David couldn't abide home-shown pictures, especially amateur travelogues, but to Claudia's surprise he put down his fork and said, " Damn it, I don't want to miss those, I'll pop down for them."

" I wish you would," said Hartley. " We're heading for trouble over there. And over here. I'd like to see you lighten up on Motors, David."

" So would I," said Julia briefly. " We're all asleep."

Claudia stopped eating with a sense of guilt. She must have been asleep, too ; so deeply involved with the collapse of her own small universe that she hadn't wakened to what was going on in a world across the sea. But probably this was only their usual Wall Street double-talk, the effect of conditions on the market. Hartley and Julia were always shoulder deep in stocks and bonds, and David was always tagging along, ankle deep. Well, she was anxious about finances, too, now that they were going to buy a house. " Julia, aren't you and Hartley interested in what we found to-day ? " she digressed, rather disappointedly.

" We didn't want to ask you," said Julia, " in case you didn't find anything that was rentable."

" We didn't——" Claudia began, and Hartley broke in before she could go on, " Then you'll stay right here ; we hate to see you leave us, anyway."

" They're nice people," thought Claudia. " Really nice." Aloud she said, " I mean, we found two houses, but they're only buyable."

" We found one house," David corrected.

" Two," Claudia insisted. " I think we ought to get Hartley's and Julia's reaction, and see if they agree with Mrs. Payne."

Julia drew a chair closer to the bed and sat down. " We love hearing about houses. Hartley, 'phone the pantry, will you, and tell Watkins to call us up here when your young newspaper man arrives."

Bertha knocked on the door while Hartley was 'phoning. " Oh," she apologized, " I do not want to interrupt, I just wanted to tell you the baby is asleep already."

" What's Matthew doing ? " David asked in quick suspicion.

" He is back in bed, too," Bertha assured him elliptically.

" Then stay, Bertha," Claudia invited her. " You didn't come to tell us the children were in bed, you want to hear about the house, and you're just in time."

" Bring over another chair," Julia smiled. " This is going to be a long story, Bertha, I can feel it in my bones."

Bertha flushed with pleasure. " Thank you. I am glad to stand, I was sitting all day. Come, Bluff, you stay with Bertha, away from the supper, like a good boy."

Hartley turned from the 'phone. " Well, let's hear all about it," he said, rubbing his hands. " Good evening, Bertha."

" Good evening, Mr. Hartley."

" Which house shall we tell them about first ? " David asked.

" Mrs. Payne's," said Claudia.

" You take that one, and I'll take the other one."

Claudia left out nothing from the plate-warmer to the lily-pool. " All right, let's buy the damn place," David scowled at her.

" I was just being scrupulously fair," she defended.

" You'll have to go some, David," Hartley advised him jocularly. " Seems like a mighty rare find. Mighty rare for these days."

" Or any day," said Julia. " It sounds absolutely perfect."

" Ach, beautiful——" Bertha exclaimed, slipping in an extra little heavy syllable that made it sound even more beautiful.

" Now you take on from here, dear," said Claudia. " The floor is yours."

" Thanks," said David sourly, and perversely, he under-sold the little house by the river, dwelling on its less attractive attributes. Claudia gave him a baleful look. " Never mind about the road frontage," she stopped him, as he grew coldly technical. " Tell them about the wild ducks, and the trees ! "

" They know there're trees. And ducks where there's water."

" You're not playing square ! "

" Facts are facts," said Julia, " with or without the trimmings, and on the face of it I'd say there's really no question about it."

"Well I wouldn't go that far." Hartley paused judiciously. "It's a close choice, and it depends on what they want."

"Exactly," said Julia firmly. "The Grey place sounds utterly enchanting, but it's not their dish of tea, and it wouldn't be mine."

Claudia was so astonished she almost fell out of bed. "Julia, do you mean it?"

"Of course I mean it. You can always build a new house with modern improvements, but you don't find an eighteenth-century hip-roof this near to New York every day in the week."

"Particularly with thirty-eight acres bordering a river, and access to two roads besides," Hartley followed up. "It sounds like an extremely sound investment, property-wise."

David didn't bat an eyelash. "What do you say, Bertha?" he asked non-committally.

Bertha clasped her hands. "I like the little house," she cried. "The other one sounds stylish but not so *gemütlich*."

"I hope we haven't influenced you," said Julia in sudden misgiving.

"Don't be silly," Claudia exulted, "we'd already planned a wing for you and Hartley to visit us!"

Hartley looked touched. "Nothing would please us more."

"Only we don't need a wing," said Julia, with a faint blush. "Just a double room will do us."

Hartley looked even more touched. "You youngsters think up anything you want as a moving-in present, and it's yours," he said.

"I only wish," said Julia, "that we could give you all the happiness you deserve."

Now it was Claudia's turn to be touched. After Hartley and Julia had gone downstairs she said, "I've grown so much closer to Julia than I ever thought I would, or could. I'm going to miss her."

"Careful," David warned her softly. "Don't let yourself miss anybody. You'll only pay for it."

"Then I'll pay," said Claudia. "It's worth it."

The next day was Sunday. It reminded Claudia of another Sunday, the Sunday of December seventh, the way David and Hartley, and even Julia, sat glued to the radio. "You knew something was going to happen," Claudia told them, with respect for their knowing.

"We weren't looking for it to happen in Korea," said David.

Korea seemed very far away, a small war with small people fighting among themselves. When Candy called to find out if they still felt the same way about the house on the river, she didn't even mention it. She said, her voice shaky with excitement, " I'm glad, too, because—what do you think? John and I are talking about buying the Grey place ! "

Claudia started to say, " Candy, be sure you're ready for it," but Candy sounded so happy that it seemed wrong to open her to doubt. " Your mother-in-law must be delighted," she offered carefully.

" Delighted is putting it mildly," Candy returned. " She's going to handle the whole deal for us, and she's sure she can get it for less, which'll make a lot of difference, because John says although fifty-five is cheap, it's much too much for a young couple to put into a home."

" It is a lot," Claudia agreed. " It's different with us. David used what he inherited from his father to buy the farm—imagine, it only cost eight thousand in those days, with a hundred acres—and we sold it for enough to buy this place."

" I wish John would use the money from the sale of Mother's apartment," said Candy, " but he won't. He says what's his is mine, but what's mine is my own, and I don't think that's fair."

" You wouldn't like him if he felt any other way," said Claudia. " David's got that kind of pride, and I love him for it, but I could kill him, too. Not that I have any money, but he won't even accept from Hartley."

" Aren't men the limit ? " said Candy. " Do you remember the powder-room curtains ? "

" Vividly. What about them ? "

" Mr. Lewellyn says he's sure they'll leave them—whoever 'they' is in a bank—and a lot of other things besides. I don't want anything else, though, except the plate-warmer, and Mr. Lewellyn says that technically they have to leave it, I mean it's screwed in or something, and that means that the person who sells is compelled to leave it for the person who buys. Not the stove or ice-box, though, unless we specify in advance."

" I wish I'd specified when we sold the farm," said Claudia moodily. " Now we'll have to buy a stove and ice-box, and that's going to cost a pretty penny. Isn't the news dreadful ? "

she digressed guiltily. How could she be talking about stoves and ice-boxes at a time like this ?

" What news ? " Candy asked blankly.

" The war in Korea."

" Oh," said Candy. After a moment she said, " John seems quite upset, but I haven't had a chance to find out much about it, I'm so excited about the house."

" So am I," Claudia confessed.

" Yours or mine ? "

" Both," said Claudia generously. " Yours almost as much as mine."

John wanted to talk to David before they hung up, and Claudia noticed that they discussed Korea first, and then the house. " Well," said David as he put the receiver back on the hook, " that was quite a surprise."

" I think it's an excellent idea," Julia approved. " Candy didn't look too well the last time I saw her, and it'll do her good to settle down in her own home and have you and David so near-by at the same time."

" She has her mother-in-law near-by, too," Claudia commented.

" Yes, it's an ideal set-up," said Julia, recognizing a wood-pile, but nothing in it. She was Boston born and bred, and was used to a lot of aunts and uncles, although, like Claudia, she had never had a mother-in-law. It was odd to think they would have had the same one if Hartley and David hadn't been orphaned when quite young. Now Julia went on, with a note of wistfulness in her voice. " You four have always made such a nice quartet."

" A nice sextet," Claudia said quickly. " Candy's devoted to you and Hartley, and so is John."

Julia was a shy person, for all her worldliness. She said, in lieu of gushing, " Suppose you let us give you the stove and ice-box as a moving-in present."

" It's too much," Claudia protested, " but if it weren't, it would be heavenly."

" It's not," said Julia.

Hartley laughed. " You sound like Claudia."

" I can think of no greater compliment," said Julia.

It went through Claudia's mind, " I wonder if Julia's getting more attached to us than she wants to let herself be."

It really seemed as if she was, because she looked really sad when she waved them good-bye on Wednesday morning, lingering on the shallow stoop until they turned the corner.

She blew a kiss to the baby, and he blew one back to her, with Bertha leading his fat hand to his lips . . . " Cheat," Claudia reproved her.

They were no sooner out of the city boundaries than Matthew announced, " I'm hungry."

" You're not," David informed him tersely. " You just had breakfast, and this isn't a picnic."

" Yes, it is," said Matthew, with a sage nod of his head. " I saw Agnes put a big box in the station wagon, and she said it was things to eat for lunch."

" Well, what do you know," said Claudia, as enthusiastic as Matthew. " Bertha and I were planning on a lot of scrambled eggs, which mean nothing in my life. And wasn't it also nice of Julia," she lowered her voice discreetly, " to say ' absolutely no tipping ' ? "

" Extremely," said David.

" It's good you intended to be so generous, look how much money we've saved."

" Are we almost there ? " Matthew broke in. " Is this our river ? "

" No, no, this is the Hudson River," Bertha explained. " We are not yet on the Parkway."

" Is our river bigger ? "

" I'll brain him," said David.

" He's never had a river," Claudia made excuses for him. " How would he know about a river ? "

" He's damn well old enough to know this isn't our river."

" Oh, pick on someone your own size," said Claudia, giving him an affectionate shove.

" Don't push me while I'm driving."

" Don't push me while I'm driving," she mimicked, and Matthew burst into an hilarious guffaw, and the baby gave his affected little snuffle, and it seemed as if Bobby were right in the car with them. " Keep Bluff off my ear," David barked.

" Bluff, off from your father's ear," said Claudia.

" Sit down, Bluff, like a good boy," Bertha urged.

" I think he wants to get out," Matthew remarked thoughtfully.

Fun was fun, and Claudia turned like a worm. " No, he doesn't," she affirmed shortly, " and neither do you."

They were there before they knew it, and without a single stop. " It's no trip at all," Claudia marvelled.

" You said that the last time," David reminded her. " Are

you going to turn out to be a bore after twelve years? If so, I want my money back."

"Anything about the house, yes I'm a bore. Do you object?"

"No," said David. "It's no trip at all."

"Seriously, I don't think you'll mind it. It's a mere nothing after the farm. I said that the last time, too."

"That commuting to the farm was a bastard. I'm glad Lewellyn arranged to get the grass cut yesterday."

"Yes, so am I; it should make a big difference, I can't wait to see."

It made a vast difference. "Oh, it is beautiful!" Bertha breathed with her first glimpse. "Matthew, pay attention, this is your new home. Isn't it beautiful?"

He withheld judgment. "I don't see the river. Where's the river?"

"We keep it out at the back," said Claudia.

"What's this log?"

"A log," said David helpfully.

"Is it going to stay here all the time?"

"No, we were waiting until you got here, so you can move it," said Claudia.

He swaggered. "I could, too, it's not too heavy——" He jumped over it, and then back again, and then over it once more, having a very good time at it.

"Don't look now," said David, "but your middle son is a half-wit."

They were so used to thinking of Matthew as the middle one. "David, it's all right," said Claudia softly, "don't look as if you wish you hadn't said it. Bobby's still our oldest, he always will be."

"You bet he will," said David huskily. He stopped short between the great watchful bride-and-groom trees and took her face between his hands and kissed her forehead like a benediction. "I wish I could carry you over the threshold," he whispered.

"Not yet," she implored him, "but next year, at this very time on this very day—we have a date to do it."

"Don't plan into the future, you might be too fat."

"I'll never get fat."

"Is that a promise?"

"Mamma wasn't."

"So she wasn't. See that you take after her in every particular."

"I'll do my best," she said humbly. It was always comforting to talk of her mother when they talked of Bobby. It gave her a feeling that he was not lonely, that her mother was looking after him.

Bertha came up behind them and gazed raptly at the house. She didn't seem to see the sagging porch, or, if she did, she made no mention of it. "The porch comes off," Claudia rewarded her.

"Unless Matthew fixes it properly," said David. "I reckoned we'd start him on the porch as soon as he finished moving the log."

Matthew drew his upper lip down over his lower, in the same little self-conscious smirk that Bobby had had at that age. It wasn't attractive, heaven knew, but it seemed to be all little boys rolled into one. Claudia thought, "I'm so glad that we carry on where we left off with Bobby." There was a time when she hadn't thought she could, and David had found it difficult, too.

Now he gave Matthew a friendly bat, and fitted the key into the latch of the door. "This is the old, original hardware, Bertha," he pointed out proudly. "And it's the old door, with the old glass in it."

Bertha's eyes shone. "It is like the farm," she said, and added, a trifle defiantly, "even nicer."

"Much nicer," said Claudia. "The farm was a salt-box house, and simpler. But it was lovely," she stood up for it loyally.

The little entrance hall gave forth a strong blend of ammonia and wax, which Claudia feared was only skin deep. "It smells very clean," said Bertha dubiously, "but I think I will change into my apron, if you will watch the children for a minute."

"I want to see the river!" Matthew clamoured.

"Hold your horses," said David, but he wanted to see it, too. "Come on along," he coaxed Claudia.

It was a temptation, but she withstood it. Now was the time to make hay and get the suitcases out of the station-wagon behind his back. Julia had suggested sending Watkins along to unpack, but David would have hated it. If she could do it herself, it wouldn't be so obvious. "Michael's sleepy, I want to pop him into bed before he gets cross," she said.

"I'll wait for you."

"I want to 'phone a grocery order, Mrs. Payne gave me a number. Go on without me. I've seen the river and I'll see it again."

" Hurry up, stop talking ! " Matthew expostulated.

" We'll ask your permission to talk," said David. He dropped a kiss on Claudia's nose, and they went off together, with Buff making sure he would not be left behind.

The suitcases weren't terribly heavy, but they were heavy enough. Bertha came downstairs in a starched white uniform and caught her at it. " Here, let me do that," she said sternly. " It is not good for a young woman to lift."

" In the first place," Claudia disillusioned her, " I am not such a young woman any more, and in the second place——" She lugged out the hamper of lunch. " Here, we'd better get this in a cooler place." She had started to say, " You forget I can't have any more children, anyway," but Bertha felt badly enough about it as it was. Bertha would have liked to have had a perennial baby in the house.

Now she picked up two of the largest suitcases, one under each plump pillowy arm, and marched off with them. " Horse ! " Claudia shouted after her in frustration, " Lady Horse Herself ! You ! Let me take one ! "

" There is plenty for you to carry," Bertha called back serenely. " Only leave the baby's bath-tub and scales until I'm ready."

Most of the rest was just dirty work—nasty little boxes and odds and ends that had a way of creeping into the best of packing in the final scramble of taking off ; Matthew's *Book of Knowledge* ; David's high boots from the mountains (" See, you wanted to throw them away," he told her triumphantly) ; a pillow-case full of the baby's overnight laundry ; Bluff's mammoth aluminium drinking-bowl. " He'll jolly well use the river from here-on out," Claudia laid down the law.

She had just finished stacking the whole lot of it in an untidy pile to be carted indoors, when Candy's tan convertible swept up in a splash of loose gravel and came to a stop beyond the fallen log. The top was down, and her thick straight taffy-coloured hair had blown itself crazy. " Hi ! " she called, puffing it out of her eyes. " Welcome home ! "

It wasn't until Claudia had almost reached the car that she discovered Mrs. Payne's small figure in the farther seat, wind-tossed but resolute, with a veil tied tightly round her hat to keep it from flying off. Claudia swallowed her surprise. " Hello, Mrs. Payne, how nice of you to come ! " she cried.

Mrs. Payne started to climb down to the ground with more than her usual difficulty, and the aid of Candy's arm. " These modern cars that have no running-board," she deplored, " were not designed for old ladies——" Once on firm land, she gathered herself together, straightened herself up, and touched her lips to Claudia's cheek. " I couldn't let you move into your new home without wishing you well, and bringing you a few posies." She reached back into the seat and withdrew a great, damp bundle of flowers, from which Claudia was not pleased to see, drooping out of one end, the limp, lean blossoms of Mrs. Payne's prize delphinium. Delphinium growing in the ground was one thing, but delphinium spitting its petals all over the house was another, and, anyway, at this stage of getting settled, she needed the additional chore of arranging " posies " like the well-known hole-in-the-head. Nevertheless, she mustered a grateful smile and said, " Thank you *very* much."

They made their way slowly to the house, with Claudia carrying the flowers smack against her bosom, because it was the only way they could be carried. Mrs. Payne had apparently gone whole-hog and stripped her garden to the bone, for in addition to an unpleasant sensation of moistness against her chest, Claudia could feel a mass of roses conspiring to stick their thorns into her. " They're so beautiful," she murmured, squirming in discomfort, " and you have such a gift for floral arrangements, Mrs. Payne——" She left the rest of the sentence hanging in mid-air, and Mrs. Payne obligingly caught it and handed it back to her. " I'll be glad to arrange them, my dear, if you'll give me the vases."

" That, my dear Mrs. Payne," Claudia inaudibly replied, " is the crux of the whole situation." Farmers who went in for goats did not, as a rule, go in for vases, but she kept the thought to herself, and turned both the flowers and Mrs. Payne over to Bertha's unsuspecting hospitality. " Find some vases somewhere, will you, Bertha ? " she suggested largely, and then hurried back to the station-wagon, with Candy at her heels. " I'd like to get the rest of the stuff into the house before David has a chance to," she said over her shoulder. " Want to give me a hand ? "

" Sure I do, and I bet you could bless us barging in with a lot of loopy flowers when you don't know what to do first," Candy panted. " Look, don't go so fast, I have something terribly exciting to tell you. Incidentally, the flowers weren't my idea, I was just starting off when Mother Payne said to wait for her, and she'd pick you a bouquet. All I was going to bring was ice-cream."

" Good. Where is it, I'd better get it in the refrigerator."

" You don't have to. I didn't stop to buy it."

" Thanks. How is it your mother-in-law came in the open car ? How come she came at all ; I thought she'd washed her hands of us for good."

" Oh, no," said Candy, " she loves you now, and loves your house. Didn't you hear her say how charming it looked with the grass cut ? "

" Yes, but I thought I was imagining it, I couldn't believe my ears."

" You won't believe what I'm going to tell you now, either. Guess what ? We've bought the Grey place ! "

Claudia slowed down until Candy came abreast of her. " Actually bought it ? " she exclaimed incredulously. " I thought you were only thinking about it."

" We were. We just couldn't make up our minds whether it was a wise thing to do, or not. And then, out of a blue sky, Mr. Lewellyn telephoned this morning while we were at breakfast, and told us that he'd finally got the price down to—guess how much ? "

" I have no idea, in fact David said he was sure they wouldn't budge from fifty-five."

" We were sure they wouldn't, either ; that's why we've been so undecided about it. But Mother Payne simply wouldn't take no for an answer. She kept right on after Mr. Lewellyn until he got the terms that would make it feasible for us to go into it."

" What are they ? "

" Thirty thousand cash, and a fifteen thousand mortgage."

" You mean forty-five thousand in all ? "

" Yes, isn't it wonderful ? I know you're not crazy about mortgages, they make you nervous, but Mother Payne says it's sound finance, something about a lot of monkey-business with the interest. Anyway, John has the thirty thousand cash, so we'd be fools, don't you think, if we didn't ? "

" Yes, I do," said Claudia. She thought, " Even if it doesn't work out, they could always sell it for more than they paid for it." Aloud, she went on, " I think it's a terrific bargain, and I only hope your mother-in-law can do as well for us. It's amazing that such a delicate-looking little old lady should have such a hard business head."

" Isn't it, though ? But don't get your hopes up. I don't think she can get the same kind of a deal on this house, because it isn't being sold by a bank to settle an estate. It was the first thing she warned me, not to talk too much about what we got ours for, because she didn't expect they'd come down very much on yours."

" Oh," said Claudia, considerably disappointed in Mrs. Payne's limited powers. " Just the same, I'm terribly pleased for you, Candy. Just think, it's only three thousand more than for this."

" But we've got less than five acres and no river," Candy comforted her.

" I'm not complaining," said Claudia. " David will be terribly pleased for you, too."

" I can't wait to tell him, where is he ? "

" Skulking round the side door like a very large and cowardly louse."

Candy gave the little giggle that so often came to her lips these days. " Talking of leopards, he doesn't know yet that Mother Payne's changed her spots overnight. Claudia, I can't tell you what a different person she is all at once. She thinks I have such a lot of common sense—me, of all people—and she keeps saying how wonderful it is that we'll be living just up the road from her. The thing I think is wonderful, though, is that you've bought a house practically next door, too."

" We haven't bought it yet."

Candy turned a little pale beneath her sunburn. " Claudia, if you leave me stuck out here, I'll never forgive you ! "

" Why, Candy, what an odd expression to use. ' Stuck out here '." Claudia regarded her with genuine misgiving. " Whether we buy this house or not shouldn't affect you one way or the other. You'll be with John, and that's the only thing that's important."

" And right next to his mother, too," Candy tacked on with a small, shaky laugh. " Oh, don't pay any attention to me, I'm not really serious, I don't think. Naturally, I have a little conflict, and naturally your being here does make a difference."

" It shouldn't," said Claudia. " You oughtn't to let yourself grow dependent on anyone or anything."

" I am, though," Candy confessed abjectly. " It worries me, I'm so dependent on John. If anything ever happened to him, I just couldn't go on living."

" You'd have to. And you would."

Candy shook her head numbly. " I couldn't——"

" I had to when David went to war. And I almost had to when he was ill last year."

" You're stronger than I am."

"I'm not. I've aways been as weak as dish-water."

"But you've been through so much," Candy protested. Her voice dropped to a little moan. "And you've lost a child. Oh, Claudia, how do people live through such things?"

"They just do," said Claudia. "Look at Bertha. She's lost her husband, and a son in the war, and her daughter committed suicide. She has no one left, and still she goes on, day after day, and you'd never know. The strength just comes."

"From God, do you think?" Candy bashfully asked.

"What difference does it make what name you call it?" said Claudia. "It comes."

Candy gave a sudden shudder. "Why did we get so serious all at once?" She quickened her steps towards the station-wagon, and picked up some odd boxes and David's boots.

CHAPTER EIGHT

DAVID was wild that they had unpacked behind his back. "What did you expect us to do?" Claudia asked him smartly. "We needed the stuff."

"You needed the stuff," he flung at her.

"Yes, we needed the stuff," she flung back.

"And you couldn't have waited?"

"No, we couldn't have waited."

The telephone bell put an end to their scintillating exchange of animosity. "Our first call!" Claudia gushed.

"I'll get it; it must be John."

There was only one instrument in the house and, farmer-wise, it was in the kitchen. Bertha was scouring the dish-cupboards, so Claudia had to lean close up against David in order to hear. He gave her a friendly pinch, and she kicked his shins affectionately. "Beast," she said.

"She-devil," he returned.

It was John, of course. "Your mother and Candy just left," said David. "That's great news about the house. It's a steal at twice that price."

"That's what I think," said John, and then he didn't say anything more about the house because the news had just come over the radio that the President had issued a statement that the United States was sending forces into Korea. "Does that mean war ? " Claudia cried, as David hung up the receiver.

" What did you do with our radio ? " David asked in answer. " We'd better attach it."

They attached it, and put it on the kitchen table. The news was still coming in. Bertha left her dish-cupboards. " Ach, no," she kept on uttering little cries of denial, " it couldn't be another war."

" We just had one," said Claudia, stunned.

David gave a short laugh. " A lot of good I'll be this time."

" You did your share," she told him passionately. She was ashamed of the wave of relief that swept over her. " If it weren't for those hideous months in New Guinea, you might never have been ill ! "

" That is true," said Bertha. " I only hope Mr. John——" She bit the words back. " I talk too much," she apologized, and turned away to her cupboards again. " Go outdoors for a little while," she urged them. " I will bring some lunch out to you and you will eat it under the trees."

" I don't like eating under trees," said David.

" The dining room is not clean yet. By supper it will be clean. Maybe you can catch some fish for supper," Bertha added persuasion on persuasion.

" I saw a perch," David admitted.

" How did you know it was a perch ? " Claudia asked.

He gave her a withering look.

" Excuse me," she murmured meekly.

" Come along," he said, " and this time Matthew stays behind."

They walked out to the river bank. " That's silly, what Bertha said about John, isn't it ? " Claudia finally plucked up the courage to ask.

" She didn't say anything."

" She began to. Is there any danger, David ? "

" Danger of what ? The whole lot of us being blown up by an atom bomb ? Sure."

" You know I didn't mean that," she returned, a little angrily. " Somehow that doesn't seem important now. It will, maybe, but not now. Not to me, anyway. All I can think of are the husbands and the sons and the sweethearts——"

" That's a female, if ever I heard one."

" So I'm a female. It's a woman's right to be a female. David, tell me about John. He's only twenty-six."

" Twenty-seven," David's jaw twitched. " My dear girl,

I know as much about it as you do. All I know is that it's a fine time for me to be sitting up here on my useless rear, nursing a goddam spot on my lung."

"The spot's healed, thank God, and for all our sakes, see that it stays that way!" Misgiving sharpened her voice, but understanding made her heart go soft. "Darling——"

"What?"

"Nothing."

"You're glad," he accused her bitterly.

"Just for me. Not for you."

He smiled unwillingly. After a little, he picked up a stone and threw it into the water, and it skimmed along like a bird, making ripples to the opposite shore. Claudia picked up a stone, too. She threw it and it sank. Like a stone.

"Here, clumsy, I'll show you."

He showed her. She tried it. "No talent," she gave up. "What else did John say about buying the house? I couldn't hear everything, Bertha was rattling shelf-paper."

"He's making a deposit."

"Then it's really settled."

"It seems to be."

"It's time they had their own home," said Claudia. "They've been married a year and a half. Just. They'll never send the men who were in the last war," she reverted tensely. "They couldn't, it wouldn't be fair."

"Maybe not," said David, "but John happens to be in the active reserve. He's a First Lieutenant in the Engineer Corps."

"I don't know whether that's good or bad," she said timidly.

He did not answer her. In silence, they watched a flock of wild ducks fly for cover, and disappear into the brush.

The next morning he said, "I think I'll go into town, I can still make the nine-twelve if we hurry."

Claudia could have wept with disappointment. He was up to his old tricks. "David, you promised to stay out here for the rest of the week," she protested.

"I'll be back on the four-ten."

"But it's such a long trip for just a few hours."

"Yesterday it was a short trip."

Wisdom told her not to argue with him. He wanted to be doing something, not just sitting up in the country "on his rear".

" Wouldn't it be easier for you if you drove in ? "

" Not particularly.   Besides, you might need the car."

" I might.   There's a long list of supplies I'd like to stock up on.   Soaps and things.   I can do it on my way to call for you this afternoon."

" Good," he said, and gave her a little pat on the shoulder for nice behaviour.

It was their first breakfast in the sunny dining room.   Mrs. Payne's flowers looked very festive in mixing-bowls and water-pitchers and milk-bottles.   Outside the windows, a bird sang, and the river looked different in the early morning.   " It's never the same from hour to hour," Claudia marvelled.

" Nothing is," said David.   " Least of all a river."

" I don't think we'll ever get tired of looking at it."

" I know we won't," he said.

It was pleasant, driving to the station.   David held her hand in his most of the way.   " It's like old times, isn't it ? " she said softly.

He nodded.   " Look, darling, be careful driving back, won't you ?   These curves are treacherous."

" I have never so much as bumped a fender," she took umbrage.

" Oh, I seem to remember one of the barn doors hanging by a thread," he mentioned off the top of his voice.

" Don't hit under the belt, that was a long time ago.   And it wasn't a fender."

" No, it was the whole front end."

The station was crowded with the kind of cars whose owners didn't have to be in New York until ten o'clock.   " I hope I'm never rich enough to have a chauffeur drive you to the train," said Claudia.

" You won't be."

He kissed her goodbye as if he meant it.   Other couples around them merely pecked, and some didn't even do that. He lingered at the window.   " Do you know how to get home ? " he queried her.

" Do you want to miss your train ? "

" You take the first turn to the right——"

" I am not an imbecile."

" And then you go past the traffic light——"

" I'm not listening," she said coldly.

As a matter of fact, she missed the road twice, because she had absolutely no sense of direction, and he knew it.   It seemed an endless number of miles before she recognized the beginning of the wall of the tooth-paste mansion. "Now I'm right," she breathed in relief, grateful that he need never know how close to being an imbecile she really was.

It was an added reassurance to see the little white house with the atrocious pink shutters sitting on the road ahead. If they wanted to take a leaf out of Elsie's and Robert's book, they could call the little house on the river, "Claudavia." She'd try that one on David when she met him at the train, this evening.

At first she thought that Mrs. Elsirob must be having carpenters and painters, because there was a row of cars that hadn't been there on the way to the station. Then, as she drove closer, she realized that there'd been an accident. She saw a black sedan lying on its back like a giant bug, and near-by the wreck of a tan car was piled up against the soft shoulder of the curve. She didn't want to see any more. Thank God, oh, thank God, that everyone she loved was safe—— Even so her hands were shaking and her foot was unsteady on the accelerator, and everything went sick inside of her. The scream of a police siren in the distance rang in her ears as she sped onward.

Bertha met her at the door. "Mr. John just telephoned from the office, and would you please call him right away—— What is the matter, you are so pale?"

"I just saw the most awful smash-up down the road. Two cars must have collided——"

"That is terrible," said Bertha. "Was anyone hurt?"

"I don't see how they couldn't have been. I was too much of a coward to stop. It brought it all back——" she faltered. "The police siren and the crowd——"

Bertha sighed. "Ja, ja, you think you are all right and very strong, and then something happens, and you live it all over again. Better you sit down a little."

"Better I 'phone Mr. John. Where are the children?"

"The baby is in his play-pen on the porch, on the safe part, and Matthew is upstairs. He gave me his promise he would not be in there long, though; he is coming down any minute."

"I'll believe it when I see it," said Claudia. "It's a good thing his father isn't here."

"He has nothing to read," Bertha mentioned helpfully. "But maybe I better take a look, anyway."

"It wouldn't hurt," said Claudia, heading for the telephone. A few moments later, John's voice came over the wire.

He was surprised to hear that David had gone into town. "Hide his pants next time," he advised.

"I'd have liked to this time. But I think he's upset about the war news."

"Who isn't?" said John.

"Hartley 'phoned last night. David said something about meeting him for lunch."

"Yes, the market's acting up, in a big way," said John. "Claudia, the reason I called is that I need a little help with Candy. She isn't over there yet, is she?"

"No, I don't expect her until this afternoon; she said she had a dental appointment at ten."

"She did, but she's not keeping it." His voice sounded harried. "She had a bad night, and I told her to cancel the dentist, and spend the morning with you instead. I know you're head over heels getting settled," he apologized, "and I hope you won't mind."

"On the contrary, I'm very pleased. We can use an extra pair of hands."

"I'm afraid she won't be much help," said John doubtfully. "That's what I'm trying to tell you. She's terribly over-wrought."

"But, John, she was in wonderful spirits yesterday! Oh. You don't have to tell me, I've been through it. It's this hideous war news. David told me you're in the active reserves; no wonder Candy's in a state."

"Candy's not worried about the war," John returned with a short laugh. "She doesn't realize that there is a war, at this point. It's something else. It's the house, I mean, not really the house, it's mother. You see——" He hesitated, and then pushed on with effort. "It's a hell of a mix-up, Claudia. We didn't get the Grey place for forty-five thousand."

"You didn't? Oh, what a shame. Why did they back down?"

"They didn't. They never did budge from fifty-five, only we weren't supposed to know it. Lewellyn, who's a little of a dope, unintentionally let it slip out when he came over after supper last night with the receipt for the deposit I made."

"I think I'm beginning to see," said Claudia slowly. "Your mother paid the extra ten thousand."

"That's about it," John admitted uncomfortably. "On the surface, it might seem like a deception, but she didn't mean it that way. I'm sure she didn't. She knew we liked

116

the place, and that we'd never find anything half as good for the money, and she wanted us to have it on terms that would save me borrowing against my life-insurance."

"She also wanted you to be near her," said Claudia objectively.

"That's true, too," said John, "and that's the only side of it that Candy can see. Now she feels that she's been trapped into getting the house, and nothing that I said, or Mother said, could make her feel any differently about it. She cried terribly, and Mother got palpitation and had to sit up with three pillows, and, all in all, it was a miserable business."

"I know how Candy feels," said Claudia, choosing her words with care, "because I'm a wife. And I can sense how your mother feels, because I have sons, and I hope that some day they'll grow up and get married. But just the same, John, they're both a little sick."

"I know it," John acknowledged unhappily. "There's got to be a show-down between the three of us, we can't go on this way. Nothing good is ever going to come of it. But I can't talk to Candy now, because she's in no condition to listen to reason, and Mother's so hurt that she won't discuss it. She insists that her only thought in paying the ten thousand was simply to do us a kindness."

"It is a sort of impasse," Claudia agreed, "and not a very pleasant one. I'm awfully glad you told Candy to tune out and come over. Maybe I can get her to see your mother's side of it."

"I hope you can," said John fervently. "I'm a little worried that she isn't there yet."

"It's early yet," said Claudia. "Wait a minute, I hear a car——" She leaned backwards to look out of the window. "No, it isn't Candy, it's another laundry—— If she isn't here soon, I'll 'phone and ask her to help us unpack."

"Do that," said John gratefully. "I'll do as much for you some day," he added, forcing a smile into his voice.

"Do as much for me now," Claudia returned in kind. "Keep an eye on David and see that he rests a little after lunch and comes home on the four-ten."

"Consider it done," said John. "Manage to give me a ring, will you, when Candy comes? The reason I'm worried is that she took two sleeping-tablets last night, and she's not used to them."

"I'll call you," Claudia promised.

It wasn't until she hung up the receiver that she remembered the fleeting glimpse of the tan car piled up against the road, but she couldn't be sure whether or not it was a convertible. Oh, God, it couldn't be! Or could it? Her legs turned to water beneath her, and her heart beat up into her throat and hammered against her ears until her head felt as if it were going to burst. She tried to think back, but she couldn't harness her thoughts. And then Matthew came stomping downstairs. "Mother!" he called loudly. Claudia wet her lips. They felt swollen and stiff and no words took shape through them. If only he wouldn't come into the kitchen. He did, of course, with an unerring instinct; he always knew where to find her, no matter what she was doing or where she was. Now he was smouldering with one of his perpetual grievances. They didn't last long, but he had a lot of them. "Bertha should knock!" he announced indignantly.

Dully, Claudia remembered that the purpose of Bertha's trip upstairs would have been defeated had she knocked, and then Bertha came in, smouldering a little, too. She carried the *Book of Knowledge* in her hand, and in silent testimony laid it down on the kitchen table. It was not often that she told tales on Matthew, but this time she had no mercy on him. She said, like an avenging angel: "Again he was reading," and waited for Claudia to discipline her son's literary interests to a more propitious time and place, but it was like having someone punch you in the stomach, so that you had no wind left to talk with. Bertha saw that something was wrong. She said, "Run and play, Matthew, but the next time you will not get off so easily."

"Matthew," Claudia's voice sounded like a croak in her ears. "Don't go near the river."

Apprehension came over his small face. "Have you got a sore throat, Mother?"

She shook her head numbly.

"See if the baby is all right on the porch," Bertha suggested, "the good part of the porch, keep away from the loose part." Then she scrapped the whole project and reverted to her original idea. "Never mind the baby, just run out and play," she said.

"You want to get rid of me," he deduced suspiciously.

"So, we want to get rid of you," she made a clean breast of it. "How about a raw prune?" She opened a cupboard and gave him three for good measure. He accepted them eagerly, unaware that they possessed hidden properties that were not entirely confectional. "I like them better than cooked," he said, and gave a great shudder. "I *hate* them cooked! Michael's a baby, he has to eat them cooked." He wandered off into his world, where the sun was out, and a squirrel was looking up a tree.

Bertha waited until he was clear of the room. "Mrs. Naughton, what is it?" she asked anxiously.

"I'm afraid something terrible has happened——" If only her throat would loosen up. Bertha helped her. She said, with a little smile, "No such terrible thing could happen in the few minutes I was upstairs, surely."

"Oh, Bertha, the accident I told you about—I have to go back there——"

"No you do not," Bertha stopped her. "You cannot let every accident you see upset you like this——"

"Oh, Bertha, you don't understand! Maybe it was Candy!"

Bertha turned a little pale. "Come now, that is foolish, Mrs. Naughton, you would have known right away if it was Miss Candy's car."

"But it was so crumpled up," Claudia faltered. "It was tan, I saw that much, but it could have been a sedan—or any kind of a car—it was so crumpled up," she reiterated in a whimpering sob. "You see, Candy never entered my head. I thought she was at the dentist's until Mr. John just 'phoned that she was on her way over."

Bertha's hand on Claudia's arm was firm. "Mrs. Naughton, you are shaking all over, you must not right away think the worst. Sit down a minute, child."

"I can't, I can't! I have to go back to find out."

"I will go with you."

"I'm coward enough to wish you could, but there's no one to leave the children with."

"We can take them."

"No, don't. I'll be all right; I'm ashamed of going to pieces like this, you'd think I'd never been through anything."

"It is because you have been through so much that it makes you feel like this. And I still say, maybe you are getting excited for nothing." Bertha turned the alarm clock on the kitchen table for Claudia to see. "Look, child, it is not yet ten o'clock. Miss Candy had to bathe the baby and give her the bottle before she leaves; I would not be surprised if she had not left yet."

"Oh, Bertha, I never thought of that, like an idiot!"

"So," said Bertha, "pick up the telephone, and I bet you twenty cents she is still there."

"If she is," Claudia quavered, "I'll wring her neck for scaring the wits out of us. What's Mrs. Payne's number, I can't think straight, Greenwich eight-seven-five-six-three?"

"Wait, I have it right here, Miss Candy wrote it down for me yesterday." Bertha consulted a paper bag neatly folded into the drawer of the table. "Eight-seven-three-five-six," she carefully deciphered. "You were almost right," she added, like a pat on the shoulder.

Claudia dialled the number. She had to dial it twice, her hand was trembling so. It seemed an eternity before the receiver at the other end of the wire was lifted. Mrs. Payne's Annie answered. Mrs. Payne was fond of saying, "Annie has been with me since John was a little tot of eight." Now John was twenty-seven. That made a lot of years, and Annie seemed perfectly happy. It was odd that Candy couldn't live peaceably with her mother-in-law for even a few summer months.

"Annie, this is Mrs. Naughton, is Mrs. Payne there? I mean, young Mrs. Payne?"

"No, ma'am. She's gone out."

Claudia's heart twisted into a sick lump. "When, Annie, how long ago?"

"I don't exactly know, Mrs. Naughton, I didn't see her go; all I know is she asked me to keep an eye on the baby."

"Did she say where she was going? Was she coming over here?"

"She didn't tell me anything. She didn't so much as say whether she'd be back in time for lunch." A note of disapproval crept into Annie's voice. "Either her own or the baby's either, for that matter."

Annie was going to be difficult. Claudia hung up. Her eyes met Bertha's. "You lost your twenty cents," she said unsteadily.

It wasn't a very long drive after she left the little river road that led into the main road. Already the dark blot of cars had thinned out to a few straggling onlookers. The accident was over and done with. It had made but a brief ripple of excitement in the even tenor of the suburban town, and people were driving away from it, going about their affairs.

The black sedan still lay on its back like a giant helpless

bug, but the tan car was gone. Far up the road, Claudia could see the vague mass of it being towed away, but before she could sweep past to gain upon it, another towing machine loomed up. She backed into a drive-way to give it clearance. Then she climbed out of the station-wagon, and approached a man who was working with a heavy length of chain. Her legs had stopped trembling, and her voice seemed to come from a long distance and not to belong to herself. " Could you tell me," she asked, " whether the other car was a tan convertible ? "

" Couldn't say for sure, Miss," he replied. " All I know is we got a call to get this one out of here, and quick ; it's a narrow road. Hi ! Mack ! Lend a hand with this, will you ? "

Mack's hulking body, clad in overalls, blocked her out. They had no time for idle questioning and curious onlookers. A middle-aged lady in a neat blue coupé, with slip covers on the seats, passed and slowed, running her window down to peer out. " Accident ? " she enquired with sepulchral interest. " Anybody killed ? "

There was nobody left to answer her. She said, " Dear me," and ran up her window again and drove on.

" I'd like to drive on too," Claudia thought hysterically, " just drive on and on and on without ever knowing——" A devasting helplessness enveloped her. How was she to go about the grim business of finding out ? She started across to her station-wagon again and suddenly realized that the accident had happened directly opposite the little white house with the pink shutters. She walked up the short gravel path gay with the home-made look of pansies and nasturtiums. The front door was pink, too. She rang the bell, and obediently the thin pink sound of chimes started up from within, and then there was silence. It was such a little house, that she didn't have to ring twice to know that it was empty. No one was at home.

A station-wagon, of a vintage outdating her own by several years, came along and started to turn up the drive, but Claudia's car was in the way. " Don't bother to move ! " a cheerful voice called out, " I'll park out here."

The occupant of the little white house had returned. She was plump and pleasant and quite young, without being youthful. She ran up the path and said, " Hello, I'm glad I got back before you left. Wait a jiff, I'll get my key out. Say, aren't you the people who moved in the house on the river yesterday ? "

"Yes," said Claudia, wondering how news got around so fast.

"Pleased to meet you, my name is Elsie Miller." Elsie fitted the key into the latch, and turned to smile. "I saw you and your husband drive past yesterday with all your luggage, and those two adorable kids, and that big huge dog. I told my husband about him, Robbie's mad for a big dog. We had a Scottie that died. Not really a Scottie. Just a part of him was, but mongrels can be so cute, I think, don't you?"

"Yes," said Claudia again, with difficulty.

Elsie flung open the door. "Come on in, but excuse the looks of everything. I had a nine o'clock appointment to get my hair done, we're having a party to-night. Married five years. Five years and no kids. Gosh, you're lucky. Just imagine, two of 'em and you're so young. Well, we're going to adopt a baby, and then maybe we'll get one of our own. It's a funny thing the way it works sometimes. The doctors say you relax or something. Listen to me rambling on, Robbie says my tongue wags from both ends when I get started. Sit down, won't you?" Elsie gestured towards a heavily flowered wing-chair in the small, overly-flowered living room. Claudia cleared her throat. "I can't stay. I just wanted to use your telephone."

"Help yourself. It's right there on the table, if you can find it under all those papers and pipes, honestly the way that man of mine strews himself all over the place—— Say, wasn't that an awful accident right outside, sort of a gruesome introduction on your first day here, isn't it?"

Claudia managed her voice. "I'm trying to find out what happened, do you know anything?"

"Not much, I was in the village, thank goodness—I'm an awful sissy when it comes to blood—but somebody on the road told me a man and a little girl got killed, isn't that awful?"

Yes, it was awful, but for a moment hope flared; and as quickly died. Candy might easily be mistaken for a little girl, with her small slim body and taffy-coloured hair. "Oh, God."

She was aware that Elsie was looking at her in consternation. "Say, is it somebody you knew or something? You're trembling like a leaf, tell me, for goodness' sake, and don't let me gabble on like this——"

There wasn't much to tell. "Now honestly," Elsie scolded her, sounding like Bertha, "you're just borrowing trouble; she might have stopped off at the village for something. For all you know, she could be at your place now, waiting for you, big as life."

Claudia shook her head. "Her car didn't pass, I was watching for it." Again a helplessness swept over her. "I'll 'phone Bertha to see if there's been any calls, I just can't stand here doing nothing!"

"Now, listen," said Elsie, "I'm going to talk to you like a Dutch uncle. When an accident like this happens, the ambulance is there in a jiffy, and the police take over and notify the family, so Bertha wouldn't know any more than you do yet."

"Then I could call the police——"

"That's what I'm getting at," said Elsie. "Only you let me 'phone instead of you. My brother-in-law's on the force, and I've got a little pull down there. Want a swig of whisky, or something?"

"No, thanks. Please—hurry——"

"Go on, sit down, that's a good girl." Elsie picked up the receiver. "Operator, I want the Greenwich police station. . . . Gosh, that's one time you get service, when you ask for the police or the fire-station. . . . Hello, is Officer Farley on duty? I'd like to talk to him. No, it's personal. . . . Charlie? This is Elsie. Say, Charlie, what was that smash-up that happened right out front of our house a little while ago? . . . Sure, I got a reason, but I'll tell you afterwards, go on, Charlie, get me the dope on it, will you?" She covered the receiver. "He's finding out. Charlie's an awful good guy. Hello, Charlie?——"

Claudia closed her eyes and gripped the arms of the gaily flowered chair. Yes, she'd been through this before. Maybe that's why she was being able to go through it again—maybe you went through things in life to prepare you for going through the next thing——

Elsie hung up the receiver. "No details yet. Charlie says an accident's been reported up this way, but that's all they have on it so far. He'll get busy and call back. So that's that. In a few minutes, we'll know. Gosh, I guess it'll be the longest few minutes you ever spent. But honestly, nothing's so bad that it couldn't be worse, I always say. Just think if it was your husband or one of your kids. Then you'd really be going through something, believe me."

Claudia nodded, in mute assent. To this pleasant, kindly stranger, the station-wagon speeding past her house yesterday had held only an enviable happiness and completeness.

123

The sharp peal of the telephone broke the air. Claudia's hand reached out, but Elsie was ahead of her. "Charlie— this is Elsie. Okay. Let's have it. . . ."

Elsie slowly put the receiver back on its hook. "It's not so good, kid," she said gently. "I guess your feelings were right. One of the cars was a tan convertible. New York licence, John Payne. They notified him about ten minutes ago. The girl's alive, but they don't know yet how badly hurt she is. They took her to the Stamford Hospital. The man in the other car seems to have been lucky, all he is is shaken up a little and maybe a busted collar-bone, they think. Gosh, kid, I'm sorry."

"Thank you," said Claudia. "I'd better let Bertha know."

Bertha was waiting for the call. She said, "Mr. David just this minute telephoned from the office. Mr. John is already on his way to the hospital."

"I'll go on over there, then, Bertha. If Mr. David telephones again, tell him I'll call him as soon as I can."

"Please, Mrs. Naughton, let me know also. And are you all right?"

"Yes, I'm all right."

"Gosh," said Elsie, "you're more than all right, you're better than I thought you'd be. Maybe that's the way it works. You know what you're up against, and you can take it."

"Thats about it," said Claudia.

"Was that your maid on the 'phone?"

It was hard to call Bertha a maid after all these years.

"What I mean is," Elsie made herself clear, "whoever she is, it's hard to move into a strange place and everything, with two small children. She must have her hands full, so if you'd like, I'll step over later and see if there's anything I can do."

"I wish you would. Bertha won't let you help with anything, but it would be nice for her to see a friendly face."

Elsie walked with Claudia to the car. The black sedan was gone, and the little country road was peaceful and serene.

CHAPTER NINE

It would always be a mystery to her how she found her way to the hospital. She must have gone through a red light at a busy intersection, because she remembered the hurried gait of the traffic policeman as he walked over to her with a ticket in his eye. When she asked him how to get to the hospital, however, he was very nice, and he gave her explicit directions, and waved her on.

Once there, the emergency ward was a labyrinth of grey corridors, and red tape. She finally ended up in a small, unfriendly cubicle with the meagre information that the patient was still in the operating room, and as yet there was no report on her condition. A busy nurse said, " If you'll wait here, I'll let you know as soon as I can." She wanted to telephone David, but there was no booth within sight, and she was afraid of missing the nurse when she returned.

After a time, the nurse passed the door again and Claudia hurried out to catch up with her. " Tell me, oh, please, is there any news yet ? "

" Oh." Recognition dawned vaguely in the nurse's eyes. " The patient's husband just arrived, I'll let him know you're here."

It seemed hours before John came. It hurt her to look at him, he was so white, and his lips were so drawn with pain. He didn't ask her how she happened to be there, it was if he had known that she would be there. "They let me see her," he said. " She couldn't talk much. But she wanted to do it, Claudia, she wanted to do it." He sank down into a hard wooden chair and buried his face in his hands.

Claudia didn't say anything. There was nothing that she could say. This that was happening to John was worse than death, it was the unfinished business of remorse. It was an even greater suffering than she had known in losing Bobby, and she had not thought that greater suffering could be.

In a little while he lifted his head and said, " Thanks for not talking. It isn't something I can talk out."

" I know."

" It's been different with you and David."

" We're older," she said.

" I hope God will give us the chance to be older, too," he said, with such childlike simplicity that it made Claudia think of the Bible, and what the Bible meant, and she could say, with honesty, " John, I think everything's going to be all right. No matter what happens."

Another nurse came to the door and beckoned from the threshold. " The doctor will see you now, Mr. Payne."

That was the hardest wait of all, and yet it was only a little while before John came back. There was no lift to his step. " They can't make a definite diagnosis until the X-rays are developed. There may or may not be internal injuries." He had to stop before he could go on, and Claudia knew the difficulty of words trying to come through a closed throat. " The doctor said the only thing that saved her was that she was thrown free of the car. She must have fallen on her left side. Her left shoulder's broken, and three ribs, and a gash on her left temple might leave a scar." He paused to swallow. " She keeps asking about the man in the other car, she doesn't believe he's only been badly shaken up, she thinks he's dead and that it's her fault. They've given her morphine, but it's had no effect."

" It stimulates her. I remember that it did when the baby was born."

" I told the doctor, and they're going to give her something else. We've got her in a private room, but no private nurse as yet, and he thinks if I sit with her, it'll quiet her."

" Would you rather I stayed here, or went home to be with your mother for a while ? "

He looked at her gratefully. " Break it to her gently," he answered.

On the way to Mrs. Payne's, she had to pass the entrance gates of the Grey estate. She drove past quickly ; she couldn't bear to look up the winding roadway, with its great massed bushes of rhododendron.

A quarter of a mile farther on, she reached Mrs. Payne's sprawling Victorian house. Thomas was polishing the outside brasses, looking quite unlike himself in a blue denim work-apron. Candy had told Claudia that Mrs. Payne had the brasses polished once a week, like a religion, whether they needed it or not, and Candy had deemed it silly to waste time and energy on things that didn't need to be done. (There were always so many little issues like that between Candy and her mother-in-law.)

" Bertha's the same way," Claudia had made a point of saying, " and really, Candy, it's none of your business, because it's not your house."

" I know, but she expects that I'm going to be exactly the same kind of a housekeeper. You'd think John couldn't live without his brasses polished."

" Well, maybe John likes his brasses polished," Claudia had retorted lightly.

" He doesn't give a hoot, but I shouldn't wonder if he'd begin to."

That was Candy, discouraged and resentful. But how different she had been the day before, lifted to the heavens in one of those pendulum swings of mood. Not that there hadn't been plenty of reason for her to be happy; it was a big moment in marriage when you bought your first home—second only to having your first baby. Claudia remembered the way she and David had been when they'd found the farm, and they were almost as excited about the house on the river. It was a never-palling excitement, this choosing of a place to live in with the person you loved, and kindness or not, it was regrettable that Mrs. Payne had intruded upon an experience that was meant for two. John had said over the telephone that Candy felt she was being " trapped " into living near his mother. It was an ugly word, an hysterical word, but knowing Mrs. Payne, Claudia felt that there was probably an element of truth in it.

" Good morning, Mrs. Naughton." Thomas leapt to the car to help her out, apologizing for his apron. He preceded her around the wide veranda, and although it would have been a simple matter to usher her through the screened door into the dim, cool entrance hall, he pressed the bell for her. Guests were never admitted, unheralded, into the Payne household.

In due time Annie appeared in one of the everlasting foulards that she affected in lieu of a uniform. Ever since the onset of Mrs. Payne's heart-attacks, Annie's self-appointed title had become that of housekeeper-companion, and it seemed to have gone to her head a little. Her rather chilly greeting to Claudia carried not only the weight of authority, but the lingering grudge of an earlier conversation that had left her hanging high and dry, so to speak. " Mr. John's wife has not come back yet," she carried on from there, " but if you'd care to see the baby, she's still out on the terrace in her carriage. And very restless, too ; she's hardly slept at all after her bottle."

" I don't want to see the baby." It was always hard to hold Candy's baby in her arms, but now it would be harder than ever. " Where is Mrs. Payne ? " she asked.

" Mrs. Payne is still up in her room. She had a very poor night. A very poor night," Annie repeated. From her tone, it was quite clear that she knew what had transpired the evening before, and it was equally clear that her loyalties lay entirely with her mistress. " If you'd care to wait," she went on, feeling that perhaps Claudia was an emissary of conciliation, " I'll go up and find out if she's able to see anyone. I must say you're looking a little peaked yourself," she added, with a trace of humaneness. " It's very humid weather we're having. Why don't you take a seat ? "

" I'd like to use the telephone, if I may."

" It's in the hall cupboard to the left."

" I know, don't bother to show me."

" And it's a dial system, you can dial the number." What Annie was really saying was that there was no charge for local calls. She would have been more disapproving than ever had she lingered long enough to hear Claudia ask for a New York number without so much as a by-your-leave. Annie shared Mrs. Payne's strict adherence to minor economies.

Claudia blessed that same sense of economy which had prompted Mrs. Payne to place the instrument within the obscurity of the coat-closet, away from open temptation. Claudia partially closed the door, oblivious of the cramped confines, knowing only thankfulness for the privacy and the darkness.

" The line is busy," the operator reported.

" Again ? " Claudia protested. She had tried to reach David from a drug-store on her way over. She hung up. Her knees were rubber beneath her, but there was no place to sit. She leaned against the serviceable brown twill of the coat that Mrs. Payne liked to wear for her walks round the garden. Next to it, in the semi-light, she could see the long, masculine outline of John's Burberry, and close to it, the gay young flare of Candy's wide-checked sports' jacket. Her throat closed up, and the tears rolled down her cheeks at last. Clothes could be such poignant messengers of grief. She remembered how it had been with Bobby, and with her mother. . . . She clenched her fists. Would she ever stop remembering ?

She tried the number again. It was still busy. If only she could talk to David while Mrs. Payne was still upstairs. She rested her elbows on the shelf that held the instrument, and cradled her head against the palms of her hands. There. That was better. The gay checked coat was behind her, and the faint, clean fragrance of Candy's favourite lily-of-the-valley perfume scarcely reached her nostrils. . . . Funny, how they had never had much luck raising lilies of the valley at the farm, even though they were supposed to spread like weeds once they got started. There were endless clusters of them growing wild along the river, though. She and David had discovered them that morning before breakfast when they'd gone out to throw some bread for the ducks. It was too late for the blooms, of course, but she had said, " Just think what it will be like next spring. I can hardly wait."

" Then you still want to buy the place ? " David had asked her, as if it were too good to be true, " in spite of no hot water for a bath last night ? "

" I didn't like no hot water," she'd admitted. " But liked what happened to us when we fell asleep."

His eyebrow climbed his forehead. " So did I."

" Be serious. I mean a sense of belonging ; I haven't had that feeling since we gave up the farm."

" I haven't either. A place is yours, or it isn't."

" And Bertha loves it. She thinks the kitchen is wonderful."

" Wait till she sees it when we get finished with it. We'd better start remodelling soon, before the world goes to pot again," he'd added grimly.

" The world isn't going to pot again ! " she'd protested. " We've hardly dug ourselves out of the last mess."

" I hope you're right. Hey, don't move, look over there, a blue heron ! "

" Where ? I don't see ! "

" Near that big clump of willows——"

Her eyes had found the slim, sweet thing before it winged away. " Oh, David," she could only breathe, speechless with the wonder of having glimpsed a little bit of God, and he, too, seemed to have forgotten the state of the world for a moment. " Pretty nice place to spend your life, with blue herons before breakfast, isn't it ? " he'd said, and to make it even nicer, a flight of wild duck had circled suddenly overhead and skittered into the water, with a small, great noise. " Buy some cracked corn in the village," he'd told her. " They'll get to know us, and they'll be coming around by the dozen for a free hand-out. . . ."

" Poor little ducks," thought Claudia now, lifting her throbbing head from the telephone stand. Maybe there'd be no free hand-outs of cracked corn. Maybe they'd go back to New York to live with Julia and Hartley again, for if anything happened to Candy all the joy and the peace of the little house would be gone.

She was aware that the heat in the closet was suffocating. She opened the door wider, and tried David's office once more. A moment later, she heard his voice. She hadn't known how much she needed to hear it, how it bolstered her flickering courage like a strong arm round her. " Look, darling," he said, " don't let a few little X-rays get you down. I don't care what they show, Candy's strong and young and she's got a lot of fight in her." A smile crept into his words. " Candy fell for that little marble powder-room like a ton of bricks, and if it's the last thing she does, she's going to powder her nose in it."

" David, no. That's all changed." Claudia lowered her voice to a tight thread of sound. " Candy doesn't want the house now. The house is at the bottom of everything."

" This must be a new turn of events. What happened ? "

" It's a long story, but the sum total of it is that they didn't get the place for ten thousand less——"

" I thought there was something phoney about that whole deal," David broke in. " I bet Mrs. Payne paid the difference."

" She swore Mr. Lewellyn to secrecy, but he let the cat out of the bag last night."

" And Candy blew her top."

" Just about," Claudia acknowledged. " She felt that Mrs. Payne had tricked them into living near her, and Mrs. Payne insisted that she only wanted to help them. John said it was a dreadful mess. She got one of her heart-attacks, and Candy took two sleeping-pills. Oh, David, I'm afraid she took more than two——"

" Nonsense, she wouldn't have been able to drive."

" Apparently she wasn't," Claudia returned on a sob. " Oh, David, I saw the car ; there was nothing left of it."

" Darling, put it out of your mind. Telling Mrs. Payne isn't going to be easy, and you've got to keep a grip on yourself."

" I dread it."

" I wish I could do it for you, but I can't leave the office until I get John's appointments squared around for the next day or two. Poor devil, he didn't have a chance to tell me any of this. The message came from the police a couple of minutes after I got to the office. It's pretty tough on him."

When she hung up, she realized that it wasn't easy on David, either ; tension and anxiety were the worst possible things for him at this point. A tonic flare of anger suddenly took the place of sentiment. Candy's behaviour was unforgivable, for there was an unreasonable and childish emotionalism in her relationship with Mrs. Payne. Granted that part of it was the reflection of a confused and modern generation, her major conflict, nevertheless, was old-fashioned jealousy, compounded of so many subtle factors that it was difficult to trace either its origin or its effect. Had John fallen in love with another woman, she might have approached the situation with a greater dignity. But no. Candy was stuffed with a lot of intellectual twaddle about John being in love with his mother, and somewhere in all the involved conversations on the subject, Claudia had gathered that Candy's security was shaken. "Damn the word 'security,' the younger generation would be a lot better off if they'd never heard it," Claudia now decided. The plain fact was that the problem of John's mother was the first real challenge to Candy's maturity, and with her basic sanity and capacity for tenderness and understanding, she should have been able to meet it. Two sleeping-pills, indeed. She should have had her little bottom spanked.

Claudia took a deep breath. Something strange and wholly good had happened to her in being able to give shape to solid thinking. It helped her through the meeting with Mrs. Payne, who was coming slowly down the stairs with Annie's careful guidance, and dramatizing to beat the band, Claudia recognized with a sinking heart. She braced herself against some immediate connection with Candy's unseemly behaviour the preceding evening, but Mrs. Payne made no allusion to it. She merely said, in greeting, " Good-morning, my dear. Candy isn't at home. She didn't say where she was going, and I thought perhaps she was over at your place."

Claudia's mouth went dry. Mrs. Payne said, "I can manage now, Annie. Won't you come into the drawing room, my dear ? "

Claudia nodded, and with her hand beneath Mrs. Payne's bird-like elbow, helped her on to the stiff Victorian sofa.

"Thank you. I'm not as young as I used to be ; I don't seem to be able to stand things very well any more." Mrs. Payne gave vent to a small sigh, which filled Claudia with an abject fear of adding the proverbial straw to the camel's back. John was right, she must break the news gently.

She sat down in a small spindly chair near-by, and cast about desperately for an opening. " Mrs. Payne, John called me from the office early this morning——" she began with difficulty.

She saw too late that it was the worst possible approach. Mrs. Payne stiffened, and the slight quiver of her delicate nostrils bespoke a patrician disdain of family problems becoming public property. There were more ways than one of killing a goose, and if indeed Claudia had come as an emissary of peace, Mrs. Payne wanted none of it.

"Tell me," she said, firmly steering the conversation towards the impersonal, " did the posies I brought you last nicely ? "

For the moment, at least, Claudia bowed to Mrs. Payne's superior generalship. " Yes, Bertha put them on the breakfast table."

" And the children ? "

" Very well, thank you. Mrs. Payne, it's about Candy——"

" I'd prefer not to discuss anything about Candy, Claudia."

" But you don't understand——"

" I understand only too well." Mrs. Payne changed the subject with facility. " Michael's such a sweet baby, I was charmed with him yesterday."

The peal of the telephone sounded through the room. Claudia started up, with her pulses pounding in her ears and the floor weaving beneath her feet. It might be John, with some further news——

" Come back, my dear, Annie will get there eventually." Mrs. Payne gave another little sigh. " I'm afraid she's getting on in years, too. She moves more slowly, I notice and she's apt to be a little short-tempered at times. I dare say it's because she's not used to having a small infant in the house."

" Then let me answer the 'phone. Oh, please——"

But Annie, for once, had bestirred herself, and all Claudia could do was to block her way as she emerged from the closet. " Annie, who is it ? " she whispered importunately.

" A call for Mrs. Payne," Annie replied, in a tone that implied that Mrs. Payne's calls were entirely her own affairs. " Miss Bixby from the garden club," she announced at the threshold of the drawing room.

Claudia went limp. " Tell Miss Bixby I will call her back later," said Mrs. Payne. She beckoned to Claudia. " Take a chair nearer the terrace, it's a little cooler. You're looking quite fagged. And no wonder. It's a big undertaking to get settled in a new place, particularly one that isn't too well equipped."

Again, Claudia felt the reins slipping from her grip. " A house is no longer important, Mrs. Payne."

" That's quite true, when one's gone through as much as you have. I hope David's not doing any lifting or moving of furniture ; we don't want him falling ill again." (Odd how Mrs. Payne managed to find one's Achilles' heel, and tread on it.) " And this war news is so upsetting," she continued. " I'm worried about John being called up. He's in the reserves, you know."

" I imagine Candy's been very worried about it, too," Claudia grasped at a new opening.

Mrs. Payne smiled faintly. " I can't say that I agree with you. Candy hasn't lived through a war, she has no significance of what it means. In fact, Candy's never really gone through anything, she's lived a very sheltered life."

" She lost her mother," Claudia interjected swiftly, " at a time when she most needed her." Perhaps the reminder would serve a dual purpose, and Mrs. Payne might realize that, with a little effort and understanding, she could fill that need.

Mrs. Payne, however, ignored the implication. " It's a natural grief to lose one's mother," she said, although if the shoe were on the other foot, she would have sung a different tune. " I just heard a car drive up, it might be Candy, she should certainly be back by now."

" Mrs. Payne, it isn't Candy's car," Claudia broke in desperately, " and please stop changing the subject, you're making it so difficult for me to tell you——"

" I very likely am, my dear, because in plain words, I'd rather not discuss my daughter-in-law."

Mrs. Payne rose, this time without aid, Claudia noticed, and carefully plucked a dead blossom from one of the many plants in the long, narrow room. " There is nothing that Candy, or John either, for that matter, can't tell me themselves if they wish to." She lifted a warning finger. " I hear Annie coming."

Annie saw at once that the atmosphere in the room was one of strain, and, resolutely, she led Mrs. Payne back to the sofa. " You should be taking it very quiet to-day," she remarked for Claudia's benefit.

" I'm quite all right, Annie, I'm enjoying Mrs. Naughton's little visit. An old lady can get very lonely at times. What is it you want ? "

" I don't want a thing," Annie replied smartly, with a toss of her head. " I only came just in to say that Mr. Lewellyn is at the side entrance."

" I don't care to see him," Mrs. Payne said tersely.

" Didn't think you did. Told him as much, and if he wasn't a big grown man I'd have said he was ready to burst into tears, he seemed so upset."

" Show him in," Mrs. Payne relented, with a degree of satisfaction.

Annie departed. " Mr. Lewellyn," Mrs. Payne explained to Claudia, " has sacrificed my confidence in him. In fact, I'm sorry I recommended him to you, for I suddenly find that his impeccable breeding doesn't mean that he's capable of handling the business end of a transaction. You have doubt-lessly heard that he made an unforgivable blunder. Un-forgivable and inexcusable."

Claudia said nothing. Mrs. Payne waited, in grim silence, for Mr. Lewellyn to make both his appearance and his amends, and his entrance, an instant later, was filled with an agitation far in excess of his crime. "Oh, dear Mrs. Payne," he cried, reaching for both her hands, "I rushed over as soon as I heard, or rather, I didn't hear, I happened to stop at the garage for gas and I recognized the car, and then of course, Karl, the garage man, told me. Oh, that poor child! Her poor husband! And it's so dreadful for you, too, poor dear Mrs. Payne. Is there *anything* I can do?"

Claudia crossed swiftly to Mrs. Payne's side. It was too late to soften the blow now, for Mrs. Payne's mind, always clear and sharp, arrived at the truth with a frightening directness. "There's been an accident," she said, in the strange, precise tone of a sleepwalker's voice. She looked up at Claudia. "That's what you have been trying to tell me. Is she dead?"

"No, no! But she's badly hurt."

"You shouldn't have spared me, my dear. I'm not a child."

"John wanted me to break it to you gently."

"John is a good son," said Mrs. Payne, still in that stunned voice. "Candy thinks he's too good a son. Perhaps she's right." Then all at once she seemed to shrivel up, and her small, frail hands clenched the air as she rocked back and forth in grief. "This is real," thought Claudia, "this isn't play-acting." She put her arm round the thin shoulders, and noticed with pity the soft vulnerable pink of Mrs. Payne's scalp. It was such an odd thing to notice, and somehow so heart-breaking. Her eyes met Mr. Lewellyn's. He was paler than pale, and his short sandy hair seemed to be standing on end. "I didn't know she didn't know!" he gasped.

He had committed another blunder.

It was just as well that it happened that way, for John called immediately afterwards, to say that Candy had fallen asleep and he had left her with the floor nurse while he went out to get a cup of coffee and to telephone. "Have you told Mother yet?" he asked.

"Yes," said Claudia. "She's standing right next to me, she wants to talk to you."

She was afraid to move too far away from the telephone.

Mrs. Payne's pallor was frightening, and the closet was suffo-catingly close with the climbing heat of midday. But at the first sound of her voice, Claudia knew that Mrs. Payne's love for her son was stronger than her body. " Put me out of your mind, John," she said, a little sternly. " There's nothing wrong with me, so stop worrying about me. And tell Candy that only one thing matters now, and that's for her to get well."

Claudia felt humbled and a little awed. Growing old was a lonely business at best, and loneliest perhaps for mothers. How easy it was for youth to sit in judgment.

Annie met Mrs. Payne at the foot of the stairs. " You'd best go up and lie down, or I'll be having you back on my hands. She thrust a bottle of smelling-salts beneath Mrs. Payne's nose. " Sniff," she said, " before you start up."

Mrs. Payne pushed the smelling-salts away, and ignored Annie's out-thrust arm. Slowly, and with dignity, she climbed the stairs alone.

Claudia watched her until she was out of sight. Annie was watching, too, with an impenetrable look on her granite face. It almost seemed as if she resented the fact that Candy's accident had lifted Mrs. Payne beyond the need of pampering. " It's been a strange and murky household," Claudia thought, with a kind of terror as she sped back to the hospital.

She was careful to slow down at the intersection. A boy was selling newspapers, with the headlines screaming war. It was incongruous that Mrs. Payne should have said, " Candy is the one thing that matters," when, at this very moment, humanity was dying by the thousands. And yet, in the final count-up, one life was all lives, and the little murky household held the infinitesimal seed of a murky world.

It was a big thought, too big to think while she was peering for the street that led off to the hospital. As it was, she went a block too far, and lost her way completely. Her beginner's luck was wearing off, and her bad sense of direction was functioning beautifully again. It somehow made everything seem more normal.

It was better, too, to go in through the private entrance of the hospital instead of the emergency entrance. There was a minimum of red tape involved in reaching Candy's room, and only a placard on the door, forbidding visitors, prevented her from going in. She knocked lightly, aware that her heart had jumped back into her throat. Carefully the door was opened from within, and in the half-dark she saw John's tall, lean, questioning figure. She couldn't see Candy, just part of the iron bed, with its white cotton cover severely tucked into neat folds at the corners.

John gave a backward glance into the room before he tip-toed out to the hall and quietly closed the door. " She's still asleep," he whispered.

" No report on the X-rays yet ? "

" No. But Dr. Hubbard's been here, he's our family physician, and he said she seemed in pretty good shape, superficially. He said a lot depends on her own come-back. He seemed to think, from the little he's seen of her at the house, that she's in a highly suspect condition of nerves, and a shock like this could easily——" He found it hard to go on.

" It won't, John," said Claudia. " Candy's got too much stamina to go down in a heap. Besides, she loves you, she wouldn't play a dirty trick like that on you."

His lips twisted, but he couldn't quite make a smile. " It would be a really dirty trick," he admitted huskily.

She patted his arm. " It's not done among the best married couples," she assured him. " What about a nurse ? You can't go on like this."

" We've got one coming from three to eleven. If a nurse isn't available for to-night, I'll stay. It's almost getting to be like the last war." His eyes wandered anxiously to the closed door.

" Go on back," said Claudia. " There's a place to wait at the end of the hall."

" Why don't you go home, Claudia ? You don't have to put yourself through this."

" How would you like a good bat on the nose ? " she enquired.

This time he managed a small smile. " All right. I'll know where to find you."

It occurred to her that he hadn't asked about his mother. It could have been because Mrs. Payne had made him believe that there was no need to worry about her, or it may have been the beneficent growing-up of a man in love with his wife. " Or it could even be both," Claudia decided.

She felt suddenly a vast tiredness and depletion, not unlike the feeling she'd had when she'd stayed with John while Candy was in labour. She hadn't left him until the early dawn, after the baby had given its first hardy salute to life. It was a little like labour now, this rebirth of their souls.

She was glad that there were no other people waiting in the small recess off the corridor. Automatically, she picked up a magazine from a table, and then held it unopened in her lap and leaned her head back against the unfriendly wicker of the eternal two-seated sofa.

"Pardon," a voice said. "Aren't you the lady I fed ducks with this morning?"

Her eyes flew open. "David!" she cried. "Oh, darling, I've been wondering when you'd get back."

"Well, now you know," he said cheerfully, and dropped a kiss on her hair before he sat down beside her. "I spoke to John just after Dr. Hubbard had been here. Any further news?"

"None. She's still asleep. John's with her." Her eyes scanned him anxiously. "David, how are you?"

"I'm fine. Why shouldn't I be?"

"Darling," she begged him, "let me get it said, and then I promise not to nag you again, because I know you can't take it easy while John's tied up here with Candy. But please, *please*, try not to overdo it. A full day's work is the worst possible thing for you, now."

"It's the best possible thing for me. It makes me feel like a man again."

"You're enough man for me just as you are," she told him tremulously. "I wouldn't know what to do with any more."

"You could try?" he wheedled.

She sighed in deep contentment. "You're such a fool. David, was it really only this morning that we fed those ducks?"

"Isn't life the damnedest thing?"

"The damnedest. Why didn't you let me know what train you were taking, ass, I'd have met you?"

"I took a taxi, idiot."

"I didn't expect you for another hour at least."

"So I'm not working hard enough."

"Oh, David, I missed you so."

"I had an idea you might have, that's why I hurried home. It was a hell of a morning for you, wasn't it?"

She nodded, speechless. "But I was glad you were on the train when it happened. It was like some hideous nightmare."

"Don't think of it, dear."

They sat for a space, saying nothing. After a time she said, "I feel so guilty, feeling the wonderful feeling of being close to you——"

He finished the thought for her. "Darling, we've had ours, and come through it. And John and Candy will come through theirs."

"I hope so, oh, I hope so. What's the good of suffering if it doesn't make you wiser in living and in loving?"

"No good," he said. "Bet you didn't have lunch."

"I didn't!" she discovered belatedly. "No wonder I feel funny in my stomach. And I thought it was love, like a fool." Indignation churned within her. "It wouldn't have hurt Annie to offer me a little something, now would it? Not that I'd have taken the time for it," she added, "but it's the idea behind it."

"I know just how you feel," David sympathized. "There's a place across the street come on. I'll buy you a cup of coffee and a sandwich."

"I hate to leave, I've gone so far I might as well wait until supper."

"You haven't gone so far. It's only half-past two."

"Is that all? Say, did *you* have lunch?" She didn't wait for an answer, she was furious. "David, you ought to have your tail kicked!" She pulled him to his feet. "We'll both go out, and maybe by the time we get back the report on the X-rays will be here. Like a pot that won't boil while you watch it."

"Fine," he said, and mentioned as an afterthought, "You're nice company to go through things with. Good and bad."

She gave a short laugh. "I'm improving with practice. Although by myself I'm not so hot. But when you're with me," she admitted modestly, "I'm remarkable."

It wasn't much of a coffee-place, and the sandwiches, guiltless of butter or lettuce, looked as bad as they tasted. Claudia drew the line at peanut butter, and ordered cheese with mustard, but David was smart and literally and figuratively stuck to peanut butter, because it came out of a glass jar and couldn't go wrong. "I didn't think that cheese could go wrong," Claudia pondered, "have a bite and see what you think."

"You're on your own," he informed her brutally.

"How long would you say that piece of chocolate cake has been behind that glass slide?"

"You're still on your own," said David.

"I wouldn't have the heart, anyway," she said, "until we hear about the X-rays."

David threw her a disgusted look. " Madame will have the cake," he told the girl behind the counter.

" You don't use ' Madame ' in a place like this," Claudia corrected him in an undertone. " You say, ' the Missus '." She eyed the cake distrustfully. " It looked better from a distance," she decided, and changed it for a doughnut.

" Dunk," David invited her, " I won't look."

John was waiting for them on the wicker love-seat when they returned. " Good news," he greeted them. " The X-rays show no internal injuries."

" God," said David, not in blasphemy but in gratitude. Claudia didn't say anything. She turned to the window and began to cry. David gave her a handkerchief. " Let her alone," he said to John, and they began to talk about the office.

Claudia blew her nose. " Damn fool."

" Go ahead," said John, " don't mind us." He looked white as a sheet, and his eyes were red, too, but his spirit was renewed. " The nurse came," he remembered to mention. " She's in with Candy now. And we have someone for the night."

" I'm so glad," said Claudia. " Have you called your mother ? "

" Not yet."

" Shall I ? "

" I wish you would," said John.

" And I'll call Bertha, while I'm at it. Let me have two nickels, David."

" Here's a quarter," said John, " and you can keep the change." He gave her a watery smile.

" Make it a dollar," Claudia bargained, " and I'll call Julia and Hartley, too. I should have let them know this morning."

" They do know," said David. " I was supposed to have had lunch with Hartley."

" Splendid," Claudia said. " That means flowers any minute."

John actually grinned. " They've already come, believe it or not. Dozens of yellow roses. The nurse is very impressed, she's got them where Candy can see them when she opens her eyes."

As Claudia started off to the booth, the nurse rustled out to tell John that his wife was asking for him, and after a time John came out to tell Claudia that Candy was asking to see her, too.

"The nurse thinks it'll quiet her if we give in to her. Don't stay but a minute, Claudia."

It was a shock, that first glance at the small bandaged figure on the bed against a bower of roses. Candy's face looked tiny and bloodless with her bright taffy-coloured hair hidden by the swathing of gauze around her forehead. Her eyes glistened, and yet there was a strange dead look in them, and her voice, when she spoke, had the sing-song rhythm of drugs and shock. "The man in the other car is dead, isn't he?" she flung out at Claudia at once.

"If he is, I didn't know it," Claudia answered. "I'd been told that he was only shaken up."

"That's the story they're trying to tell me," said Candy, "but I know they're lying, I know he's dead, I felt the crash of the car and I saw it turn over and over——" her voice mounted to a scream, "and I killed him, I killed a man! It was my fault, all my fault——"

"Now come," the nurse said, "you have to quiet down, Mrs. Payne. It's the morphine and the other medicine they gave her," she explained in an aside to Claudia. "We just have to let her rave until it wears off."

"She thinks I'm raving," Candy wept helplessly. "I'm not raving. I killed a man. . . ."

Claudia took Candy's right hand, the one without the bandages, and held it, firmly. "Listen to me," she said. "I'm sorry to disappoint you, but you didn't kill anybody, and you're not so very much banged up yourself, more luck than brains."

"I wanted to do it. I was going as fast as I could, I didn't care any more—and then the other car was coming towards me all of a sudden, and I couldn't stop. It was awful—awful—awful——" Her breath came sobbingly. "Claudia, I'm so ashamed."

"Well, you ought to be ashamed," Claudia said crisply. "David would wring my neck if I ever went above fifty."

Candy's voice dropped to a croon, "John's been so sweet—so wonderful——"

"I don't doubt it," said Claudia. "Better than you deserve. I always said he was too good for you."

Candy's eyes widened with another kind of shock. "You're fooling, aren't you?" she whispered.

Claudia patted her hand. "Sure. Now go to sleep again, and to-morrow everything will look different."

"I don't want there to be a to-morrow."

"Now that's not very nice talk," the nurse inserted, and then she saw that Candy's lids were drooping and she was asleep. Cautiously, Claudia unloosed her fingers, and immediately Candy's eyes flew open again. "I was dreaming of my mother, I thought you were my mother—and I got myself mixed up with my baby. Don't leave the baby with Annie—that's what I wanted to tell you and I couldn't think any more—*Claudia!*"

"Yes, dear, I'm right here."

"Take the baby, won't you? John's mother spoils her and Annie doesn't love her, and they're both too old for a little tiny baby——"

"I know, dear," said Claudia softly. "David and I will keep her until you come home."

"Promise——" Candy breathed.

"I promise," said Claudia.

"Cheer up," David said, as they drove away from the hospital.

"I'm trying to."

"Well, do. What's a few broken bones?"

"Nothing. Broken bones heal up, but mental agony doesn't."

David swerved out into the road, and stepped on the accelerator. "I don't want to be behind that car in front, it's weaving all over the place," he muttered. "You drive like a woman!" he shouted raucously as he passed it.

Claudia looked back. "It *was* a woman!" she told him in dismay.

"I knew it," he said complacently, "that's what burns 'em up. As for Candy's mental agony, she's cooking up a lot of imaginary problems, including the man in the other car."

"But telling her so isn't going to help her, and her suffering is worse than if she had real troubles, because she has nothing tangible to pin it on."

"Except herself."

"She can't find herself. That's what's so hard."

David shrugged. "That's why there are so many psycho-analysts on Park Avenue."

"Free clinics, too," she retorted, "so don't be so intolerant of the leisured class."

He chose to let that one slip by. "Well, what are you getting at—that Candy needs mental treatment?"

"I don't know. I was worried about her even before the accident. I thought the new house would straighten her out. It might have, if Mrs. Payne hadn't done what she did."

"I'm not excusing Mrs. Payne, but that was only the trigger. If Candy didn't blow her top at that, it would have been something else."

"Maybe."

"No 'maybe' about it. Anyway, cheer up," he reverted. "I'm wondering how I can be tactful about taking the baby."

"You've got your troubles," said David, "and they're not imaginary."

It turned out, though, that there was no trouble about taking the baby, and the tact was all on Mrs. Payne's side. Claudia found her in the upstairs sitting room, bending over the perambulator, giving little Elizabeth her bottle. The bottle wasn't tipped enough, and the baby was getting air, but Claudia made no comment. "Candy held quite a conversation with me," she said.

"I'm so happy."

"And John says to tell you he'll take a taxi home, and have supper with you, and then drive your car back to the hospital."

"Yes, he'll be needing it until he can get his own repaired."

There was no point in telling her that the convertible was beyond repair. "Mayn't I finish giving the baby the bottle?" she asked instead.

Mrs. Payne straightened up with effort. "If you would, my dear. I can't bend over too well, and I was afraid to lift her, my arms aren't steady enough to-day."

"Where's Annie?"

"Annie has her hands full, and I didn't like to ask her, News of the accident has got around, and people have started being attentive." Mrs. Payne's brow puckered anxiously. "Annie wanted to telephone the local employment agency for a baby's nurse, she says she can't be up at night and work all day, and she's right, I dare say. Still, I'm afraid to trust the baby to a total stranger."

"I don't blame you. I wish I could send Bertha over, but I'd hate to be so tied down that I couldn't go over to the hospital every day."

"My dear child, I wouldn't permit it for a moment. Besides, Annie wouldn't tolerate another person in the house. I was thinking——" Mrs. Payne hesitated, and a slight flush stained her cheeks. "No. It's an imposition, and I mustn't ask it of you."

"You can ask anything," said Claudia. "You seem to forget that John took care of the office for almost a year while David was ill. So nothing in the world that we could do would be too much."

"It's very generous of you to put it that way. It makes it much easier. Claudia, could you possibly manage, with Matthew, and a baby of your own, and all the work of moving, to keep Elizabeth until Candy comes home?"

"Of course we can!"

"But what will Bertha say?"

"Bertha will say that two babies are no more trouble than one."

"Are you sure?"

"I'm sure."

Mrs. Payne gave a great sigh of relief. At the very end, though, she wept a little to see the baby go. She lifted one of the petal-like hands, and covered it with kisses. "Grandma's little angel. Grandma will miss you."

"Thomas can drive Grandma over to see her little angel," Claudia suggested, "just as often as you want."

Annie said, "The easier Mrs. Payne takes it, the better. Maybe she'll get more rest, now. I've got everything packed, and Thomas can begin piling things in the back of your station-wagon."

"Just the bassinet. We don't need the scale, or the tub."

"Best have them," said Annie.

"We do not need them," Claudia repeated firmly. "We have Matthew's."

A small running stitch needled its way around Annie's lips. It was more than obvious that she wanted to get everything belonging to the baby out of the house.

They drove off at last. "Our friend Annie," David remarked, "would be a picnic for a psycho-analyst."

"Wouldn't she, though."

"How long? Eighteen years?"

"Nineteen. Since John was eight."

"No wonder he doesn't see it, he's too close to it."

"Candy sees it. But she doesn't know what she's seeing."

"Do you?"

"I think so." She took a deep breath of sweet fresh air. "Just smell how clean and fragrant. Honeysuckle."

"How does it feel to have a baby on your lap?"

"I'm trying not to feel. I suppose I'd be a little of a picnic, too."

" No, you wouldn't. You've done yours the hard way, darling. Bit by bit."

She smiled grimly. " Up one step and back two."

" No matter. You're getting there. Homely little monkey."

" Who ! "

" The baby, who'd you think ? "

" You're crazy ! " Claudia exclaimed indignantly, " this baby is beautiful." She glanced at him out of the corner of her eye. " Don't look so pleased with yourself. You're as subtle as an elephant."

He slowed down as they approached the gates of the Grey house, and without asking her, turned up the winding drive-way.

" What are you doing that for ? " she asked a little sharply.

" Why not ? It'll only take a minute."

" You think they'll really buy it ? "

" They have bought it."

" They've only paid a deposit, and they can lose it, if they have to. Or Mrs. Payne could probably wangle it back for them under the circumstances."

" What circumstances ? A few busted ribs ? "

" They'd be better off in another house. Preferably in another town."

" Rats. If Candy and John are looking for freedom, they'll find it in themselves, or they won't find it at all."

" That's just the point. They're not free enough to be tied. Oh, David," she broke off, " it is *really* a lovely place ! Look at the garden in this misty light."

" I am," said David.

The old Italian caretaker was nowhere to be seen, but he had done a good day's work, and the grass shone like velvet, and the flower beds were islands of colour, set in brown peat-moss, freshly raked and edged.

" The house is lovely, too, in this light," said David.

" Yes. But so empty. It breathes emptiness, as if it were waiting for people to move in and make it come alive."

" Now don't go whimsical on me," he warned her. " Look, stop by to-morrow morning and pick some flowers for Candy, and tell her that they're from her own garden."

" Now who's being whimsical ? "

" That's not whimsical. It's sensible."

" She'll say that she wants no part of it."

" She was in love with it yesterday."

" That was yesterday."

" But they'll have to have some place to live, and this is far better than anything they'll be likely to come on, in addition to being central. John wouldn't like her to be off in the country like we are."

" You talk as if she were going to be alone," said Claudia slowly.

David lit a cigarette. " Darling, with a war on, men like John are valuable. He's trained. And necessary."

Her heart stopped. " There's something you haven't told me, David."

" There's a lot that John hasn't told Candy."

" I didn't ask you what John hadn't told Candy. What haven't you told me ? That he's going to be called ? "

" He has been called. Yesterday."

" David, no ! Not so soon ! "

" He was expecting it. That's why he was so glad that Candy wanted the house. He'd like to leave her in a home of her own, and he'd like to have that home to come back to."

" Oh, God," Claudia cried in a choked voice. " It's so unfair ! "

" It is. And then again, it isn't." David threw away his cigarette, unsmoked. " I'd give my eye teeth to trade with John. And that doesn't mean that I don't love you."

" I know," she said, a little wearily. " By this time I've learned that a husband and a man are two different beings."

" Not so different. A husband wants to see his wife and children live in a decent world."

" You sound like a pamphlet, so I'll sound like one, too. Is bloodshed the only way we can get a decent world ? "

" It shouldn't be. But it is."

He slid the car into gear, and they were past the gates, and headed towards home. " I suppose," Claudia ventured, in a quavering voice, " that you think you've been a help to my general morale."

A smile tugged at his lips. " You asked for it. Besides, I thought you might as well get it all at once, and have it over with."

" Thanks."

The baby stirred within her arms. " Shhhh——" she whispered. " Keep sleeping, darling." After a moment, she said, through gritted teeth, " Sweet Annie, she didn't put the rubber panties on."

David caught her hand in his. " I'm a lucky devil."

" I am, too. How can I say that ? " she asked him wonderingly.

He pressed her fingers, hard. " Because the more there is behind us, the more we have to look forward to."

" I'll have to think that one out," she said.

CHAPTER TEN

THEY didn't talk again until they reached the wall of the tooth-paste king. " I've never used his paste. I suppose the least I can do is to buy some, since he's a neighbour," Claudia mentioned.

" The least," David agreed.

The wall went on and on, and then abruptly the little white house with the pink shutters was winking at them with one dim light in the living room window. " Elsirob." David tasted the name anew. " I wonder if their names really are Elsie and Rob."

" They are, I forgot to tell you. She calls him Robbie. She's so nice, David, and I know she's going to be awfully friendly, and you might as well face it that she says 'goo'bye-now ' ; and when she wrote her name and telephone number down for me, she dotted her i's with little circles, but it's time we stopped being snobs about things like that, and tooth-paste kings."

" It's high time," David acknowledged.

" In fact, I meant to tell you that if we should buy the house on the river, we could call it Claudavia."

" Should buy it ? " he echoed. " I didn't know there was any doubt in your mind."

She was miserably aware that his disappointment was second only to the fact that she had let him down a little, but she couldn't lie to him about the way she felt. " Well," he said, after a moment, " there's no hurry about a decision. She's really a good baby, isn't she ? She hasn't cried once."

" Very," said Claudia. She was grateful to him for not talking any more about the house. " Do you think I should have telephoned Bertha we were bringing a boarder ? "

" I thought you did."

" I changed my mind, I wanted it to be a surprise."

" It will be," said David.

They turned in at the river road, and for a space of magic

146

it was country, deep and wild, with Nature lavishly tossing trees and flowers and berries into an indiscriminate tangle of beauty. A rabbit skittered out of the bushes and froze in the middle of the road and looked at them.

"Hey, you stupid!" David expostulated.

"He's no intention of moving, the sweet little trusting fool!"

David obligingly went over to the side. "There ought to be plenty of deer around here, too," he said.

"I'd kill anyone who killed one on our property."

"You would," said David, looking pleased.

"I would," she affirmed.

The rabbit hopped off into the bushes, like a busy little club woman going to meeting. "Some day I'd adore to catch one and just hug it," said Claudia.

"Let me know when you do," said David.

The glint of diamonds began to show through the tangle, and suddenly there was the river, and although no tidy driveway led up to the door of the little hip-roof house, there were bright lights in the kitchen, and smoke coming out of the chimney. "Bertha must be using the coal stove," said David. "The electric range isn't good enough for her."

"Couldn't you slap her," Claudia scolded affectionately, "with all she's got to do!"

Bluff heard them first, and came galloping out, and then Matthew was racing behind him, and finally Bertha stood in the doorway, with Michael in her arms.

"The porch might be loose, and the house might need painting," said Claudia, "but it isn't empty."

"That it's not," said David. "Hello, Bluff, old boy, glad to see us?"

"Please, Bluff," Claudia begged, "keep your tail to yourself. Matthew, your father's too busy with his dog to say hello to you—Hello."

"Hello," said Matthew. "What's that?"

"What's what?"

"What you're carrying?" he demanded suspiciously.

"I'm not carrying anything."

"You are so!" He stood on his tip-toes. "It's a doll!" he discovered in disappointment.

"This doll is alive."

He pulled at her arm. "Let me see."

She let him see. "It's a baby!" he said, in outright disgust. "We have a baby."

" I know, but ours is getting so old," said Claudia, " I thought we'd get a new one."

He seemed a little confused, and she could see him trying to put two and two together, and arriving nowhere. " I guess it's Candy's," he deduced.

" Yes, it's Candy's," said Claudia. " She's lending it to us for a little while."

" What do we need first out of the car ? " David asked her.

" Just the box with the napkins," said Claudia. " Here comes Bertha, I knew she couldn't stand it."

Bertha looked as if somebody had lit a candle behind her eyes. " Ach ! " she cried. " Give me ! "

She thrust the old baby into Claudia's arms, and took the new one. Claudia couldn't get over it. " All of a sudden he feels like a ton, and looks like a giant," she said, and remembered that the same thing had happened with Bobby after Matthew was born ; and after Michael was born, Matthew had suddenly seemed grown up. It was strange, and quite wonderful, to know that feeling all over again. It made Candy's baby feel like her own.

It was a rather mixed-up supper, for which Bertha was deeply apologetic, but David said they'd excuse doing without finger bowls just this once because, after all, she wasn't expecting an increase in family the day after they'd moved in. " I am so happy," she exulted, " it is like a present for me to have the baby, and I feel it in my bones that Miss Candy will be all right. And that is also a beautiful stove," she added, with her cup running over.

There were clouds to Bertha's silver linings, but Claudia decided that nothing could be gained by thinking about them to-night. There was the war, and the fact that Bertha would be sad when she had to give the baby up, and when they did the kitchen over, her heart would be doubly broken because they were certainly not going to have a dilapidated coal range standing around like a poor relative.

" I wonder," Claudia said to David, while Bertha was upstairs shifting things around to accommodate the baby's bassinet, " whether we could possibly keep it."

" This time I'm lost," said David. " Keep what ? The baby ? "

" No, the coal stove. When we do the kitchen over."

" Oh," said David.

" Well, you can't walk out on a house that's as nice to us

as this one is," Claudia defended. "When I came in the door this evening, I left all my unhappiness outside, like a pair of rubbers on a bad day."

"It's not exactly poetry," David smiled, "but it's as good a way as I know of calling a house a home."

Bertha came down in time to serve the dessert. "I baked an apple pie to try the oven," she said, "but we also have nice cookies, if you want them."

"Bertha, you half-witted woman, you didn't bake cookies, too, to-day !" Claudia protested.

"No, I did not get the time," Bertha admitted reluctantly. "Mrs. Miller, who lives in the pretty little house with the pink shutters, brought them for the children."

"That was lovely of her," said Claudia.

"She is a lovely woman," said Bertha. "It is nice to have nice neighbours. The cookies are different than I make, though," she added with a slight reservation. "They are not rolled with a rolling pin, they are only dropped from a spoon."

"Bertha, dear, nobody rolls any more when they can drop," Claudia enlightened her gently.

Bertha's mouth almost looked like Annie's for a moment. "I roll," she insisted flatly, "and I also like a coal stove."

"Bertha, when you're with us nineteen years you're going to be a pain in the neck," said David. "But in the meantime, you're the joy of our lives ; I don't know what we'd do without you."

"You would manage," Bertha modestly returned.

"Like a lame duck," said Claudia. "Oh, Bertha, by the way, would you have any cracked corn on you ? "

"If you haven't," said David, with a magnanimous gesture, "we'll overlook it this once, but see that you have some to-morrow. In the meantime, we'll borrow a few of those dropped cookies."

"No more than three," Claudia stipulated. "My conscience would bother me."

The ducks were charmed with them. "There's nothing," said Claudia, "like putting your best foot forward."

They stayed outdoors until the mosquitoes drove them in, although they were loath to admit that there were mosquitoes. "Let's go in and telephone the hospital," said David. "I told Julia and Hartley I'd keep them posted."

"Tell Julia her flowers came, and thank her for Candy,"

said Claudia, " and don't you think it would be nice if I called Mrs. Miller, too, and thanked her for the ducks ? "

" I think it would be very nice," said David.

Mrs. Miller was so pleased that everybody enjoyed her cookies, that she offered to take care of Matthew the following day. Claudia relayed the offer to Bertha, who was properly appreciative, but firm in her refusal to accept. " I can manage," she insisted. " Matthew is no trouble."

" Bertha's certainly looking a gift-horse in the face," Claudia commented to David. " Her pride is a disease."

The next morning, though, Bertha wasn't quite so proud, for suddenly there weren't enough hours in the day. She was in the kitchen at half-past five, making the baby's formula, and Claudia was furious. " Now, honestly, Bertha, couldn't that have waited until seven o'clock ? I'd planned to do it ! "

" You have plenty to do," said Bertha, " running back and forth to the hospital. This way, I can get Michael out of the way early."

" Poor Michael," Claudia duly informed David, " his schedule's been advanced, willy-nilly, and I could see his security shaking like nobody's business."

" If that's all that's shaking, he's lucky," said David. " Wasn't it a hell of a night ? "

Claudia was dismayed. " Bertha and I closed all the doors, and hoped you didn't hear. It must have been a little colic from the change of water."

" It sounded like quite a lot of colic," said David. " You must be dead on your feet."

" It's Bertha who's going to be dead if she isn't already. I can get away from it most of the day. Do you want to see her get a bath ? "

" Bertha ? "

" That's not terribly funny."

" I thought it was."

" Well, do you ? Speak up. Bertha's issued a special invitation for the event."

" You use my ticket," said David. " I'm shaving."

The children's bathroom was a pretty good-sized one, but it seemed crowded, because Matthew was there, too, with his eyes taking up most of his face. Bertha realized that it was a topographical error of sorts, to have included him in the audience—cold, as it were—but it was too late to do anything about it now. " Run ask Papa," she said, blushing hotly.

"No, I'll attend to it," said Claudia, resigned, and after Elizabeth had been rolled in a towel and powdered, she led Matthew out into the warm, lovely sunshine, and pointed out to him that the drakes—"The little boy ducks, darling "—were of an entirely different colour.

"The baby isn't a different colour," said Matthew, quite doggedly.

"No, I know she's not, but it's the same idea," said Claudia lamely. "We'll go into it more thoroughly some other time, I have to take Daddy to the station now. Look. Why don't you run and ask Bertha if you can go and spend the morning at Mrs. Miller's ? "

He came back in a little while, pale with an extra dose of soap-and-water, and with a clean handkerchief sticking up out of his pocket. "Bertha says I can stay as long as Mrs. Miller wants me," he announced.

"How the mighty have fallen," said David.

"It really makes me feel much easier about leaving the house, though," said Claudia. "At least one in a bassinet and one in a carriage can't throw things at each other."

"I see what you mean," said David.

Mrs. Miller was all smiles when Claudia left Matthew at the door. "We're going to have so much fun," she exclaimed brightly.

"That's what you think," Claudia replied silently. "Mrs. Miller was delighted," she told David, as she scrambled back into the station-wagon. "Bertha's right, it's nice to have nice neighbours."

"But it's not a nice thing to do to nice neighbours," David commented. "Are you going straight to the hospital from the train ? "

"No, I thought I'd stop off and pick the flowers for Candy first, and as long as I'm so near, I can kill two birds with one stone."

"Give Mrs. Payne my love," said David, " and tell her to grow up and be a big bird, and let bygones be bygones."

"I have a sense she's ready to," said Claudia.

She decided to step in to see Mrs. Payne before she picked the flowers. There was no use in letting them lie in the car and wither, and visits to older people were something that shouldn't be hurried. Candy hadn't learned that yet. Old people didn't like to feel you were perched on the arm of a chair for a moment of compulsory chatter, but that you were really interested in talking to them. And given half a chance,

Mrs. Payne actually was interesting, especially when she forgot to call herself an old lady, which, in terms of years, she wasn't. What would happen if Candy, and John, too, were to begin to treat her like an ordinary human being who didn't have to be catered to and appeased ? " I'm going to try it this morning," Claudia decided. " I'm going to ask her to have Thomas drive her over to give Bertha a hand with the baby." Bertha wouldn't want the hand, of course, but she'd like the company, and Mrs. Payne would probably enjoy the change and the feeling of being needed. " My, what a little girl scout you're turning out to be," Claudia told herself wryly, as she rang the bell and peered through the screen door. After a moment she heard Annie's voice from the region of the dining room. " Go on with your dusting, Thomas, I'll answer, it can't be anybody this early."

" It's only me," said Claudia, ready and willing to bury the hatchet.

" Oh," said Annie. " Mr. John left for the hospital a good half-hour ago."

Claudia blinked. Was it possible that Annie wasn't opening the screen door, or was it an optical illusion ? " I came to see Mrs. Payne," she said, as civilly as she could.

" Why, I haven't even taken Mrs. Payne's breakfast tray up to her yet," Annie stood her ground. " I told her she needed to sleep until nine o'clock, and it's barely that now."

A choice of rejoinders leaped to Claudia's lips, but she controlled the impulse to lash out at Annie. " Very well," she said, and turned on her heel, ashamed to find that she was shaking with outrage. She started the station-wagon with a great splash of gas that would have set David's teeth on edge, and whisked through the *porte-cochère* with a fine splutter of gravel against her wheels. She was still fuming when she turned in at the gates of the stone house. Tony was tying some annuals that were already tall enough to stake ; he recognized the car, and came towards her. " One nasty word out of him, and I'll let him have everything I'm saving for Annie," she muttered.

There wasn't a nasty word in Tony, however. Every wrinkle in his leathery face held consternation and sympathy. He had heard about the accident and, in his broken English, he begged Claudia to believe that he would do anything and everything to be of service to the poor little lady. " Just a few flowers to take to the hospital," Claudia smiled at him.

He all but stripped the garden, and when he laid the

fragrant masses in the back of the station-wagon, he said, " I clean the windows and wax the floors, and then you can move furniture in before the little lady come home from hospital."

Claudia stared at him. " Tony, you're inspired ! "

She could hardly wait to get to the hospital to talk it over with John. He was sitting in the waiting-room, studying some blueprints, which was a good sign. " Once an architect, always an architect," she greeted him blithely.

He looked up, " Oh, hello, there ! Candy had a pretty good night."

" Better than we did," Claudia amended to herself. Aloud she said, " Here are some flowers from your own garden."

" Oh. Mother's ? "

" Your own, I said. The house you just bought. Remember ? "

" Yes, I remember," he returned a little heavily. " But I don't think Candy wants to remember. She hasn't even spoken of it."

" She's had other things on her mind. How's the man in the black sedan ? "

" He's been discharged from the hospital with only a few minor bruises. The accident was in the paper this morning, and Dr. Hubbard showed Candy the account of it, so now she believes us. That's one thing out of the way. But the house is something else ; I don't want to talk to her about it yet."

" Do you think Candy should go back to your mother's when she's ready to leave the hospital ? "

" What else is there to do ? If the apartment in town weren't sold, we could go there, except that most of the stuff is crated for storage. That's what was so perfect about buying the Grey place," he went on. " We'd have just moved everything in, instead of storing it until we'd found a place."

" You talk as if that were impossible."

" It is. The house holds no joy for Candy now. I think you'd better tell her the flowers are from your garden."

Claudia laughed. " Candy's seen our garden. It'll be a long while before we have any prize specimens like the ones in that bunch."

" You're really buying your house, aren't you ? " John asked a little wistfully.

" We really are."

" I spoke to Mother this morning. She wants to take the loss on the deposit rather than have Candy go ahead with something she doesn't want to do."

" Your mother must be disappointed," said Claudia. She frowned. " John, did you say it was this morning that you spoke to her ? "

" Yes. We had a nice talk, and got a lot of things straightened out between us. Why ? "

" I stopped by——"

" That was thoughtful of you——"

" But I didn't see her."

" You didn't ? "

" No. Annie gave me to understand that she was still asleep."

" That's ridiculous. Mother's always up early. I'll have to talk to Annie. Mother had quite a run-in with her last night."

" About Candy ? "

" Yes. How did you know ? "

" Annie doesn't like Candy. That's one of the reasons why you shouldn't go back to your mother's house, it would only mean a great deal of friction."

" Not now. Mother said she'd rather let Annie go than tolerate any disloyalty."

" That takes courage, after all these years," said Claudia.

" Mother has courage. And I'm not sure that it wouldn't be the best thing for her. Only I wish there were more time to work things out. . . ." His eyes met Claudia's. " We haven't got much time left to us."

" I know you haven't. David told me. That's why you'll have to make do with what little time there is. It's that way in a war. Years become days, and days become years. You have to live every minute that you're together as if it were your last."

" You and David ought to know," said John humbly. " But I can't tell that to Candy, Claudia. She isn't ready for it, it would be too much for her."

" Then that's her tough luck, John. She'll have to know it, sooner or later. And if you wait too long, she'll never forgive you. I know that, too. Because even if you only live in your first house together for a day, or a week, or a month, you will have had it. Nobody can take that away from you, and every moment stands for something precious."

" Yes," said John.

She picked up her pocket-book and gloves. "I don't think I'll wait to see her this morning, I'll come back on my way to call for David. You take the flowers to her, John. Tell her that Tony sent them, with his love."

John cleared his throat. "Do you think Tony would stay on?" he asked unsteadily.

"I think you couldn't get rid of him," said Claudia.

He must have made quite a little headway in talking to Candy about the house, because she somehow had the impression that the whole thing was her idea. "I told John that it was the only thing to do," she discussed it drowsily with Claudia that afternoon. "So silly to lose a big deposit like that. . . ."

"Of course." Claudia's lips twitched. "Money doesn't grow on trees, as the saying goes."

"John said we could easily pay that extra ten thousand ourselves from the sale of the apartment—his mother wouldn't mind. . . ."

"I wouldn't mind either," said Claudia.

Candy's lids flickered with a faint amusement. "You know what I mean. I wish the doctor would stop giving me medicine to make me sleep. . . ."

"It's for the pain," Claudia explained. "It makes you sleep on the side."

"I'd rather have the pain on the side, and not be sleepy," Candy grumbled. "I want to talk about my house."

"I don't blame you. I'd like to talk about my house, too, if anybody would be kind enough to listen."

"I'll get around to your house later," said Candy. "Claudia, how's the baby?"

"Mine, or yours?"

"It hurts when I laugh. Mine first."

"She's fine. Bertha swears she gained three ounces so far to-day. When you get her back, she'll be positively obese."

"'Obese'. That's fatter than fat. I love fat babies. Claudia, could you please measure the powder room for a little rug? It's the first thing I have to buy."

"It's the most important thing to buy," Claudia assured her solemnly.

"Don't tease me . . . it could be fun. . . ." Candy's lids drooped heavily. She was alseep. . . .

" Darling make it fun," Claudia whispered, and lightly touched her lips to Candy's cheek.

Julia intended to drive up the following day on the chance of seeing Candy, and if not, certainly to see the house—both houses. It was gratifying that she took such an interest. " Julia's getting more and more human," Claudia told David. " I really have come to get away from the feeling that she's just a relative."

" She's mellowed," David conceded. " Considerably."

The next morning, however, Hartley telephoned that Julia couldn't come. She'd wakened with a high fever, and the doctor didn't know what it was. " A high fever doesn't sound at all like Julia," Claudia frowned. " Now I don't know who to worry about first."

" Worry about yourself," David advised. " You're trying to do the work of six people."

" You've got me mixed up with Bertha."

It wasn't until that evening that Julia's ailment developed into, of all things, a conspicuous case of mumps. If it weren't so serious, it would have been funny, for the most unlikely person in the world to have the mumps was Julia. " Where on earth did she get them ? " Claudia commiserated with Hartley over the telephone.

" I can't imagine," said Hartley. " Although the doctor says there've been several cases in the district this summer."

" Is she terribly miserable ? " What she wanted to ask was, did Julia look very peculiar with her cheek swollen, but she didn't think it was kind. " She's wretched," said Hartley. " And very disappointed not to be able to see your house. I'm afraid it'll be a few weeks before she's able to go out."

" It'll still be here," said Claudia, sounding like Mrs. Payne. " And tell her I'd come right down to see her, but mumps is one thing we can do without in this household."

" I should say it is," Hartley fervently agreed. " I was saying to Julia, you just moved out in the nick of time."

" We certainly did," said Claudia. " What would happen to Hartley if he caught them ? " she asked David as she hung up the receiver.

Ostentatiously, he unwound the telephone cord. " Why do women always knot it up ! " he fumed.

" It works knotted," she assured him. " I asked you, what would happen if Hartley got the mumps ? I mean—it wouldn't be as bad as if you caught them, would it ? "

" Thanks for the compliment."

" Just don't get them," she entreated, trying not to look panicky at the thought.

" I wasn't planning to," said David.

A day or two later Julia was able to talk over the telephone herself. She was still running quite a temperature, and sounded like it.

" How is Candy ? "

" Coming along fairly well," said Claudia.

" And how's your house ? "

" At a stand-still. I mean, we haven't a minute's time to give it any thought as yet, what with David trying to get the office squared around before John leaves, and Candy's place to get ready."

" You must have your hands full. I wish I could help."

" I'm glad to be busy. Julia, does it hurt awfully ? "

" When I chew, but I don't chew. Does Candy know about John leaving yet ? "

" No, the doctor says to wait until she gets home, which ought to be soon, now. Julia, isn't there anything I can do for you ? I know there isn't, but if there were, I'd love to."

" Not a thing. Hartley's been an angel. He stands at the door—the doctor won't let him come near the bed—and looks so unhappy that I can't bear it." A note of happiness crept into Julia's voice. " It's the first time I've ever been really ill except for my operation. Which doesn't count."

Claudia knew what she meant. One was in a hospital with an operation, and the burden of responsibility was removed, in a way. But there was something very sociable and intimate in Julia's having the mumps at home.

" I forgot to ask her if they were going ahead with the solarium," Claudia said after she'd rung off. She glanced at her watch. " Nine o'clock already, time to go to bed."

" Let me finish my pipe," said David. " I asked Hartley about it. They can't tear the place apart until Julia's up and around."

" That's a shame, they were so anxious to begin. When do you think we'll be able to start in doing the porch, and the hot water, and things ? "

" After John goes, and Candy's more or less settled. You've got enough on your mind for the present."

" So have you. Anyway, there's no hurry about it. It'll give us something to look forward to in the autumn. In the meantime, I'm having a good time with Candy's house.

It's like saving my cake and eating it, too. To-morrow," she went on, with a lilt of anticipation, " the first van load of Elizabeth's furniture's going to be delivered."

" Don't kill yourself."

" I'm not. It's wonderful to be tired at night, with a good healthy physical tiredness." She could have bitten her tongue out the minute she said it. The one thing that David was not supposed to get, was tired. She studied him closely out of the corner of her eye, and surreptitiously reached for the maple rung of a nearby chair.

" I saw you," he said dryly. " And just how much longer do you think I'm going to coddle myself ? "

" I don't call going into New York every day irom nine to five coddling yourself."

" Most of it is desk work stuff with John. It looks like the same thing is going to happen as happened in the last war."

She didn't have to ask him what had happened in the last war. That had been when the firm was Killian and Naughton, and David had been to Roger Killian what John was to David. Roger had closed the office and retired when David had gone overseas, and after David had come back there had been months and months of marking time, until finally, with the mammoth era of the new housing projects, the partnership of Naughton and Payne had become one of the most active and important firms in the east. That kind of intensive and demanding work was over now, as far as David was concerned, so, in a way, Claudia was glad that all building would probably slow down again. With a new war looming up on the horizon, shortages and curtailments could cut off the very breath of an architect. It would be hard sledding financially, but at least David wouldn't be slaving himself to death.

" John's talking about not drawing anything from the firm while he's away," David broke into her thoughts.

She sensed an edge of strain in his voice. " Oh," she said, non-committally.

" Damn fool," he went on gruffly, " with a new baby and a mountain of doctor's bills behind him, what's he going to use for money ? His army pay won't go very far."

It was just as well to get it said. " Candy's already talked to me," Claudia told him quietly. " She says that John's going to let her use her own money to pay for the house, and she's very happy about it. So am I. He's at peace with his pride. He said something about the business not having to support two families while he's away."

"It means," David supplied grimly, "that I'm still not much good. While I was away, the firm was able to support two families."

"When you talk like that," Claudia upbraided him, "I could kick your silly tail. Things were booming, and you know it." But she realized that his sense of inadequacy was a hard and bitter pill for him to swallow. Just as it was hard for John to accept the use of Candy's money. "There must be whole cycles of living," she decided with a little sigh, "when things are hard for everybody." Aloud she said, "Someday it's got to be."

"Got to be what?" he asked.

"Less like walking a tight-rope."

"First," said David, who could follow her even when she didn't make sense, "you have to get to the other side."

"Something tells me we're half-way over."

"In that case," he said, "let's go out and take a look at the river before we go to bed."

There was a moon, and every tree was two—one reaching towards the sky and the other shimmering deep into the dark, clear water. "It's an omen," Claudia whispered softly.

"I hope you're right," said David.

She put her arms round him. "It is," she said. He was like a child, suddenly, bruised and rebellious, and his weakness gave her strength. She felt, not like a wife, but like a mother. It mattered little whether it was Matthew or Michael or Bobby within her arms. All of them was one, and one of them was all.

There were ups and downs to Candy's getting well. "Her physical weakness is largely an evasion of reality," Dr. Hubbard told John. "It'll take time before she's herself again."

"Time is the one thing they haven't got," Claudia fretted to David. "The house is ready now, and the sooner she comes home, the better. John's mother feels the same way about it."

"Incidentally, John's mother told me you'd done a wonderful job with the furnishing."

"She was nice not to interfere," said Claudia.

Actually it had been a rather simple matter to place Elizabeth's lovely pieces of Chippendale and Sheraton in the spacious, welcoming rooms. "They sing in here," Claudia exulted, and thought how lucky it was that Candy wasn't stuck with a lot of unexciting furniture. It was lucky, too, that Candy had admitted that she wasn't the sort of person who wanted to supervise every slightest detail herself. " Funny, isn't it ? " Claudia marvelled to David. " It would burn me up to have anyone else having a finger in my house."

" If everyone was like you," David remarked, " interior decorators would go out of business."

" The two things she really loves are that silly powder-room and that magnificent piece of nonsense that calls itself a plate-warmer. She'll never use it after she gets it out of her system, but she loves it. And I guess that's maybe the beginning. Maybe she'll go on from there."

" She'll go on from there," David prophesied. " Another year, and she'll be haunting country auctions."

" And I'll haunt with her," said Claudia.

It was a sunny morning in mid-July when John finally brought Candy home. There was no one in the house. Claudia had arranged it that way. She and Tony had filled the rooms with flowers, and then she had locked the door, so that John would have to use his latch-key. And then, if he had good sense, he would pick Candy up in his arms and carry her over the threshold, and together and alone they would wander through the house and savour the wonder of their first home. " There'll be a salad and a cake and everything ready in the kitchen for your lunch," Claudia instructed John. " And I'll bring Martha over later with the baby." Martha was one of Bertha's unexhaustible supply of cousins. Bertha had already trained her with the baby, and Martha could cook, and naturally she boiled her dish-towels and kept the pots brightly scoured, being Bertha's blood relation. " I'm keeping my fingers crossed," said Claudia, " for Candy to like her."

When the shadows were deepening on the lawn, she drove Martha up the winding driveway, and Martha, holding the baby in her arms, rang the door-bell, and Claudia drove away again to call for David at the station.

He kissed her. " Well, how did it go ? "

" I don't know. There was a sale of soaps and canned goods in the village. I marketed like crazy to keep my mind off."

" You deserve a medal."

" I think we can stop by now. Enough is enough."

" Your hands are like ice," he said. " I don't think you could stand it another minute."

" I couldn't," she confessed.

They rang the bell, like strangers. Martha opened the door, looking as if she had always been there, and belonged there.

"Good evening, Martha. Are Mr. and Mrs. Payne at home?"

"I believe yes," said Martha, who had a sweetness of humour. "I'll tell them that you're here."

Claudia knew, when she saw their faces, that in the quiet hours of their being together, John had at last told Candy that the war had come very close to them, and that he would have to leave her for a while. There was something so pitifully young and vulnerable about her, with her arm still in a sling, and the ragged wound across her temple, not quite healed. "As if," thought Claudia, with her throat choking up, "she'd been in a war, too."

"Hello," said David, breaking the small silence, "welcome home."

"Thank you for everything," said Candy. "It's beautiful, every bit of it. And the baby looks wonderful." She smiled at Claudia. "Really obese."

They sat on the terrace, not any of them saying very much. Their hearts were too full. In a little while, Martha appeared, carefully coached by Bertha. "There is plenty for you to stay for dinner," she said.

"I wish you would," said John.

"So do I," said Candy.

"We fully expected to," said Claudia, and then they laughed a little.

"Candy asked Mother, too," John mentioned after a pause. He glanced at his watch. "I'll go over and call for her."

"I'll go with you," said David.

Claudia and Candy were alone. Candy said, "John says his mother's known for quite a while. It must be almost as hard for mothers."

"In a way, it's harder," said Claudia.

"She's been through it, and she knows that she has the strength to go through it again. But will I be able to go through it?"

"Yes," said Claudia.

They were silent for a space. "But what will I do when he's gone?" Candy whispered out of the breaking of her heart.

"Look forward," Claudia said.

"Are you able to look forward? Even now?"

"There's nothing else to do."

"I love the house. But not without John. I hate it without John." Candy bit her lip. "What if he never comes back to it?"

" I'm sure he will. As much as you can be sure of anything."

" That's true," said Candy. " Oh, Claudia, if only it were a year from now, two years from now."

" Don't trade the future. I thought the same thing last year when David had to go away."

" And this year he's well, and you've lost Bobby," Candy finished softly.

" Yes."

" And you're still happy."

" Learning to be."

" You're a better person than I am."

" Just older," Claudia said using the same words she had used to John.

" How does anybody get through the hard years," Candy cried on a little moan.

" Some people don't, but you're one of the ones that will."

" I wish I was sure of it."

" David and I are sure of it. John's sure of it. And I even think your mother-in-law is sure of it."

" She was awfully nice while I was in hospital," Candy offered. " I got so that I enjoyed her visits. Especially when Thomas brought her instead of Annie. Annie still doesn't like me. She never will."

" Oh, nonsense," Claudia told her without conviction. " She's just old and crotchety. Crotchety's a nice word, isn't it ? "

" Not very," said Candy. " Personally, I don't care for it."

It was that same evening that Annie gave notice. She had walked up the road to take Mrs. Payne home, and Mrs. Payne, who knew that there would not be too many more evenings with John, told her, with a small lift of pleasure, " You needn't wait, Annie. My daughter-in-law and son said they'd drive me home a little later."

Annie's gaunt face took on a purplish flush. " It seems you don't need me any longer," she said, in a trembling voice, " so you'd best find yourself somebody else who doesn't mind being kicked around."

She was gone before anyone could speak. " This is a sickness," said John, shocked.

" I suppose all things must come to an end," said Mrs. Payne, " or they turn into a sickness."

" Mother, don't be hasty. I'd hate to think of you alone in that big house."

" I won't be alone, there's Thomas for the heavy work.

Don't worry about it. I'm not helpless. It'll be good for me to be on my own."

"Maybe Annie will come to her senses," Candy suggested. "A lot of people lose their balance at times," and with a little laugh she added, "I ought to know."

"I ought to know, too," said Mrs. Payne, and suddenly they smiled at each other.

Claudia glanced at John. In spite of being sad, he looked quite happy.

"If you haven't gone through it," Claudia said, as they drove home later that evening, "you can't know what it's like. You might think you do, but you just can't."

She could have been talking about any one of a dozen things that had happened to them in the twelve years of their marriage, but he seemed to know that she was thinking only of Candy, and John's going off to war. "It's a good thing she has the baby," he said.

"It doesn't really help. When you left for the Pacific——" She made herself go on. "Even Bobby was too young to be any real comfort."

"I know," said David. "It was only in the last year that he began to be a person, grown-up enough to meet on your own level."

She couldn't do anything except nod her head. David could bring the words out, he was stronger than she was. Her lips moved. "I miss him so."

He put his free arm around her. "I do, too, darling."

"I guess these are hard days for all of us." She gave a watery smile. "Even for Julia with her mumps."

David slowed the car, and turned off to the river road, and the dark night was suddenly full of stars, like sleigh-bells in the distance. Off through the trees, there was a glimmering of light from the little hip-roof house. And then David said, "Sometimes I feel sorriest of all for them."

Odd that she should know that he was thinking of Julia and Hartley.

CHAPTER ELEVEN

ACTUALLY, nobody took Annie too seriously. True, the obvious explanation for her behaviour didn't hold water, as she had already passed that crucial period in her life. Claudia gathered that during that time she hadn't been any bed of roses to live with, but neither had Mrs. Payne, so they had sort of counterbalanced each other, and eventually one, or both, had blown over so to speak, and a truce had always been re-established.

This time, however, Annie didn't blow over. She must have worked at fever heat behind the locked door of her room, because by the time John and Candy took Mrs. Payne home after dinner, she had packed all her possessions, called the local taxi-company, and disappeared into the night. Thomas met them at the door, looking dazed. Candy gave the details to Claudia over the 'phone the next morning. "I have a feeling he's not going to stay long, either, without Annie. Isn't it sad for it to end like that after all these years? I feel terribly sorry for Mother Payne. It's hard to be so completely dependent on people that you pay."

"That was the first really grown-up thing that Candy's ever said," Claudia reported to David, who was prancing into his trousers, ten minutes late.

"What's Mrs. Payne going to do? Damn it, darling, why did you let me oversleep?"

"I had fun watching you. So you'll catch the next train, what of it? Candy offered to give her Martha, who's awfully good, but Mrs. Payne wouldn't hear of it."

"Hasn't Bertha got any more cousins?"

"It seems not. I asked her first thing. So Candy's already 'phoned the Greenwich employment agency and she says that there are quite a number of companions for elderly people on file."

"I bet," said David.

"I bet too," said Claudia soberly. "I think Mrs. Payne is right, she'd be better off being alone, but Candy says John would worry, so Mrs. Payne said all right, have somebody."

It seemed almost too easy. Mrs. Payne " had " Mrs. Selby by the time John returned from New York that evening. Mrs. Selby looked fifty, was really sixty, and acted a playful forty. She was a gentle-lady from Kentucky, with a great deal of *joie-de-vivre*, a bureau-ful of cosmetics, and she called Mrs. Payne " pet," in two syllables.

"I must say," Claudia kept David duly up-to-date, " that Mrs. Payne is more of a thoroughbred than I thought. She just smiles, and takes it, and pretends to like it."

"Maybe she does like it, after Annie," David suggested.

"She doesn't. She told me as much. But she doesn't want

164

to be a burden to Candy and John. One thing she balks at, though—she won't put up with being read aloud to, and Mrs. Selby likes to read aloud, so it mightn't work out after all. Did you 'phone to see how Julia was to-day?"

"Yes, I spoke to Hartley. It'll take a little while before she's herself again."

"Oh, dear," said Claudia. She sighed. "I wish the news from Korea was better."

He ruffled her hair. "You certainly do have your troubles," he teased her.

"There's so much unrest in the world. Big and little."

"There always has been."

"Isn't it more than usual now, though?"

"Maybe," he admitted. "How soon is supper ready?"

"It makes no difference. It's chops. Do you want to walk down to the river?"

"How'd you guess?" he said.

They sat by the water's edge until a sudden thunder shower drove them indoors. The electricity went off, and Bertha said now were they glad they had a coal stove, and they said they were.

They ate by candle-light, which was lovely, thought Claudia, but sad. The ache of an uneasy world was still in her heart, but the tiredness had gone out of David's face. The place was good for him, there was no doubt about it, and yet she was glad that nothing could be done about buying it for the present. Mr. Lewellyn was the only one in his office who was capable of handling the sale, and he had gone off to Nantucket for a month's vacation. However, he had left specific instructions with his assistant to show Mr. and Mrs. Naughton all the new listings. Most of them, Claudia didn't even bother to look at, especially if they featured a large rumpus room, or a swimming pool, or a greenhouse, which most of them did. "Still, you can't tell," she said to David. "The perfect thing might come up any moment, and we'll be glad we didn't settle on this place so fast."

"I never knew you to shilly-shally like this," he upbraided her gently.

"I didn't, either," she confessed.

He tried not to show that he was disappointed in her shilly-shallying, for he would have liked to start work on the house before the cold weather set in. In the meantime, he sketched out some plans and submitted them for casual estimates, even the cheapest of which was staggering. The way it shaped up, they'd be into another ten thousand dollars, just for the fundamental necessities without any of the trimmings. "It's a good thing," said Claudia, "that we don't have to pay an architect's fee to boot." Secretly, she was beginning to feel that the ideal thing would be to find a house like John and Candy's that didn't need any doing-over.

"Wait until Miss Julia and Mr. Hartley come up to see it," Bertha advised sagaciously. "They will tell you whether it is good to buy it or not."

"We're the ones to live in it," Claudia moodily returned. "I ought to be able to make up my own mind."

"It is hard to make up your mind with so much dirt around," said Bertha, and decided that she would no longer put off cleaning up the cellar.

"I think you're crazy," said Claudia flatly. However, there was a fascination about a dark cellar full of old stuff, and before she knew it, she was pitching in, too.

The telephone rang while they were knee deep in grime and dust one afternoon. Matthew, opportunely, was getting himself a drink of water from the kitchen, and Claudia called to him to answer.

"It's Aunt Julia!" he shouted down.

"Ach," Claudia muttered. Couldn't it have been somebody nice and plain, like Elsie Miller, or even the wrong number? She was glad to hear from Julia, but there was nothing quite so shanty as a child answering a telephone and then yelling out who it was.

"Sorry, we were in the cellar," she explained, a little breathlessly. "How are you, Julia?"

"Out of bed at last," said Julia, "and the doctor says I can drive up with Hartley next Saturday morning, if you'll be home."

"That's wonderful, of course we'll be home! And we've really been holding off making up our minds about buying the place until you both see it," Claudia added on a sudden impulse.

"I don't know how much our judgment is worth," Julia said, but Claudia could tell that she was pleased, anyway. "We won't stay long," she went on, "so please don't dream of having lunch for us."

"Miss Julia said absolutely no lunch," Claudia promptly relayed the information to Bertha, but before she could go any further, a pot roast leapt to Bertha's eyes. "I bet you twenty cents," she gloated, "that Mr. Hartley has not had potato pancakes since we sold the farm, and that is almost a couple of years."

"It'll be a couple of years more then."

Bertha was shocked. "They are coming all the way from New York, and you are not asking them to stay for lunch?"

"Stop the dramatics. I asked, but they're not. And they're right. It's no fun for us, and no fun for them until we're settled."

"We are settled enough," Bertha stubbornly maintained. "What is it to put two more plates on the table? Also Mr. Hartley loves my cooking."

"Also his gall-bladder doesn't."

"That was before he had it taken out."

"Out or in, he still gets the same pain. When he 'loves' unwisely and too much."

"I will anyway have a pot roast and potato pancakes ready, just in case," Bertha planned. "And some dressed cucumbers with sour cream that he likes, and an apple strudel."

"Bertha. For God's sake. Be refined. You know perfectly well that Miss Julia never has more than a jellied soup for lunch, with a spot of fish or a soufflé."

"Ja, and I think maybe they are both a little tired of such stylish cooking. They will enjoy something really to eat for a change."

"I hate you," said Claudia.

"It's not nice to hate anybody." Matthew's voice reeked of virtue. Claudia wheeled on him. "Get back upstairs out of this dust. You were told to go out and play."

"I played."

"Play again," she adjured him crisply.

He spied a pile of rubbish, and eagerly pounced upon a rotted length of garden hose. "I want that," he exclaimed. "Don't throw it away."

She slapped his hand down. "You and your father. Birds of a feather."

"Who does it belong to?"

"The garbage man. He should have toted it away years ago."

"These too." Bertha dumped a mountain of miserable rags into a wooden box. "Very dirty people lived here; the attic is worse, even."

"If you think you're going to tackle the attic next, you've got another think," Claudia laid down the law. "I'm not going to do one more thing until we decide definitely whether we're going to buy the place or not."

"We already bought it," Matthew remarked.

Claudia raised her brows. "We did? How nice. What did we use for money? Now run along like a good boy, and see if the baby's all right."

"He is. He's still in his play-pen."

"We did not expect him to walk out," Bertha mentioned mildly.

"He's so dumb," said Matthew, disgusted. "All he does is throw his blocks around. He thinks that's fun."

Claudia sensed the loneliness in his rebellion. Bobby and he had just begun to stop fighting and to be companions. Pity softened her voice. "I'll tell you what, put on a fresh shirt and wash your face and hands, and I'll take you to the station with me to call for Daddy."

"My shirt's clean," he objected.

Pity vanished. "*March!*" she commanded.

He read the handwriting on the wall, and dissolved up the cellar steps bit by bit. "He is, anyhow, much better than he used to be," Bertha defended, when he had finally disappeared from sight. "He does not argue quite such a lot any more. And Mrs. Naughton, you are right, the apple strudel is too heavy in the middle of the day; I could make just a plain apple pie."

Claudia snorted. "Look who's talking about arguing." She poked gingerly at an old garden chair, blanketed in cobwebs and mouldy with dampness, and suddenly had enough of cleaning up other people's mess. "You'd better get ready yourself for the station," Bertha gave her an out.

Claudia glanced at her watch. "Quarter to five already," she discovered on a bleat, "I can barely make it, even if I hurry!"

"You have a smudge on your face," Bertha called after her urgently. "And be careful of that loose step!"

"Stop being such an old hen," Claudia called back. "And get out of that hot cellar; you did enough for one day!"

"I will rock on the porch with my hands in my lap," Bertha got in the last word.

Matthew had given himself a lick and a promise, and looked better without it, but, like Bertha, who was she to call the kettle black? "Button your button," she said, as she covered her own multitude of sins with a silk muffler and a loose jacket.

"It is," he said.

"It's not. And don't think because you wet your hair that I think for one moment that you combed it."

He flattened a few damp wisps with the palm of his hand.

"Lovely," she complimented him dryly. "I'm sure Daddy will be proud to own you. Both of us," she amended silently.

The station-wagon was none too presentable, either. She and Bertha had hosed it down the day before, but it had to go and rain afterwards. There was no getting away from it, it was hard to live in the country without being able to afford a handy man for the outside work. It was one of the things she wouldn't admit to David, or he'd start doing odd jobs around the place that he had no right to do. As it was, it was against the doctor's orders for him to go to the office every day, although it was a wonder that he kept to his word about catching the four-ten home each afternoon. It was anyone's guess how long he'd be able to go on doing it, once John was gone. She put the thought away from her with a little shudder. What was there to be done about it? A war made one's personal problems insignificant and unimportant.

"What's the matter?" Matthew asked.

"What should be the matter?"

"You looked funny, like you had a headache."

She was surprised, and touched by his sentiency. It was new to him, born, doubtless, of the insecurity of his own small universe. "Now, since when did I ever have a headache?" she retorted. "Hop in, we have to step on it."

He hopped in. She started the motor, and out of the blue, Bluff was there, with his great paws scrabbling against the side of the car, panting to go along.

"Let him," Matthew begged.

"All right. Open the door." After all, there was nothing like a Great Dane to dress up an out-dated station-wagon.

He did more than dress it up, he occupied it utterly. "Hey!" Matthew expostulated, "don't push me out, you!"

Bluff might have been nailed to the ground, so difficult it was to hoist him off the front seat into the back. He went over in reluctant sections, and finally settled himself, silly with bigness, in drooling anticipation of a pleasant ride. "Close your mouth and put your tongue in," Claudia exhorted him through the mirror. She glanced at Matthew. He, too, was settling down. She recognized that brooding thoughtfulness in his face which meant that he was about to pop with questions. "Shoot," she said as they left the little white house behind them.

He quickened.

"Shoot what?"

"Nothing. In other words, never trouble trouble until trouble troubles you. Look at that fat squirrel."

His interest in the squirrel was perfunctory. "There's lots around here," he said, a little bored with them.

"I know, but it's always a sort of a lovely surprise to me, anyway, when I see one."

"I like the ducks on the river better. Why didn't we have a river on the farm?"

"We thought we were lucky to have even a brook."

"I wish we'd buy this house; can't we?"

"We'll see."

"If we don't buy it, are we going back to New York to stay with Uncle Hartley and Aunt Julia?"

"We're off. No. Next?"

"Why not?"

"Why not what?"

"Didn't you like it at Uncle Hartley's and Aunt Julia's?"

"Very much. But it was only for a visit. Until we found a place of our own."

"Maybe we'll go back to the farm," he hazarded. "Could we?"

Her nerves gave a warning crackle. "Matthew, you know perfectly well that we sold the farm."

"Are you glad that we did?"

It was a hard question to answer. "Everything happens for the best," she said, with a forced cheeriness, and was instantly aware that she had left herself wide open for the unhappy groping of his next question. "Did it happen for the best that Bobby was killed?" he asked in a muted voice.

Her soul cried out in negation, but it was wrong to confuse him with her own struggle toward peace and acquiescence. "It was for the best that he didn't suffer," she answered evenly. "And he's happy now, and that ought to make us happy, even though we miss him so much."

"Is he happy because he's with your mother, and Bertha's husband, and everybody else who died?"

"It's nice to think so, isn't it?"

He wasn't too sure. "I'd be afraid to be dead. I don't like the word 'dead'."

"Neither do I," she agreed. "Let's just think of him being where he'll never know any pain or illness, like most people who have to stay on earth."

"Like Dad being sick, and Aunt Julia having the mumps?"

"Yes."

"Why is there sickness?"

"Sometimes it's a way of learning how to stay well."

"Like you learn lessons in school?"

"Quite a lot like it."

"And then when you graduate, do you die?"

It was a new way of looking at it, and a rather disturbing way. Bluff saved her from going into the various ramifications of the idea by barking at a brace of stray dogs ambling down the road. He wouldn't have done anything about it, but the dogs didn't know that he was a big bag of wind, and took to their heels, which made Bluff feel very powerful indeed. He kept on barking louder and louder, and there was no use in trying to talk over the din.

"Bluff smells," Matthew observed at length.

"Run your window down a little more."

"Are we going to stop off and see Candy?"

"We haven't time."

"I'm glad Candy wasn't killed like Bobby was. Why wasn't she?"

"I guess she has a lot more lessons to learn before she graduates." Claudia swallowed the lump that came, unbidden, to her throat. "Matthew dear, admire the pretty country."

"I saw it. Will Dad get another partner when Uncle John goes to war?"

She shook her head. "No. He wouldn't. Even if he could."

"When will Uncle John go?"

"He expects his orders any day."

"I bet Candy will cry."

"Many women cry when there's a war."

"Did you cry when Dad went to the last war?"

"At night."

"I think Dad would like to go to this war, too," said Matthew sagely.

"I think maybe he would. But he can't," she added with a degree of thankfulness, "and that's what you call a cloud with a silver lining."

"With a what?"

" Skip it.—Oh, *Bluff!*—Matthew, run your window down all the way."

Matthew ran down his window, and racked his brain for more questions. " What are we having for supper ? " he brought out at last.

" Turkey hash from last night's roast of veal," she told him.

By the time he thought that one through, they were threading their way into the crowded village street toward the station.

The train was ten minutes late, and it seemed an hour. It was indecent to feel like that after twelve years, for most of the women in the parked cars appeared to be rather bored with the daily ritual of meeting husbands. Some were reading behind smart spectacles ; some were just sitting, idle and irked, and all of them were expensively tanned, with good-looking sport-dresses exposing smooth brown backs and shoulder-blades. A fairish number of nicely washed children disported themselves quietly while waiting, and the prevailing dog was Poodle. " Never mind," said Claudia to Matthew, " we have the only Great Dane."

Matthew was an opportunist. " I wish we had a pony," he said gloomily.

" Wish," said Claudia. She eyed him without pride. " If anyone asks who you are, you're the gardener's child."

" What gardener ? "

" Here comes the train."

He craned his neck. " It is not."

" I heard it. Far off."

" I don't hear anything."

She smiled secretly, betting with herself that her ears had not deceived her. Meeting David at the station each evening was one of the nicest things about living in the country. She remembered how, at the farm, six o'clock had brought the joyous crowning of each day. She remembered the year of empty twilights when war had torn their lives apart. Perhaps, she thought, if you hadn't known separation, you could never experience the fullest joy of being together. It was a bitter price to pay, but worth it.

The train came to a groaning stop. Matthew kneeled on the seat, the better to peer out. " There's Uncle John ! "

" It can't be, Uncle John always takes a later train."

She would have got out of the car to look for David, but her coat and muffler kept her in her seat. " One of these days," she resolved, " I'm going to drive down in my white linen—when it gets a little dirtier." For the moment, however, she contented herself with scanning the crowds, and suddenly he emerged from the stream of commuters, and waved to her. " There's Daddy, too," Matthew discovered belatedly, " right in front of Uncle John."

" Why, it is Uncle John! " Claudia exclaimed. " Something's wrong," she decided at once, and her heart lurched with the ever-present fear that he might have taken ill, and John had come home with him. She forgot that she looked a sight, and leapt out of the car and ran to the platform. His arm around her and the touch of his lips reassured her. He'd never have kissed her like that if anything had happened. . . .

" Hello," said John. " I didn't let Candy know I was taking an earlier train; can you drop me off? "

" Yes, of course." She knew, all at once, why he had taken the earlier train. " When? " she asked through lips gone suddenly dry.

" I have to go to Washington in the morning. I'll know more about it after that."

" Oh, John," she could only say.

" Don't let on to Candy. I'll tell her to-night."

" Then better not discuss it in front of Matthew," said David. " God, look at that beast's head."

" I hope you mean Bluff," Claudia essayed over a heavy heart.

The car was too small for Bluff's welcoming tail. David caught it on the way. " Hey, stop it, you big clown, you'll hurt yourself. . . . Hello, Matthew."

" It never fails ; first his dog, then his son," said Claudia. " John, you sit in front with David so your suit won't get full of hairs."

" He won't be wearing it much longer, anyway." There was a mixture of emotions in David's voice, and more than ever, Claudia realized the special impact of John's going. He kept his eyes on the road ahead. " Everything all right at home? " he asked, without turning.

She leaned forward. " Yes, fine. We began to clean the cellar. What a mess."

" Leave it. I'll help you on Sunday. There might be some things there that oughn't to be thrown out."

" That's what Bertha and I are afraid of. You'll want to keep every old latch and key."

" Did you find any ? "

"No. Just old rags."

John forced a laugh. "You two have a good time over anything, even junk."

"Especially junk ; David should have been a junk-man."

Silly conversation, she thought. Anything to hide what we really feel. . . . Even Matthew must have sensed that something was in the air. He sat quietly, watching the countryside, green-heavy with full summer.

"We were certainly fortunate to inherit old Tony with the property," John remarked, as they turned in at the drive-way. "There's nothing like a fine Italian hand with lawns and shrubs."

"We've got a sixteen-year-old schoolboy half-time and half-witted," said David.

Claudia said nothing. She hadn't told David, yet, that Fred hadn't showed up the last two days. "John and Candy are entitled to a little good fortune," she said lightly, "to last them over the next few months."

Candy came running around the side of the house before David had a chance to turn the motor off. Her arm was free of a sling now, and the gash above her eye scarcely showed beyond its ridge of healing. She still looked like a tow-headed little girl in her yellow sunsuit, but womanhood came into her eyes when she saw John. "When ? " she whispered, just as Claudia had asked.

"That's a fine welcome for a man who happens to come home a little early."

"Don't fool me, John——"

He held her close. "Nothing definite, darling ; I leave for Washington in the morning. How's the baby ? "

Candy smiled with effort. "She doesn't know when to stop, she gained another eight ounces this week. And your mother's here. Don't let's tell her yet ; let's keep her for supper and not say anything to spoil her evening."

He kissed her again.

"So long," said David, clearing his throat. "I'll 'phone you sometime to-night."

"Oh, stay a minute," Candy begged.

"Not the way I look," said Claudia ; "I'm not fit to get out." It was true, but at the same time she couldn't bear the vicarious sharing of such futile, needless anguish. "There's no *reason* for it," she protested chokingly to David as they drove away. "Homes disrupted, people who love each other torn apart, and for what ! And don't give me that business

about a free world—it may be all right for the men to understand it on those terms, but not for women ; it's happening
too often ; there's something wrong someplace and we're
paying for it."

" Finished ? " he asked her patiently.

" No, I could go on for ever. Particularly since I'm not
grousing about myself, but about Candy. And John's mother.
And thousands and thousands of wives and mothers who are
going through the same thing."

" What alternative would you suggest ? "

" None," she admitted. " I suppose we're doing the only
thing we can do. But it's not much comfort to Candy."

He forgave her for being a woman, and therefore lacking
detachment and the taste for heroism. " That it's not," he
agreed.

" Are we going home now ? " They turned guiltily. They
had forgotten all about Matthew, he had been so quiet.

" Yes, darling, we're going home," said Claudia, and marvelled that gratitude had come to take the place of grief and
bitterness in her heart. Perhaps, in time, the same miracle of
living would happen to Candy, too.

" It would be nice," Bertha blandly suggested on Saturday
morning, " to ask Miss Candy over to lunch. She must be
very lonely with Mr. John away."

Claudia deposited a handful of undistinguished roses in the
kitchen sink, and picked a thorn from her finger. " You
can't smell these flowers for the onions," she remarked coldly,
" and it will serve you right if nobody eats your precious
pot-roast."

Bertha smiled in unperturbed good-will. " It will be
eaten," she said. " It smells good, no ? "

" I just had breakfast, I'm no judge. These roses haven't
been sprayed for years, the beetles have had a holiday." She
plucked off all the outer petals, and stuck the remnants of
bloom violently into a cut-glass celery bowl. " *Voilà*, buds."

" Nobody could tell they were not," Bertha complimented
her.

" Don't try to get around me with sweet words. Here, this
is the best I can do for your centrepiece ; take it or leave it."

" I take it," said Bertha. " We need something to make
the table look nice. I think I will set for Miss Candy, just
in case."

" If you're looking for work, go ahead. But I already

asked her yesterday, and she said she didn't feel like going out."

"Ask her again. She will have to see that life must go on, no matter what happens."

"Life doesn't mean coming over here to eat your pot-roast," Claudia retorted, although she knew what Bertha meant. "However, I'm calling her, anyway, to find out how the baby is," she added nastily, so as not to seem to be giving in too easily. "Really, why you insist on killing yourself with three extra, and barely a pot to cook in and no two plates that match, I can't imagine. Except that you're an awful show-off."

"So I am a show-off," Bertha cheerfully acquiesced.

It was as good an opening as any. "Bertha's a show-off," Claudia started off to Candy. "She wants you to come for lunch with Julia and Hartley."

"Not to-day I couldn't." Candy's eyes were red even over the 'phone.

There was no point in reminding her that John hadn't gone into battle yet, he was only in Washington. "I know how you feel," Claudia said instead, "I'll drive over later with David."

"I wish you would," said Candy gratefully. "Julia told me she and Hartley intended to stop by, too."

"Before or after they come to us?"

"Before."

"Then you'd better prepare them for a shock when they see this place after yours."

"I wish this place wasn't so perfect!" Candy burst out. "Even beauty hurts without the person you love."

"How well I know that," thought Claudia. Aloud she said, "What kind of a night did the baby have?"

"Awfully restless, and a little fever, but John's mother says it's only teething. She says John always got an earache with every tooth."

"My babies never ran to ears, thank goodness. How's Mrs. Selby working out?"

"Thomas says she drinks," Candy replied starkly. "I think Mother Payne ought to get rid of her, and come over here to live."

Claudia was so surprised that for a moment she couldn't say anything. "Do you think it's a bad idea?" Candy asked anxiously. "I haven't suggested it to her yet. I didn't even mention it to John when I spoke to him over the 'phone last night."

"I think it's a magnificent idea," said Claudia slowly. "In fact, it's such a good idea that I don't think it's necessary to use it. Just having it in reserve, in the back of your mind, is enough."

"Oh," said Candy. After a small silence she said, "I'm not quite sure, but I think I see what you mean. One thing, though, I'm not being noble about it. We're both so alone with John away, that it would sort of be nice for the three of us."

"The four of you," Claudia corrected. "It's a wonderful thing for a baby to grow up with a grandmother around."

"Books on child study don't say so," Candy offered doubtfully.

"Oh, never mind books." Claudia dismissed them with a wave of her voice. "They'll be making a new-fashioned circle and getting back to old-fashioned theories one of these days. There weren't half as many nervous wrecks with big families and long dining-room tables as there are with no families and kitchenettes."

Candy laughed shakily. "Maybe you're right. How's David?"

"He's fine."

"I bet he misses John, too." Her voice broke a little and Claudia decided that Candy had had her quota of growing-up for one day, and she was glad that Matthew bounced in and announced importunately that he wanted a screw-driver.

"Wait a minute, Candy. Be quiet, Matthew, can't you see I'm talking? We'll see you later, Candy, the 'phone's still in the kitchen, and I can't hear myself think.—If you should change your mind about lunch, Bertha says, drive over at the last minute."

"I will," said Candy, "except that I'm sure I won't."

"Did she say she would?" Bertha asked as Claudia hung up.

"I wouldn't bother to set."

Bertha sighed, heavy with the sense of Candy's aloneness. "Poor child."

"She's not such a poor child," said Claudia crisply. "Let's stop pitying her."

"Where's a screw-driver?" Matthew persisted. "I'm helping Dad fix the lawn-mower. Is that stuff going to be cookies?"

"No, it is dough for pie," Bertha told him.

He gave a violent shudder. "I hate pie."

" That's just too bad," said Claudia. " Go tell your father that I don't happen to have a screw-driver on me at the moment."

" I saw a rusty one in the cellar," Bertha recalled. " It is in that box with some old tools to be thrown out."

" I'll get it," Matthew volunteered. In passing, he dipped into a bowl of sliced apples and snaked a sliver, only to have Bertha deftly disengage his fingers of it. " Those are green, they will give you a stomach ache."

He tripped on the bottom step of the cellar and scraped his knee, which meant iodine and a wail of protest. David presented himself at an uncrucial moment. " I thought I sent you for a screw-driver," he began an instant offensive.

" I hurt myself on the cellar step," Matthew defended himself.

" Nobody should use those steps," David ordained. " They're rotted out. The whole flight needs to be replaced."

" In the meantime," said Claudia, " we'll use a rope and swing ourselves down every time we need something from the cellar. David, seriously, everything has to have so much done to it, whatever you try to do now will only be a drop in the bucket."

" Drop or not, the grass has to be cut."

" Fred promised to come on Monday. But he says the mower's no good."

" That's why I'm fixing it," said David, and marched off to wrestle anew with the worn-out machine.

It wasn't the sort of job that was good for him, but he wouldn't take kindly to being told so. " I wish you'd catch some fish for supper ! " Claudia threw after him.

" Oh, yes, that would be a big help ! " Bertha added an enthusiastic two cents.

" Yippee ! " Matthew shouted. " I want to go, too ! "

David dragged to a halt, filled with conflict. The river was no fisherman's paradise, but there were plenty of bass and too many pickerel, and an occasional perch, and so it was that Hartley and Julia arrived some time toward noon, and the three of them stood watching David and Matthew fishing in deep absorption from the river bank, with Bluff sprawled out beside them. " It's like something you'd see on a picture post card," Julia smiled.

" They've been at it for two hours," Claudia whispered, as if they could hear her.

" Great ! " Hartley applauded. " Best thing in the world

for David. Splendid buy, river land. We stopped off to see Candy; that's a fine place, too, lovely house, handsome grounds, but this is great. Great."

"The property is wonderful," Claudia conceded, "if only there weren't so much to be done to it, inside and out."

Julia threw back her light summer fur, and a little whiff of her favourite perfume sweetened the air. "The porch seems to be falling off," she observed, "which is just as well." She knew her old houses, and her appraising eye had already registered the doorway, and the old glass in the mullioned windows. "It's a find," she said. "The house itself is so pure and beautiful."

"Never mind the house," said Hartley. "You don't come on land like this every day in the week. My advice right off the bat is to buy the place. I'll leave you girls to talk, and I'll go down and join the men. Don't let her get over-tired, Claudia. This is her first day out."

Julia really did look as if she'd been through a lot more than mumps. There was about her a special and rather ethereal quality that Claudia couldn't quite put her finger on. "Do you want to rest before you look around?" she asked, solicitous of the paleness of Julia's fine-boned face.

"Of course not. I want to see everything."

Claudia devoutly hoped that Julia wasn't carrying any left-over mump germs around with her—it would be all that David would need to add injury to insult. "Hartley was lucky," she said, although it really wouldn't have mattered so much if Hartley had gotten them.

"So I hear," Julia murmured elliptically.

Bertha greeted them in the hall, with Michael plastered unwillingly to her hip. She wanted to put him down in front of Julia, and make a dramatic production of showing how nicely he could walk all by himself.

Julia's admiration was all that Bertha could wish. "I simply can't get over him!" she exulted, and sat down in a chair and lifted him to her lap. "I bought one of those little French hand-made suits for him; it's in the car. I hope it fits; I didn't realize he could get so big in just a few weeks."

"I always buy a size too large," Bertha warned her thriftily. "I will try it on him, after we have lunch."

Smart Bertha, the way she slipped it in behind Julia's back as it were, but Julia was a match for her. "Bertha, we have no intention of staying for lunch," she said firmly. "That was clearly understood before we came."

Claudia settled back to watch the fun, and in the end, of course, Julia lost out, and they stayed. Hartley ate too much and enjoyed every minute of it, and Julia acknowledged that it was the first time that food tasted good to her since she'd been ill. "That's the truth," said Hartley. "I think I'll leave her up here for a few days to get some colour in her cheeks."

Bertha couldn't take a joke, and it was all that Julia could do to persuade her that it was out of the question. "Matthew, run ask Watkins to give you that big package we left in the car," she suggested, in order to change the subject.

Matthew's disinterest was only skin-deep. Julia never failed to produce a present for him, but she'd certainly been a long time getting around to it to-day, what with so much talk about houses, and Candy, and what was going to happen with John. Finally, however, the big moment had come. "All right," he said, with a vast nonchalance.

Once out of sight, he must have run all the way, because he was back in no time, completely out of breath. "Is this it?" he asked, trying once more to seem very unconcerned.

"Yes, go ahead and open it," said Julia. "There are two boxes tied together. The little one's for the baby, and the big one's for you."

"Oh, boy!" Matthew smacked his lips in anticipation, for Julia had a genius for selecting the perfect gift; but in this particular instance she had apparently suffered an odd block in her unconscious, for she'd bought him the exact duplicate of the airplane she'd given him last Christmas. It was a very superior airplane, to be sure, equipped with twin motors, sleeper berths and crew, but, as far as Matthew was concerned, it was a wasteful gilding of the lily, when he'd been hankering for ice-skates. However, it was a sign that he was growing up into a nice person, because he didn't say, "You already gave me one of those"; he said, "Boy! Gee! Thanks!" Then he ran out to show it to David, who was talking to Hartley on the porch.

"Matthew's getting to be more like Bobby every day," said Claudia.

Julia nodded. "I was just thinking the same thing." She reached out, and put her hand over Claudia's. "I can't believe he's not here. At moments, it's just as if he were standing beside me."

"I often have that feeling. Other times—I can't seem to find him. Then it's like death."

" I know," said Julia softly.

Julia had never lost anyone who was dear to her, and Claudia wondered how she knew.

CHAPTER TWELVE

THAT was on Saturday, and on Monday morning Julia 'phoned Claudia to say goodbye.

" Why goodbye ? Where are you going ? "

Julia's usually controlled voice held a tremor of excitement. " Hartley and I are sailing for Paris to-night."

It was a funny thing for Julia to be excited about, since sudden trips to Paris, or anywhere in the world for that matter, were no novelty in her life. " How long will you be gone ? "

" About a month. The contractors are tied up and can't begin on the solarium until then, anyway, so it all works in beautifully."

" Yes, it does. We'll probably both be doing over our houses at the same time. Is this a business trip for Hartley."

" No, pure pleasure," said Julia, with a note of pure pleasure in the way she said it. " He thinks the change will do me good."

" It will," Claudia concurred, and heard herself add, " We'll miss you."

" So will I," Julia returned, a little shyly. After so many years, it wasn't easy for in-laws to discover each other ; indeed, it was worse than beginning from scratch. " I'm going to drive in and see her before she goes," Claudia decided out of a clear sky. It wasn't a purely single-purposed decision, however. David had taken an earlier train than he should have, and she'd call for him and see to it that he came home earlier to make up for it. Then, also, all her sheets and pillow-cases were on their last legs, and most of the New York stores were having August sales.

Bertha was delighted to hear about the sheets and pillow-cases. Moreover, she thought it highly proper that Claudia should see her relatives before they took off to Europe. Seeing people off to Europe, in Bertha's traditional mind, still came under the same category as hot-house grapes for operations. " And as long as you are going to New York, anyway," she mentioned, " you could stop in and exchange the baby's suit ; it will not fit him at all by next year. Maybe you could get something for the house instead."

" Now, really. Aren't you ashamed ? " said Claudia, who'd had every intention of doing just that.

" No," said Bertha brazenly.

" You're just bad all the way through," Claudia pointed to the meat order that Bertha was unwrapping from its soggy wrappings. " Are those bones you begged from the butcher for Bluff, or for a family soup ? "

" Both," said Bertha. She eyed them lovingly. " They are beautiful. Sometimes there is not enough marrow in them to make marrow balls."

" What a nerve of them," said Claudia. " And now, if you will excuse me from this mundane conversation, I'll get dressed to leave."

Matthew drifted upstairs a few minutes later. " Who's taking a bath ? "

" I am. Any objections ? "

" Why ? "

" Why what ? "

" Are you taking a bath ? "

" Why not ? "

He whimpered in frustration. " Are you going out ? "

" Yes."

" Over to see Candy ? Can I go along ? "

" No, I'm going to New York."

Claudia could see the bottom drop out of his small world. " I'll be back in time for supper," she assured him quickly. " Daddy and I will drive home together."

" I wish I could go with you."

" No, you don't. New York's horrid in the summer. So hot and stuffy."

" Then why are you going ? "

She didn't tell him Julia and Hartley were leaving suddenly for Europe. So much had happened to destroy the security of his universe that there was no point in adding to a sense of shifting foundations. He didn't realize that he was attached to his aunt and uncle, but some day he would look back upon them and discover that they had been a part of the pattern of his childhood. " I'm going to exchange Michael's suit," she said.

" I have two airplanes."

" I know." She wanted to give him a great hug and kiss, but she didn't. Matthew was growing out of kissing—he used to be all over the place with it—easy little sloppy kisses, that he kept on tap like a kind of stock-in-trade. " Men don't kiss," he had discovered for himself, and David had been quite relieved. He felt that masculinity was one thing a man couldn't develop early enough, or have too much of. Claudia, on the other hand, wasn't afraid of Matthew being a sissy. Her heart ached for him as he turned away, inarticulate with a loneliness he could not explain. Was it better to let him struggle through these hard spaces of adjustment by himself, or to give him a hand across the rough spots ? She wished that, like Candy, she could go to a book for the answer, but she never had, and it was too late to begin. She'd just have to go on calling on something from within herself to handle each problem as it arose. She said now, downing common sense for instinct, " Look, Matthew, I met Mrs. Miller in the village yesterday, and she has her little nephew visiting her. Would you like to go over and play ? "

He was cagey. " How old is he ? "

" About your age. Now stop looking a gift horse in the face."

Matthew's eyes lit up. " Has he got a pony ? "

" No, but you can bring over one of your airplanes."

" Why not both ? "

" Don't be *nouveau riche*."

" What's that ? "

" People who have two airplanes. Shall I 'phone Mrs. Miller or not ? "

He gave a magnanimous shrug. " If you want to."

" Many thanks.—Run and stop my bath water while I call her."

Mrs. Miller was delighted, and said she'd make a picnic lunch on the lawn. " Honestly," she said, " I was getting desperate, it's so lonesome for a child all by himself. Shall I pick Matthew up ? "

" Oh, no, I'll be passing in a little while, I'll drop him by."

Bertha tried not to seem too glad to be rid of Matthew for the afternoon. It was fairly obvious that she intended to make hay with the attic in his absence, but she looked as if butter wouldn't melt in her mouth. She said, " He needs other children. It will be good when he starts school here and begins to get acquainted."

" Starts school somewhere," Claudia qualified. It was important for Matthew to grow roots, but was this the right place to grow them ? They had already been asked to join the country club, and she and David hadn't even bothered to confer about it. "You didn't want to, did you?" he'd remembered to ask after he had refused.

"You know how I pine for those Saturday night dances," she'd replied.

"That's what I thought."

It occurred to her suddenly that Matthew and Michael might want the Saturday night dances and the tennis and the beach parties some day. "Not while Elsie Miller keeps on having nephews and nieces," she decided. David liked Elsie and her husband, and the brother-in-law who was on the police force, and Claudia was glad. David was as much of a real snob when it came to people as she was.

It was so nearly lunch-time that she ate a sandwich while she dressed. Bertha frowned on filling one's stomach with sandwiches, but she'd learned the kind that Claudia liked— full of lettuce and magnetism. "Delicious," Claudia congratulated her on a concoction of cucumbers and minced something or other. "Now, for goodness sake, take it a little easy this afternoon, will you?"

"Oh, sure," Bertha obliged at once.

"I don't trust you. Promise you won't touch the attic."

"I promise," said Bertha readily.

Claudia narrowed her eyes. "I still don't trust you. What other piece of mischief have you got in mind?"

"It is no mischief; I am just going to make a little jelly from the grape vine."

"Putting up jelly with all you've got to do!"

"I found some old jars, and if I don't use the grapes, the birds will get them. I will put the baby outside in his pen, and I will enjoy picking them. What's so hard about that?"

"Go ahead," said Claudia. "Kill yourself. See if I care."

She was really furious when she discovered that Bertha had managed to polish up the station-wagon while Claudia was taking her bath. "That idiot woman!" she exploded.

"Who?" Matthew asked with interest. "Mrs. Miller?"

"No, Bertha."

His face clouded. "Don't you like Bertha?"

"Don't be silly. I adore her. Only she spoils us. I don't know what we'd ever do without her."

A load rolled off his shoulders. At least his world was safe in one respect. "She's waving at the door to us," he said.

Bertha's wave was broadly innocent. Claudia shook her fist at her and drove away.

Matthew couldn't quite make head or tail of it. " Why does Bertha work so hard ? Do you make her ? "

" She makes herself."

" What for ? "

Claudia pondered it. She had never analysed the reason for Bertha's wonderful and amazing compulsions, except that she had lost her husband, and her daughter had committed suicide, and a son had been killed in the first war.

" Why ? " Matthew insisted.

" Because," said Claudia soberly, and somehow Matthew seemed satisfied with the answer.

Elsie Miller was waiting for them on the small patch of lawn in front of her house. Bertha would have been pleased to see that her nephew was about half Matthew's size, and a whole year older. He had a pointed little face and pale, straight, silky hair. Like a coward, Claudia was glad that he did not remind her too sharply of Bobby.

It was her first trip alone to New York in the car, and David scowled his disapproval when he realized that she had parked in front of the office. " How many fenders did you scrape ? " he wanted to know.

" None," she informed him coldly. He didn't deserve to be told that a kindly taxi-driver had backed in for her. Nor was it necessary to humiliate herself by confessing that she had almost gotten a ticket for going East on a West-bound street.

" What did you come in for ? " he pursued ungraciously.

" To change the baby's suit."

" Very important."

" It was. It came from one of those hand-made shops on Fifth Avenue and cost thirty-two dollars. Everything else was so expensive, too, that I just left the credit there."

" On what theory ? "

" Some day they'll have a sale. Although all the stores are having sheet sales, and even so, they cost a fortune, so I didn't buy any. I reckoned we'd have enough to slide through on, if we were careful not to use both beds every night."

She was rewarded for her silly chatter by seeing a smile twitch at the corners of his mouth. He looked strained, not because of work, but because of the lack of it. The telephone hadn't rung once during the half-hour she'd been there, and Miss Spencer, a newish secretary, appeared to be spending most of the afternoon in the lavatory. " I suppose I might as well leave now," David admitted, after making a pretence of going over some papers on the desk. " There's not much activity in building these days."

" Thank goodness," said Claudia. " I've absolutely prayed that things would let up a little with John gone."

He gave a snort. " So it was you. And I was taking for granted that it was the summer-time and the war combined." He slapped her backside. " I'll thank you to mind your own business hereafter. We have to eat, you know."

" We'll eat," she said. " Especially with Bluff around. We can always share what Bertha manages to buy him free of charge."

This time he grinned quite openly. " Come on, but don't think I'm going to leave the office every day in the middle of the afternoon."

" I don't," she placated his pride. " It's just that if we want to say goodbye to Julia and Hartley, we'd better hurry."

" You mean we'd better hurry if we don't want to get a parking ticket."

" We won't. I found a policeman and told him I'd be right down."

" He must have been charmed."

" Actually, he seemed more surprised than charmed."

When they finally emerged to the street, the policeman was putting a white tag in the window of the car in front. Claudia gave him a sunny smile and said, " Thanks ever so much."

He regarded her sourly. " You've been gone fifty minutes, lady."

She was deeply contrite. " I didn't mean to be, I'm terribly sorry."

" Thank you, officer," said David, who, for a courageous man, was apt to be a little too humble to traffic policemen.

" It doesn't pay to be afraid of them," Claudia pointed out as he settled himself behind the wheel.

" That's what you think," David muttered. " He let you get away with it because he thinks you're a nit-wit."

" It takes a special kind of brains to be a nit-wit."

He gave her the same look as the policeman had given her. Then he grudgingly remarked that she had improved in parking. She knew, of course, that she hadn't. When she went marketing in the village, she could recognize the car a mile off, because it always stuck out from the others like a crooked tooth. It was too bad she wasn't a good liar. Two blocks later, she told him about the kindly taxi-driver who had taken pity on her.

Fanny opened the door for them. "Hello, Agnes," David greeted her.

Claudia poked him with her elbow. "That was Fanny."

He had the audacity to argue about it. "Agnes," he repeated stubbornly, as Fanny departed with his hat and coat.

Julia's dressing-room was full of handsome luggage, just enough banged up to improve it, and Agnes was packing. "Good afternoon, Fanny," David said.

"That's Agnes," Julia said. "Claudia, come in my bed-room with me, and David can go in Hartley's room, and talk to him while Watkins packs. We decided so quickly, we're in a turmoil."

"We shouldn't have barged in," said Claudia. "We'll only stay a minute, though."

"To think of you taking that long drive in from the country just to say goodbye," said Julia, much moved by the gesture.

There was a limit to honesty. It would have been a shame to disillusion Julia by telling her that she was only a part of the drive. "How is it you could get accommodations at the last minute?" she digressed. "I thought this was the heavy season."

"It is. And actually, we couldn't. I mean"—Claudia was certain that Julia blushed—"we could only get one large double room. It'll be the first time Hartley and I have shared a room since we bought this house, fifteen years ago."

"It ought to be fun," said Claudia.

This time there was no mistaking Julia's blush. "It will be," she said. "We're rather looking forward to it."

"I'm glad you had the mumps," said Claudia.

"So am I," said Julia. And then she delivered herself of what was, for Julia, a rather daring admission. "And I'm glad that Hartley didn't have them," she said.

Claudia repeated it to David, driving home. "Maybe love is catching," he said, with one of his left-handed compliments, and squeezed her knee.

She lifted his hand to her lips. It was a silly thing for an old married woman to do, and he told her as much. "Watch your driving," she adjured him.

It was good to get beyond the city limits. Claudia

187

marvelled at the greenness and the sudden peace. "Why do people live in cities?"

"I thought you hadn't made up your mind yet," said David.

"All I need is a couple of hours in New York to make me make up my mind. The minute I get there I seem to have three feet in one shoe. Incidentally, Julia told me that we should be sure and use the house any time at all; she's leaving it fully staffed."

"We won't, but it's nice to know we could. And again, incidentally, Hartley offered to put up the money to buy the place out here and do it over. He doesn't like to see us spend everything we got from the sale of the farm."

She had to be careful, knowing David's pride. "Don't you think he's right, in a way?" she suggested, a little timidly.

"In a way. Only you know how I feel about accepting."

She was wise enough to give in. "Me, too." After a space, she said, "No matter what we decide to do, though, New York is out of the question with rents sky high, and nothing to show for it at the end of a lease. At least if you own your own home, you own it."

"That's the point."

Invariably, they talked themselves around to the same conclusion.

They fell silent, until they were past the toll bridge entering Connecticut. "I forgot to tell you, stop for Matthew, I left him with Mrs. Miller."

As always, her heart relayed when she saw him catapult out of the house at the first toot of the horn. Words tumbled over each other in his excitement. "I'm invited to stay for supper, I want to stay, can I stay for supper?"

"I should say not," said Claudia. "Mrs. Miller's had enough of you by now."

"But she asked me to!"

Elsie Miller appeared with her small nephew close behind. "We sure did," she said. "We're eating early, so we can catch an early movie. We'll bring him home around nine."

"Oh, boy!" Matthew gulped.

"I didn't tell him we had a movie up our sleeve," Elsie explained. "In case you said no, I didn't want him to be disappointed."

"Please let him," Elsie's nephew piped up in a pale sweet voice. "Can't he, please?"

Claudia glanced at David. He didn't believe in children

188

living at the movies, but the eager, imploring look in Matthew's eyes must have made him change his mind. " If Mother's willing," he said.

" I'm willing," said Claudia.

" Yippeee ! " Matthew shouted.

" Yippeee ! " the little nephew echoed, and Claudia saw that a friendship had been born. It was good, and she was grateful. " If Matthew goes to the public school here, they'll probably be in the same class," she said, as they drove off.

" What's bad about that ? "

" Not a thing."

He turned the car into the little country lane that led off the main road. The sun was setting in a great ball of glory and laid its colours deep into the river. " Oh, Lord," Claudia whispered, in a kind of awe.

Again, David put his hand on her knee. "Isn't it something?"

They heard Bluff bark before the little house showed out from the trees. " He hears us coming," said Claudia. He galloped toward them, still barking loudly.

" I never saw him so glad to see us," said David.

Claudia wasn't paying any attention to Bluff. " That's awfully funny, the baby's still in his play-pen on the lawn."

" It's warm, the air won't hurt him."

" But the grass is damp. Stop the car here, and let me out, will you ? It's shorter."

" A little dampness won't kill him."

He let her out, anyway, and Bluff jumped in. She ran across the lawn. Michael pranced in his pen like a small caged animal, his rompers bellying out from the rear. Yes, they were quite wet with the dew off the grass. She lifted him up, and carried him into the house. " You big fat thing, you. What's the matter, Bertha didn't take you in ? "

In answer, he stared at her opaquely, and twisted the middle button of her dress. " Hey ! Stop that, you ruffian ! "

He laughed then, and bounced down out of her arms. " Come along, we'll look for Bertha."

The front door was open. " Bertha ! We're home ! " she called out. There was no answer. Bertha was probably in the bathroom, and hadn't heard the car come in. Claudia walked the baby upstairs, and deposited him in his crib. The bathroom door was open, and she noted that the big towels she had used before she'd left for town had already been whisked away, and fresh ones hung in place. " That woman can make work for herself like nobody's business," she muttered. " They'd have been good for two more baths."

She ran downstairs again, through the dining room, into the kitchen. " Bertha! Where in earth are you!"

Bertha wasn't in the kitchen, but a platter of little marrow balls were, blonde and tempting. More luck than brains that Bluff hadn't found them. . . . She sniffed. There was a sweet, burning odour of sugar. She rushed to the stove and moved aside a large pot of the rich purple juice of grapes. " There goes your jelly," she said aloud. " It serves you right, I bet you went back on your word and began on the attic——"

She rushed upstairs again, ready to give Bertha a piece of her mind. The sun was a blinding fire in the attic window. She had to shield her eyes from the glare. " Bertha, are you here?" There was no answer. " Bertha, where on earth are you! The baby could have been kidnapped!" With the words, fear clutched suddenly at her throat. So many horrible things happened in the paper, not only to babies, but to grown women. Crime had no respect for age. Suppose—— Her thoughts recoiled. No, it couldn't be—— She'd find David, he'd tell her how silly it was—— Maybe Bertha was picking more grapes—— " I'll break her neck," Claudia whimpered through parched lips, " for scaring the wits out of me——"

She ran down the back stairs into the kitchen. Through the window, she could see David, walking towards the river with Bluff behind him. How could she summon him back from that moment of replenishment by the water's edge? " Quack, quack!" she could hear him call to the ducks— and she saw them swoop like a Japanese print against the darkening sky. No, Bertha wasn't outdoors, or he would have seen her. " Oh, God," she cried aloud. " Bertha! Where *are* you! Bertha!"

The sun had disappeared all at once, and all at once evening had come, drawing its soft, quick blanket of darkness around the little house. It was then, and only then, that she noticed a streak of light from beneath the door leading to the cellar. Somehow her legs carried her across the kitchen floor, and someone's hand, other than her own, reached for the knob. For a moment, she saw nothing but the broken wreckage of a box of old jelly glasses, and then she heard Bertha's faint call from just beyond the turn of the steps.

It could have been a dying call, but it wasn't. Bertha might have been a bleeding wreck, tied to a post by some violent marauder, but she wasn't. She was merely squatted, in a rather ludicrous mass of helplessness, on the cellar floor. "Don't be frightened, it is only my ankle," she explained feebly, before Claudia could bring her vocal chords to function. "Did you bring my baby in ? "

Claudia's voice came back in a rush, and her knees stopped shaking. "Never mind the baby, yes he's in, he's upstairs in his crib, Bertha did you fall, what happened ! "

"I did not fall exactly, my foot twisted, and I dropped my tray of glasses, and then I could not get up again."

A tentative try at Bertha's solid shoulders felt as if they were nailed to the ground. If only something could be done before David found them. Bertha read her thoughts, "Mr. David must not strain himself, I am too heavy."

"Claudia ! " A moment later she could hear him go from the kitchen to the dining room. "Where's supper, where's everyone ! "

"He is hungry," Bertha moaned. "And the baby has not had anything to eat either, and Matthew—where is Matthew ? "

"Nobody's starving and Matthew's having the time of his life at the movies," Claudia broke in brusquely. "David, we're down here ! Surprise ! "

A ghost of a smile flickered along Bertha's set lips. "A fine surprise. But I am glad you are not scolding me for making the jelly."

"I'm coming to that later, I'm going to feel nothing short of murder when I begin to scour that big evil purple pot."

"Throw the pot out," Bertha advised her brazenly. "Just throw it out and I will pay for a new one ! " Then they both laughed, which was all David needed to make him mad. "I warned you not to use those stairs ! " he bellowed, when he saw Bertha on the floor.

Bertha seemed to have gained strength from laughter. "I was not near the steps ! " she denied indignantly.

"Her ankle gave way, she was probably too tired to stand up straight," Claudia inserted grimly. "She didn't have enough to do, she had to use up some sour old grapes and a batch of somebody's old jelly glasses ! "

"I am punished," Bertha submitted meekly. Then she winced and bit at her lips. "You must excuse me. The pain stops me from talking."

David knelt beside her, his fingers encircling her wrist. "Get her a little whisky, Claudia, and 'phone Dr. Hubbard. She oughtn't to be moved until he examines her."

It must have killed Bertha not to protest that she didn't need a doctor; instead, she said that she didn't need the whisky. "Shut up," said Claudia.

Dr. Hubbard's number was tacked conspicuously over the telephone. Mrs. Payne had already laid the ground for Claudia to call him night or day in any emergency, and although Mrs. Payne hadn't said it in so many words, Claudia knew that David's "trouble", as she was prone to put it, was in the back of her mind. Now an emergency had arisen, and Claudia "touched wood" before she dialled the number, thankful that the emergency wasn't David. It was something to touch wood about, too, that it was only Bertha's leg, and not a stroke or a heart attack. For once, life's bark seemed to be worse than its bite.

Misfortune ran smoothly in all directions, for Dr. Hubbard was at home, and said that he would come at once. "Don't move the patient," he cautioned, "until I see her."

It occurred to Claudia—not for the first time—that David should have studied medicine, which was an implicit compliment to the man you loved to feel that healing lay within the quietness of his hands and the strength of his presence. He stayed with Bertha through the painful ordeal of lifting her on to a stretcher, and he was with her in the hospital when her leg was set and placed in a cast. Later, Bertha told Claudia with tears in her eyes, that it was as if God were standing beside her, and Claudia knew what she meant.

It was close to ten o'clock before Matthew returned from the movies, full of "yippees" and "oh-boys". "We stopped for a soda," Elsie apologized at the door, "and then I dropped Robbie and Alan off on the way. I hope you don't mind Matthew getting home so late."

"Not a bit, I was glad to be rid of him," Claudia replied, with more truth than wit. "Matthew, your bed's turned down, run on up and pop into it, but fast, and don't wake the baby, and wash your teeth."

He wanted to argue, but didn't, under the assumption that irreproachable behaviour might lead to more movies in the future. "Good night," he said obediently, and then lingered half-way up the stairs. "I want to tell Dad about the horse in the movie."

"Tell him to-morrow. He's not home, he went to the village."

"For what?"

"He had something to attend to. Now no more conversation, kindly."

"I left my airplane at Mrs. Miller's, I have to get it to-morrow."

"It's safe," said Elsie, "I put it away ; it's such an expensive toy. Alan's going to stay another couple of days, so maybe Matthew can come over in the morning again."

"Yippee ! " said Claudia. "Matthew, march."

Matthew marched.

"Come on in the kitchen with me, Mrs. Miller, I'm pouring some jelly into glasses "—Elsie was too diffident to use Claudia's first name, so Claudia couldn't very well call Elsie "Elsie ".

"I ought to get home," Elsie demurred. "What kind of jelly ? "

"Grape."

Elsie followed her. "I love grape, though, personally, I don't fuss with making my own. But, of course, when you have someone like Bertha to put it up for you, you'd be foolish not to."

"I haven't," said Claudia succinctly.

"Haven't what ? "

"Got Bertha."

Elsie's jaw dropped open. "Don't tell me that after all these years she walked out on you like Mrs. Payne's Annie ? "

"No," said Claudia, "but the effect is the same." Then, while she poured the jelly into an ill-assorted collection of any old glasses and containers she could find, she recounted what had happened. "Bertha will only be in the hospital for a day or two, but she'll be laid up for a long time. It's a compound fracture."

Claudia felt embarrassed because Elsie took it so hard.

"Oh, Mrs. Naughton, how awful ! " she cried. "Why, you poor thing, you've just gone through one thing after another, and yet you're so calm about it, that's what I can't get over ! "

"Mother ! " Matthew's voice floated down the stairs in a hoarse stage-whisper designed to be inaudible. "Where's Bertha, I have to have some more toothpaste, it's all gone ! "

Claudia hurried to the kitchen door. "Matthew, will you hush ! You'll wake Michael !—Bertha's down in the village with Dad, you can use my toothpaste, but don't squeeze from the middle ! And put the top back when you're through with it ! There's no need for Matthew to know until the morning," she said to Elsie.

"Honestly." Elsie sat down abruptly. "I'm just so shocked, and here you are, as cool as a cucumber ! "

Carefully, Claudia filled the last glass, and poured the little that was left in the bottom of the pot into a saucer to be used up for breakfast. Yes, she supposed, in Elsie's eyes, she really was as cool as a cucumber, finishing the jelly as if nothing had happened ; washing the pot, too, until little bright streaks of glistening metal began to show through the blurred surface. There was a kind of intense satisfaction in getting it shiny enough to join the rest of Bertha's immaculate utensils. Maybe going through one thing after another, as Elsie said, made you strong for each new thing that happened, so that nothing really seemed as if you couldn't live through it, because you had lived through so much already. Elsie hadn't lived through anything, except not being able to have a baby. It almost seemed as if she were trying to pay off her debt of gratitude to life by a vicarious participation in other people's troubles. Using one's heart that way made it big, but not strong. "It could be a lot worse," she heard herself comforting Elsie. "Do you want a glass of jelly to take home ? "

Elsie shook her head numbly. "No, thanks."

"Oh, come on, you said you liked grape." ("How stalwart I must sound," she thought with a grimace. And yet how could she make Elsie see that, apart from feeling badly for Bertha, this was very little of a catastrophe ?) She opened the drawer where Bertha kept a neat stack of used bags and neat little wads of string, and wrapped the jelly so that it could stand upright. "Don't spill it," she cautioned, "or you'll bless me."

"Thank you," said Elsie. She rose. "I'll call for Matthew in the morning, and I'll take the baby, if you'd trust him with me."

"It'll be a big help if Matthew's off my hands, but I've already arranged to leave the baby at Candy's, while I see Bertha and go to the agency."

Elsie lifted her jelly from the table. "I couldn't take things the way you do, I think you're wonderful," she reiterated lamely.

David returned from the hospital a few minutes after Elsie had gone home. He hadn't had any supper, so Claudia gave him a plate of soup, with the little marrow balls floating on top, and some crackers. "A nice lamb chop?" she tempted him further.

"No nice lamb chop."

"Scrambled eggs?"

"No, this is more than enough."

"You don't look tired," she said.

"I'm not."

"That's good.—How was Bertha when you left her?"

"Upset, because you're all alone."

"She shouldn't be."

"The doctor told her that it's going to be weeks before she can go back to work."

"She's never had an idle day in the whole twelve years she's been with us."

"She's in for a hell of a feeling," said David, with the remembered taste of incapacity bitter on his lips.

"I'm afraid so."

"It won't be too easy for you, either. What are you planning to do?"

"It won't kill me to do my own work, and take care of my own children, like a million other women."

"And wait on Bertha to boot?—We're not that broke."

"We're not broke at all," she said hastily. "I was just showing off, the way Bertha does. It's contagious. I'll get someone to-morrow."

"You're an opimist."

"Not at all. Candy says the agency's already replaced Mrs. Selby with a very capable widow who ran her own corset business for years."

"She sounds fascinating."

"Doesn't she, though. But it's sad, isn't it, so many women who've had their own homes having to earn their living by going into other people's homes?"

"When you think of it, yes."

"Mrs. Selby had her own home down in Kentucky, with servants to do her slightest bidding. And I believe it." She gave a little shudder. "Maybe I'd drink, too."

"Look, darling, it's too late to brood on the sad state of humanity. Let's go to bed."

"Let's," she agreed. "You go ahead, it'll only take me two minutes to rinse off these few dishes."

He was in bed by the time she got there. "Did you wash your teeth?" she queried him sternly.

"You can feel my tooth-brush," he said.

"That's sweet of you.—David, do I seem by any chance to be unusually wonderful?"

"Not to me," he promptly replied.

"That's a relief. Just give me a good kick in the pants, will you, if I ever do?"

"With pleasure," he agreed. As she put out the light, he said. "Who thought you were so wonderful?"

"Elsie Miller."

He pulled her down to him. "I like that woman," he said.

"What woman?"

"Elsie Miller."

"That's who I thought you meant," she murmured.

"*Whom?*"

"Elsie Miller."

"What are you laughing about!" Matthew bellowed from the next room, struggling awake, so as not to miss anything.

"Shhh——" Claudia silenced him. "We're asleep!"

They almost were.

Everything ran like clockwork the next morning. She'd bathed the baby, got Matthew dressed, fed everybody, made the beds, dusted with a paper napkin, and had both children in the car ready to drop them off, one by one, on the way to the station with David.

"Who gets Bluff?" David asked, in the middle of closing the front door.

She clapped her hand over her mouth in dismay, for hadn't she gone and forgotten all about Bluff! "I'm sure that either Elsie Miller or Candy would adore to have him," she covered herself quickly, "but I'd rather take him along with me." It was a downright lie, of course, because she was wearing her white linen—just for morale—and the last thing she wanted was to spend a morning with Bluff drooling in the front seat beside her. However, that was the way it would have to be, and even so, David had a nerve and wasn't satisfied. "Suppose someone steals him?" he objected.

"Would you?" she asked succinctly. "Nobody knows he's a sissy. I don't think I'd even get a ticket if I were parked in front of a fire-hydrant."

"Don't try it," he advised.

It wasn't nine o'clock yet, but fortunately the little house with the pink shutters was wide awake, with its blinds up, and its door open. Claudia could see Elsie carpet-sweeping the hall, and a toot of the horn brought her quickly to the car. " Hello, how's Bertha ? Oh, that *baby* ! Can't I really keep him for the day ? Hello, Matthew, you'll help me take care of him, won't you ? " Matthew wasn't everjoyed at the prospect, but Elsie rushed ahead without noticing. " Good morning, Mr. Naughton ! I sure wish Robbie was still home to see this wonderful old doggie——"

" Do you want Bluff, too ? " David smiled.

Her nice, full lips opened to a laugh. " No, just the children, please. Matthew, you can run on, darling, Alan's upstairs in the spare room, changing his socks, he stepped in a puddle. He'll stop dawdling if he knows you're here. Can't I have the baby, really ? Honestly, I'd just love it."

" All right," said Claudia. " Here's a box with everything in it—a change of panties, and his lunch ; it's all mixed already—not the panties—the vegetable and chicken. All you have to do is heat it. And a scraped apple for dessert. I'll 'phone Candy from the hospital that you're keeping him."

" I could 'phone her.—How did you say Bertha was this morning ? "

" I didn't. I'm going to see her after I drop David. Yes, I wish you would call Candy for me, it'll save time.—Here's your baby——"

" He's so *solid* ! Look at him go for my button, will you ! "

" That means he likes you," said Claudia shamelessly.

" Oh, you *darling* ! " Elsie cradled him ecstatically, only to have him try to scramble loose from her arms. " He can walk," Claudia mentioned. " Just hold on to his hand."

David started the car. Claudia looked back at them as they slowly made their way up the pansy-bordered path, with Elsie mincing her steps to Michael's.

" What made you leave him ? " David asked. " At least Candy has Martha to help her."

" Candy doesn't want to get pregnant," said Claudia. " Not now, anyway."

" I see," he said, meaning that he didn't see.

" It's a new theory. Elsie's planning to adopt a baby, and borrowing Michael plus Matthew might just possibly do the trick instead."

" It'll do something," David hazarded.

" It's done one thing ; it means we don't have to make another stop, you'll be in plenty of time for your train.— Bluff ! Stop drooling on my shoulder ! "

" Look at my suit," said David. " I'm one mass of hairs."

"Oh, dear. He's such a nuisance. Let's get rid of him."

"All right, let's get rid of him."

It could have been that Bluff was smiling, the way his tongue hung foolishly from between his opened jaws. "Vicious-looking teeth," said David fondly.

Claudia kissed his silly face, and Bluff kept smiling.

There was time to spare when they arrived at the station. They got out of the car and walked Bluff up and down the platform, and everybody looked at them, and a little girl cried out, "Oh, Mummy, is it a lion?" Mummy looked at Claudia's white dress and said shortly, No, it wasn't a lion, so come along. She was one of the wives who would be all made up that evening when she called for her husband, but this early in the morning, she wasn't. "I think happy women don't wake up puffy," Claudia remarked.

"I'm glad you're happy, darling."

"David, how can I be happy?" she asked him in wonder.

"I don't know." His eyes were a caress upon her face. "All I know is, you're not puffy." He yanked Bluff away from a black poodle. "Mind your manners."

They kept on walking until the train came in, and what with David's good looks, and Claudia's white linen, and the size of Bluff, they felt immensely prosperous. "I'll catch the four-ten home, but don't send the chauffeur for me, I'll take a taxi," David said as he kissed her goodbye.

"No taxis, the chauffeur will call for you," she said, and again he told her she was an optimist.

Bertha had been taken to a different hospital than Candy. "I'm getting around quite a bit," thought Claudia wryly, as she found the correct entrance and parked the station-wagon. "For heaven's sake, don't bark!" she remembered to caution Bluff. It might be better to take him in with her, and then again, it mightn't.

David had left orders for Bertha to be put in a private room, which was causing her untold anguish of spirit. Indeed, Bertha was in such anguish of spirit when Claudia walked in the room that it was difficult to tell where one torment left off and the other began. It was strange to see her in bed with the great hulk of the plaster cast making a small mountain beneath the covers. "So early!" she cried out. "What did you do with the baby?"

"Left him home and told him to answer the 'phone and write down any messages.—Bertha, does it hurt much, how do you feel?"

"It does not hurt at all, and I feel fine!" she replied in a fury.

"Oh, that's too bad," said Claudia.

"I only wish it was more serious, and I could be up in a few days!" Bertha made a tardy pact with fate.

"I met Dr. Hubbard in the corridor. You'll be home in less than a few days," Claudia promised her.

"I cannot go home," said Bertha flatly.

"Oh, you can't, can't you? What's the matter, aren't we good enough for you?"

The tears rolled down Bertha's cheeks. It was shocking to see Bertha cry. Deep and soul-shaking tragedy had happened to her in her life, and she had shed no tears, she had been like a great, proud ship, slowly making its way into harbour. Now Bertha was crying because her leg was broken. "She's afraid," thought Claudia. "For the first time in her life, she's afraid." It was the most hideous of all fears, the fear of having nothing to do, the fear of having to face oneself. David had gone through it, and that was what he had meant when he'd said, this morning, "It's going to be a hell of a feeling for Bertha."

Unobtrusively, she gave Bertha a tissue from the box on the bureau. "It is not the pain," Bertha protested angrily. "That stupid jelly! I could whip myself!"

"The jelly was delicious, we had some for breakfast.—What's this nonsense about not coming home?"

"I will not be able to work for a long time. The doctor told me."

"If you mean you can't clean the attic or wash the car, you're right. But you're not going to get away with doing nothing, you can mend, and shell peas——"

"We eat so many peas," Bertha interrupted with a snort. "No. I will go to Hedwig until I am on my feet again."

"Hedwig! Listen, Bertha, she's your one cousin I can't abide. She looks like a mean lobster, with her little eyes over a nose without any bridge. And I apologize to lobsters, because I like lobster. Why, you'll be miserable with Hedwig! In fact, I'm not even sure——" She couldn't go on. It was hard to say it to Bertha, but Bertha said it for herself. "You are not sure that she will want me? No, she will not want me. But Hedwig will do anything for money to buy herself pretty clothes, and she will want the money that I will give her for my board and room."

Suddenly, Claudia wanted to cry, too. This was a different

kind of tragedy, but it was tragedy none the less. This was another case of Mrs. Payne, in reverse. "Money can't buy any of the things that really count," she thought. One thing was certain, she wasn't going to let Bertha go to Hedwig's. Naturally, there'd be a period of trays, and helping Bertha in and out of bed for a while, but it was small payment in return for twelve years of devotion and service. "Don't be an ass," she said. "We need you more than Hedwig needs you."

"Nobody needs me," said Bertha starkly.

"Such self-pity!" Claudia scoffed.

"It is not self-pity," said Bertha quietly. "It is something I see all of a sudden. I need to be needed, more even than you need me."

"Bertha, we all need to be needed."

"Not so much as me," said Bertha.—"That dress could stand a washing."

"That's why I wore it."

"Do not try to do it yourself."

"Do you think I'm crazy? I'll send it to be dry-cleaned. You're the only person I'd trust to launder it."

Bertha sighed. "I have been thinking and thinking of somebody to help you, and there is just one niece, but she is too young, she is eighteen and wants to stay in New York. I thought of her for Miss Candy."

"Too bad Martha was the last of your good relatives."

"Ja," Bertha sadly agreed. "What will you do?"

"Get someone from the agency, I'm on my way there now. I'll let you know what luck I have."

"Do not kill yourself running back and forth," Bertha begged. "Did you hear from Miss Julia and Mr. Hartley yet?"

"Hear from them? They only left last night!"

"Last night——" Bertha echoed incredulously. "It seems like a year——"

Claudia patted her cheek. "Have a little patience; any minute, now, time will pick up its feet and begin to move so fast you won't know where it's gone to." She wished she could be sure of it. There wasn't even any mending that she could bring to while the hours away, for Bertha was chronically caught up with mending. If only she could play solitaire. . . . No, Bertha wouldn't play solitaire, even if she could. The minutes would stretch slowly into hours, and the hours into days, and the days into weeks. Something that Matthew had said came back to her, something about learning lessons

in school, and graduating. " Out of the mouths of babes."
It was funny how, as one grew older, proverbs kept boomer-
anging into truth.

CHAPTER THIRTEEN

MISS GOODE'S Elite Employment Agency hid itself down
a long narrow corridor on the third floor of an old-fashioned
building, with a dental mechanic's laboratory on one side
and a chiropodist on the other. Once, so far back that it was
hard to recall too clearly, Claudia had had occasion to go to
an employment agency in New York. It had been quite
different, with an enormous room, so to speak, for the em-
ployers, and adjoining it, another enormous room filled with
employees. No such magnificence existed at Miss Goode's.
The office comprised a single, stuffy cubby-hole subdivided
by a low partition, where Miss Goode presided at a shabby
oak desk with two telephones on it. She was a small woman
with spectacles and poor hair, and her name wasn't Miss
Goode, it was Miss McCabe. It appeared that there wasn't
any Miss Goode.

" Good morning. What can I do for you ? " she asked, as
Claudia entered.

There was no point in using Mrs. Payne as an introduction,
for Mrs. Payne herself had so newly availed herself of the
services of the Elite. " I need a maid," Claudia stated merely.

Miss McCabe took in the white linen, with more and more of
Bluff on it, but still bearing that magical signature of a " Flora
Rosenbach." She brightened. " Not five minutes ago," she
confided, " I spoke to one of the best lady's-maids we ever
placed. She'll be available for an interview to-morrow. She's
an excellent person, and has nice references. Also, she'll assist
with the chamberwork, and she'll help out in serving, once in
a while, which is unusual." Miss McCabe squared around in
front of the desk and withdrew a fresh card from a filing
cabinet. " May I have your name and address ? "

" Thank you," said Claudia gratefully, for it was certainly
nice to be mistaken for Julia's sort. " I didn't mean that kind
of a maid, though," she explained. " I meant a cook.—The
name is Mrs. David Naughton. Still Pond Road."

Miss McCabe took the information in a miniscule handwriting, her forefinger deeply bent. "Any particular preference

201

as to nationality? I have a very fine Finnish cook, but she won't be free until the end of the month. And possibly not then. The lady who employs her might let the butler go instead, and then, of course, Inga will stay on. Her name is Inga. I've placed her several times."

" I see," said Claudia, kissing Inga goodbye on both cheeks. " I need someone right away." It was just as well to let it slowly unfold that she and Miss McCabe were apparently not using the same dictionary. " And I don't keep a butler," she mentioned gently.

" Oh." Miss McCabe used the eraser end of her pencil. " That makes it much easier. So many girls don't like to work with male help, these days."

" They don't have to work with any help," Claudia elucidated.

Miss McCabe gave a visible swallow. " You mean you just keep the one ? "

" Just the one. We're a very small family," she added, to soften the blow.

" Then you're alone ? "

" No, I have my husband."

" Two in family," Miss McCabe made note.

It was Claudia's turn to swallow. " And a couple of children," she threw in nonchalantly.

Miss McCabe placed her pencil quietly on the desk. " What you want is a general houseworker."

" Why, yes," Claudia innocently agreed, and couldn't resist adding with extreme affability, " Is there anything wrong with that ? "

" They're hard to find," said Miss McCabe, with pursed lips, and Claudia could have almost sworn that she said in effect, " They are extinct in the higher brackets of society."

" A lot of people must have them," Claudia offered tentatively.

" I m'ght refer you to our Stanford branch," Miss McCabe suggested, as if Stanford were a poor relation. " Unless you're interested in a girl who sleeps out. No Sundays, of course, and you furnish the transportation."

" No," said Claudia, on all counts.

Miss McCabe tried again. " I don't have a single general houseworker. How about a kind of housekeeper-companion ? I have a delightful Southern woman—a lady—who could be helpful to you in the house, and would be nice with the little ones. I placed her recently, in one of our very finest families here in Greenwich, but it just didn't work out. The lady was quite elderly, so perhaps a change to young children might be exactly what this particular person would like——"

" Is her name Miss Selby ? "

Miss McCabe blinked. " How did you know ? "

" I'm that way," Claudia murmured.

" Oh." Miss McCabe edged a little farther back in her chair. " I still feel," she went on, not to be daunted, " that your one chance of being suited is the kind of person who is a lady in her own right, and will appreciate sharing a home. Also, the salary isn't quite as much as the specialized cook, or chambermaid-waitress, or butler."

Claudia happened to know that Mrs. Payne had paid Miss Selby two hundred dollars a month, and her mind balked at going into still higher astronomical figures. " Now I have in view," Miss McCabe continued thoughtfully, " someone whom I have just placed, but I'm quite certain that it isn't going to work out very well. With the same elderly lady, as a matter of fact. She is an extremely fine type of woman who has had her own home, and her own business."

" The corset business ? " Claudia suggested.

This time Miss McCabe did not swallow, she gulped, and she was still staring wordlessly at Claudia when the door opened and somebody walked in. Miss McCabe jumped up from the desk. " Katie ! " she exclaimed, " I thought you were in Nantucket ! "

Claudia turned. Katie was the beginning and end of all Katies, from the top of her excessive permanent wave to the tip of her bumpy, short-vamped toe. " I came back," said Katie with finality. " I didn't like it up there."

" Well ! " cried Miss McCabe, so full of a delighted astonishment that she neglected to probe further into Claudia's mysterious powers of deduction. " Katie, this is a coincidence if ever I saw one ! Why don't you sit down and talk to this lady, Katie ? She's looking for someone right away, and it might just happen to work out ! After all, you've worked before where they had children, and you didn't mind——"

" Okay," said Katie, with the large air of a gambler.

Miss McCabe officiated. She led the way towards a brace of cane chairs somewhat removed from the vicinity of the desk, and then left them to become further acquainted with each other. " How many rooms ? " Katie led off at once.

" I've never really counted them," said Claudia. " Have you any written references—may I see them ? "

"Okay," said Katie, willing to bury the hatchet. She dug into her purse and withdrew a much folded piece of notepaper, which stated somewhat meagrely that the bearer, Katie Manus, had been employed as houseworker for a period of ten months, and was willing, sober, and honest, Sincerely Mrs. George Loeser, tel. Bridgeport 8-4563.

Claudia folded the paper. " Why did you leave ? "

" Because I only got every Thursday off from Wednesday night to Friday morning, and every other Sunday from after breakfast."

" Oh," said Claudia. She'd forgotten that there were such things as days off. Bertha hadn't bothered with them. " How much time did you *expect* off ? "

" Every Sunday instead of every other."

" Oh," said Claudia again, trying to reckon out what was left of the week. " And how did you get to your days off ? "

Katie shrugged. " Car. You got a car, haven't you ? Or sometimes I can take a bus."

" We have no bus," said Claudia.

Miss McCabe inserted herself into the interview. " These are all minor considerations," she took over capably. " Mrs. Naughton, why don't you drive Katie out to see the place, and if it's satisfactory, we can go on from there. How does that strike you, Katie ? "

" Okay," said Katie.

It was just one okay too many. Claudia was about to say that she and Katie were not meant for each other, when Miss McCabe caught her eye. " May I talk to you a moment ? "

" Me ? " asked Katie.

" No. Mrs. Naughton.—You wait here, Katie."

There was nothing subtle about Miss McCabe's approach. She drew Claudia into a corner and said in a sibilant whisper, " Take my advice and grab Katie, if she's willing. It was just a miracle she happened to walk in like that ; I can place her ten times over in the next half-hour, don't let her slip through your fingers ! "

Claudia hesitated. Maybe Katie would grow on one. And did it so much matter whether Matthew said okay or oh-boy ? " Very well," she agreed, feeling like a milk-sop.

Katie followed her to the station-wagon which was parked half-way down the block. The day was climbing to mid-day heat, but Claudia hadn't dared to leave the window open more than a crack, for Bluff thought nothing of squeezing his head through, and choking himself. From a distance, she could see the black blob of his nose against the rear glass, and at the same moment he caught sight of her, too, and gave a great leap over the seats, panting with welcome. He must have been jumping back and forth like that for some time, for the windows were running with the steam of his breath, and the leather seats were encrusted with the dusty imprints of his paws. "Oh, Bluff!" she protested, peering in from the outside, "just look at the looks of this car!"

He answered her in a series of deafening barks, accompanied by frantic attacks upon the door. The furore attracted a small crowd. "Carefully, lady, you got a mad dog in there," some friendly voice gave warning, and when she turned to assure the voice that Bluff was glad and not mad, she saw Katie fleeing towards the direction of the Elite Agency as fast as her solid legs could carry her. There was no point in going after her, that was clear. If Katie didn't like Nantucket, she was going to be equally temperamental about mad dogs.

For a moment, as she started to open the door, she had a sudden misgiving that Bluff actually could have gone crazy with the heat. She could feel his tremendous weight ready to pour out into the street, and it was all she could do to push the door closed again. "Bluff!" she entreated him. "Be quiet! Calm down!"

He barked the louder, and spun around and around the seat, which wasn't broad enough to hold all of him at once, so that he kept slipping and scrabbling. "Oh, dear," thought Claudia. If he was fool enough not to realize that a policeman might come along and shoot him—as policemen had a perfect right to shoot mad dogs, and big ones at that—this was no time to argue with him. The thing to do was to get herself into the car without letting him get out of it, because one thing was certain : he wanted to be out, for one reason or another, and probably both.

No one had the temerity to help her accomplish the difficult feat. On the contrary, the crowd drew back a little as, like a lady animal-tamer in the circus, she again put her hand on the knob and, in a single shove of sheer dexterity and strength, held Bluff back by his collar while she slid into the seat, and pulled the door closed behind her. Her senses reeled with the stifling aroma of dog and heat. "You idiot!" she shouted at him, "get off my lap, and let me get the car started!"

She made for the open countryside as fast as she could, and then she stopped the car again and let him out into a deserted back road, leaving both doors ajar to clear the atmosphere.

She drew a deep breath, filling her lungs with the freshness of fresh air. " *Bluff!* " she protested. " How can you *be* like that?"

He told her how he could be like that, and all at once her heart melted with gratitude, and she put her arms around his powerful neck, and said, right in the middle of the road, " You're an angel and a gentleman."

Gentleman or not, he was suddenly a millstone around her neck. She had wanted to try her luck at the Stanford agency, she had wanted to stop back to look in on Bertha again, she had wanted to do a lot of marketing ; but she didn't dare to leave him alone again for any length of time. Maybe Candy would keep him for a while in lieu of Matthew.

She stopped for petrol, which was the last thing she needed in the car, as it was full up. She had the oil checked instead, but as the car didn't need oil either, she had water put in the radiator and air in the tyres. The bill for all this service was exactly nothing, therefore it was rather embarrassing to ask the attendant to wipe off the wind-shield into the bargain. She drove off again, flying blind as it were.

It was the first time that Bluff had called on Candy in her new house, and he was much pleased with the great clumps of hardy rhododendron, and the vast expanse of smooth, green lawn. Fortunately Tony was nowhere in sight, but Martha was polishing the door-knocker, with the baby asleep in the perambulator close by. " He remembers me ! " she cried.

" Of course he does," Claudia assured her. It was important that Bluff and Martha be friendly, for they might be seeing a lot of each other for the next several days.

" How he wags his tail ! " Martha marvelled, rubbing her thigh. " He hurts," she added ruefully.

" He loves you," said Claudia. " Where's Mrs. Payne ? "

" It is too bad, you just missed her. Her mother-in-law telephoned a few minutes ago for her to go over, but I will call her." Martha put the bottle of polish on the ground, and then thought better of it, and stuck it beyond reach of Bluff's cavorting. " How is Bertha, Mrs. Naughton ? I have been so worried about her. Mrs. Payne said I could go down to see her this afternoon, if it is all right for her to have company."

" I'm sure it is," said Claudia, " it's the best thing for her." Inwardly she thought, " There goes my chance of leaving Bluff here." It would be too much for Candy to take care of the baby and the dog at the same time, with Bluff so "ausgelassen," as Bertha would say. "Don't 'phone Mrs. Payne to come home," she said. " I'll stop by for a moment. Come along, Bluff ! "

She lingered to peep at the baby, doll-like and remote beneath the white canopy of mosquito-netting. "She's gained," she congratulated Martha.

"Nearly six ounces," Martha bragged.

Claudia tried to recall the thrill of it. It was a long time since she and Bertha had thought of Michael in ounces. They had almost stopped thinking of him in pounds.

It was safe now to wave to Tony on the way out, but he didn't see her. He was busy nipping the dried blossoms off the laurel. She sighed. What sheer luxury to have a gardener who had time to prune.

She paused at the gates, undetermined. Turning right meant home, and left meant Mrs. Payne's. She turned left, for if Candy had been called over there, Mrs. Lancy, or whatever her name was, had probably given notice, and having so nearly inherited her, Claudia decided that she might at least see what she looked like.

As Thomas admitted her into the cool foyer, she caught a glimpse of Mrs. Lancey, not too well corseted (like the shoemaker's child going barefooted)—having a sizable luncheon in solitary state at the long dining room table, with a magazine propped up against her glass of milk. So she was a milk-drinker, Claudia made note. It was an improvement on gin, but why not water at her age?

Thomas appeared to be churning with similar grievances. "Wouldn't budge to answer the bell," he unburdened himself on the threshold of the drawing room. "Expects to be waited on." There was an importunity in his manner that urged Claudia farther into the room, away from the door. "Mrs. Payne's upstairs with Miss Candy. Annie's up there, too."

"Annie!"

"She came in a taxi about half an hour ago. She told me before she saw Mrs. Payne, she's sorry for everything that happened and wants to come back. The one in there"—Thomas jerked his head towards the dining room—"she's smart, she knows when she's got an easy place and she doesn't want to leave."

"How do you know?" Claudia asked curiously.

"She told me when I was serving her lunch. Oh, she's a smart one," he repeated, "she knows something's going on upstairs."

"So," said Claudia. "Would you tell Miss Candy that I'm here."

" I will," said Thomas, with alacrity.

He came down a moment or two later. " Mrs. Payne and Miss Candy would like you to come up," he said. " They're in the sitting room."

The sitting room was the pleasantest room in the house ; it was small and square, and held a sewing machine that Annie had used on and off throughout the years. Mrs. Payne was sitting in a comfortable little arm-chair, which made her look less frail than the big Victorian wing chairs in the drawing room below. Candy was standing beside her, almost protectively, Claudia thought, and Annie was seated stiffly on the very edge of the divan. She looked awful, as if she hadn't slept for weeks. Impulsively, Claudia held out her hand, and Annie rose and gave her hand in return. It was moist and cold.

" Why, hello, Annie, how nice to see you ! "

" Isn't it ? " Candy agreed.

" Annie wants to come home," said Mrs. Payne, quite simply. " We're discussing the problem of Mrs. Lancey. I dare say the only thing to do is to say I'm sorry and pay her a month's salary, and let her go."

" I don't want to put anybody out of a place, though," Annie broke in nervously, " especially if Mrs. Payne likes her."

" But I don't like her, Annie ; she gets on my nerves. I don't suppose I ever will like anybody but you ; we've been together for too many years to start new relationships at our age."

Annie blew her nose. She couldn't talk with the emotion that flooded her. " I would like to pay her the month's salary," she offered tremulously. " It's the least I can do for the way I behaved."

" Ridiculous ! " Mrs. Payne put an end to that idea, and went to her desk. " I'll write out a cheque. Candy can take it down to her, if she doesn't mind."

" I don't mind," said Candy. " I'd like to. I think it's lovely that Annie's going to be here, with John away and everything. I mean—you know—Annie's someone we can all depend on."

" Thank you, Miss Candy," said Annie humbly. " And that goes for you, too, Mrs. Naughton. I heard about Bertha, and I'm very sorry. Any time we can keep the children for you, or I could come over and help out, I'd be only too glad. That is, if Mrs. Payne can spare me."

" I can spare you," said Mrs. Payne, tartly. " If it wasn't for my daughter-in-law worrying about me being alone, I wouldn't need anybody at all."

" You look fine ; I was surprised," Annie admitted.

Mrs. Payne waved the cheque dry, and handed it to Candy. " This is the best two hundred dollars I ever spent," she smiled graciously.

" It seems a great deal for just a few days," Claudia finally interfered. " Why don't you let me 'phone David and find out if it's necessary, Mrs. Payne ? "

" It might not be necessary, my dear, but it will save unpleasantness. I engaged her on a monthly basis, and I'm dismissing her through no fault of her own."

" But you're not dismissing her," Claudia insisted. " She was leaving anyway. I've just come from the agency, and Miss McCabe mentioned that she had a nice woman who would be available, and it turned out to be Mrs. Lancey."

" Oh the nerve ! " cried Candy. " She must have called the agency on the sly, and now she won't let on ! "

Mrs. Payne said nothing. She merely tore the cheque in small, slow pieces, and dropped them in the waste-basket. " I believe I have sufficient cash in my pocket-book," she remarked, " to pay Mrs. Lancey for the three days and a half she's been here." She paused at the door. " I trust that she has finished her lunch."

Annie stepped after her quickly. " Mrs. Payne, why not let Thomas do it ? The woman's apt to be unpleasant, as you say, if she's the scheming sort."

" I can be a little unpleasant myself, Annie," Mrs. Payne assured her.

" She can, too," Annie murmured respectfully, as Mrs. Payne left the room.

In a very short while, Mrs. Payne returned. " Will you call a taxi, Candy ? Ask him to be here in fifteen minutes." She glanced at her watch. " It's almost one o'clock. I know that Candy hasn't had lunch, and I daresay Annie hasn't.— How about you, Claudia ? "

" I'm terribly hungry," Claudia discovered.

Mrs. Payne said, " Annie, take off your hat and coat, and we'll both go down and see what we can do to help Thomas."

Annie's pale face took on a little glow. " I'll just put them in my room, and tidy up a bit." Then she hung back, uncomfortable and awkward. " I'll wait until Mrs. Lancey's gone, of course."

" No need to wait," Mrs. Payne told her crisply. " Mrs. Lancey didn't have your room, Annie. Your room is exactly as you left it. And it wasn't left too tidily, either, as I recall."

"I thought about it afterwards," Annie apologized. "I was in such a hurry to get out, I couldn't leave fast enough."

"Now you can't get back fast enough," said Mrs. Payne, rubbing it in a little. "Suppose you get a move on, and we can have a soufflé. I'll go down and tell Thomas to light the oven, and grate the cheese for you."

Alone, Candy and Claudia looked at each other. It wasn't something you could laugh about, or even smile about. "She's quite a person, my mother-in-law," Candy said at length. "I guess people don't really change, they just become more, or less, of the same thing they were born."

"I guess that's true," said Claudia, "and it's the time in-between 'the more' or 'the less' that's hard to take. Incidentally, you've got to be quite a bit 'more' yourself."

Candy shook her head. "'Less.' I cry myself to sleep every night. I have no courage. I can't face a future without John."

"Candy, don't be a fool. Why should there be a future without him?"

"Because there's a war. And John's in it. He won't stay in Washington for ever, I'm not that much of a fool. One day he's going to come home to say goodbye. It's like a sword hanging over my head. Sometimes I almost wish it would drop, and the agony would be over with."

"Those are the kind of swords that don't drop, half the time. By the way, I hate to seem unsympathetic, but I must inform you that you haven't 'phoned the taxi yet."

"Oh, heavens!" cried Candy in dismay. She dialled a number. "I'll have to 'phone Martha, too, to tell her I'm staying for lunch. Did you see the baby when you were over? What were they both doing?"

"The baby was asleep, and Martha was cleaning the outside brasses."

"Martha's almost as wonderful as Bertha," Candy said. "She never lets a week go by without polishing even the door-knobs. She knows I love them when they're bright and shiny."

Claudia smiled to herself. And Candy thought she hadn't changed——

She felt like Cinderella in reverse when she called for David that evening. There'd be no platform parading this time. Firstly, she couldn't get out of the car, because she and

Matthew were being book-ends to Michael, who was anchored between them on the front seat, and secondly, denim overalls, and dirty ones at that, borrowed no swank from a messy station-wagon full of children. She'd tried to remove as much of Bluff as possible—hence the overalls—but the job had lacked a professional touch, and the windows were still smeary.

" This is the first time Michael's called for Dad, isn't it ? " Matthew commented with indulgence. (The children were clean, at least. They were all bathed and ready for bed underneath—— Lord, how she'd hustled all afternoon.)

" It's the first time for Michael for quite a few things," she said, and hoped devoutly that this cataclysmic disruption of his schedule would not result in a restless night. If there was one thing she could do without, it was an interrupted night's sleep, for the next few days were beginning to pile up like relentless payment to a neglected household. There was already a not inconsiderable accumulation of the children's laundry, and no house could go very long on paper-napkin dusting. " I'll vacuum after supper," she planned, which would leave her free to leave early in the morning to go to New York, where employment agencies stretched out, one after another, for endless blocks. Of course, there was the small matter of supper and breakfast in between, but thank goodness the children needed only cereal, and fortunately David hadn't eaten the lamb chop last night. There was soup left, too, which was very clever of it, and half a tin of Bertha's butter cookies, and a special kind of potato-flour cake that improved with age.

" Here comes the train ! " Matthew shouted.

" I hear it, I'm not deaf," said Claudia. " You sit in the back now, and I'll hold the baby."

" Look, he's scared, the sissy ! "

" He is not." She took him on her lap. " See the nice choo-choo, Michael ? Hear the pretty noise ? "

It was difficult to sell him that particular bill of goods. His face puckered up, ready to cry. Claudia diverted him hastily, " There's Daddy ! " She tooted the horn, and then picked up Michael's hand and waved it vigorously. " Say hello to Daddy ! "

" Well, if it isn't the chauffeur's brats," said David. He ruffled the gold silk of Michael's hair, and gave Matthew's nose a friendly punch, and then he caught Claudia's lips in a quick, hard kiss. " I gather you had no luck," he said.

" You gather right."

" Where's Bluff ? "

" I left him with Elsie Miller when I picked up the children."

He grinned. " Elsie'd better watch out, she's apt to have twins.—Matthew ! Down in back there, I can't see through you.—Whose is the suitcase ? "

" I'm leaving," said Claudia. " I don't like the job, it's too much work."

" It is," said David sombrely. " You look tired."

" Oh, don't be silly, I was just being funny. I'm not a bit tired.—Bertha sent Martha over to pack some of her things and I said I'd leave them for her at the hospital in the morning, but we'd better leave them now, because I'm planning to drive in town with you to-morrow."

" Fine ! " said David. " Who takes the children this time ? "

" Candy. And Elsie Miller takes Bluff, provided he hasn't wrecked the place this afternoon. Really, I don't know what's got into him ; he think he's a pup again, the way he cut up all day."

" It must have been the poodle this morning," said David. " Can Candy handle both children all right ? "

" Annie said she'd lend a hand."

" Annie who ? "

" I forgot to tell you. There's always so much to tell when you come home, you'd think you'd been away a year." She began to give him a blow-by-blow report, with the little pitcher behind them listening with big ears. Too late, she decided that it was hardly the thing to do if Annie was going to be exposed to him the following day. " Anyway, Annie's back from her vacation now," she concluded emphatically, " and everybody's chastened, but not too chastened."

" What's chastened ? " Matthew demanded.

" You know what chasing means," said David.

" No, I don't."

" I've seen you chasing a squirrel," said Claudia mildly. " For all the good it did you," she added.

He pondered it. Somehow, he must have lost the main thread of the conversation on account of being in the back seat. " Can we go up to see Bertha ? " he changed the subject.

" Come to think of it, I don't see why not," said Claudia. " That is, if Dad's not too tired."

" I'm not tired," said David. " There wasn't enough doing down at the office to make me tired."

" That's the worst kind of tired," thought Claudia un-

happily. Aloud she said, " It'll put Bertha's mind at rest to
see the children, and it'll save me a trip to-morrow.—
Matthew, you're a smart fellow, why didn't I think of it
myself ? "

It wasn't until she felt the amused eyes of a young doctor
upon her that she realized why she hadn't thought of it.
She felt her cheeks grow hot. " David, why didn't you
remind me I had on overalls ! " she ground out under
her breath.

" I thought you knew," he said.

" This is going to embarrass Bertha to death."

Bertha didn't notice the overalls, however. She was so
happy to see the children that, for all she knew, Claudia
might still have been wearing her white linen.

The next morning, everything didn't run quite so much like
clockwork as it had the morning before. Claudia and David
slept in one bed, to save making up the other one, but cheating
showed because Matthew stuck his foot through his lower
sheet, which was on its last legs, anyway, and made a big rip
in it. " Matthew, what do you *do* with your feet while you're
asleep," she queried in exasperation. " Why don't you keep
them in your pocket."

" That's hands," he said.

She yanked the sheet from the bed. " Now I have to make
it all up fresh. Why didn't you rip it to-morrow night ? "

He got a little lost on that one. " Run and bring me another
sheet from the linen cupboard," she told him.

" Where ? "

" What do you mean ' where ' ? We only have one linen
cupboard. Never mind, I'll get it——"

" No, I'll get it," he said.

The torn sheet presented a problem. Was it worth mending ?
Emphatically no. Especially with no Bertha to do it. Then
if it wasn't worth the mending, it certainly wasn't worth the
laundering. So she tore it all the way across. It tore like a
dream. She tore it again. And again, and lo, it became
wonderful rags. Great big ones, and a few little ones along
the hem, where the tearing wasn't so good. Why, she could
wallow in soft white rags until Bertha came back. Then
Bertha could wash the whole batch at once.

" What on earth are you doing ? " David demanded from
the doorway.

" Giving myself a catharsis."

"What about a little breakfast instead? It's after eight."

"You go down and start on your orange juice. Everything's ready but the eggs."

"I don't want any eggs. Where's Matthew?"

"Don't begin that egg nonsense. In the linen cupboard. —Matthew! What are you doing so long?"

Matthew came back with a sheet in his hand. "I saw my other airplane on the top shelf," he explained. "I looked at it. Couldn't I take it over to show to Alan?"

"You're going to Candy's to-day."

"Oh, boy!" said Matthew.

"Don't think this gallivanting is going to keep up," said David. "To-morrow we stay home and mow the lawn."

Claudia couldn't believe her ears. "David, really? Do you mean you're going to take a day off?"

"I thought I might."

Her heart stopped. Was he keeping anything from her? "You're all right, aren't you?"

He gave her a look. "My God!" he said. "You're still a bunch of fear, aren't you?"

She nodded abjectly. "On and off."

"All right, I'll eat my eggs."

"Thanks," she said humbly. "Scrambled or boiled?"

"Boiled."

"Come on, I'll put them on.—Matthew, bathroom."

"Where's Michael?" David asked.

"Other bathroom. Always. Right after breakfast."

"The army's lost a good general," he complimented her.

For all her system, however, they were late in starting. The garbage had to be put out for the garbage man, and she'd started a split-pea soup for supper, which, in the past, had proven a godsend when a lot of nourishment was needed in one fell swoop. Occasionally, Matthew might detect a bit of carrot or onion floating around, and he'd shy away from it in horror; but for the most part it would go painlessly down everybody's throat, including the baby's.

"Good coffee," David mentioned, from the kitchen table.

She dumped some bits of toast into a bag for the ducks. "I treated ourselves to heavy cream," she confessed. "I wasn't taking any chances.—Do you know how much cream is? Thirty-six cents a half-pint. Remember how we practically bathed in it at the farm for nothing?"

It hadn't been for nothing, exactly, and they both knew it, but it was nice to think so in retrospect. "What I wouldn't give for a private cow," she sighed. " Milk is twenty-four a quart. And calves' liver ! David. How much do you think ? A dollar eighty-nine a pound."

" If you had a cow you couldn't have your milk, and eat your liver, too," he reminded her.

" No, but we could have butter and milk at the same time, and butter is ninety-eight."

He folded his paper napkin meticulously. " You're not serious about it, are you ? "

" About what ? "

" Farming again."

" How could we ? On thirty-eight acres."

" There's over fifty acres adjoining us. And two silos, and a barn——"

" David," she interrupted in a panic. " Are you crazy ? "

He crumpled the napkin and tossed it aside. " I suppose so,—You're not dressed yet."

" I'm all fixed underneath. It won't take me a moment. —Why don't you run Bluff over to Elsie Miller's in the meantime, and when you come back we'll all be ready."

He glanced at his watch. " It means a double trip."

" But it'll save time anyway," she urged him. Anything to get him out from underfoot, anything to get his mind off farming. Couldn't he take a joke ? A cow was all she needed to simplify her life.

By a miracle of what he had called generalship, they were finished with everything, and waiting on the porch for him when he returned. He delivered himself of a small whistle, for she was wearing the white linen, somewhat the worse for yesterday's hard use, but replete with the big hat and all the tangerine accessories, to make up for it. Even Matthew had regarded her appraisingly. " You look nice," he'd said. And what with David's whistle, she was gullible enough to believe it.

CHAPTER FOURTEEN

She suspected the worst as soon as they turned off the parkway and drove across Fifty-seventh Street towards Fifth Avenue. It was only the middle of August and hot—the same as it was when they'd left the country less than an hour ago, but nobody was wearing white dresses and big floppy hats. Everybody was wearing navy blue, or black, and most of the shop windows showed tailored suits and short fur coats. Bitterness flooded her. The Flora Rosenbach had played a dirty trick on her. It had gone out of season before she'd had half a chance to wear it.

" What's the matter ? " David asked her.

" What should be the matter ? "

" You were frowning.—Where'll I let you off ? "

" Anywhere along here. There are agencies all the way up Madison."

He stopped the car and kissed her fondly, still thinking, doubtless, that she looked like a fashion plate, and she didn't have the heart to disillusion him. " Call me at the office around one," he said. " If I'm free, we can have lunch. And be careful crossing, wait for the light."

She could feel his eye on her, so she waited, trying to remember the name of that big agency that went all the way around a corner. She walked up a block or two, and there it was, staring down at her from a second floor of a large office building. *The Cosmopolitan. Select Help in All Nationalities.*

She didn't waste time waiting for the elevator. She could have, though, because she was much too early. There wasn't a soul there, except a little man with a big moustache. He said, " The girl's don't begin to come in until eleven o'clock."

" Oh, dear.—What time is it now ? "

He pulled out a watch from his pocket. " Exactly nine forty-seven," he informed her weightily.

This was a fine business. What was she going to do for the next hour and a quarter ? She needed sheets more than ever, especially if she was going to make rags out of them while Bertha wasn't around to tame her down. But the department stores weren't open yet, either. The speciality shops might be, though, and she could use up the credit on the little suit that Julia had bought Matthew, by buying something for Elsie Miller. A gift—and a nice one—was definitely in order, and she was sure that Julia wouldn't mind.

She tried to dawdle, but she was there in no time. The bronze door swung open to her touch. The shop was air-conditioned. She shivered.

" Yes, Madame ? " The saleslady wasn't shivering, she wore immense pearl ear-rings to keep her warm.

" I want to buy a gift."

" A baby gift ? "

She shook her head. That would be jumping the gun.

" No. Something in a luncheon set, I think."

The cheapest luncheon service for four was twenty dollars. She'd never dream of spending it for herself, but Elsie was worth every penny of it, especially since it didn't really cost anything ; in fact, there was still ten dollars left of the credit. She debated whether or not to use it up on Bertha, and decided against it. Everything was so terribly hand-made and expensive, it would only upset instead of please her, so she finally settled on three uncomfortably miniscule guest towels for Candy's marble powder room, and a frighten-ingly fine handkerchief for Mrs. Payne. Buying a gift for Mrs. Payne was somewhat of a luxurious inspiration.

" Where shall I send them, Madame ? "

" I'll take them. All three in separate packages, please."

The saleslady beamed as she made out the bill. " Yes, Madame, I'll have them gift-wrapped. Thirty-three dollars and nineteen cents, including tax. Is this a charge ? "

" No," said Claudia, " I'll pay for it." She counted out the money, gratified to use up all the loose change in her purse. " Oh, dear," she discovered, " I'm short a penny."

" Oh, Madame, that's nothing ! " The saleslady gave a deprecating smile, accepted the dollar and eighteen cents, and waited.

" I know I have it with me," Claudia affably assured her, and finally fished out the credit-slip of thirty-two dollars-and-something from the very bottom of the bag.

The saleslady looked as if she'd been robbed and the smile faded from her face, beam and all. Her thin lips as much as said that if she'd known what she knew now, she certainly wouldn't have bent over backwards to have the stuff boxed and ribboned. Claudia, on the other hand, felt that the day had started off very auspiciously, and hurried back to the agency in high spirits.

She went to six agencies, to be exact—one after another, and all within a radius of a few blocks. Indeed, two agencies, a French one and a Scandinavian one, were in the same building.

Mrs. Johansen was a kindly woman, large of heart and bosom. " The girls are beginning to come back from the country now," she took the trouble to explain, " they don't want to go away. It's too lonesome, unless you take a couple. I have a very nice couple, they're over there in the corner, and I don't believe they're going to be suited with the lady who's talking to them."

Claudia followed the direction of her glance, and at that very instant the couple rose and stalked off without a word, leaving the lady who didn't suit them talking to herself with gestures. Claudia could see her wondering what she had said to offend them.

"Would you care to interview them?" Mrs. Johansen suggested.

"Yes," Claudia decided on an impulse. She might as well see what it was like to talk to a couple.

"Just take a seat, and I'll bring them right over."

The couple refused to be brought. They stared over at Claudia and shook their heads. Mrs. Johansen returned. She said she was sorry, but she didn't think it would work out. They were looking for a place in the country where other help was kept, as the man wasn't very strong. "I really think your best chance," Mrs. Johansen concluded, obviously anxious to be rid of her, "is to look in the paper for a house-worker."

"Thank you," said Claudia. Why hadn't she thought of it before? A paper cost five cents, and the employment fee was twenty dollars, single, and forty dollars for a couple. And if they didn't stay, where were you? Of course, the agency promised to give you someone else within thirty days, but if they couldn't give you anybody good the first time, how could they do it the second time? Or the third, or the fourth? Especially if their hearts weren't in it.

She bought the morning *Times* at a near-by stationer's. They had already been taken off the stand to make room for the evening papers, but the storekeeper dug one up from under the counter. What was all the rushing about? One of these days the world would meet itself on the way back.

There was no place to open the paper. She wasn't deft at opening newspapers even when she had a lot of room to work around in. She might as well find a park bench. Or, better still, go to Julia and Hartley's, where she could do some other things besides. She wanted to 'phone David to tell him she couldn't spare the time to meet him for lunch.

Watkins opened the door for her, and seemed not at all surprised to see her, so she gathered that Julia had left word that she and David might wish to stay at the house occasionally. "I just want to read the paper," she explained, and, fittingly, he led her to the dim, cool library.

" Would you care to have lunch ? The cook is off to-day, but Fanny's here ; she'll be glad to fix you something and bring it up to you on a tray."

" No, thanks," said Claudia. She had an odd feeling about going to Julia's house in her absence and ordering luncheon. Julia would have been delighted, of course, and Watkins wouldn't have offered if he hadn't wanted to, but, just the same, it wasn't quite the thing to do. Not even when they had lived here with Bertha and the children had it ever really seemed like home. Though maybe she hadn't known when she was well off ; it would be mighty restful to be in the middle of a soft Louis XV bed, and have Agnes bring in breakfast every morning. " It must be nice to be rich," she thought, particularly nice after a taste of what it meant to worry about money. She'd never actually worried about money before, even when David had had to go away. They'd been able to live so cheaply in the mountains that they'd even managed to save a little, but now, with John away, and David talking about cutting down his drawing account, it wasn't going to be easy to make ends meet ; every penny would have to be watched. " And I can't let him see me watching them either," she cautioned herself.

" Are you sure there's nothing else, Mrs. Naughton ? "

" What ?—Oh, no, thank you, Watkins. I'll just slip out when I'm ready. Don't bother about me."

" Shall I pull up the dark shades ? "

" No, I like it dim, it's so cool."

Alone, she kicked off her pumps, turned on the desk lamp, and tackled the paper. What a lot of HELP WANTED ads ! She glanced through them to see what other women were offering. Quite a few offered two-in-family, no laundry, no Sundays, and fifty dollars a week. How long had this sort of thing been going on ? Did Candy realize how fortunate she was to have come by a completely unspoiled Martha so painlessly ? If only Bertha could conjure up another cousin for a few weeks. It would probably be longer than a few weeks at that, for Bertha would be on crutches for a month at least. What an enticing position to offer a new maid : " Two adults, two children, one great Dane, and one invalid.—And would you mind sweeping up the porch, doing a little laundry (just a small mountain of it every day)—and we have to be very careful of the garbage, because the man collects only once a week, and, of course, I like the dish-towels boiled every night after supper."

"I stand a great chance," she muttered as she rustled through the paper, trying to find the column of SITUATIONS WANTED. She found it a last, tucked away at the bottom of the page. Quite a difference from the long, long HELP WANTED columns. She scanned the meagre list at a glance. A caterer, two companions, a cook (No cleaning, serving—just what I need), another cook with downstairs work (Bravo, I could do upstairs!). Oh, no, you couldn't, my mistake, "City only."— Oh, this is more like it, a *houseworker*! Oh, dear. Sleep out, 9 to 5. Another houseworker! Fond of children, by golly, no objection to country.—And a telephone number into the bargain!—WA-5, or was it WA-8? Surely she wasn't going to need glasses to read fine print? She leapt to her feet and pulled the shade up. There, that was better. WA-8. What a nasty shock. David said he was getting to the point where he had to back out of a 'phone booth to see what number he was calling from. But David was seven years older than she was, so there was an excuse for him. "We're neither of us as young as we think of ourselves," she reflected soberly. As a matter of fact, she was entirely too old to wear overalls around the house . . . which was beside the immediate issue, so why bring it up?

She dialled the number. It was engaged. She found a gold pencil on a memo pad with Hartley's initials engraved on both, and wrote the number down for later use, and turned back to the column. One more general houseworker, also with a telephone number. She blessed Mrs. Johansen for her sound advice. This, undoubtedly, would be the answer to her prayer, and for all of a nickel, with the telephone calls thrown in for nothing.

There was only one thing wrong with the solution. The numbers kept on being busy. Busy, busy, busy. The busy little busy signal began to get on her nerves. She'd better call David, and tell him not to wait lunch for her.

He said he wasn't waiting, he couldn't get out before quarter-past one, anyway.

"Oh, good," she changed her mind, "that still gives me half an hour."

It was a good thing she hadn't asked Fanny for a sandwich. It was a long, long while since she'd had lunch with David downtown.

She tried the numbers again, and still they were busy. Finally one of them answered. "I'm suited," a cold voice replied, and banged up the receiver.

She ached with an ignoble lust for retaliation. How nice it would be to have the shoe on the other foot. All she had to do was join the ranks of HELP WANTED, and then her line would be the one to be busy. She picked up the gold pencil again and started to compose an ad. After a few abortive attempts she concluded that it would avail her nothing to hide the essential facts, so she decided to inflate them.

"HOUSEworker. Young couple, two children, charming old house on river, own room, bath, unusual opportunity for right person. Telephone collect. Greenwich 7–0489."

Seeing it in black and white, she couldn't help but feel that it would be a little more accurate if she changed the adjectives around. " Charming old couple on river with double-size dog, complete with children. Unusual opportunity for person not in right mind."

Oh, well, it didn't hurt to try, especially since she could telephone the advertisement, and charge it to Hartley and Julia's number.

" There's a special rate for three days, Madame."

That didn't augur well. Didn't they expect the ad to work before three days ?

Meticulously, she asked for the charges on the ad. Four dollars and eighty-six cents ! " How does it come to so much ? " she demanded.

The voice at the other end of the wire was patient. " Four lines, Madame. Six words to a line. Plus tax."

" Have I used the whole twenty-four words ? "

" No, Madame."

" Could I cut out something to bring it down to three lines ? " she enquired thriftily.

" Whatever you say, Madame."

" Read it back over, would you ? "

She jotted the ad down, and studied it again.

" Madame, why don't you cut out the charming old house ? " the disembodied voice suggested.

" What would I do with the river ? "

" You could leave it, Madame. Two children, river, own room, bath."

She re-counted the new version. " That gives me an extra word. What can I say in one word ? "

" Why not say ' references,' Madame ? "

" Yes, of course ! Now what are the charges ? "

" Three lines, Madame. Three dollars and forty-four cents."

She hung up, quite pleased with the saving, and counted out three bills, four dimes, and a nickel. She'd left a penny short on the credit, but now she was leaving a penny too much, so by some involuted method of thinking, she was square with the world. She found stationery in the top drawer, wrote a little note to Julia, addressed it, stuck the money into an envelope, and laid it on the blotter. It was simpler to do it that way. She might forget she owed it, otherwise.

She tidied up in the small gem of a washroom concealed behind a panel of the library. It would save her doing it at David's office, where you had to use a key down the hall, which she wasn't crazy about. Some day, David planned, they would expand and have a private washroom, but not with space at five dollars a square foot.

As usual, Miss Farley was nowhere to be seen. " Come in ! " David called from his room. " The Duchess is out for lunch, she ought to be back any moment." She kissed him, noting that his desk was pretty well cleared of its usual mountain of blue-prints and papers. " It's lonesome without John, isn't it ? " She brought it out into the open.

" Very," he agreed. " But he's not missing much in the line of work. If this lull keeps up, I'll close the office and function from the country. I'll build little houses with one picture window looking into another picture window," he added with a grimace.

Her heart quickened. If only he could function from the country, with time and energy to do all the big things that he dreamed of doing—that he'd begun to do before he'd had to go away. How he hated ugly little houses that were a desecration to the beauty of the countryside. Once, a long while ago when they were first married, he had talked about building a modern cathedral. There were still cathedrals, and not houses, in his soul. " Do you really mean it ? " she asked him seriously.

" The only thing that would lure me to close this office," he harped back, almost seriously, " would be a farm.—I was a damn good farmer, if anyone should happen to ask you. I was going over our old accounts while I was waiting for you, and we showed quite a profit towards the end."

" But not enough to live on," she reminded him.

" No, not enough to live on," he conceded.

" David, are you terribly worried about money ? "

" Not terribly," he said. " We'll scrape by. But I'm

afraid if we buy the house (she noticed that he said " if " instead of " when ") we won't be able to do all the things to it that we wanted to do. Labour and materials have taken another jump."

" We can get by in it, the way it is," she said, and let it go at that. When Mr Lewellyn returned from his vacation— and it ought to be any day now—perhaps the thing to do was to rent it for another six months ; the rent was far cheaper than anything they could get elsewhere, even in the country.

The outer door opened and closed. " Miss Farley's back," he said. " Come on, let's go, where do you want to eat ? "

" Anywhere," she said. She would have been satisfied with a drugstore counter, but no, he had to take her to an expensive French place off Park Avenue. " David," she expostulated, when she saw the prices, " this is sheer piracy ! "

He didn't bat an eyelash. " What do you want to begin with ? Soup ? "

" We're having soup for supper."

" Oysters ? "

" NO ! " she exploded.

" Will you stop looking at the right-hand side ? "

" I'm fascinated at their nerve. Ninety cents for six oysters. Ninety-five cents for a shrimp cocktail ! "

" Look," he argued patiently, " I don't take a girl out very often, you know, especially one that looks like a million dollars."

Poor darling fool. Couldn't he see she looked like a piece of left-over fruit in her droopy picture hat and tangerine scarf ? " I'll have the oysters," she said gently, and felt that they had both reached new heights in love.

He ordered clams for himself. She was filled with conflict. But as they were only a nickel cheaper, why should she spoil his pleasure for a nickel ? You couldn't do anything with a nickel these days, anyway.

It broke her heart, however, to see him order an omelette when he'd had eggs for breakfast. " Scallops ? " she cajoled. They hardly ever had scallops at home, for Bertha felt that she didn't put her best foot forward with scallops. As a matter of fact, she didn't believe in them, insisting that they were nothing more than a large piece of halibut cut into little pieces by a designing fish-man.

" All right, scallops." David gave in. " Scallops for two, and Madame will have a mixed green salad."

" David, I don't want the salad *or* the scallops ! " she broke in importunately.

223

The waiter waited politely.

"Darling, make up your mind," David said, a shade too evenly.

Her spirit swooned. He'd kill her if she ordered the omelette, and yet everything else was so outrageous.

"Madame would care for a lamb chop?" the waiter offered helpfully. "Or the sole bonne-femme?"

Two and a quarter for a lamb chop, which anyone could fix. And two-seventy-five for the bonne-femme, which was nothing but a cream sauce over a piece of fish, fancied up with a canned mushroom, sliced to death. No, thank you.

"Scallops," she surrendered weakly.

"You always were, and still are, hell in a restaurant," David told her in a savage undertone, after the waiter had departed.

"You don't understand. You never see my point."

"I see your point.—Now listen, there's a time to spend, and there's a time to save. And the once in a blue moon we go to a decent restaurant, please don't make an issue over a few cents one way or the other."

He was in earnest about it, and she could sense that again his pride was at the bottom of it. "It isn't the price," she defended. "I told you that you didn't understand. It's just that I hate for us both to order the same thing."

"So we can share," he threw in. "Well, I'm not a sharer. You ought to know that by this time."

She was really angry at him. He was too high and mighty to be a sharer, was he? "I suppose you wouldn't deign to go into a restaurant where you can get a whole lunch, either!" she flung at him.

"I prefer à la carte," he told her shortly.

"So you can pay extra for bread and butter and coffee!"

It was very nearly a quarrel, a silly one, but with a principle at stake. And then the oysters came. They were warmish, and slid around in their shells like a limp hand-shake. David tasted one, and put his fork down. "This is inexcusable," he announced, and summoned the waiter in a voice that was positively kingly. "These are not fit to eat," he said.

The waiter was all theirs from that moment on. "I'm sorry, sir. What can I bring you instead, sir?" He whipped out the menu again.

"Nothing!" Claudia took over quickly. "Nothing, we're in a hurry, just the scallops."

"Yes, Madame. Immediately."

She drew a breath of relief. Now if David only wouldn't bend over backwards on a tip, they'd get by quite reasonably after all. She smiled at him beguilingly. " Don't be mad," she said. " Oysters and scallops are too much of the same, anyway."

He pinched her knee beneath the table. " Devil."

He didn't call her " devil " very often, but when he did, he got an awful lot into it. It was the sort of thing that kept them feeling like a young couple.

He had to get back to the office for a two-thirty appointment. " What are your plans ? "

" I've got a busy afternoon," she lied. " What time will you be ready to leave ? About four ? "

" Make it half-past," he said.

Again she was going to be at a loss for something to do, but she didn't want him to have her on his mind. It was as if she no longer had any roots in New York, for ten years on the farm and a year in the mountains had made her a stranger to the city. It would have been different if her mother were alive, for her mother had always been the one abiding tie that had given meaning to her trips to town. Suddenly she felt, out of nowhere, a great yearning for her mother, and with it one of those sudden, overwhelming waves of loneliness for Bobby. How nice for them that they were together, somewhere—it was only she who was the lonely one. And then, as always, she asked herself what more a woman could demand of life than David, Matthew, and Michael ? " Bertha home again, if you don't mind, please," she petitioned some vague, all-powerful Presence.

In the meantime, she had two hours on her hands with nothing to do. In the middle of the most exciting city in the world, she had nothing to do. Shameful admission. Would it hurt her to go to a museum or an art gallery ? Yes, it would hurt her very much, including her feet. High heels on hot pavements were an abomination. Some day, she knew she would have to make up for the intellectual lapses in her life, but not now. Now she just wanted two hours to pass quite painlessly, and without too much walking. Going to a movie was one way of doing it. A lot of people went to the movies in the afternoon by themselves. It took courage to do it. By some odd association, she thought of Miss Rose, alone in her little flat, with her radio, and a book from the lending library, and her memories. Maybe it was memories that eased the pain of loneliness, maybe memories sat beside you in a darkened movie house, and held your heart like a comforting hand. Maybe that was why Miss Rose could go on fitting day after day, her tape-measure hung around her neck, and the little rosette of pins a badge against her waist. Because memories held her heart from breaking.

It took one step of thinking to go from Miss Rose to Miss Tate. Well, why not ? She'd need an autumn dress sooner or later, and heaven only knew when she'd be able to come to town again. As a matter of fact, Julia would be home by the middle of September, and even if the white linen were spanking clean and the day boiling hot, she wouldn't have the nerve to meet her in it. Nor in her old navy blue, either, that Bertha had so cagily hung back in the closet for a rainy day. It would have to be a very rainy day indeed, what with the new styles pinching in at the waist, and billowing out around the hips. Not that she was hankering to billow, she merely wanted not to disgrace Julia ; she wanted also to atone for her psychological ineptness in the restaurant. Looking back upon the incident, she felt like kicking herself for making an issue over the inconsequential cost of a luncheon. What David needed at this point was a luxury-loving wife to boost his confidence, not a prudent nag to remind him of a curtailed earning power. " Have enough sense," she took herself to task, " to act like a parasite instead of an Amazon." Which could easily be the elaborate sophistry of a woman who wanted a new dress.

Whatever it was, she was aware, suddenly, that her infirmity of purpose was blocking the sidewalk, and suddenly the quickest short-cut to the dress, now that she'd thought of Miss Rose, was to place the burden of responsibility on Miss Tate's capable shoulders. Then Julia couldn't complain, no matter how she looked, though of course she'd have to tie Miss Tate's hands, by making it clear that Rosenbach originals were out of the question.

The vast store was almost deserted through the late August lull of shoppers, and the sixth floor, to her disappointment, showed not a single sale-rack to mar its carpeted perfection. She was tempted to turn around and take the next elevator down, when, to her astonishment, the floor-manager recognized her, or perhaps he just recognized the white linen ; or perhaps it was his sole business to stand by the elevator and remember anything and everything. At any rate he murmured, " Miss Tate, of course ? " And she nodded. There wasn't anything she could do about it. The fat was in the fire, to borrow Bertha's expression.

The damned packages added to the fire. Miss Tate's alert brown eyes didn't miss a trick, much less the label. "Buying pretties?" she chirped, as she led Claudia off to the big corner dressing-room.

"You'd better put me in a little one," Claudia wanted to warn her, but Miss Tate, who happened not to be busy—who happened, indeed, to have just that day returned from her vacation with an impressive coat of tan—was performing exactly as if Julia were along. "Oh, dear," thought Claudia, "this is a big mistake." She knew Miss Tate was going to have a great shock when, finally, she would stand revealed in a five-dollar slip, mended to the screaming-point by Bertha's thrifty fingers. Ignominiously, she put the moment off as long as she could. "I'm not sure I'll be able to get what I want," she began, a little hesitantly, "and in that case I don't want to take up your time."

Miss Tate gave a gay little laugh. "You cute thing, we'll find *exactly* what you want, some stunning new things just came in. I've got the best of them tucked away for my special customers. What about a navy three-piece suit? I have a precious little Nella Hilton—she's really doing some wonderful designs; I shouldn't say it, but I prefer her to Rosenbach, this fall. Although," she added tactfully, "that white linen did very nicely for a summer frock, and you'll be glad to start on it this winter if you go south. But just wait till you see this little suit, you'll adore it!"

"I already have a navy blue," Claudia managed to get in edgewise, and hoped to God that Miss Tate didn't remember it.

If Miss Tate remembered it, she preferred not to. "You can't have too much navy blue for fall," she declared firmly. "But for an extra ensemble, I want you to see a cocoa-brown two-piece dress that's simply out of this world."

Claudia shook her head. "Miss Tate, you don't understand. I want something very inexpensive."

Miss Tate gave the impression of poising in mid-air. "Something around a hundred and fifty?"

"Less," said Claudia starkly. "Much less. I can't afford the same kind of clothes my sister-in-law wears, and that's why I probably shouldn't have bothered you, but I thought there might be a sale."

Miss Tate's eyes narrowed, and she didn't say anything

for quite a long while, and then, finally, she spoke—almost harshly, Claudia thought. "I want to tell you something about that sister-in-law of yours," she said, and before Claudia could open her mouth in Julia's quick defence, Miss Tate swept on in a voice that fairly shook with emotion. "Somebody," she said, "must have told her that my husband's been an invalid for a number of years——"

Claudia felt a pang of guilt—she recalled having mentioned it to Julia the day they'd bought the white linen—"I'm sorry," she murmured.

"It's nothing I ever talk about myself," Miss Tate quickly explained, "and if it weren't for what I'm going to tell you, I wouldn't be mentioning it now.—But do you know what she did?"

Claudia shook her head abjectly.

"There hasn't been a week," Miss Tate went on, in her funny little way of keeping her lips from moving in lieu of emphasis, "that she hasn't sent flowers—he adores flowers—and when she sailed for Europe last week, she left a standing order for them. And in addition—just listen to this—in addition, her chauffeur calls every afternoon to take him for a ride in the park. Now is that something, or is that not something?"

"That's something," said Claudia humbly. It didn't add up to so much when you came right down to it, but it added up to a great deal that she hadn't known about Julia.

Miss Tate flicked at her eyes, and gave a dry sniff. "Now look," she got back to business, "don't take off your dress, we're going down to the débutante shop. It's not my department"—she gave a little wink—"but I can get away with murder occasionally."

The débutante department was two floors down, but Miss Tate knew her way around, anyway. She produced a smart little cocoa-coloured twill dress at twenty-nine fifty, a tiny hat with a gold feather for eight dollars and seventy-five cents, and a pair of brown shoes for twelve dollars. It all fell together in no time at all, and Miss Tate stood back and admired her handiwork with the detachment of an artist. "You couldn't look more adorable no matter how much you spent," she announced. "I mean it."

Claudia gazed at her reflection in the mirror with a sense that she wasn't so old after all, if she could get away with a débutante's outfit.

"The only thing it needs," Miss Tate squinted, "is just to pinch it up a wee bit more on the left side."

" Could Miss Rose do it ? "

Miss Tate lowered her voice. " Miss Rose isn't allowed on this floor, she's a custom-fitter. And, sweetie, on second thoughts, do you know what I think ? I think you can get away with that skirt just as it is. Look. We'll draw the belt one notch tighter.—Oh, what I wouldn't give for a figure like yours !—There. I wouldn't *dream* of spending money on an alteration. Why, you could wear the whole ensemble right out this minute, just as it is ! Why don't you, and I could send the white linen for you ? "

It was a good idea. The cocoa-brown would be excellent for David's morale. And for her own, too.

Miss Tate walked with her to the elevator. " Sweetie, you look a little tired," she remarked with concern. " Too much vacationing ? "

" No, I haven't been away," said Claudia.

" Neither have I," said Miss Tate. " I couldn't leave my husband."

" But where did you get that wonderful coat of tan ? "

Miss Tate did her little trick of making her voice disappear and using her lips instead. " The roof. And a sunlamp.

" Oh," said Claudia. What a nice woman Miss Tate had turned out to be. On an impulse, she gave her the handkerchief that she'd bought for Mrs. Payne. What Mrs. Payne didn't know would never bother her.

David thought she was somebody else coming in, and the beauty of it was that she was hardly late. " Turn around," he said.

She turned around.

" That's not all you, around the hips, is it ? "

" I'll slap your face," she said. " It isn't any of it me.— How much ? "

She could see that he was shell-shocked when it came to guessing what she paid for things. " It isn't reduced," she helped him along. " This is strictly new merchandise, as they say."

" A hundred and twenty-five," he played safe.

She was pleased to think that she looked so expensive, and he was pleased that she'd spent so much on herself. Later, after the tonic effect of it had penetrated, she would tell him that the whole business came to less than fifty. Then he could spend what she hadn't spent on the new suit he needed, and they'd just about break even.

He had a surprise for her, too. Instead of parking the car, he had had it greased and washed. The windows glistened. She had the grace to blush when, later, they picked up the children at Candy's and stopped at Elsie's to call for Bluff. Elsie's station-wagon was in the driveway. "It's a fine mess," said David. "The least we can do is to have it washed for her."

"It's all right, I bought her a luncheon set," said Claudia.

CHAPTER FIFTEEN

THE advertisement began to work towards noon of the next day, and what with four collect calls and two train fares, Claudia glumly decided that she might just as well have paid an agency fee. She engaged the second train fare, chiefly because she didn't want the whole experiment to be written off to a total loss of money, time, and effort.

Her name was Lena. "Is she a witch?" Matthew whispered, as she took over the kitchen on the morning of her arrival.

"Shhh. Everybody can't be pretty."

"Why does she wear those shoes?"

"They're not shoes, they're carpet slippers," Claudia enlightened him morosely.

"Why?"

"Because she gets forty dollars a week instead of fifty, I suppose."

"What?"

"Nothing."

"I said 'hello' and she only said 'hello' back."

"Be grateful for small favours."

"I hate Lena," he gave forth his verdict. "What time is Bertha coming home?"

"In a few weeks."

His face fell. "But I thought she was coming to-day!"

"Excuse me. I forgot to report to you. Bertha's niece called for her while we were in New York yesterday and took her to Brooklyn."

"Why did you let her?"

"I didn't know about it. Martha told me when we got home."

"Were you mad?"

"Only technically.—Now, Matthew, please. No more questions. I have to show Lena where everything is."

She spent a good part of the next day cleaning up after Lena. "You'll burst a blood-vessel," David cautioned her, when she opened the oven before supper. "Come on, let's go out for a breath of air before we eat."

She closed the oven door with alacrity, for she could see the sun setting over the river, outdoing itself. She found half a dozen thick, uneven slices of bread that Lena had cut for no good reason, and they fed the ducks, and then sat on the bank watching them.

"Another ad called up this afternoon," she mentioned as they drifted back to the house.

"Why ? " David asked, sounding like Matthew.

"I guess she reads slowly. But I told her to come, anyway, sight unseen, and bring her clothes. She has a short reference, but a nice voice."

So Bessie arrived at noon-time the following day, richly dark in complexion as well as voice, and resplendent in a purple dress and large gold ear-rings.

"What's that smell ? " Matthew asked, in a loud whisper.

"Perfume. Mostly."

"I don't like it," he said.

Claudia didn't like it, either. She didn't like a number of things about Bessie—the way she left her bed unmade the next morning, or the way she ran through a pound of butter in no time, nor the way she put the string beans on to cook at three o'clock in a big pot of water, and then let them sit until they became limp and dreary.

"She's a congenital par-boiler," Claudia told David on the way home from the station that evening. "It's in her blood. Like chewing gum."

David said, "You're just spoiled after Bertha. Also you're dead tired."

"I'm tired of cleaning up after them. It's easier to manage by myself."

"You're not going to. Overcooking string beans is no reason to dismiss anyone ! "

"It isn't the only reason," she blurted out. "She eats too much ! "

"Shame on you," he said.

She could feel her cheeks grow hot. "I don't care how it sounds, it's true. I've spent more on food in two days than Bertha's bills came to in a week. There was plenty in the refrigerator for lunch, including split-pea soup, but she ordered two pork chops and ate the baby's apple-sauce. She also used up almost the whole bottle of cream for breakfast over her cereal, and had bacon and eggs besides. And took half the morning over it, too."

"You don't sound pretty," he said.

"I don't feel pretty. I can feel myself getting mean around the lips."

He softened. "Look, darling, watch your lips, and keep her."

His own lips could have stood a little watching at supper. The leg of lamb was over-salted and raw in the middle, the potatoes were sodden with grease, and his fork had egg on it. It was the fork that did it. The same as the oysters had done it. David was like that.

She kept up a pretence of looking for a maid, just to make him feel better, but she didn't bestir herself. "It doesn't pay go to through this upset, Bertha will be back before we know it," she placated him. "And, anyway, the secret of doing your own work is to make up your mind that you're going to like it."

"You also have to make up your mind that you're not going to be able to do anything else," he said.

"Oh, that isn't necessarily true." Nonchalantly, she dabbed the last of a bottle of expensive perfume behind each ear. "I hope Julia brings me more perfume from Paris."

"When's the last time you read a good book ? " he persisted.

"You flatter me. I was never much of a reader."

"When's the last time you went over to see Candy ? "

"I haven't. Purposely. She drove her mother-in-law and Annie over here yesterday, and it was the first time since the accident that she's taken anyone in the car. It was quite a step for her."

"That's a rationalization if ever I heard one.—When's the last time you went down to the village ? "

"What is this, an examination ?—I market by 'phone, it's much easier.—Isn't it nice of the grass," she forestalled him quickly, "to stop growing in August ? Next week will be the second Saturday you won't have had to cut it."

"It'll make up for it in September," he said. "If I were sure we were going to buy the place, I'd begin to have those white pines moved, this is the best time for transplanting evergreens."

Again she found herself wishing that she could say, " I think we ought to buy the place." But if they used the money from the sale of the farm, they'd have nothing to fall back on, and the uncertainty of the future was beginning to frighten her. It was beginning to frighten David too. She could tell that, without his saying so. " Oh, I think I like the evergreens where they are," she replied lightly.

" Except they'd be in the way of the library wing. The wing we're not going to build on," he amended wryly.

She had no answer for him. He put out the light, and opened all the windows, and the room was filled with sound. " Noisy damn place, isn't it ? Listen——"

" I am.—Did you ever notice how peepers sound like sleigh-bells in the distance ? " She was glad that there were just the frogs and katydids. She still couldn't bear the sound of the whip-poor-will, it tore her heart to pieces.

One thing she hadn't reckoned on, and that was that there would be any urgency about deciding whether or not they would buy the house. And then Mr. Lewellyn returned from his vacation and drove over to see them the following Saturday morning. A malicious rainfall had put ideas into the grass, and David was mowing it in the high spots, when Mr. Lewellyn's dusty sedan drove up. Claudia recognized it from the kitchen window, and kept on making a spaghetti sauce for lunch. Elsie Miller had got the recipe straight from the mother of an Italian policeman, and had presented it to Claudia complete with herbs, so it had that superior flavour that came from special seasoning and long simmering. It would never be Bertha's idea of a Saturday lunch ; therefore Claudia figured that it was just as well to get a lot of it under their belts before she came back.

Matthew burst in. He smelled the garlic, looked into the pot, and gave one of his better shudders. " You don't have to eat it, I have a piece of calves' liver for you," she said pleasantly.

He looked more than ever agonized. " Daddy says will you come out," he remembered hastily.

She wasn't pleased to leave the sauce at a crucial point, simply to hear that Mr. Lewellyn had probably unearthed another of his endless rumpus-rooms or swimming-pools for their consideration. David met her halfway across the lawn. " I have spaghetti sauce on," she enlightened him curtly.

" You may have spaghetti sauce, but you also have no house

to live in," he informed her. "It seems that somebody's dickering for the adjoining fifty acres."

"Do they want this place, too?"

"It's a possibility."

She felt like Mrs. Payne. "Is this just a scare to get us to make up our minds in a hurry?"

"I don't think so. In any case, our deal is off. The man who wants to buy the property has a development project in mind."

"What kind of a project?"

"Little houses on quarter-acre plots."

"Picture windows," she supplemented.

"Exactly," said David. "Even if we buy this place, our property value is shot to hell."

"Oh," said Claudia.

Mr. Lewellyn came hopping over to them with his invisible little limp. It was a novelty to see anyone who had just come back from a vacation looking paler than ever. Mr. Lewellyn didn't sunburn, he freckled sparsely, and in a way that added little, if any, lustre to his pallid skin. "This is just a crying shame," he commiserated, with a dampish handshake. "I was just telling your husband that the only way to really protect yourselves is to buy the adjoining property, but what you'd do with nearly a hundred acres is more than I can imagine."

"This used to be a fine farm," said David. "It's a crime to tear down those barns and silos."

"Surely," Mr. Lewellyn agreed. "I hadn't thought of that. I wonder if it would pay to move them?"

"It wouldn't. Not with costs what they are."

Mr. Lewellyn sighed. "It's just too bad. It isn't my client, so it's out of our hands. That's why the minute I got wind of it I thought I'd better come right over and tell you."

"I'm glad you did," said David, who looked anything but glad.

"Of course, if you did buy this place, anyway," Mr. Lewellyn went on thoughtfully, "it might be a very shrewd investment, because you could probably turn it over at a considerable profit for an extension of the housing estate. Any sort of land with water on it is at a great premium, and the price on this place is considerably lower than the adjoining property. Fortunately, your five hundred dollars rental constitutes an option until September eighth, if I recall correctly. So all in all, it's still a good investment, as far as real estate goes."

"We're not buying a home for real estate investment," David returned tersely. "We'd buy it to live in. On the other hand, we don't want to live next to an estate of fifty or more houses."

"Surely *not*," Mr. Lewellyn fervently agreed. "I daresay the only thing to do is to find you another place, probably much nicer, because, as I always say, everything happens for the best."

"That's what I always say, too," Claudia commented dryly, after Mr. Lewellyn had driven off in a cloud of dust instead of on a broomstick.

"I'll go down for the mail," said David.

"Can I go, too?" Matthew put in out of the blue.

Claudia jumped. Her nerves were probably more frazzled than she realized. "You scared the wits out of me, please knock before you talk," she reprimanded him.

"Can I?" he insisted.

"No," said David, and meant it.

"I need you to help me, anyway," Claudia inserted quickly. She pinioned his arm as David walked off towards the station-wagon. "Let Daddy alone," she said in an undertone.

"What's the matter, is he mad?"

"No, he's just disappointed."

"Why?"

"Somebody might buy the property next door."

He couldn't see the connection, that was obvious. "Daddy loved those big silos and the barn," she explained. "Want to shell some peas for me?"

"No," he said in David's voice.

"I didn't think you did." She gave him a friendly shove. "Go on and play."

"I have nothing to play with."

"Too bad about you."

"Can I have my new airplane?"

"No. Save it for a rainy day."

"I can't use it in the rain."

"Not that kind of rain."

"What kind of rain?"

"You've got the old airplane," she evaded.

"I could have a race with both of them."

"I wouldn't."

"I would."

This was one of his better moments. She kissed him, and then pulled his hair to take the curse off of it.

235

" Hey ! " he protested. To hide his emotion, he pulled away and stomped off, engaged deeply in some imaginary project of his own. " Come on, Bluff ! " he called out importantly. Bluff dashed out from around the side of the house, and they stood for a moment looking at each other, all dressed up and nowhere to go. " C'mon ! " said Matthew, with a large gesture. Bluff followed him trustingly. Poor Matthew. Poor Bluff. Poor David. All three of them had little empty places in their hearts.

Like a fool, she began to cry.

David was a long time getting the mail. There was no doubt in Claudia's mind that he was driving around the property next door. It was almost noon, so she fed the baby and gave Matthew his lunch on the kitchen table. The calves' liver was for supper, so he was agreeably surprised to find a piece of yesterday's chicken, flanked by a baked potato and some spinach, which, by some strange miracle, Matthew had suddenly begun to like. " All I need is for some smart alec to find out that spinach is injurious," Claudia had once remarked menacingly to David. " It is," replied David, who couldn't bear the stuff.

And now Matthew, with a loud scraping of his plate, was demanding more spinach.

This was a sheer embellishment of the ridiculous, particularly since there wasn't any more. " Have some apple sauce," said Claudia.

" Is that all there is for dessert ? "

She produced a cup-cake.

" It has no icing on."

" Sue me," she said, and thought what an unattractive expression it was.

" What does soomee mean ? "

" There is no such word. I meant, ' Dear me '." She glanced at her watch. It was time for David to be back. She certainly wouldn't take any chances and put the spaghetti on, rather it were undercooked than overcooked.

She cleaned out the ice-box while she waited for him. What a lot of doo-dabs were left, now that there were no Lenas or Bessies around to eat them up. She put them all together, and married them with some bacon fat. It would save opening an extra can of dog-food.

Bluff read her mind. " Knock me over, why don't you ? " she said.

He was almost completely wooed by the bacon fat. Except for two slices of beets remarkably untouched, he licked his aluminum bowl clean with a great deal of sliding and pushing. Claudia regarded the beets with annoyance, and picked them up and fed each slice to him by hand. He accepted them. She found them later, laid daintily by the pantry door, still intact. " Phooey," she said.

David wasn't talkative when he got back, and she didn't ask him anything. She said, " Spaghetti," and he said, " Fine." It was nice of him to say " fine," because she could tell that he didn't feel like eating.

" Any mail ? "

" Oh, yes." He dug into his pocket and produced a handful of bills and a letter from Julia. She opened the envelope, Paris posted, and thinly important. What good-looking handwriting Julia had—slim and aristocratic, and like herself, difficult to decipher at a glance. Now was no time to try to do it, though, with lunch half on. She put it aside, and then promptly forgot about it. " Oh, Julia's letter ! " she remembered, tardily, and brought it to the table. " Funny for her to write, she never writes letters when she's away. Read it aloud."

" I don't like to read aloud," said David. He glanced through it while he drank his coffee. " Nothing too important," he said. " They just want to know if we've bought the place, and if not, why not."

Claudia didn't say anything. He went on reading. " Julia says she bought you a coat which she's sending on with their trunks ; they're flying back instead of taking the boat."

" I suppose they want to get started on the solarium." The coat would be a life-saver, but she refrained from mentioning it. She said, " One of the nicest things about having money is to be able to buy people presents.—I had a taste of it with the credit. Elsie hasn't got over that luncheon-set yet.—She doesn't look well, but it's only sinus.—What else does Julia say ? "

" Read it for yourself."

She took the letter. " They seem to be having a lovely time," she kept up a running comment, " sort of a delayed honeymoon after all these years.—It's the first time I can remember that they've been away together. It's always been either a business trip or a fishing-trip for Hartley, or a social cruise for Julia."

" Are you making conversation ? "

" Yes. Like mad. I'm almost as disappointed as you are about the house."

" I think you're relieved."

" In a way," she confessed. " Maybe living in New York for the winter would simplify life."

" Back to Julia and Hartley's ? "

" Don't tempt me !—No, seriously, once Bertha's home again, I can begin to look for an apartment."

" What makes you think you'll find one ? "

" You can't tell what'll turn up.—Do you think we'll ever land in Paris ? "

David gave a short laugh. " Not at the rate I'm going."

" I don't think I'd be very good at sight-seeing," she said. " Cathedrals would get me down."

" You'd see Chartres," he told her firmly. " And La Sainte Chapelle."

" I've never heard of La Sainte Chapelle."

" A lot of people haven't, or if they have, they don't bother with it, they go a few blocks on to Notre-Dame."

" Or the Louvre," said Claudia.

" Or the Louvre."

" How long since you've been to Paris, David ? "

" Fifteen years."

" Two years before we met."

" Yes."

" I'm glad you had it, anyway. It'll do for both of us." She finally slipped the letter back into its envelope. " I'd answer it," she said, "but they'll be back by the time they'd get it."

" Two weeks from next Monday," said David, and then he added, " Maybe we could manage to go out to the airport and meet them."

" I'd like to," said Claudia, and found to her surprise that she meant it. She felt a sudden small lift of happiness. It was pleasant to look forward to meeting Julia and Hartley.

She cleared the table, and sent David and Matthew off to catch some fish for supper—which she was reasonably sure they wouldn't catch, or she wouldn't have sent them.

As luck would have it, though, they caught two perch —puny little bony things that weren't worth the cleaning. " I'll fry them for you for breakfast," she put it off.

" Broil is better," David advised her. She contained herself with effort. He didn't know a blessed thing about cooking, but just the same she had a feeling that he was going to be a nuisance about those nasty little fish.

Her feeling was right. "Have you got a slice of lemon in the house?" he followed up.

"Yes, I have a slice of lemon in the house," she replied. "What are you biting my head off for?"

If he didn't know, she wasn't going to try to explain anything as subtle as the emotion that flooded through her. "You can just take your slice of lemon and your perch," she said coldly, "and shove them back in the river."

"You told me to catch some fish, didn't you?"

"You didn't have to go and do it."

She served the perch that evening as a separate course, so that they wouldn't be hanging over her head all night. They weren't very good, basically, but David certainly went overboard about them. He'd been the same way on the farm. Chicken could be tough, or beef could be stringy, but if it was their own, he'd insist that it was wonderful. Although these perch "might have been a little too small to broil," he reconsidered, tentatively, through a mouthful of bones. And then the telephone bell rang, and they forgot about the fish, because it was John on the wire.

"He just got in," David reported, replacing the telephone. "We'll give him a little while with Candy, and then I think we'd better go over."

"How long can he stay?"

"Over-night."

She said, with effort, "I can't leave the children." She was a coward to be glad that she was to be spared the look on John's lean young face, and the anguish in Candy's eyes. It brought it all back. For as long as she lived she would never forget the twilight evening when she'd said goodbye to David. She hadn't known that he was heading for New Guinea. It might have been Africa or Italy. But Candy knew that John was going to Korea.

It must have brought it all back to David, too. He sat up reading for a long while after he came back. She didn't ask him to go to bed. There were times when a man wanted to be alone, and this was one of the times.

They drove over to Candy's the next afternoon with the children, and Matthew, without being told, never once mentioned Uncle John. They didn't stay very long. "I have to give the baby an early supper, or he won't go to sleep,"

Claudia said. She couldn't talk on the way home, and Matthew was frightened. He said, " Are you crying ? "

" Of course not ! "

" Mamma has a little headache," David said.

He saw to it that she could lock herself in the bathroom to cry it out. She felt so helpless. There was nothing she could do for Candy, or say to Candy, to lessen the torment in her groping young soul. Candy had even turned away from God.

CHAPTER SIXTEEN

MICHAEL woke the next morning with a sniffle and a slight fever. " It's nothing," Claudia said. " I'll keep him in bed, and he'll be all right by to-morrow."

" You're improving," David told her. " There was a time when you'd magnify a sniffle into everything from measles to pneumonia."

It was true. It was as if, without knowing when or how it happened, she had achieved an inner security, invulnerable to panic.

" How are you going to manage to see Candy to-day ? " he went on. " Call Mrs. Miller to come over for a while ? "

" Elsie's been having those awful sinus headaches. I'll tell Candy Michael's laid up, and ask her to come over here to lend me a hand."

David nodded his approval. " Do that. Keep an eye on her for the next day or two. It'll be tough going for her until she gets used to it."

" It's not something you get used to," said Claudia. " You just learn to accept it."

Candy didn't come over, however. She sent Martha instead. It was a wasted trip. " But everything is all finished already ! " Martha exclaimed in surprise. " You have nothing for me to help ! "

" No, I haven't really," Claudia admitted. " I just wanted Mrs. Payne to get away for a little."

" I wish she would," said Martha sadly. " It is terrible to see her so white and quiet. During the night, I heard her crying."

" I know," said Claudia.

" She does not want anyone around her," Martha went on. " Yesterday she took the baby over to her mother-in-law's, and told me to have a day off and go to Brooklyn to see Bertha. I did not like to leave her, so I did not stay long."

" I wish I could get over to see Bertha.—How is she ? "

" Worried. Always worried about how you are getting along. She would be surprised if she knew how good you manage." Martha smiled. " She would be worried you are getting along too good without her."

" She needn't," said Claudia. " It's just that you have to learn to manage without people, whether you like it or not. And I don't like it. I'll be mighty glad to see her again."

" It will not be long, she thinks. The doctor says she can walk soon without her crutches. And already she is beginning to help Hedwig with the cooking."

" I must 'phone her this evening," Claudia reminded herself.

They talked a little more and then Martha went home. " Thanks just the same," said Claudia.

Michael's four-o'clock temperature was normal, and the next day he was out in his play-pen. It was a pretty day with the trees dappling patterns on the grass, and the river throwing a thousand diamonds back to the sun. " Oh, Bobby ! " her heart cried out, " where are you——? " Then Michael tripped against the rail and she ran to pick him up. Matthew stopped loading twigs on the barrow, at five cents a load. " He's bleeding ! " he announced, respectfully.

" Just a little cut where his tooth hit his lip," she said. " Run in and get me the bottle of iodine from the medicine chest."

" It's going to sting," Matthew said with relish.

It was in the middle of stinging when Mr. Lewellyn's grey sedan appeared. " That man has a way of coming at the most inconvenient times," Claudia muttered.

" What ? " said Matthew.

" Nothing.—Run and tell him I'll be right there."

Mr. Lewellyn was in a chatty mood. He told her he'd just stopped by to see Mrs. Payne—" Mrs. Payne, senior," he made clear, and she was a brick. Simply a brick. He'd thought maybe she'd want to sell that big house now that she was alone, but no, she was going on just the same as always. " I ad*mire* that kind of spirit," Mr. Lewellyn earnestly proclaimed.

" So do I," said Claudia, wondering if Mr. Lewellyn had driven over on a hot day just to call Mrs. Payne a brick. " Has the property next door been sold ? " She came to the point.

"No, it hasn't!" Mr. Lewellyn's tenuous voice took on a new lease of breath. "That's what I came to tell you.—In fact, it's all up in the air, because Mr. Jameson—the big estate down the road, you know—got word of the deal, and he's terribly against the development, naturally. So he's going to fight it on the grounds of a zoning law that he insists takes in this particular area of river road. One-acre or two-acre building lots, I'm not certain which, but, either way, it's surely going to affect the sort of housing this dreadful investment corporation wants to put up.—I thought Mr. Naughton might be glad to know it."

"He will be," Claudia assured him, but inwardly she thought, "This leaves us just where we were before."

David used almost the same words when she told him about it that evening. "Mr. Tooth-paste objects," she said, and David said, with a one-sided grin, "Now where do we stand?"

"I wish I knew," said Claudia. "David, do you realize that this is the first time we've ever dawdled over a decision?"

"Yes," he said. "It must be a sign of age."

"Or something," she amended. "What kind of a day did you have?"

"I was busy for a change," he returned, with a degree of contentment. "What kind of a day did you?"

"Fine. I had so much time on my hands, I almost read a book."

"Maybe there's something in what you say," he commented soberly, "about putting yourself in a frame of mind to do what you have to."

"If you ask me, it's easier to do than not do," she offered, for what it was worth.

He gave her a quick glance, started to say something, and then changed his mind. "It looks as if things are going to pick up," he remarked, after a moment.

"That's good," she said.

He found his pipe, and packed tobacco into it in a way he hadn't done for a long while—as if he and the pipe were one with each other. He'd hardly ever smoked a pipe in the last year; he'd even gone over to cigars, like Hartley. "By the way," he said (again, as if he'd read her thoughts), "I forgot to tell you that Watkins 'phoned the office to let me know he got a cable to meet Hartley and Julia at noon next Monday. Do you still want to drive in with me?"

"Yes, I do. I suddenly realize it's nice to have family. I used to scoff at it. And I'd like to have flowers in the house when they get there. There's a florist in the village that can take the order. I'll send a dozen of the longest stemmed yellow roses I can get, Julia loves them."

"That would be nice," said David, and she was glad he didn't tell her that it was a foolish extravagance, since flowers were a routine part of Julia's housekeeping.

"Are you going to leave the children with Candy?" he asked.

"No. Ever since John's gone, I can tell it's a strain on her to be with them. Anything that's normal or part of her old life seems to upset her. She said she could spare Martha to stay with them.—Or if anything slips up, Annie says she's always willing to come over. Only I hate asking."

"So do I," said David. "But it'll do you good to get away from the place for a few hours."

"At least," said Claudia, "I can wear my new dress before full skirts go out of style.—I wonder if Julia will spot that it came from the débutante department?"

"You have your worries," said David.

She kicked him, and they felt very close.

Monday turned out to be a perfect day for an autumn dress of cocoa-brown, not one of those Indian summer days that were hotter than July, and stickier. There was more than a hint of autumn in the air, with a real wind tossing a skittering of leaves underneath the shrubs and bushes. Claudia called David to the window. "Do you see what I see across the river, or do I imagine it?"

"You'd have to be blind not to see them."

"What?"

"Those two ducks."

"I don't mean them, I mean that row of elms, they're beginning to turn already."

"It could be blight," said David, who was being arbitrary. "What time do you expect Martha over?"

"Nine. It's only five to.—Planes aren't ahead of time as a rule, are they?"

"They're more apt to be late. I want to stop off at the office first, and I'll check with the airport from there.—I hear a car coming. Ready?"

"Gloves. Handkerchief. Yes, I'm ready.—How do I look?"

"Fine."

"You're not looking. Look!"

"I am. Fine."

That was as much as she was going to get from him. She

243

took it out on Bluff. "Will you get away, you big clown! Don't drool all over me!—Oh, darling, you didn't mean to—go ahead and drool if you want."

David said, all of a sudden, "You look very pretty."

She knew it was just because she'd kissed Bluff. "You don't fool me," she said, "take a peep at Michael, will you, and see why he's so quiet?"

"He's thinking," David reported. "Why is he in his crib?"

"I'd rather have Martha keep him indoors until it gets a little warmer."

"Mother!" Matthew shouted up from downstairs. "Candy's here!" There was a note of relief in his voice. Martha was somewhat of a bore, but Candy was fun; or she used to be.

"That's odd," said Claudia. "I wonder why she didn't send Martha?"

And then Candy was running up the stairs, and she stood there, staring at them, with her back against the door. Claudia's only thought was that something had happened to John. Her knees went weak, she wanted to go to Candy, but it was like being in a bad dream, trying to move and not being able to.

David reached her first. He, too, must have thought that something had happened to John, the way he steadied her with both hands on her shoulders. "What is it, Candy?"

"The radio!" She had to swallow before she could go on. "The radio. It just came over the radio."

"You can't go by the radio," said David. "You don't even know where he is."

Candy shook her head. Her voice, when it finally came, was hardly a voice. "It isn't John. There was a plane crash at Gander an hour ago. A Paris plane, on the way to New York. I rushed right over because I thought you'd have heard something."

The colour left David's face, but that was all that happened to him. He stepped to the radio on the table between the beds and turned it on. There was only the nine o'clock chatter about this and that. He turned it off again.

Matthew's voice banged at the door. "Mother!"

Candy opened it part way. "Mother's dressing."

He got his toe in, anyway. "Who's Dad 'phoning to?" he wanted to know, with that odd sentiency that Claudia had noticed in him of late.

"The airport, to see if the plane's late," said Candy.
"Now run along, I'll be right down."

"Are you going to stay here to-day instead of Martha ? "

"Yes. No. I'm going to take you and Michael home with
me. So run and get whatever you want to bring along to
play with."

"Oh, boy ! " said Matthew. " I'll bring my airplane.
There's lot's of room to fly it over at your place."

Candy closed the door.

"I can't reach the airport," said David. He turned to
Claudia. " I won't wait. You stay here, darling. I'll call
you."

"I'm going with you."

"Don't give a thought to the children," Candy said. " I'll
keep them over-night. Or as long as you want." She caught
Claudia's hand, and pulled her back into the room. " Does
God really know what He's doing ? " she asked tremulously.

"I think He does," said Claudia.

"Even though it doesn't seem so ? "

"Even though it doesn't seem so."

"You ought to know, "said Candy.

They hardly talked during the ride to New York. Once
or twice Claudia glanced at the set profile of David's face,
and turned her eyes away again, not wanting to intrude,
even in spirit, upon a grief as private and as special as this.
No matter how separate their ways of life had kept them,
Hartley and he were brothers, and in the hours of crisis they
had come close to each other. She remembered how the war
and David's illness and Bobby's death had drawn them
together, and although David was strong and his emotions
leashed, she knew that he could not help wishing at this
moment that Hartley and he had always been close, other
than in the spaces of need. A little vein that twitched in his
temple and the way his jaw-bone worked told the sorrow
that was reaching deep into his soul.

There wasn't much traffic at this hour of the morning,
and what with David's driving fast and steady, it didn't
seem long before they saw the skyline of New York taking
shape. As they turned into Madison Avenue, David slowed
down. " It's not ten o'clock, the afternoon papers aren't
out yet," he said.

They drove up to Hartley and Julia's house. It looked
just as it always looked, with the proud lions guarding it,

and the soft net curtains uniform throughout, with the dim sweeping outline of drapery shadowed from within. David rang the bell. " I can't live through the next few minutes," Claudia thought. But she knew that she would, because she had lived through enough to know that she could. She felt the touch of David's hand on her arm. " Here we go again," he said, with a small, twisted smile. She wet her dry lips. " Here we go again," she said.

Watkins opened the door. One look at his face, and hope died. " I telephoned the country, sir," he said in a low voice. " Miss Candy said you were on your way in."

They were all there, gathered in the back of the hall— Fanny and Agnes and the cook, white and blotched with weeping. Claudia was glad that they were weeping. She was glad that there were flowers—the yellow roses she had sent, and white chrysanthemums with Miss Tate's card attached, and many others besides. " We didn't have to order any," Fanny gulped. " We were going to, but we thought there was enough. Her room is full." The tears ran down her cheeks. " Oh, Mother of God," she cried, and covered her face with her hands. Fanny was the closest to Julia. " Fanny looks after Julia," Claudia remembered explaining to David. Now her grief made her not a servant, but a friend.

Watkins motioned David aside. Claudia could hear what he said. " There's a reporter in the library, sir."

" I'll talk to him," said David.

There were pictures of Julia and Hartley in all the evening papers. Fanny and Agnes and the cook hung over them. They were pictures that they'd never seen before, pictures taken quite a while ago. " So pretty," Agnes said, blowing her nose. " Like a honeymoon couple. I always thought she was beautiful. Maybe not beautiful, but fine-looking. From the top of her head down. And Mr. Hartley, too."

The cook didn't say anything. She turned away, and went downstairs. " Cook's taking it hard," said Agnes. " Awful hard, poor thing."

It was a strange day. There was nothing to do, nothing that could be done. Agnes served lunch for them in the library. " Please try to eat," Claudia coaxed. " These are brook trout. Julia loved them."

David smiled a little. " They look almost as good as the perch you fixed." Still, it was hard to swallow and they left the table with the food scarcely touched.

There was an envelope on the desk. He picked it up. It

was the note she had written to Julia, telling her about the advertisement, and enclosing the money for it. Claudia wondered why she didn't cry. It was poignant things like this that broke your heart. . . .

Later, friends began to come, and Julia's two elderly aunts from Boston, and some members of Hartley's club. They were all deeply shocked. They said, each in his own way, that it was hard to believe that anything like this could happen to someone you knew, someone who was close to you. How true that was, Claudia reflected. How many times in the past year the same thought had occurred to her. If you hadn't lived, you didn't know what life was about. That was why so many people with souls still untried, shied clear of sentiment, and scorned it, even. They could not know that sentiment was the ultimate distillation of life.

As for herself, she wasn't afraid of sentiment; she felt, quite unashamed, that Julia and Hartley were together now, and that their honeymoon would go on and on. That was why she could not cry for them, as she had cried for Candy. Candy had so much to learn; and John, too. The years ahead would be full of the pain of learning. "David and I have years ahead, but we have years behind us," she thought. There was that to be said for growing older. "I want to go on, not back," she suddenly realized, and with the thought the past and the future became inexplicably one. All the things that had ever happened to her, all the love that had ever filled her heart, was hers for ever. She was glad that Hartley and Julia had finally become a part of that love. This was a strange kind of death, robbed of its sting, disembodied, somehow, from all the accoutrements of death. It was simply that Hartley and Julia were no longer there. In a way, it was quite wonderful.

At five o'clock David came back. He had been out with Watkins. There were things to attend to. "Do you want to go home, or shall we stay?" he asked her.

"Agnes has the guest-room ready for us," she answered, "but I'd rather not have the children sleep at Candy's overnight; she can give them supper and drive them back."

"I'd rather go home, too," said David.

Fanny followed them to the steps, wistful and disappointed. "We were all saying we hoped you'd be bringing Matthew and the baby down real soon. Watkins heard one of the aunts say you'd be owning the house, now. And that's good, we're all glad, it'll be a bit of life around."

Claudia hadn't thought about bringing the children down. "I hadn't either," said David. "But it's something to think about."

"There's a great deal to think about," said Claudia. "Knowing Julia, she'd want us to see that Fanny and the rest of them were taken care of."

"They will be," David said.

It was a sweet night for driving. "I'm so happy for Julia and Hartley," Claudia said at last. "They hadn't built up enough memories together for one or the other of them to have gone on alone."

David pressed her knee in answer. After a time, she said, "Bobby must have been surprised . . . and pleased . . . to see them."

He stared ahead of him. "I can't go quite that far."

"I can. It's so logical. How can there be much difference between where they are and where we are, when scarcely an instant separates us?"

"You go on thinking that way," he told her huskily.

"Maybe some day your pride will let you think that way, too."

"Maybe," he acknowledged.

They turned into the little lane that led to the river. "Slow down a moment," Claudia said. "There's nothing lovelier than a barn and silos reaching up against the sky at sunset."

"Nothing lovelier," he agreed. "There's so much promise of living on a farm."

"I'm glad we belong here."

This time he took her hand. "Do we?"

"We do, David," she said, almost as she remembered saying it in the marriage ceremony.

He cleared his throat.

"I'm glad that Julia and Hartley saw the place before they left."

"So am I. They loved it, too. They really wanted us to buy it, didn't they?"

"They really did," said David.

"Then they'll be happy for us. Darling, we're rich, aren't we? We always have been."

"We always have been," David said.

Long before they reached the house, they could see lights

in the windows, like little beacons. "I hope Candy hasn't been lonely," Claudia said.

"I think I see her waiting at the door," said David.

Claudia leaned forward to peer through the deepening shadows. "That's not Candy," she cried, "it's Bertha!"

It was somehow right that Bertha should have been there. Claudia put her arms around her, in welcome and in gratitude. "Thanks for having them for lunch," she merely said.

"I thought of that all day," said Bertha.

"Are the children home yet?"

"Yes. Miss Candy put Michael to bed for me before she left.—Matthew is in the bathroom."

"I'm going to yank him out," said David. Bertha and Claudia smiled faintly at each other. "We have to go on like always," Bertha said. "I have some supper ready for you when you want it."

"I think we'll take a little walk along the river first with Matthew," Claudia said. "He'll have to know."

Matthew emerged from the bathroom, woebegone and reluctant to confess catastrophe. "My airplane smashed. I was flying it at Candy's and it stuck in a tree, and then it fell and smashed."

Claudia's eyes met David's. "Never mind, Matthew," David said with effort, "you have the other one Aunt Julia gave you."

Matthew's face looked suddenly as if someone had lit a candle behind his eyes. "Boy!" he said. "Can I have it?"

"That's what it's there for," David told him.

"Boy," he said again, and softly, "I'm lucky."

"Yes, darling, you're lucky," Claudia murmured. She held him close and kissed him, and, for once, he did not pull away.

THE END